7

The TRUTH Undiscovered

Copyright © 2018 by J. Kathleen Cheney,

Dream Palace Press

1st Digital Edition, 2018,

cover design by J. Kathleen Cheney.

All rights reserved.

No part of this book may be reproduced in any form or by any electronic or mechanical means, including information storage and retrieval systems, without written permission from the author, except for the use of brief quotations in a book review.

This book is a work of fiction. Names, characters, places, and incidents are the product of the author's imagination or are used fictitiously. Any resemblance to actual events, locales or person, living or dead is coincidental. The author acknowledges the trademarked status and trademark owners of various products referenced in this work of fiction, which have been used without permission. The publication/use of these trademarks, is not authorized, associated with, or sponsored by the trademark owners.

For more books by J. Kathleen Cheney, please visit her website: www.jkathleencheney.com

Foreword

This novel covers the first meetings and the problems that the group of four specialists—The Lady, Inspector Miguel Gaspar, Inspector Gabriel Anjos, and Miss Nadezhda Vladimirova—tackle together. Among their other assignments, they are tasked with finding the killer of Alessio Ferreira, the next-older brother of Duilio Ferreira in **The Golden City**, and a friend and confidante of the infante of Northern Portugal.

Originally published as a serial, this book came out over a span of thirty-one months. It was originally broken into three parts, but that's been removed for this version.

It was an interesting experiment for me, as I often sat down to write a chapter without having any idea where I would end up. I am generally more of an outliner, but I made a conscious effort in this book to fly by the seat of my pants. (I'd like to think of this as a growth process.)

I did, however, have one big constraint; this book takes place months before **The Golden City** begins. Nothing could be revealed in this book that isn't already known at the outset of **The Golden City**, nor could I mention anything that would, in the end, spoil the plot of that book. I suppose that's the challenge of writing a prequel. It makes the ending a bit less definite because it's not quite the end.

I have always wanted to talk more about these four, whom I've secretly called my *Torchwood*. (If that reference is lost on you, think of it as a shadowy group that protects mankind from the shadows.) In addition, there's a Bonus Scene at the end of this book which tells something of what happens after the conclusion of **The Seat of Magic**, so if you haven't read that book, you might want to skip the Bonus Scene.

I hope you enjoy this story as much as I enjoyed writing it.

FOR MY PATRONS:
Past, present, and future

Writers can't write without love.

I do not know what I may appear to the world, but to myself I seem to have been only like a boy playing on the seashore, and diverting myself in now and then finding a smoother pebble or a prettier shell than ordinary, whilst the great ocean of truth lay all undiscovered before me.

—*Isaac Newton*

Chapter 1

THURSDAY, 19 SEPTEMBER 1901
PRAIA, CABO VERDE

Miguel Gaspar sat in his darkened study, contemplating the missive on his desk. The letter fascinated him. It had come from Portugal, from Lisboa. It was written in Portuguese, in a firm, slanting hand. No smears. Right handed, he was certain. The fine cream-colored stationary smelled faintly of myrrh. And when he touched the page, glowing strands of gold reached up from the black ink to clasp his fingers. They followed his hands if he drew them away, like a spider's web pulled taut.

He must be tied to this woman. That was what those strands of glowing energy always meant.

And yet... he'd never met her before. He was sure of that. Even if she didn't give her name—she'd signed it only *The Lady*—he knew she was someone he hadn't met.

He picked up his glass and swallowed a sip of brandy. Bitter and orange-colored, it slid down his throat. Red flames briefly flickered on everything about him—along the edges of the bookshelves, the top of his desk, on each portrait framed on the white-plastered walls. The flames paled to orange, then yellow, and faded away completely as the taste faded in his mouth.

Brandy was orange, cognac more golden. Rum was brown. Sherry, a sparkling pink.

He passed a hand over the paper again, watching as the golden threads reached for his dark skin.

He *was* tied to this woman.

Not in the future. His gift never showed him possibilities. It only showed him what was. What existed. And if it wasn't showing him the future, it could only be showing him the past. Or the *absolute.*

She had offered to hire him to 'provide aid in a political transition,' as she called it. She wanted his gift. He wasn't sure if she wanted him to hunt witches, provide information for blackmail, or overthrow a prince. She hadn't been specific. One never could be when writing a letter like this, a letter that could be seized or stolen. The ink told him nothing further about what she wanted him to do.

Whatever it was, he was likely going to do it. Not because of the words on the paper, but because of the strands. If her words alone had created a link to him, then he could only imagine what she could do in the flesh.

Or rather, he *could* imagine.

THURSDAY, 3 OCTOBER, 1901

Miguel had nothing else planned that afternoon, so he climbed up onto the roof at William's house to watch the ships come in. Near the edge of the plateau, William's home had a better view of the harbor than his own. The afternoon was crisp, and wind whipped dust into the air on the streets. Women hurried by, clutching at their headscarves.

Most of the pedestrians below were normal, more or less. Some bore the sickly taint of ritual magic about them, clasping their skin like burgundy vines, but nothing so marked to make him consider telling a priest, who would be wrapped in vines of his own that spoke of the Church and ownership and pride of station. One man walked by on the street, lines draping off his form that told Miguel he had more than one woman waiting for him. And he'd clearly just left another woman's bed, something Miguel didn't care to know. *Too many ties, that fellow.*

He tore his eyes away from the street below and made himself watch the harbor, where people would be distant enough that their foibles didn't ~~to~~ twist his perceptions. It was calming to watch the sea.

The ship arrived as scheduled, the blue and white flag of Southern Portugal easily visible with a spyglass. He double-checked the name written on the stern and then waited while the ship was moored. More time passed as the crew secured the ship, but Miguel was finally rewarded for his patience with the sight of the steamer's first passenger debarking.

It was *her.*

Generally, he had to be closer to a person to see what was in their soul, but this woman had such a presence that he could spot it even through the spyglass. She glittered golden in the sunlight, her white dress nearly obscured by his mental impression of her glow. He wasn't even sure of the color of her skin or hair. Everything about her proclaimed her exceptionality.

He drew back from the telescope and closed his eyes, savoring the sugary taste of anticipation in his mouth.

"Did you see the ship you wanted?" William bellowed from the stairwell.

Miguel turned back to see his friend waiting there, not quite committed to coming out on the roof. Despite being in his early thirties, William was nearly deaf, a reminder of a terrible ear infection in his youth. At times he shouted, unaware he was doing so.

An Englishman, William dwelt on these islands by virtue of having fallen sick aboard ship and, after being left on Santiago to either recover or die, falling in love with the young woman who'd nursed him. His English family was scandalized by his marrying an African woman, so after one uncomfortable visit, he'd never returned there. As that woman was Miguel's cousin, Catarina, he and William had eventually become close friends.

There was nothing special about William, not a gift or talent nor a shred of inhuman blood. When Miguel looked at him, he saw only William, one of the things that made him good company. The man belonged to his wife and two little daughters—a simple, straightforward fellow. *If only he wouldn't yell my business across the rooftops for all the servants to overhear, he would be the perfect friend.*

Miguel faced William directly, since his friend couldn't follow his voice without seeing his lips. "Yes, the ship came in an hour or so ago."

"What are they carrying?" William gazed out in the direction of the harbor, so before answering, Miguel waited for him to look back.

"Passengers," Miguel said when he had William's attention again. For most, this was merely a stopping point on their way to the Cape of Good Hope.

"Aha! The woman who wants to hire you away?"

"Yes," Miguel said. "I am considering going."

He'd been an inspector with the police here on Santiago for a few years, but there wasn't enough to keep him busy. Not as an inspector, at least. With his father gone, there wasn't much to hold him on this island, either. He wanted to see something more of the world before he died, and this might be his best chance. That was without even considering what the *bearer* of the offer wanted of him—or might offer herself.

"We would miss you," William said, face serious now.

"I would miss you, too, but I think the time is right." It had been a year and a half since his father's death. If there was any time ripe for him to move on, surely this was it.

Chapter 2

SUNDAY, 6 OCTOBER 1901

It took her three days to contact him.

Careful questioning told Miguel she'd been ill aboard ship. During the voyage from Lisboa, she'd mostly stayed in her cabin and had barely eaten when she did emerge. The three days since landing had likely been so she could recover. She hadn't emerged from her hotel, not so far as his investigator knew.

Praia might be a capital, but it wasn't Lisboa or Paris. Miguel doubted the lady in question had plans to tour the other islands. Cabo Verde didn't offer much for tourists. The islands were generally no more than a stopping place, a convenient spot to warehouse items needed for sea travel. Or in the old days, slaves.

No, the first time she emerged from her hotel was to meet with him.

The taverna wasn't crowded, not mid-afternoon, and that made it simple for him to recognize the person with whom he was supposed to meet. But he could never have missed her anyway.

Standing in the taverna's doorway, Miguel watched the woman for a moment… when he could keep her in his sight. She faded out of sight if he wasn't looking directly at her. Instead of being obscured by her aura this time, she was shrouded in shadow, which served the same purpose, he supposed. It hid her, not only from his inner sight, but from his actual sight as well. Judging by the responses of the few others in the taverna, they didn't see her either.

That was a shame. She was stunning, with dark hair and ivory skin and long, pale eyes a bit wide-set. The cool way she watched the room spoke of self-assurance. That was money and influence... and age. She was forty or so, but certainly didn't look that age. The brown shadow-striped silk suit flattered a mature figure. She had no ring on her finger, which might indicate a momentary inclination toward an affair, but he thought it meant no husband at all. He saw no ties of that sort about her. She wasn't the sort who needed a husband. She was content without one. He was sure of that.

The glittering gold of her skin made sense now that he saw her this close, the mark of fairy blood. A lot of it, although she was human enough to pass unremarked by those who did see her. That explained the glamour as well, cloaking her from most people's view. It *almost* worked on him, as human magic never did.

He had the strangest feeling he'd met her before, although he certainly would recall it if he had. No one forgot meeting a woman like her. It was more than that, though. He felt like he knew her—like he knew her *well*. He recalled the strands of connection from her letter, and decided it must be the truth, even if it defied logic.

She looked directly at him then, as if weighing his abilities just as he weighed others'. A flare of recognition crossed her features, quickly schooled back to coolness. There was intelligence in her eyes, but he'd expected that. She would be smart and outspoken, a gift afforded to a woman most people simply never heard or saw. He felt sure of that trait, too.

He'd learned enough. He crossed to her table, drew out a chair, and sat. As he did so, lines of connection lifted from her form and reached out to him, carrying the smell of myrrh and the earth after rain.

One of her dark brows rose like the wing of a gull. "You're not going to ask my permission?"

The question had been intended to unsettle him. Her voice carried the tinkling of silver bells under its words. He wondered what she sounded like to normal people. "Why go through the pretense that this is a casual encounter, Lady?"

She leaned back in her chair with an ease that made him wonder if she was wearing a corset. Her delicate brows drew together in what might be wariness. "No, this is a business meeting, Inspector Gaspar," she said. "I appreciate your directness."

He wasn't going to grovel to this woman. "Then tell me who you are and what you want."

"Who I am is unimportant," she said with a shrug, a gesture that seemed familiar to him. "As to what I want, I'm putting together a cadre of... I'll call us *specialists*. I heard there was a Meter here on the island and wondered if I could entice you to join my little group."

Miguel stretched out his legs. *Could* anyone else see her? No one stared at him as if he was insane, so apparently they could either see both of the table's occupants, or neither. They would not see the golden lines that now bound him firmly to her, making his ultimate response certain, but he didn't intend to let *her* know that. Not yet. "Why should I come with you?"

"Better pay, perhaps more excitement," she said. "You would be working for the Portuguese throne. In the Portugals, primarily, but also wherever else we're needed. From here I go to Brazil, then back to Europe. You could find out what winter is."

He didn't care much about the Portuguese throne. His Portuguese grandfather was long gone, and he doubted that any kin he had in Portugal would be interested in meeting their long-lost *mestiço* cousin. There wasn't anything holding him here. She would have had that investigated before sending for him. She would know he had no family left. He only wondered whom she'd used to investigate him. Whoever it was, he'd been discreet—probably Eduardo Cunha. "What exactly would I be doing?"

"Investigating," she said, her head tilting exactly as he expected.

Who did she remind him of? "More."

"Northern Portugal," she clarified. "The Special Police, which means you'd be working directly for the throne."

"They have investigators already," he pointed out.

"Not like you," she said easily. "And you wouldn't be investigating *for* them. You would be investigating them."

He sat back. That made a huge difference. The Special Police of Northern Portugal were charged with keeping non-humans out of that country. It was their primary duty, one which didn't sit well with him. He'd heard about the excesses practiced against sereia and selkies who wandered into their territory. It had long been whispered they would begin hunting witches next. "To what end?"

She laced her gloved fingers together and set them in her lap. "There are elements within that body that need to be rooted out. In time, the ban against non-humans will end, and the Special Police must know which officers might be unwilling to let go of that particular mandate."

In other words, they were to dig out villains entrenched in those offices for two decades. That would *not* be pleasant. There would be resistance. In truth, the attempt stood a good chance of being fatal. And it made no sense, since the prince himself commanded those officers—*he* had leveled the ban. This woman was working against the prince, then, despite her claim that she served the throne.

She returned his level gaze, lovely eyes unflinching. It was almost as if she knew what he was thinking. Not a *talent*; he didn't think that. Instead Miguel had a strong feeling that her mind worked much in the same way as his own—cool and analytical, with the emotional aspects of the argument stripped away. A rare find was a woman who allowed others to see that in her.

Perhaps that similarity in thought was what kept making him think her familiar. Perhaps she was too much like him. He gazed at one of the ties binding them, a golden strand that started on her hand and clutched his wrist. *No, there's something more.* "For whom do you work?"

"If I were to say," she told him, "it would be treason, would it not?"

Miguel set his elbows on the table, laced his fingers together, and set his chin upon them, an uncouth posture in polite company, but he wanted to see her reaction. "How much?"

She didn't flinch at his intentional rudeness. "To start, four times your current pay. Plus we'll cover all expenses for your removal to Portugal and pay you any monies currently owed to you by the garrison."

The way she suggested that exorbitant allowance told him it was pocket money for her. He didn't need it. He had no wife or children to provide for, no addictions to feed, and while it was true that the garrison was often in arrears with their payments to the locals, he wasn't starving either. His Portuguese grandfather had left him enough money to assure he didn't need the pay. "I see no reason to accept."

"It's a challenge, something new and different," she said, surveying the customers about them. "I don't think you get much of that here."

Could he stare her out of countenance? Miguel doubted that.

She gazed back for a time, then asked, "How do you do it? How do you know what gift someone has?"

Ah, curiosity. "Most people who have a gift glow with it," he offered. "Seers tend to have a bluish glow, healers more of a golden one, for example."

"So it's in your eyes. Do you see a difference for selkies as well? Are they a different... color?"

Miguel was rarely asked to explain his gift. "No, a selkie is intrinsically different. They *are* magic, rather than being gifted with it."

Her dark brows knit together. "But they can bear a child with a human. How is that possible if they're innately different?"

As she was not entirely human, *that* question was a loaded gun, ready to backfire should he handle it carelessly. "When I meet someone who has selkie or sereia blood, I can see it melded in with their human side. *How* that happens is a question for another sort of witch."

"A scientist, perhaps?"

He chuckled. "I doubt one would find enough willing subjects to make a study."

"You could help with that," she pointed out.

Yes, he could. He could walk through the streets of Praia and point out each witch, half-breed, and non-human that crossed his path. But he didn't intend to do so. Labeling them pushed them one step closer to persecution. The Spanish Church with its continuing crusade against witches would pay a great deal to get their hands on Miguel Gaspar—not to kill him, but to use him to their own ends, to betray others into their hands. He felt certain this woman wasn't leading him down that path. She wouldn't. He didn't know if she had a telltale trait to reveal her inhuman origin, like a selkie's musky smell or a sereia's gills and scale-patterned skin. Even so, he didn't attribute her trustworthiness to her inhuman blood. He simply *knew* she was trustworthy. "I won't," he finally said.

"Not even in the interest of Science?" she asked, sounding incredulous. "Do you not want to know what makes *you* different?"

"I am far more interested in what makes me the same as any other man," he said.

"Hmmm," she said. "You said that seers were blue-tinged. How do you see *my gift*?"

"It's not like the others," he said. "It's more as if you're draping shadows about you or holding the light around your body like a curtain."

"No particular color?" She seemed disappointed.

"It's from your inhuman blood," he said. "So it doesn't work the way a human gift does."

A split-second passed before she answered. "I don't have any inhuman blood."

"Yes, you do." He gazed at her ivory features, where the substance of magic seethed just under the skin. "Your family might never have known they weren't human, but you're part fairy."

She sat up straighter, her lips pressed tightly together. No, she definitely hadn't known. Or she'd refused to acknowledge it. He knew dozens of witches and parti-breeds who lived in ignorance of their blood. Most of the time it was better to leave them in that ignorance. But he found it fascinating that this woman didn't *know*.

She turned to look at him. "There was an old joke that my father was *fe*. He was from Galicia, originally, I think."

An odd statement, but that explained her ivory skin. Galicia was the Spanish province directly north of Northern Portugal, if he recalled correctly, and the people there were Celts. "I don't understand your point."

"Not *fe*, like in church," she said, stressing her words carefully. "*Fae*, like the English say it. They have fairies there."

Since he had no better explanation for her inhuman blood, he didn't argue her conclusion. He needed to do some research. "I wouldn't know whether that was the case, as I have no basis for comparison."

"Then perhaps you should come to Portugal and find out." She rose, forcing him to rise with her. She stepped around the edge of the table and stopped when she stood only inches from him. She pressed a small brass key into his palm, warm from her fingers. "I'm in room 312. If you want to discuss it further, I'll be there. "

Then she brushed past him, bearing the scent of myrrh with her... and a hint of rosemary. That last was her actual scent, perfume or soap, not supplied by his gift. He'd expected something heady, perhaps lily. Then again, if she didn't want people to see her, it would be spoiled if they smelled her. Miguel pocketed the key. He hoped no one else had seen that last interchange. No one saw her walk out of the bar, not that he could tell.

He wasn't going to waste time supposing that her suggestion was, in any way, innocent. It had been a prelude to seduction. What he did want to know was whether she offered her body as a further enticement to join her unnamed enterprise or whether she merely found him attractive. Perhaps she was bored with proper Portuguese gentlemen and thought a *mestiço* man might prove a more interesting lover.

He wouldn't mind a night or two of dalliance with this woman. He approved of her looks and had no doubt she would make a wonderful lover. He had a sense, almost like déjà vu, that he'd been her lover at some point before.

But the very fact that he was having such a reaction, one he couldn't remember having before with any other woman, told him he should proceed with caution.

Chapter 3

SUNDAY, 6 OCTOBER 1901

"You had a key," she said when she opened the door. "Why knock?"

When she moved back, Miguel stepped into her room and waited as she locked the door. It was nearly midnight now, and he'd had some time to reflect on their earlier discussion. "I left the key at the front desk," he explained. "I didn't want any confusion as to whether or not you let me through that door of your own volition."

"Cautious, too," she said with a wry smile. "I like that."

Miguel surveyed the room. It was one of the hotel's best, with a screened off area for the white-draped bed and a seating arrangement before the windows that allowed a view of the beach. He didn't perceive anyone hiding in that space with them, which meant he was truly alone with this unknown woman. She gestured toward the sofa that faced the window. A low table before it held a bottle of white wine and a pair of glasses. "Join me," she said softly as she settled onto the sofa.

It wasn't quite an order. Miguel suspected she was simply so accustomed to giving orders that everything she said came out that way. He sat across from her, turning on the seat so he could look directly at her. Strands of gold reached from her ivory skin toward his dusky hands.

She now wore a dressing gown of old gold satin. No ruffles. Very austere. The underskirts that peeked from underneath the gown were edged in Brussels lace, though, hinting at a sensual, but not frivolous, nature. A man's signet ring adorned her right hand, but she wore no necklace or earrings. She poured a glass of wine for each of them and then leaned back, sipping at hers. "I'm glad you came."

He didn't think that was an inane social comment. She meant those words. "I'm curious as to why."

"I like the way you talk to me," she said, gesturing vaguely with the be-ringed hand. "You don't stumble over your own feet trying to be polite, nor do you think it necessary to couch everything in simple terms so as to make them comprehensible for a woman. You seem to think me equal to a man."

Most women thought him handsome first and gave less consideration to his character or behavior. "In my profession, one learns that a woman can be just as capable as a man."

"Of committing crimes?" she asked.

"Of anything, lady. Women can take heroic risks, make hard decisions, kill when necessary. It's never wise to discount a person merely because she wears a skirt."

She nodded. "Very true. History has proven that over and over, and yet women are still treated as too feeble-minded or too weak-willed to walk their own way."

Definitely no husband. That signet ring must have belonged to her father. "Foolishness. Why would you need to clean out the Special Police now?"

"Down to business. I like that you don't waste my time, either." She set her glass back down on the table. "The seers in the Golden City are predicting that Prince Fabricio's death is imminent. They're all too afraid to say so publicly, of course, but there are a few who will talk for a price."

"Are *you* his death?" Miguel asked.

"Heavens no," she said with a light laugh like the tinkling of bells. "No one knows exactly how that will happen. What is important is that change is coming. When the prince dies, the infante will assume the throne and the ban on non-humans *will* be lifted. We have to clear out the Special Police before that happens."

The implication was that she worked for the infante... or one of the numerous noble families who hoped to influence the man once he became prince. His political views were unknown. Since his elder brother had kept him under house arrest for the better part of two decades, it seemed unlikely that the infante would continue his brother's policies. Either way, this might change the country's relationship with Cabo Verde, currently a protectorate rather than a colony. The Portuguese garrison was here primarily to keep Spain and France off the islands, not to govern the people of Cabo Verde, who had been democratically ruled for decades now. The change would hit closer to home for him, then.

"And other parts of the government?" he asked. "Do you intend to investigate them?"

"I have been charged with the Special Police, not anything else at this time."

Miguel took a sip of the wine, a dry white. Crystals of ice seemed to form on the surfaces near him, then faded from his vision as he considered her words. It would be treasonous to undermine their prince. Then again, the reclusive prince of Northern Portugal was rumored to be insane. "I will not cooperate on anything which goes against my interests."

"What specifically concerns you?"

She was what bothered him. "That's to be determined on a daily basis, lady. If the situation becomes too questionable for me, I will walk away."

"*I* would not stop you, Inspector."

Not an absolute answer, that. "Who would?"

She gave him a very direct look. "If necessary, my executioner."

He recognized that expression; she wasn't joking. "Executioner? You have your own?"

"Yes." The lady shrugged again. "She's a healer who's lost her gift. She can kill with a touch, though, as all healers can."

Powerful healers lived on the knife's edge of becoming dangerous. They had to guard their talents more vigilantly than he did, even. The fact that this one *knew* she had crossed the line made her especially dangerous. "What does she do for you when not executing your foes?"

The lady shifted on the sofa. "Her primary function is to question people. After a few minutes with her, they would sell their own mother's secrets. She's dead, you see, and any human sitting down with her innately senses there's something unnatural about her."

Dead? The dead didn't sit down and question others. They rotted. "I've never heard of the dead moving about."

"She calls herself a *rusalka*," the lady said, "a thing the Russians believe in."

Something about the way she said it made him question

THE TRUTH UNDISCOVERED

whether she believed in the woman's claim, but he wasn't going to delve into the business of a dead woman. He would rather keep his distance. "Will I have to work closely with her?"

"No," she said. "That will be the place of the Truthsayer I'm going to Brazil to find. The Jesuits say he's the best. Are you interested in coming along?"

He wanted to see more of this world before he died. He had long wanted to visit Brazil, but had never gotten around to it; he'd been taking care of his father. This offer would take him to both Brazil and Portugal... a good start. That reeked of letting Fate make the decision for him, but he wasn't going to turn down such an offer merely to hold to an illusion of personal autonomy. "Yes."

She smiled a smile worthy of a well-fed cat. "Good. I would have been disappointed if you'd decided otherwise. I like you."

Ah, so now they'd reached the seduction. It surprised him that she intended to pursue him even *after* she'd gotten his agreement to go with her. He doubted she was a woman of low morals, although he wouldn't put it past her to use her body to get what she wanted. "Why?"

"As I said, I like the way you talk to me. You treat me like an equal. I distrust men who feel compelled to scrape and bow for me, and disdain the ones who condescend to me."

Well, at least she knows how she feels about men. He didn't think she'd told him all the truth, though. Very little of it, actually. "Who are you?"

"I won't say," she said with a brief shake of her head.

"Not even your given name?"

She considered that for a long time. "Adela," she finally admitted, "is one of my names, Miguel."

Well, *that* was an interesting step to have taken. Given her hesitation, she probably gave out that name less frequently than she took lovers. Why had she told *him*? "And what now?"

She reached her hands up and began removing pins from the braid looped at the back of her neck. It fell down her back as she rose and crossed to the window, wrapping shadow about her as she did so. She wasn't trying to keep him from seeing her, only people beyond the glass. Miguel rose, crossed to the window, and gazed out at the last of the evening's light. There were boats in the harbor, their lanterns shining faintly. "Who *can* see you when you're doing that?" he asked.

She chuckled. "Well, it's obvious that you can. Usually it's only witches who have the second sight. The ones who see things as they truly are. And they have difficulty."

"I have the second sight, Adela, simply far more than others, which is what makes me the Meter."

She smiled when he used her given name. Not a dry, sardonic smile, but a soft smile, a private one. She didn't smile like that often, did she? "I didn't know that," she said softly.

"A day without learning something new is wasted. My mother told me that."

"Was she bookish?" she asked.

"Yes."

She tore her eyes away from the harbor to gaze up at him,

laying one pale hand against his chest. "Are you?"

Miguel had no doubt that Adela was a reader, too educated not to be. "Why seduce me? You have my agreement. I'll join your little excursion. Why persist?"

She dropped her hand back to her side and her head tilted in vexation. "Why should I not?"

Not at all repentant. "I see no reason a woman shouldn't seduce as many men... as men do women," he said, "but I'm not the sort of man to take a lover casually. Nor do I think you're that sort."

She regarded him narrowed eyes. She didn't look offended. More like she was plotting. "Perhaps not."

"Then why pursue *me*?"

She glanced toward the glass again. "I told you. I like the way you talk to me."

That wasn't a lie. But it wasn't the answer he wanted either. He wasn't sure what he was fishing after, but there was something missing from this conversation, some truth left undiscovered. "There's more to it than that, I hope."

Her eyes flicked back toward him. They were green, like his own, but a clear green. Like everything else about her, they were *familiar*. "You hope? Do I take that to mean it's not an absolute 'no'?"

She hadn't answered his implied question. "It's 'not tonight,' Adela. Give me some time to consider."

She licked her lips. "Very well. We leave for Brazil Friday morning. I'll book a cabin for you as well. On the *Ferreira*. I assume you have arrangements of your own to make. Will you join me for dinner tomorrow?"

Here on the island, he was considered an excellent catch. He had a decent inheritance, a fine house, and good family and political ties. Miguel doubted those facts meant anything to Adela, so he didn't see any advantage in her pursuit of him. Even so, he wasn't going to snub her. That he would be her lover seemed almost inevitable. He just didn't know *why*, and that bothered him. "Here at the hotel?"

She pondered that for a moment. "Is there another restaurant you'd recommend?"

"I know one with better seafood."

They made arrangements to meet, a shockingly mundane thing to do when she stood there in her dishabille, her hair loose. Then Miguel took his leave of her, the golden strands between them stretching until too thin for even him to see.

But he knew they were still there.

Chapter 4

MONDAY, 7 OCTOBER 1901

A night's fitful sleep hadn't improved Miguel's understanding of the woman. But he had business that demanded his time that morning: visits to his solicitor, his banker, and a couple of his friends. It kept his mind occupied instead of fretting at the problem that Adela presented.

The last of his visits was to William's house. If there was a book on the island that would tell Miguel about fairies, it would be there. The butler showed him into the library to wait, so Miguel began surveying the shelves.

William came striding in a moment later, his blond hair tousled and his waistcoat buttoned askew. He threw his arms about Miguel as if he hadn't seen him in months. "My friend," he bellowed. "So have you decided? Are you leaving us?"

Miguel scowled at him. *Poor timing.* He'd apparently interrupted his friend in the midst of some morning play with his wife. It was the oddest part of Miguel's gift, its most embarrassing aspect. He could always tell who'd been having sex... and with whom. He'd learned very young it was something he should never mention. "Yes, I'm afraid. Are there rumors already?"

William went over to his liquor cabinet, counting off points as he went. "That you are getting your house in order. That you are going to Brazil. That you are going to Portugal. That you are going to England. That you will sell your house."

"I don't know how long I'll be gone." Miguel said once he was sure William was looking at him.

William shook his head. "I will miss you, my friend."

"And I you. And Catarina and the girls. I will write to you all when I can."

William sighed dramatically. "Why, Miguel? I didn't think you were serious about going."

"She made an excellent offer." He would like to run his previous day's experience by William, but he didn't have the time to explain his reaction to the woman. He was still puzzling over it himself. And what she claimed she wanted him to do. It would take a late night and a bottle or two of cognac, particularly since treason might be involved. "I did want to borrow a few books for my journey, though."

William gestured widely. "What I have is yours, my friend."

"Do you have anything about fairies?"

William's blond brows drew together, barely visible against his pale skin. "Did you say *fairies*?"

Miguel nodded. Sometimes William 'heard' him wrong, and it was an odd request. "Anything about how their magic works or what they're like."

William laughed. "Do they actually exist?"

"Let's say I consider it a possibility."

William shook his head disbelievingly. "Well, if anyone would know, it would be you."

He handed Miguel a glass of brandy, and then took his own and went to examine his shelves. He pulled off a book and handed it absently to Miguel, his eyes fixed on the shelves.

Miguel peered down at the fabric-covered tome. It was in

English, *The Fae*, written by someone named Armstead-White. That should be a good starting place. He set it aside when William wordlessly handed over another book—a volume of fairy tales in French by the Comtesse de Ségur. *Children's stories*, Miguel decided.

"You don't read Russian, do you?" William asked as he peered at another shelf.

"I don't know," Miguel admitted. He'd never tried. Perhaps he should, given the Russian creature who awaited them in Portugal.

William drew a book out from among its fellows and handed it over. Miguel glanced at the spine. *Russian Folk Tales*, it read in neat Cyrillic, by Alexsandr Afanasyev. *Apparently, I do read Russian. Handy to know that.* Miguel set that book on his stack as well.

William's wife Catarina bustled into the room then and came over to kiss Miguel's cheek. Unlike Miguel, she was as dark as her husband was fair. She cast an exasperated glance at William and made a complicated gesture with her hand that prompted William to glance down at his waistcoat and then quickly re-button it. She turned narrowed eyes on Miguel. "I hear you're leaving."

"I'm afraid so, my dear. Tomorrow."

She came and laid one hand on his shoulder. "The girls will miss their godfather. Will and I might even miss you, too. Can you at least stay for luncheon?"

That had been his ulterior motive behind putting this visit off until last—Catarina had an excellent cook. "I would be happy to do so."

The Silva family had a small restaurant on Constituição Street. While it might not be as urbane as the hotel's restaurant, the food was better, the seafood that morning's catch, and they had a couple of private dining rooms, one of which Miguel had already secured for that evening.

He met Adela in the lobby of her fine hotel, a shadow-wrapped figure that smelled suspiciously of myrrh and rosemary. She'd only worn the rosemary, in truth. His mind perceived the smell of the myrrh, but it wasn't actually there. His gift was creating that smell in his head, he was sure, a perceived stimulus possibly related to her unusual heritage.

"Are you hiding?" he asked her as he watched strands lift from her skin and reach toward him, their gold muted by her shadows.

"Not from you, of course," she said, the gloom about her fading away. A European man in a fine frock coat and tall hat paused mid-stride to stare, but when he saw Miguel there, he quickly glanced down at his moving feet and walked out the hotel doors. "I didn't want to attract speculation," Adela said.

Miguel was caught again by that feeling of familiarity, as if he'd expected her to say just those words. To tilt her head exactly that way. He pinched the bridge of his nose and shook his head, trying to drive away that sensation. It was not one of his normal aberrations. He dropped his hand and found that she was watching him with a line of worry between her brows. "Not a headache," he supplied, extending his arm for her to take if she wished. "Shall we go?"

THE TRUTH UNDISCOVERED

She wrapped her hand about his forearm, her kid-gloved fingers coming to rest on his dark sleeve as he led her out of the hotel. Gold strands wrapped about him, encircling his arm and then his chest, and the smell of myrrh grew stronger. Perhaps the smell came from the connection he sensed between them. He'd never experienced the like before. He wasn't even certain how he knew what myrrh smelled like.

She walked along at his side, her eyes taking in everyone about them, as people darted from work to home or out for a meal. A group of ragged children ran by, playing football in the street. The fact that they didn't run over to beg pesetas off him hinted that they couldn't see the two of them strolling along Constituição Street.

"Am I inside your illusion?" he asked.

"Yes," Adela said, a smile tugging at one corner of her lips. "Why?"

"I can no longer see it," he admitted. "How wide can you extend it?"

"Several feet more than it is now, and yes, whatever is inside my sphere is hidden, save from those who have the sight like you."

"Interesting."

She smiled down at the dirt road between the neat plastered buildings as she walked. "I hope so. Tell me, then, what you see out there. Are there dozens of witches about us? Or are they rare?"

"Here in Praia I'd say about five percent, perhaps." That was actually a conservative estimate, but he preferred not to expose others.

"So many? I'm amazed."

He steered her past a large pile of mule dung, the scent of which made him taste brownness. "Many of them don't realize it, though, or have powers so slight it hardly matters."

She was shorter than him and thus had to look up to meet his eyes. "How could they not know?"

He could lecture her on this all day, and there was no chance of her gainsaying him. After all, his talent was shockingly unique. He could say almost anything, and she would have to take it as truth. "Many witches don't use their gift or deny to themselves that it exists. Seers seem to be the most often unaware of their talent."

She shook her head. "Unaware? How?"

Miguel shrugged. "They think they're simply lucky. Weak seers are quite common, the most common of all witches. At least that's the case here. It might prove different in Portugal or Brazil."

"How fascinating."

He led her down the street and around to the back door of Silva's restaurant. Silva's wife, Teresa dos Santos, let them in before Miguel had a chance to knock, her seer's gift glowing faintly blue about her. She led them up the stairs to the private dining room. It wasn't a fine room, certainly not like the ones this wealthy woman ate in regularly. The curtains were thick enough to obscure them from view, though, and the white-dressed table and chairs were clean. Honest businessmen regularly used this room, and Silva kept it tidy.

"Serviceable," Adela said as he took her wrap and handed it to Teresa. "I caught a whiff of the kitchen as we came upstairs, and I expect you're correct about the food, Inspector. It smells wonderful."

She directed that last sentence at their hostess, showing a touch of diplomacy.

"Thank you," Teresa said in a businesslike tone. "I'll bring up the wine." She swept from the room, wrap over her arm.

Miguel held out a chair for Adela. She sat, looking down as she did so and exposing her neck to him. He fought a flickering urge to place a kiss there, almost as if obligated. As if that was something he regularly did, a habit. He brushed two fingers against that spot instead, and she stilled. *Not offended*, he thought, merely startled.

As he came around to sit across from her, her long eyes followed him. "So tell me about you and Teresa."

He laughed. He was impressed she'd picked up that there was still, even a decade later, a tie between him and a former lover. He could see it still, faint as it was, a fragile red strand that bound him and Teresa. "That was long, long ago, before she married. And Silva doesn't know, so it would be better not to mention it to him."

Adela's head tilted as she surveyed his face. "Did the two of you part well?"

"Yes," he said. "It was never meant to last beyond a week. Teresa is, by the way, one of the best cooks on the island. I offered to help fund a restaurant for her, but she'd rather not take money from me. People would talk, she thinks."

"Hmmm," Adela said. "If her cooking is as delectable as you

claim, she shouldn't have trouble finding another investor."

Unfortunately, investors weren't as common here on the islands as they must be in Portugal. Miguel talked with her about the island's business, about money—about everything but magic and her mission in Portugal—as they worked through the courses of the excellent dinner. Afterward, she sipped coffee, watching him with her clever eyes.

"So, have you made up your mind?" she asked once Teresa's waiter had taken away the last of the plates, leaving them their privacy. She reached over and placed her free hand over his.

Miguel sat back, watching her narrowly, but didn't draw his hand away. One thing his gift didn't tell him was another's intention or veracity. "Tell me, why are you so interested in me?"

She drew her hand back, her face tilting downward as if she might be blushing, if she possessed a blush at all. "I am a modern woman. I do as I want regarding men."

"That didn't answer my question."

Her pale eyes flicked up to meet his. "Are you interested or not?"

A harsher bell sound had accompanied those words—she was vexed. "I am… but I'd rather you answer the question. Why me? You've just met me, and yet you don't seem like an impetuous woman."

She licked her lips, gathering her thoughts. Finally, she said, "When you're a child, you have strange fancies. Strange ideas. I always felt I was missing something, as if I was half of a pair of gloves." She sighed. "Other girls would have a best friend, but I never did seem to find one. I was convinced that sooner or later I would meet that girl who was meant to be my best friend, like the other glove I was missing."

This speech was a long way from her desire to seduce him, but Miguel suddenly had a strong suspicion where this was heading. He'd had strange fancies as a child, too. He'd long since put them all behind him. At least he thought he had. "Did you ever find that friend?"

"No. I would meet another girl, and think, 'perhaps she will be my friend,' but I would know immediately she wasn't right. When I grew older, I gave up on finding that best friend and turned to lovers. But even in the first moment when I met a man, I knew he wasn't right either."

"You have impossible standards, then?"

She shook her head. "No. I gave up after that, thinking that I must be the problem. I expected nothing but discretion from my lovers."

"A bleak way to approach love," he said.

"Pragmatism." She rubbed two fingers absently across the knuckles of her other hand, touching that signet ring. "It was never love. Love is for poets."

An answer he might have given. "So your interest in me is purely pragmatic?"

She cast him a dry look, as if exasperated that he'd even proposed such a thing. "Of course not, Miguel."

He'd merely wanted to prod her. "Then?"

"You walked into that taverna yesterday and I thought,

'There he is. After all this time.'" She chuckled. "It is the strangest thing. I *recognize* you."

Miguel gazed at her, calculating. He'd had dreams as a young man—vivid dreams of living in other places and times. His mother had urged him to write down every detail he could remember. He still had those journals.

Adela reminded him of those dreams. *That* was what kept triggering that sense of familiarity.

She was waiting for some manner of response from him. There was no hint of fear on her face. No, she didn't show her emotions to others, did she? That pragmatism was her armor, keeping her safe from the world's censure over her lack of conventionality. But he knew she was afraid. She'd admitted more to him than she would to any other. It was a gesture of trust, like revealing her true name.

That was one thing he'd managed to learn in his afternoon's reading. Fairies could be controlled through their names. She'd given him a name, and he could use it to control her. Not an action she would have taken lightly.

"You think I'm your missing glove," he finally said, careful to keep his tone neutral.

"That makes it sound trivial," she said, a hint of regret in her voice. "I meant no insult."

"When we met yesterday," he offered, "I experienced a sense of déjà vu, like I'd met you before."

Her eyes narrowed. "But we've never met. I'm sure of it."

"No. We haven't."

For a moment there was silence. Miguel reached over to

touch her cheek. She didn't flinch away. Her eyes dropped and she turned her face so that his palm cupped her cheek. He rubbed his thumb over her lips and her eyes drifted closed. "I would like to take you to my house," he said. "There's something I want to show you."

A smile tugged at her lips, a wry one. "Of course, Miguel."

He knew how that sounded, an invitation to be seduced. "Shall we go now?"

She set her napkin to one side and rose, apparently not as interested in coffee as she was in him. He held out his arm and a moment later they were on the street.

"I've seen a photograph of your house," she said.

"I'm not surprised to hear that."

"It's lovely. I've never visited Cabo Verde before, so I didn't know what to expect of houses here."

"Many are in the Portuguese style," he said, and they proceeded to discuss local architecture—a very safe topic—until they stood on the steps of his home.

He unlocked the door and ushered her inside. A single lamp burned in the foyer, his staff already turned in for the night, so he led her by one hand down the main hallway to the library, their footsteps the only sound in the house. He picked up the tin of matches to light the gaslights. The gloom in the room lifted, although it was far from bright without all of them lit.

Adela stood near the doorway, looking perplexed. Her hands were neatly folded together. "You wanted me to see... your library?"

Miguel hid a smile as he surveyed the handful of journals on one of the upper shelves. He pulled down two and turned back to her. "Did you expect something else, Adela?"

"Frankly, yes. I expected to admire your fine bedroom furniture."

He gestured for her to sit at the table. "When I was young," he began, "I had very vivid dreams. In them I was always off on adventures. Sometimes I was Portuguese, sometimes French. I was even Chinese in one, I recall. My appearance changed, but it was still me inside. My mother, thinking I might one day become a writer like Jules Verne, encouraged me to record them. So I did." He opened the first book and began flipping through the pages, looking for a particular passage. "The dreams faded away as I grew older. By the time I went to university, they were gone."

"Do you intend to write adventure stories one day?" Adela asked, laughter in her voice.

Her tone provoked the taste of caramel in his mouth this time. "I am not as bookish as my mother hoped I'd be, and I only completed a year at the Sorbonne before she took ill and I had to return home."

"Yes, I was told that."

Eduardo Cunha had been thorough. It hadn't been a secret, though, why he'd returned. "In any case, I no longer dreamed. I didn't want to. But occasionally I would pull one of these out and recall what it was like. I've not done so in years, though."

"Fond thoughts of your childhood?"

"I had a very pleasant childhood," he said. "I had wealth,

THE TRUTH UNDISCOVERED

privilege, and friends. The dreams were something else, though. Other children didn't have dreams like mine. Did you ever have such dreams?"

"Not that I remember," she said after considering for a moment. "Certainly nothing vivid enough to write down."

Too much to expect. Miguel sighed. "In my dreams," he told her, "I was never alone. I always had a companion. No matter how much I changed, there were some things about her that stayed the same. As a young man I thought of her as the perfect woman."

She smiled wryly again. "A woman in your dreams? That little Austrian doctor would probably say you're lusting after your mother. Have you read his book?"

"Yes." William had lent him his copy of the book on interpreting dreams. A hefty volume written in German, it had taken some time for Miguel to get through it, but the doctor's theories hadn't applied in this case. "The woman in my dreams was very little like my mother, Adela. No matter if we were both Portuguese or French or Chinese, she always had black hair and fair skin. And pale eyes. Some things about her never changed."

Adela regarded him warily now. "What do you mean?"

He handed her the journal he held, wondering if she would pass the test. "I apologize for the hand," he said. "It's never been good, but I was fourteen when I wrote that."

She leaned closer to the lamp to read the page, her eyes flicking back and forth. After a moment of reading silently, she shot a questioning glance at him and then checked the page again.

"So tell me, Adela, is there a heart-shaped birthmark on your right hip?"

Her eyes rose to meet his. "How did you know?"

That was an admission. For a moment he found it nearly impossible to breathe. Then he managed to speak. "I'd forgotten all about that passage," he admitted. "Buried that memory. All my adult life though, I have found myself unwittingly comparing every woman to *her*, and found them all lacking. Not that they were not as fine, but they simply weren't..." he nodded toward the journal she still held, "...that woman."

She sat back in her chair, gazing at him wordlessly.

"You have a mole," he added, "beneath your left breast."

She swallowed. "You dreamed about me when you were a boy."

"Or someone very like you," he said. "I have been thinking for the last two days that you were strangely familiar, but didn't think of this until you mentioned your childish fancies. And I now understand. Those lives I dreamed were all mine... and you were with me in each of them."

"How is that possible?" she whispered.

"How is it any more unlikely than your believing I'm your missing half?"

"They're both illogical," she agreed.

Miguel rose and offered a hand to help her up. She stood, stepping without hesitation into his arms. Miguel kissed her, and wasn't at all surprised to discover that she kissed exactly as he'd always believed a woman should, her lips exactly as he remembered. She sighed and said his name, which only inflamed him further. He set one hand on her hip—right where she would have a small heart-shaped mark. "Shall I take you to bed now?"

She drew back, but only far enough for her eyes to meet his. "Yes."

Chapter 5

TUESDAY, 8 OCTOBER 1901

None of the servants had questioned Adela's presence, so they were very discreet... or she wasn't the first woman to breakfast with him here.

Seated on the terrace overlooking the gardens of Miguel's home, Adela enjoyed the mild temperature and the breeze off the sea. One of his servants had fetched her luggage from the hotel, so she'd donned a dressing gown and short jacket. He wore the white trousers that were so common here on the island, with only a white tunic over that. Not at all formal this morning. It was... *comfortable*, as if they'd done this every morning, forever.

Adela watched Miguel as he calmly ate his breakfast, By the standards of Cabo Verde, he was wealthy—one of the wealthiest men on this island. His servants had brought a breakfast of steamed cornbread and honey, though, which wasn't a European choice. *Local fare.* It was heavier than her normal breakfast, but she could stand to eat a little more than usual, given that she'd not had much sleep that night.

Miguel did things the way she'd always thought a man should. He kissed her the way she wanted to be kissed—the right way. Everything last night had played out precisely how she always felt her first time with the perfect lover should. It defied logic. There shouldn't be this strange connection with a man she'd never met before. She should be keeping him at a distance, only that would be a waste of time.

Because she believed Miguel's theory, no matter how improbable it was.

She'd lain in his arms in the darkness while he told her of his short time at the Sorbonne in Paris, when he'd only been eighteen. He'd often slipped away from the Latin Quarter to roam the streets. And on one street he'd stopped, mesmerized, staring at a rundown house of three stories. It was on an old street, one not destroyed by Haussman in his zeal to recreate Paris. He said it felt like he'd been in that house before. An ancient housewife in the adjacent home told him of the previous owner, a man who'd worked for the Jesuits, a man with a name that seemed familiar to Miguel.

That encounter *had* stirred his desire to reexamine his childhood dreams, the ones he'd tucked away in the far corners of his mind. But his mother's illness forced him to return home to Cabo Verde, and caring for his parents had taken all his time. He'd set the idea aside once more.

I was in Paris in the fall of 1886.

Adela hadn't told him that yet. She had been in Paris to find a vampire supposedly hiding in the library of the Sorbonne. The library had begun renovations the year before, and a persistent rumor of a lurking shadow in the stacks had provoked her to visit. She hadn't found a vampire, though; she'd found a rusalka instead.

She'd been a very strong-willed twenty-five then, and if she'd run across an eighteen-year-old gentleman student from a former African colony, she didn't recall it. Would she have noticed him if they'd met then?

Perhaps not, but she also remembered seeing a house as she strolled along St. Lazare Street and feeling the strongest sense of déjà vu. At the time she'd believed it was merely

THE TRUTH UNDISCOVERED

something she'd seen before, perhaps a photograph. She walked that street several times over the winter, wondering why that one house seemed to call to her. She might have missed Miguel by minutes.

She wondered what the Jesuits made of him. They'd tracked the Meter for hundreds of years now. There had to be records of birth dates and death dates, things easy to compare. The Jesuits would surely have put together what they knew of the Meter and reached the same conclusion Miguel had last night, that he was being reborn over and over, and her with him.

It might be impossible, but it was the only conclusion that explained the evidence of her senses. Her intuition—one of her most reliable friends—told her it was the truth.

That conclusion, however, would play havoc with the Jesuit's mission to protect orthodoxy. The Catholic Church didn't believe in reincarnation in this earthly realm—not for most people, at least—so the discovery of a powerful witch who defied their teachings must cause them to question... and to fear him.

She watched Miguel a moment longer, noting that he drank coffee in a way that seemed, to her, *correct*. How there could be a correct way to drink coffee, she didn't know, but he was clearly a master of it.

And the coffee *was* excellent. Strong, with just a hint of milk. Exactly how she liked it.

Adela took another sip as she decided how to broach the topic she wanted. In the end, she chose directness. "What do you see our relationship in the future? Will we continue as lovers? And would it be clandestinely, or openly?"

Miguel sat back, smoky eyes appraising her. "I notice you're not demanding marriage."

"Legally, I don't have a name," she said. *Interesting, though, that he brought up marriage immediately.* It hinted at a taste for the traditional. "I can't sign my name to a license, nor can I write anything in the church's register."

He nodded sagely. "Being part fairy would make that dangerous for you anyway. Anyone who learns your name can use it to control you."

Adela licked her lips, annoyed. At her father, of course, who kept the truth secret even from her. She'd never known why her father refused to have her baptized, why he'd always insisted that she never sign a document or take a man's name. She'd assumed that it was a concern of magic—human magic. But Miguel's suggestion that she had fairy blood meant...

She'd already told Miguel Gaspar her name.

It was the name her father had used for her, which made it as close to a true name as she had. She had handed Miguel power over her, and he knew it. She set down her cup. "Is that what *you* intend to do? Control me?"

He smiled. "I admit that I prefer to be in control at times. But I will never use your *name* to force you. I will swear that on my mother's soul, if you wish."

She wondered if that carried any weight with him. She wasn't a child of the Church. She'd never actually crossed the threshold into one. But she did believe that people had souls. Given what he believed about having lived before, he surely did as well. "No need for that drama."

Whether or not she felt tied to him, she had lived this long without him. She could survive perfectly well in the future without him again. If he crossed her, she would simply avenge herself later. The twist of his lips suggested he knew that about her, that she would walk away rather than be coerced. "I enjoy being in control as well."

"I expected nothing less," he said. "I can make it happen without your signature, or your name being said."

"Make what happen?" she asked picking up her coffee again.

"A wedding," he clarified, now gazing at her over the rim of his own coffee cup. "It wouldn't be that difficult to find a priest to perform a ceremony without saying your name, and outside the church itself."

Despite not being a child of the Church, she knew quite a bit about the *laws* of the Church—she worked with the Jesuit Brotherhood, after all. Marriage was one of the Church's seven sacraments, one not taken lightly. "There is an impediment," she pointed out. "I've never been confirmed."

He laughed. "Are you actually concerned about that? Spiritually, I mean."

Adela took a deep breath. "No, I suppose not."

"I ask because if you were to become pregnant, I would prefer that the child become my legal heir."

"Do you think that likely? How old do you think I am?"

"Forty-one," Miguel said easily.

Adela set down her coffee. Most people wouldn't guess that high, but he wasn't like most other people, was he? "Did your gift tell you that?"

He laughed softly, the corners of his eyes crinkling. "I had no intention to offend, Adela. The mistress of Etienne de la Cour died seven years before he did, so it seems logical to me that you'd be seven years older than I am. I am thirty-four. You are, therefore, forty-one."

Etienne de la Cour, the Frenchman he now believed he'd been ~~his~~ before being Miguel Gaspar. She had apparently played the part of his mistress in that conceit, not a wife. He was correct about her age, though. She had no certificate of birth and no baptismal records, but she knew when she'd been born. She was the only person alive who knew.

Or so she'd thought. "People will say that I'm pursuing a younger man in hopes of regaining my youth."

"Are you seeking a compliment?" Miguel asked. "You bear your age very well, my dear. I doubt that others would guess as I did."

She picked up her coffee again and took a sip, wondering if Miguel had ever bothered to court a woman before. As wealthy as he was, he could likely have any woman on this island he wanted. He certainly didn't bother to flatter *her*. She preferred plain speaking, though. "You understand that if I am willing to enter into a marriage that the Church considers invalid, that I'll have no compunction about ignoring such an agreement if I wish?"

"As I said, I have no intention to force you to my will."

"Then with that caveat, I'll accept," she said. "If, however, you're expecting me to birth child after child, I doubt that will happen. I've never come with child before, and I haven't been celibate."

He shrugged. "I'm being pragmatic, Adela."

THE TRUTH UNDISCOVERED

She toyed with her coffee cup. "Yes, I could tell you weren't trying to be *romantic*."

He leaned forward and took one of her hands in his, his fingers dark against hers. "I am not a romantic, Adela. I see the world as it is. No matter what we'd prefer life to be, if a Portuguese woman enters a relationship with an African man, she will feel the censure of others. I prefer that you have some protection should our relationship come to light."

She sat up again, startled. "You intend for us to continue to be clandestine, even after the paperwork is signed—or not signed, in my case."

"Yes, I do," he said. "There are those who will think less of you once they know."

Her mouth fell open, prepared to protest, but he held up one hand to stop her.

"My closest friend, William," he said, "is English, and when his family learned he'd married my cousin Catarina, they told him he could return home, but she was not welcome. He took her anyway, and although my cousin does not speak of it, I know the treatment she received from his family was unkind. They felt that he should have taken her as his lover, but never married her."

"But I am Portuguese," she began.

"The prejudice exists in the Portugals as well," he said, "although not to the same extent. People there will think better of you if they only suspect that I'm your lover, rather than your husband."

Her coffee cup was empty now, so she couldn't lift it to her lips as a cover for taking a moment to think. She dealt on a regular basis with both the Freemasons and the Jesuits, mostly due to her reputation as her father's heir. Her father had been an expert on magic, someone the two antagonistic groups used as a go-between. He'd negotiated a truce between the Portuguese factions, and she'd managed to keep the two groups in balance. But there *had* been prejudice against her because she was female... especially among the Freemasons who didn't wish to admit a woman among their number. She'd had to work hard to hold her place in the two Portugals.

While there were a number of citizens of African descent, or partially so, in Southern Portugal—the two Portugals had once held African colonies, after all—her team would primarily be operating in *Northern* Portugal. Miguel Gaspar, even half-Portuguese as he was, would be remarked upon there.

She gazed at him for a moment, weighing the chance of social disapproval against the fact that this man fit with her better than any she'd ever met before. And in the end, that won. "I will deal with that issue when it crops up."

His brows rose slightly. Perhaps her delay in answering had convinced him that she would be swayed by the opinions of her countrymen over her own sensibilities. But he didn't question her answer. "I will arrange it then."

That afternoon they were married in the courtyard of his house by a priest whose robes were suspiciously tattered about the hem. Miguel's friend William and his cousin Catarina served as witnesses, and no one mentioned the fact that the priest never once asked for her name.

It wasn't romantic, but she wouldn't have trusted Miguel if it had been.

Chapter 6

THURSDAY, 10 OCTOBER 1901

"I'd like you to reconsider." Miguel knew better than to think Adela would do so because he simply asked her. She wasn't the sort to give in to a man's whims. "I have a plan."

Her eyes flicked toward him, and she ran one finger down his bare chest. "And you want to discuss this in bed?"

He'd put off this conversation for days, but they were to leave on the *Ferreira* in the morning. "Would you suggest talking about it after we're aboard ship?"

She laughed softly, stretched her arms over her head, and then rolled onto her side to face him. "What is your plan?"

"I will go to Brazil alone, find your Truthsayer, and bring him back." He ran his hand up her side and shifted closer to her. "You stay here. You can use my house. Or not, if you prefer. And when he and I return, we borrow William's yacht to sail to Lisboa."

She rubbed her cheek against his chin. "And why?"

"The *Ferreira* is a wooden ship, but the hull is reinforced with steel beams."

"And this is important, why?" Her lips moved to his neck, and the touch of her teeth sent images of red daggers along the edges of his vision.

Miguel forced himself not to give in to the distraction. "You were ill for days after you arrived here. Some part of that is crossing moving water, but I suspect traveling on a steamer was the worst part of it. All that steel."

She drew back and regarded him with a rumpled brow. "I suffer from motion sickness."

"On trains?"

"Yes."

"In carriages?"

"Not usually," she admitted.

Over the last few days, he'd discovered she held some prejudice against the idea of the fae side of her blood. There were stimuli that clearly bothered her, easily explained if she had fairy blood, and yet she refused to acknowledge that as a possible cause. The chiming of church bells troubled her not because she was part fairy, she maintained, but because she had delicate ears... and yet the sounding of a foghorn caused her no discomfort whatsoever. She could tell when she handled items with iron content, but put that down to refined taste. She avoided churches and graveyards but claimed that was because she disapproved of aspects of the Church's control over her people.

It was a difficult topic to broach, because she saw herself as the most rational person in any room. Not only did she not want to admit her weaknesses, but she didn't want to admit that was where they'd come from.

"You don't suffer from motion sickness in carriages because they're primarily made of wood," he said. "And they're traveling over land."

Now he'd vexed her. She fixed him with a hard gaze, the sort she probably used to intimidate men. It wasn't as effective with her hair tumbled about her face, and the glittering of her skin belied her next words. "I know what makes me ill," she insisted.

"And you can't be open-minded about any other possible cause?"

"Are you calling me narrow-minded?"

"Hmmm," he said. "I said what I meant. You're not open-minded about this single topic. Otherwise I find you quite willing to listen, or you'd not be in my bed."

"Hmmm," she returned.

Miguel thought she might be softening. "Your father had some dislike for his own kind, perhaps?"

"You might be right," she allowed. "I should be willing to give this more study. If I were to stay, what do you suggest I do? It would be at least three weeks there and back, would it not?"

"That depends on the doldrums, and how thick they are this time of year."

Her eyebrows rose. "The doldrums?"

"The place where the wind doesn't go. To get to Recife, we might not have to cross them. That would save us time."

"Ah. Sailing has never been an interest of mine."

"You don't live on an archipelago," he said. "Even if I don't travel, it's all I hear at dinner parties."

She turned to lie on her stomach, propping herself on her elbows to gaze at him. "You don't sound like you enjoy sailing, either."

"I dislike the inconveniences of travel," he said. "That doesn't mean I don't want to see what's at the end of the road. The *Ferreira*'s sailors tell me their *Pequena Camisola* is a fast ship, capable of sixteen knots. If they catch the currents and avoid storms, we could be in Recife in a week."

"*Pequena Camisola*? Whatever do you mean?"

"The sailors think it unlucky to change a ship's name, so they still call it by its old one, hoping it will ignore the name painted on its stern."

"A charming superstition," she said, "but hardly valid. I'm certain the shipping company doesn't care for it, since it's their name on the ship."

He laughed. Sailors were among the most superstitious creatures on earth. "They allow it if it will keep the sailors aboard."

She ran a finger down the length of his nose, one of those oddly familiar gestures. "I think I shall stay here," she said. "Offer the man whatever he wants to get him back here. Your blunter speech should appeal more to a Truthsayer anyway."

He'd had no intention of saying that aloud. "I'll bring him back."

"And I will stay here," she said, tracing her finger across his lips, "and become very familiar with your friends. I intend to learn all your secrets."

That didn't surprise Miguel at all.

THE TRUTH UNDISCOVERED

MONDAY, 14 OCTOBER, 1901
THE OPEN OCEAN

The deck of the *Ferreira* heaved under his feet, and Miguel made his way to the bow, keeping out of the path of the sailors as he went. The ship was making good speed, although not the promised sixteen knots. Even so, they would weigh anchor in Recife in two more days. The doldrums had been narrow, sparing them the days of sitting still, and now they'd caught a current that bore them south along Brazil's coast.

The sails snapped in the breeze, a sound like a deep bell accompanying each snap—it would be a cacophony if he didn't like it. The sea air tasted green and salty in his mouth, and the wind ran blue-green fingers along his skin. The Portuguese sailors were an easy bunch, two with a faint seer's glow and one with the mark of a finder, but otherwise no witches among them. Most were friendly enough, and although a couple looked askance at a wealthy African man, they said nothing.

It was splendid to be at sea. He would have enjoyed having Adela with him, but she couldn't appreciate this the way he did. He hadn't been on a voyage in over fifteen years, and he'd forgotten the sheer joy of sailing, seeing nothing ahead but sea. It made it seem as if there were still unknowns in this world, something his jaded soul often forgot.

He gazed up at the fore-mast. The rigging plan was familiar. He knew the name of each of the sails: the sky-sail, the royal, the topgallant, the topsails, and the foresails. He'd stood on the deck of a similar ship before. He must have been a sailor, not a passenger, or he wouldn't know the names of the lines and the sails. And he only knew those names in English. That told him that at one point or another, he'd been an English sailor.

He hadn't taken the idea of rebirth seriously until Adela came along. He'd always passed it off as coincidence or wishful thinking. He'd never had *proof.* She was as near to proof as he could get.

CHAPTER 7

WEDNESDAY, 16 OCTOBER 1901
PRAIA, CABO VERDE

Adela went to Catarina. Despite Miguel's clear affection for William, she found the man's volume a little tiring. His wife, however, was clever and curious, and that meant she might know what Adela needed.

Catarina poured the coffee, and Adela added a touch of milk to hers, careful not to splash anything on her skirt. She wore white today, better to handle the temperatures here. "Now," Catarina began, "what exactly are you looking for?"

Adela took a sip of coffee. Catarina's coffee *was* better than that served by Miguel's cook. "I am looking for a Jesuit."

Catarina sat contentedly, not uncomfortable with her, a good sign. "A Jesuit? There is no monastery here, you know."

No, the Jesuits didn't live that way. Even in Lisboa, their Brotherhood was not monastic, preferring to be out among the people. "He will be... somewhere on this island. Close enough that he can keep an eye on Miguel. He will most likely not identify himself as a brother, to keep from drawing attention. He would have arrived here as soon as they figured out that Miguel is the Meter, might have followed him when he went to France, only to return here when Miguel did."

"Perhaps a land owner?" Catarina asked with a coy smile. "One who mysteriously had to return to France for that year, but hasn't gone back since? No wife or children?"

Adela smiled, thinking she'd chosen well. "He's French? Ah,

I suspect he's the one I'm looking for."

Catarina sat back. "When Miguel and I were children, Miguel was always reserved, old for his years. He spoke very well from the beginning, Portuguese coming to him early."

"Not Crioulu?" Crioulu was the pidgin spoken here, created by the merging of Portuguese and several African languages.

"No, not with *his* grandfathers," Catarina said. "Our mutual grandfather was the Portuguese governor when the colony was given its independence, but Miguel's other grandfather was a Portuguese businessman. Both sides of his family spoke Portuguese in their home. My other grandfather was a tradesman, so I spoke both."

"Probably wise."

"It never hurts to know more than one language. But that was exactly the problem with Miguel. His parents hired a tutor, but when the tutor started him on French, the man found that Miguel already spoke it, more fluently than he did. The tutor thought some trick had been played on him and quit in a huff. One of the local landowners, a Frenchman by birth and newly arrived, offered to practice French with Miguel until his parents could find a... more challenging tutor. Marcel DuBois is his name."

Now that was interesting to know. "And how old was Miguel then?"

"Five?" Catarina touched the tip of her nose. "Perhaps six."

Fluent in French at five. Impressive. "I would appreciate it if you could give me his direction. I need to speak with him."

"I'll have my man take you there after our lunch," Catarina offered.

THE TRUTH UNDISCOVERED

The land owned by Marcel DuBois sprawled atop one of the plateaus overlooking the city of Praia and its harbor. The Achada Grande was barren, attractive in the way of wilderness, but not fruitful like the Portuguese countryside. It hadn't taken long for Adela to learn that the previous year had been one of drought, the rainy season almost nonexistent. Unfortunately, save for a terrible storm a few months past, 1901 wasn't looking much better for the area.

Catarina's driver deposited Adela at DuBois' door and promised to wait for her, so she went up the steps of the white-plastered house and pulled the bell chain.

The sound of the bell didn't set her teeth on edge. It wasn't a church bell.

A barefoot servant in garb more suited to the fields than to a fine household answered the door. He took her card and bobbed a bow before running away to find his master. Adela stood in the entry hall and waited. The house itself was clearly in the Portuguese style, with azulejos coming up the mid-point of the plastered walls, a festive blue, white, and yellow.

She traced fingers along the vining pattern in the tiles, waiting to see the homeowner's reaction to her questions.

She didn't have to wait long. A handsome silver-haired man in the white trousers and linen shirt common here came hurrying along the hallway. She would guess his age as past sixty, but he looked like a healthy specimen for that age, the kind of man who stayed alert and strong. "Monsieur DuBois," she said, "or should I call you Frère Marcel?"

"Madame," he began in pleasantly accented Portuguese, ignoring her insinuation, "you have the advantage of me, I'm afraid. Your card, it says nothing." He held out her calling card, which was, indeed, blank.

"You know exactly who I am, Brother."

"I'm afraid you must be mistaken," he said.

"You're afraid of the wrong thing, then. How long have the Jesuits known that Miguel Gaspar is Etienne de la Cour... and so forth?"

Although Miguel had hinted she should use her time studying the scant understanding humans had of fairies and their nature, she'd chosen to study his nature instead. His journals recording his dreams had given her material to put together a timeline that was easy enough to follow. Every time one of the previous Meters had died, somewhere else in the world, the new Meter was born within a year. That could be coincidence, but she had her doubts. And with an organization as widely-spread as the Church, it wouldn't be difficult for them to track witches of interest.

DuBois gestured for her to step into a sitting area off the entryway hall. The sunny room had comfortable-looking leather arm chairs and an impressive wall of bookshelves set so that the sunlight wouldn't strike them. Adela picked one of the chairs—the one that looked more worn, indicating it was his normal seat—and sat down.

"Madame, may I ask your name?" he asked as he settled in the other chair, mouth pursed like he'd eaten sour grapes.

"An amusing attempt," she said, "but since there's a telegraph line between here and Sierra Leone, I'm certain you were notified the moment I stepped aboard ship in Lisboa.

You also know that I have no intention of giving you my name. Then again, we knew each other long ago, didn't we?"

"I have never met you before, Madame, of that I'm sure."

She leaned one elbow on the arm of the chair and set her chin on her fist to gaze at him. "Not in this incarnation, of course. But you are French, and of adequate age to have been Etienne de la Cour's assigned watcher. When a local priest noticed Miguel Gaspar's unusual abilities, you were sent here to observe him. You even managed to wriggle your way into becoming his *de facto* tutor, did you not?"

The landowner laced his fingers together over his belly. "Yes, I know who you are. As to your first question, I have no idea."

She shifted back into the chair and gazed at the man. She was surprised he'd given in so easily. He'd maintained his disguise as a landowner for over thirty years, a long time for a Jesuit to be out of the world. "No idea about Gaspar and de la Cour? Or no idea about the entire string of deaths and births?"

"The second, Madame. We were watching closely for de la Cour's return, and thus it only took a few years to identify Gaspar."

"But as to identities prior to de la Cour?"

"We tracked the Meter, Madame, but as to whether he was the same man, if there were those among the Brotherhood who calculated that before, the information would have been suppressed."

The Jesuits lived to spread their faith, and as the idea of reincarnation flew in the face of the Church's beliefs, they would surely not want the idea that the Meter was the same person, simply reincarnated, to be true... or even known. Miguel Gaspar was a walking contradiction of Church doctrine. That alone explained setting a man to watch over the Meter at all times. "And your God would not allow one exception to His rules?"

"The Meter exists to serve God's will," DuBois said, a non-answer.

"One man cannot pose such a danger to your Church."

"There are two of you," DuBois said, a hint of acid in his tone.

Of course. She would not be surprised to learn that her own ease with garnering access to the Jesuit Brotherhood in Lisboa had its basis not only in her father's history of working with them, but also that the Jesuits wanted to keep track of *her*. How long had they known about her previous association with the Meter? Since she was a child? "Ah, so you worry over me as well?"

"Of a certainty."

"I have been giving it a great deal of thought, and I suspect it was the Jesuits who made my father so determined to hide what he was."

"I had nothing to do with your father," DuBois said defensively, proving that her suspicions were correct. The Jesuits *had* influenced him to deny his kind for some reason, although the specifics of that could vary widely. He could have been trying to protect her from them, and himself, or he could have conceived some aversion due to the teachings of the Church.

With her father long dead, Adela doubted she would ever have a clear answer. "In the fall of '86, I was in Paris, as was

Miguel. Both of us frequently walked past the same house, one that had belonged to de la Cour. I wonder now why I never crossed paths with Miguel there. Did you prevent it?"

His jaw flexed, a sure sign of irritation. "I was charged with watching him. I didn't need you interfering with him."

"And yet here I am, fifteen years later."

"Yes. I'm aware you managed to convince one of the Franciscans to marry the two of you. I am also aware that you didn't sign those marriage lines, and I can render those invalid, as they should be."

Now that was fascinating. "Why bother? I intend to share his bed whether or not we have the sanction of the Church. I saw no harm in making the union legal for the sake of any children who might be born. Then again, having read his journals, I know there won't be any children."

"There never have been," DuBois said. "Not in our reckoning."

"Then why interfere?"

DuBois' face hardened. "Because one way or another, you are always his death."

Chapter 8

**WEDNESDAY, 16 OCTOBER 1901
PRAIA, CABO VERDE**

Adela ran her fingers along the arm of the chair in which she sat, considering the accusation DuBois had made. "How am I his death?"

DuBois gave a bitter laugh. "He thinks he can't live without you, an idea you have always fostered, I suspect. You die and, if he doesn't die with you, sooner or later he takes his own life."

That *was* what had happened to Etienne de la Cour in the end. "But his mistress died seven years before him."

DuBois' shoulders squared. "And it was a fight to keep him in this world that long," he said. "He wanted to die, every day, and I had to remind his of his purpose, and of the mortal nature of the sin he proposed."

Adela licked her lips, thinking. That would have worked on Etienne de la Cour because he was a good son of the Church, but how many of those other identities were not? How many were Buddhist or Pagan or... or simply had no faith at all? Despite his insistence on a wedding, she wasn't sure Miguel had strong feelings for the Church. That must rankle DuBois.

It did, however, explain the seven-year gap in their ages. DuBois had been hanging on to the Meter, influencing him. *Was that for the power that being the Meter's watcher brought? Or was it true concern for Miguel's soul?* Once again she found herself wishing for a Truthsayer's insights into DuBois.

On the other hand, she'd gotten what she came here to get—an acknowledgement that the Jesuits had known all along, not only about Miguel, but about her. DuBois had directly interfered in Miguel's life, and hers, which hinted that they would at every chance they had in the future as well. And they had interfered with her father, somehow, which had in turn tainted her entire life.

On the whole, she had great respect for the Jesuits, but this tarnished her perception of them. She would watch them more closely from now on. "So what do you intend to do about me now?"

DuBois favored her with a contemplative expression. "We need him alive," DuBois said. "Our seers say that there is a terrible war coming, something the like of which has not been seen in centuries."

In the last century, there had been wars in Europe, the Americas, China, Russia; it would be harder to find a country that *had* been spared. The Chinese were fighting an uprising now, another war had sprouted in southern Africa between the Boers and English, and the Spanish had recently fought the Americans, much to Spain's regret. To surpass all of those, it would have to be a terrible war, indeed.

Adela set her chin on her gloved hand and regarded DuBois with concern. "Be clear on this, DuBois. I don't intend to let you have him back, but I will do everything in my power to keep him whole. For myself, not you."

"When you become pregnant, you will die in childbirth," he predicted.

She'd already noted that pattern among Miguel's journals. That wasn't always the cause of her death, but when she did become pregnant, it had never ended well. "How fortunate that I'm not a child of your faith, then, and know how to prevent that from happening."

His jaw clenched, but he didn't respond. His position was difficult, she supposed, being forced to rely on someone he disliked who would use methods he found morally questionable to achieve his goals.

Unfortunately, he would never be completely gone from their lives. She could get rid of him, but the Jesuits would simply replace him. She preferred the devil she did know, as her father used to say.

Adela rose and walked from the room, not bothering to take her leave of the man.

RECIFE, BRAZIL

The city of Recife was a bustling one, many times larger than Praia, and not nearly as dusty. Dozens of canals and channels had given the city the name of the Brazilian Venice—the port was built around a trio of rivers coming together to empty lazily into the sea. Miguel hadn't ever visited the *European* Venice, but he'd seen photographs and doubted they were much the same. Recife had a very Portuguese look to it. Except for the palm trees, which swayed in abundance over the white-plastered buildings and along the streets.

He watched the city come closer as the *Ferreira* came into the port, sails sliding down with the groaning of lines. Recife sprawled in every direction, with Olinda to the north and Jaboatão farther to the south. Ships loaded at the busy docks, shipments of sugar cane, coffee in huge burlap bags, bales of cotton. Unlike Cabo Verde, Brazil had many valuable crops to support its people, making Miguel once again wonder how his islands could improve their lot. The recent years of drought had taken a toll on everything grown in Praia, making Brazil look like a veritable jungle in comparison.

When he left the *Ferreira*, Miguel hired a porter to take his bags to the hotel on Bom Jesus Street. The hotel admitted him, but he had no doubt the clerk at the desk had reservations on seeing his dark skin. Miguel could almost taste in the air an aversion for those of African descent, something he never felt at home in Cabo Verde. When he handed a missive over to the concierge and asked that it be delivered to the police station, the concierge—a man who bore the glowing ties to both a wife and a mistress—scowled at him. Against his inclination, Miguel handed the man twenty réis. The concierge took the bill grudgingly, but agreed to dispatch a boy to the station with the letter.

After that, he had only to wait.

A note *was* returned to him that afternoon, although it wasn't sent up to his room. Miguel only discovered that when he went down to eat dinner, too late to visit the police station. That irritated him. In Cabo Verde, the errand boys would have vied over the chance to do favors for him. In the years since he'd visited France, he'd forgotten that other countries were less inclined to believe that an African man was wealthy. The French had been willing to accept him, but here in Brazil where so many Africans had arrived as slaves, there seemed to be an expectation that anyone with brown skin shared that heritage.

The white-aproned waiters in the hotel's restaurant were all

THE TRUTH UNDISCOVERED

of African descent, like him. A young man with a hint of the seer's gift directed Miguel to a white-draped table near the back of the restaurant, and then seated him in the chair where Miguel could observe the door. Other patrons of the hotel chattered away, most of them Europeans, Miguel guessed. They weren't as offended by his presence as Brazilians might be.

The young waiter brought Miguel a glass of the local *cachaça*—a sugarcane-based drink that tasted white in his mouth—and rattled off a menu where little sounded familiar. On the young man's recommendation, Miguel ordered something called *moqueca* to start—a delicate fish soup that, interestingly enough, included coconut milk. He added a steak, followed by a sweet roll and coffee. He sipped at the last, and was surprised when one of the other waiters gestured a slow-walking man toward his table.

The approaching man was a Truthsayer; Adela hadn't been wrong in her information. Miguel had never seen one with an aura like this, though. His body was surrounded by a blue-white glow that someone other than the Meter might mistake for a halo—the man's name was *Anjos*, after all. Gabriel Anjos.

But what hadn't been in the information given Miguel was the man's state. Adela had mentioned in passing that the man might benefit from working with a healer since he was ill. That was wrong.

Gabriel Anjos was *dying*.

In Miguel's sight, blackness clung to Anjos' lips, the mark Miguel had come to associate with consumption. The man was near his age, but looked a decade older. He walked like an old man. Anjos' gray suit, not well made in the first place, hung from his shoulders, showing he'd lost a great deal of weight. His breathing was shallow and the scent of cigarette smoke followed him about.

It took a second for Miguel to realize he was smelling *actual* smoke, not some manifestation of his gift.

Once the young waiter drew out the cane-backed chair, Anjos slumped down into the seat, his face ashen from the effort of walking across the room. He was about the same height as Miguel and handsome despite his illness, but had the sort of features that would blend in anywhere. Brown hair, brown eyes, medium skin, and no scars or marks to distinguish his features. He would be excellent at tailing criminals... if he had any chance of keeping up with them.

"The dinner is first-rate," Miguel told the man, "and since my patroness is paying, order whatever you wish."

He held out a vague hope that Anjos would order a large meal and surprise him, but the man said, "I have no appetite."

Miguel waited while the waiter set down a glass of water for Anjos, but then nodded the waiter away.

Anjos drew out a silver case, took out a cigarette, and lit it from the candle burning in the centerpiece. He lifted the cigarette with shaking fingers and took a puff, and the smoke curled about his face like a lover's fingers. He exhaled and said, "It helps me forget the pain."

His brown eyes stared into Miguel's, as if daring him to contradict that statement. The man was an addict, and that meant he would love his cigarettes more than almost anything else. Possibly more than his own life, since there seemed to be so little life left in him. Another thing to factor into his calculation of how to convince Anjos to come with them to Portugal.

"May I assume you're the person who's had me investigated?" he asked then.

Miguel shook his head. "No. My patroness."

"Ah," Anjos said. "And why did you—or she—want to meet with me?"

The tricky thing about Truthsayers was that if you didn't lie, at least a little, they weren't sure if they could trust you. *No basis for comparison.* "While I admit to being curious about you—and you are, indeed, what the investigators claim—I am here on her behalf. She becomes ill when she travels and dispatched me to meet with you instead."

"And what do the Jesuits claim I am?" Anjos said after taking in another breath of smoke.

"I didn't ask if the Jesuits were her tools in this, so I can't answer that, but she told me you are supposedly the most powerful Truthsayer alive."

Anjos coughed into a handkerchief. "I question the *alive* part."

Miguel smiled. Well, the man had a touch of humor about his condition. No one recovered from consumption. They usually had enough time to put their lives in order and then died. He would put Anjos near the end of that downward slope. "My lady has a healer who works for her."

Anjos took another drag on his cigarette, and smoke wreathed his face like a second halo. "You don't believe she can help me."

One always assumed a healer as female. Male healers did occur, but they rarely had much power. "I don't," Miguel answered. "Her healer is dead, which makes all of this problematic."

That caught Anjos' attention, his dark eyes narrowing. "And yet you believe that being dead makes it *problematic*, rather than impossible. Why is that?"

Miguel shook his head. "I can't lie to you about this. No healer has ever healed consumption that I know. And this healer of hers is dead already. My gift tells me it cannot work."

"What is your gift?" Anjos asked.

"I am the Meter."

"Meter? What is a Meter?"

"I see what others can do, what they are, what binds them," he explained. He sat back and studied Anjos' weary face. After a moment, he offered, "You have no wife or lover, although there are ties somewhere in your past, years gone. Your only lover now is those cigarettes. You've cut yourself off from everyone, save one person, but that one is... family... blood. No, it's more like two people, twined together. Your obligation."

"You believe every word of that," Anjos said. "Then again, a charlatan wouldn't do worse."

"If you wish me to perform for you like a circus acrobat, you will be disappointed. I've no need to prove to you what I can do."

Anjos stubbed out the end of his cigarette, plucked another from his case, and lit it. "And who exactly is your patroness? Why have me investigated?"

This was where delicacy would come in, and that wasn't his strongest trait. "My patroness prefers to remain anonymous, to some extent. She is known as the Lady. As to you, she hopes to hire you away from the State Police."

"To do what?"

"That's a little vague," he admitted. "She wants a group in place in Northern Portugal who can… ease the transition of power when the old prince passes."

Anjos laughed dryly. "My father cared about the Portugals. I don't."

If he recalled correctly, Anjos was the son of a wealthy Portuguese gentleman and one of his kitchen maids. Apparently, that gentleman hadn't felt any need to pass wealth on to his by-blow. But stepping into that topic would likely prove unhelpful, so he tried another tack. "I'm not going for love of the Portugals," he said. "I wanted to see something of the world. I've lived most of my life on one island."

"But not all," Anjos said after taking another breath of cigarette smoke.

It was interesting that Anjos had picked up that distinction so easily; his abilities as a Truthsayer must be truly amazing. "I spent one year at the university in Paris," Miguel admitted, "before my mother took ill and I had to return to the islands."

"Not enough of the world for you?"

"It's not the only reason I'm going. There's the matter of a woman."

"Ah. Running toward or running away?"

"Toward."

Anjos nodded. "I would not mind getting away from the legacy of my wife. She left me, you see, and others never let me forget that."

This was likely another problem area—it was one of the things the investigator had mentioned. Since Anjos had brought it up, Miguel asked, "Why would she leave you?"

"I was too boring," Anjos said. "Too set on being an inspector and too little on pleasing her whims."

That the woman had left him for a criminal in the town in Olinda was a matter of record. When that man later murdered her, he managed to cast suspicion on Anjos. The accusation was eventually disproved and yet *still* made it into the investigator's report years later. The persistence of that accusation was likely a constant irritant for a police inspector. "Policing is a business that requires one's whole heart."

Anjos laughed shortly. "There are all manner of policemen who don't care about their work."

"But not the good ones," Miguel said, spying the opening he needed. "I served on a municipal force for twelve years. There are good policemen and bad ones. That's what we're being hired to do—to weed out the bad."

Anjos blew out smoke wearily. "And who determines how *bad* is defined?"

"If I'm not much mistaken, we will," Miguel said, leaning closer. "That's why *you* are needed for this, Anjos. You have a gift, one uniquely suited to question other officers. These

THE TRUTH UNDISCOVERED

are men accustomed to thinking their prince's mandate to hunt non-humans and witches makes it right. They think their choices are honorable, reasonable. A less-skilled Truthsayer would be fooled if they withheld the truth."

"All they have to do is remain silent," Anjos pointed out.

"And that's where the healer comes in. Are you aware of the true abilities of a powerful healer?"

"This is the dead one you mentioned earlier?"

He nodded. "Powerful healers can compel an answer."

"You're suggesting torture," Anjos said with a tilt of his head.

"It's not pain," Miguel explained. "It's a compulsion. However, I'm told most people are so frightened by this woman that they comply. She is, after all, dead and yet not dead."

The other man's eyes narrowed. "You have doubts about that."

"I've yet to meet her, but I do have faith in my patroness' word."

Anjos coughed again, pressing his handkerchief against his lips. When the fit passed, he brought away the handkerchief, now stained with blood. "I will consider the offer, but be warned... I might not survive the sea voyage."

Miguel watched the man rise and slowly walk away. Never once had Anjos asked about money.

The money didn't matter to Miguel because he had money of his own. Anjos clearly didn't. *Money means nothing to a man who knows he won't survive to enjoy it.*

Chapter 9

WEDNESDAY, 16 OCTOBER 1901
PRAIA, CABO VERDE

Catarina knew nothing of Miguel's reincarnation, so Adela couldn't divulge her actual reason for visiting DuBois, but she did report that DuBois was, indeed, an incognito Jesuit brother. Over a late dinner, Catarina took that news calmly, merely shrugging and moving on to what Adela planned to do about the man.

"Nothing," Adela admitted. "If I have him killed, another will merely take his place. Perhaps two."

Catarina's dark eyes peered at Adela over the rim of her coffee cup. "Would you truly have him killed?"

During the return carriage ride, Adela had given that a great deal of consideration. "I admit, it was my first thought. But I've yet to order *anyone* killed, so it's unlikely I would start with an inconvenient Jesuit."

Catarina laughed. "I'll never be able to stop thinking of DuBois that way, now—the Inconvenient Jesuit."

Adela found she was liking Miguel's clever cousin more and more. "I am assuming he does good works here on this islands, so that is one reason not to end him."

"True," Catarina answered. "He does help many of the poorest families here, particularly since the drought began. He hires some whom others would not. He makes certain that many of the indigent receive medical care when they cannot afford a doctor. And thus, I must try to think well of him."

Adela poured another cup of the coffee and stirred in a dollop of milk. "It would be simpler if I could just despise the man."

"Well, many of the wealthier men of this island here do the same," Catarina noted, "including Miguel and William, so do not think DuBois singular in his charity. The poverty here is overwhelming, especially in bad times, so the work is never done. One person, one family at a time, it's the best we can do."

Adela leaned forward. "Speaking of which, there is a woman who cooks for a restaurant, Teresa dos Santos. Do you know her?"

"I do," Catarina said, the corners of her eyes crinkling.

"Miguel tells me she refused the funds from him to open a larger restaurant. Would she, do you believe, accept an investment from me?"

"You wish to invest here in Cabo Verde?" Catarina set her coffee aside.

"I am considering it. You own cook is excellent, but I have to admit, the meal at Silva's restaurant was... absolutely splendid."

"Not merely the company?" Catarina teased.

"I'm able to differentiate," Adela said with a slow nod. "So, do you think she would accept funding from me?"

"I think that would be tolerable to her."

"Then will you help me put together a proposal? I'm sure you'd have a better idea of the legal hurdles I'll have to surmount here."

Catarina smiled and sat back in her chair. "I do, indeed."

OLINDA, BRAZIL

Olinda was, without doubt, far more charming than Recife itself. Olinda had once been the capital of the state of Pernambuco, Miguel knew. Thus, it had retained many of its lovely old colonial buildings, most built by hands as dark as his own. But he wasn't headed to that part of Olinda.

He'd come here following Gabriel Anjos. Anjos had been surprisingly difficult to track, not because the man was elusive but because the man was *slow*. It was harder to stay hidden from a man who moved at such a limping pace. Miguel had been grateful when Anjos finally caught a cab. He hired one of his own to follow the vehicle out of Recife.

Where Anjos was going, he didn't know, but he suspected it was to see the source of that tie Gaspar had noted about him. Not a woman, not a child, but something held him here... that was what Miguel wanted to discover. If he knew the reason why Anjos wanted to stay, then it would be easier to pry him loose.

I did assure Adela I could get the man to come with me. It would be a shame to fail her so early in their relationship. And Anjos was an exceptionally talented man. That was also a consideration.

The cab carried him all the way to Olinda. The driver pulled into a court to one side where he could see the cathedral, an old white-plastered building that looked quite impressive for its age. Not much different than some of the churches in

Cabo Verde in style, either. Anjos stepped down onto the cobbled street before the cathedral, paid the driver, and then began limping down the street, heading into a residential part of the city. Miguel waited until Anjos had gone around the corner, then exited his own cab and followed the man.

When he came around the curve of the road, he could see all the way down to the sea. Anjos limped on, walking carefully on the cobbles. Miguel pursued him past several larger houses that seemed to be let out as individual flats, each balcony hosting drying laundry. It was a section of town that showed ties to the church, the faithful bearing ties of power about them that glowed purple in Miguel's sight. He could almost smell the censers—although he was actually catching whiffs of cigarette smoke from the watchers leaning over the cast-iron rails of the balconies. A group of children ran up the road past him—mostly African, that lot—and ran on toward the cathedral.

Anjos stopped at the door of a yellow-painted house, drew out his keys, and moved to open the door.

Miguel paused, catching something in the air. A warning. Perhaps one of those watchers on the street's balconies had flinched. Something smelled wrong.

He turned to look back up in the direction which he'd come just in time to see a form all of fire barreling toward him, the smell of brimstone rising with it. The creature of flames roared at him, bellowing out a breath of strong-scented air.

Miguel heard people fleeing, chairs scraping on the balconies, windows banging shut. The creature came closer to him, its size swelling as it did until it stood twice the height of a man. It grabbed Miguel's wrist, sending flames up his arm. He gazed curiously at those flames, feeling a suggestion pushing at his mind, one that reminded him of the tentacles of a jellyfish slipping past his skin, faint stings but no real grasp.

"It's a good illusion," Miguel told the creature, and kicked it in the balls.

The illusion of fire shrank like a hot-air balloon collapsing, folding down into the shape of an African man on his knees, clutching his privates.

Miguel stood his ground, wondering why he'd been singled out. That was when pain exploded through the back of his head. Darkness enfolded him before he hit the cobbles.

Chapter 10

WEDNESDAY, 16 OCTOBER 1901
OLINDA, BRAZIL

"Ezequiel, what have you done?" the voice came from the other side of the room, meant to be hushed and low, but Miguel still heard it.

"He was following you, Gabriel," a second voice returned. "What was I supposed to do?"

"Let him follow me," the first man said.

That was Gabriel Anjos, Miguel could tell now. Even hushed, his voice had a distinctive sound in Miguel's ear. The other man? Clearly related somehow. Given the familiarity between them, brothers, perhaps. Miguel continued to listen, lying still so as not to draw attention.

"I know you're awake," Anjos said, and then began coughing, that hacking, wet cough that made Miguel think the man was coughing up blood. He stilled after a moment, and the other man—Ezequiel—said something to him in a low voice.

"I am not going to the hospital," Anjos said then. "And I know you're awake, Inspector Gaspar, so you might as well sit up."

Miguel sighed heavily and pushed himself into a sitting position. When he opened his eyes, he beheld a small room with tatty furnishings. He'd been lying on a worn cane-backed settee with a hand-made quilt of brightly colored fabrics over it. The workmanship was filled with a glow of love and magic—probably made by a woman. The recently painted walls of the room were yellow to make it cheery, and two other cane chairs stood across from where he sat. A small hearth was unlit and immaculately clean. "Who cares for this house for you?" he asked Ezequiel.

The third man in the room, an African man whose face bore some similarity to Anjos about the jaw and nose, folded his arms over his chest and lifted his chin. "You have no business bothering Inspector Anjos."

"I was offering him a job," Miguel said. "Are you brothers?"

The other man—Ezequiel—shot a terrified glance at Anjos, who was still folding up his soiled handkerchief. Anjos merely nodded, so Ezequiel asked, "Who are you?"

His voice was similar to Anjos', but Anjos had a more cultured tone, his accent less broad. Anjos had been educated, but Ezequiel had not. In most cases, that would be a source of jealousy. Ezequiel had used a club on Miguel, but it was out of a desire to protect Anjos, so that spoke of loyalty between them. Now that Miguel's eyes were open, he could *see* the ties of brotherhood between them, a faint cloud of strands of different colors built up over many years. Friendship, obligation, anger, jealousy, love, patience... all there between the two men.

Ezequiel was Anjos' younger brother, although clearly of a different mother. Apparently, the Portuguese gentleman who'd gotten Anjos on a kitchen maid had also taken an interest in his slave women.

And just as clearly to Miguel's eyes, Ezequiel wasn't a Truthsayer like his brother. That meant Anjos inherited his gift from his mother, not their mutual father. Ezequiel did show a healer's touch, but not of a level that he could help his brother in any way. He was the sort of healer that aided others with aches and pains, the sort old women sought out to help them with sore hands in the cold months.

Miguel smiled at Ezequiel. "I am Inspector Miguel Gaspar, currently of Cabo Verde, but I've recently taken employment with a Portuguese faction. My employer wants to hire your brother as well."

Ezequiel shot a big-eyed glance at Anjos. "Portugal? They want you to go to Portugal?"

Anjos made a calming gesture. "You know very well I cannot go."

Ezequiel shook his head. "Gabriel, you must not refuse because of me. You have always wanted..."

Anjos raised one hand to stop him. "I would not survive the journey," he said. "There is no point."

There was more to it than that, Miguel could tell. This brother was the reason that Anjos stayed. Then again...

Miguel heard halting footsteps coming down the steps from the rooms above the sitting room in which he'd found himself. Dark skirts wrapped around thin ankles. The woman wore a lace-trimmed ivory shirt, and gray threaded her wiry hair. And all about her form showed the golden aura of a healer, far more powerful than the son's pale light. Now Miguel know who'd made that quilt that lay on the old settee. It was part of her, imbued with a bit of her magic as she'd sewn it.

"Mamãe," Ezequiel protested, "you must rest."

Ah, so this is the real reason. Anjos could not leave his brother, who in turn would not leave his mother. Having returned to Cabo Verde to nurse his own mother through her final illness, Miguel understood that faithfulness.

The older woman wasn't far off the age his own mother would have been today, and had once been quite beautiful, but she was worn out before her time. Miguel wasn't sure if that was simply the demands of working for a hard master, or whether she'd simply given too much of herself in her work as a healer. Looking about the sitting room again, Miguel could see that it was a waiting room, a place for her clients to wait while she worked with another. The quilt held enough of her magic to calm her visitors, to make them feel better merely for having sat there.

"Nonsense," the woman said in a soft voice that still bore tones of her African birthplace. "I heard your brother. And who is our guest? Who hit him?"

Guest? Miguel rubbed the back of his aching head. Interesting that the healer knew someone had hit him. Or perhaps she'd merely overheard the same conversation he had.

"Tia," Anjos said, "he's come here to hire me. Ezequiel was surprised, no more."

Anjos is willing to cover for this brother. Miguel wondered if Anjos had been covering for Ezequiel his entire life. And he didn't know what had happened to the other man, the one who'd thrown the illusion of a demon about himself.

The healer came closer to Miguel. She stopped and peered into his eyes. "If you'll sit down, boy, I will make your headache go away."

"Mamãe," Ezequiel tried again. "You must keep your strength."

The woman grasped Miguel's arm with one hand and gently

drew him toward the settee. Not wanting to fight her, Miguel went. He sat politely on the settee and waited while the woman stood with her palm to his forehead.

He knew what she was doing. She was trying to use her gift to sense the forces flowing throughout his body. He'd had this done before, and always with similar results. Healers found him... *frustrating.*

And nothing would convince Anjos that he was what he said he was like this woman's reaction.

After a moment, she drew back and eyed Miguel. "What *are* you?"

Gabriel Anjos considered the mestiço man before him. Tia Ana Maria lifted her hand from his forehead, her warm eyes slitted in suspicion. "I cannot move your energies," she told Gaspar. "Why is that?"

Gaspar gingerly rubbed the back of his head. "I am immune to magic. Of all kinds, madam, so not even a healer can affect me."

An interesting thing to know. When Gaspar spoke, his voice had revealed nothing, falling strangely flat on Gabriel's ears. He had encountered criminals before who were like that—who simply had no emotion about anything at all. Their words didn't register as true or false in his ears when they spoke, only as... *words.* Gaspar sounded the same, but he clearly had some care for the others about him, so there must be a different cause. Perhaps his claim of immunity from the talents of witches was true.

Tia Ana Maria tuned her head toward him. "I feel his flows, Gabriel, but I am being held back from touching them."

"I am, as far as I know, unique," Inspector Gaspar told her.

"I cannot sense him either, Tia," Gabriel said, taking her papery-dry hand. "But I don't believe he's dangerous." Miguel Gaspar struck him as... civilized. Likely a gentleman, and wealthy based on the quality of his clothing and his hotel. Well-groomed, confident—a difficult thing for a mestiço man in Brazil.

"I have never heard of a man who withstands magic before," she said over her shoulder.

"He knew Feliciano wasn't a demon," Ezequiel added. "And that he wasn't burning."

Gabriel sighed. "Feliciano was with you? I've told you..."

He didn't bother to finish, though. He'd never had any luck convincing Ezequiel that Feliciano didn't care whom he involved in his problems. Feliciano didn't care who was caught, either, which was why Ezequiel had spent time in the jail in Olinda. Feliciano had begged Ezequiel's forgiveness, and Ezequiel had given it, blissfully ignoring the truth that his so-called friend would do the same again the next time the need arose.

"Tia," Gabriel said instead. He shoved one hand in his pocket and fingered the cigarette case there. She didn't like his smoking, said it made his lungs worse, but it distracted him from the pain, and in the last year he'd begun to need it more and more. *Once I get in the cab*, he promised himself. "This man claims he is a *Meter*. Do you know that that is?"

Tia Ana Maria's dark eyes slid toward Gaspar again. "That

is only a legend."

"I assure you, I am not," Gaspar said. "It's not precisely an honor."

"And he wants you to go with him?" Tia asked. "Gabriel, you *must* go."

She must have overheard that part of his conversation with Ezequiel. "Tia, you know I cannot travel that far."

She crossed her arms over her chest and fixed him with a one-eyed gaze. "You will go, son."

In the culture from which her mother had come, women ran the family, and because she'd nursed him after his own mother's death in childbirth, Ana Maria considered him *her* son. Gabriel walked a careful line between offending her and going his own way. "Tia..."

"You will go."

Ezequiel glanced back and forth between them. "Mamãe, you cannot send Gabriel away."

"You will go with him," she told her son firmly. "In Portugal, you will have a new start."

Gabriel glanced over at Inspector Gaspar. The man seemed utterly unconcerned about the addition of Ezequiel to the party travelling to Portugal. Then again, perhaps Gaspar already knew Ezequiel would balk at going.

"Mamãe," Ezequiel began, flushing, "I cannot go..."

"How much money do you owe him?" Gaspar asked tactlessly. "I see that among all your other ties, young man. You owe him money, and he holds that over you to buy your allegiance."

Gabriel had suspected that money might come into it, but whenever he'd asked Ezequiel, his brother denied it.

"I don't owe him money," Ezequiel insisted, paler now.

Gabriel sighed. *A lie, as always.* Sometimes Ezequiel forgot he was a Truthsayer. "Ezequiel..."

"No," Ezequiel said forcefully, "you will not make me leave him." He turned and walked out the front door before Gabriel gathered the energy to chase him.

For a moment, there was silence. Gabriel coughed despite trying to hold it in. He sat on the nearest chair, pulled a handkerchief out of his jacket pocket, and dabbed at the corner of his lips. "Don't even think it, Tia."

If he let her, Tia Ana Maria would give him all her energies and die in his place. And there was no point to that. His sickness was a sentence of death. She was weak, but might live for years to come. There were others who needed her help. She came and stood next to him, a solicitous hand to his shoulder.

"Their relationship is more to him than just money or friendship," Gaspar said then.

"It is none of your concern," Tia Ana Maria said, a note of defensiveness creeping into her tone. Her fingers tightened on Gabriel's shoulder.

Gabriel sighed. He understood exactly what Gaspar meant. He'd known that for some time. He wouldn't mind Ezequiel's attachment to Feliciano if it wasn't so one-sided. Gabriel was sure Feliciano would dump his brother without hesitation if a wealthier and more subservient victim came along.

Gaspar held up one hand. "I meant only that he will not walk away willingly from this other man."

"It is none of your concern," Tia repeated, hand shaking now.

"Let me take you back upstairs, Tia," Gabriel said. "You need your rest for tomorrow's visitors."

With one more baleful glance at Gaspar, she conceded, letting Gabriel escort her back up to her room. Climbing stairs always winded him, and he had to stop on the landing to catch his breath.

"He has no business seeing into private matters, that one," Tia Ana Maria groused.

"He may not be able to help it," Gabriel said, "just as you must heal others, he must do what he does." It was more a case that she preferred to keep their family's business private. When Gabriel's wife left him, quite publicly, Tia Ana Maria had been incredibly annoyed. "Now, promise me you will lie down and rest, Tia."

"You know I will, Gabriel." She patted his cheek and went into her bedroom, closing the door behind her.

After a moment on the landing spent simply breathing, Gabriel started back down, praying that his knees wouldn't buckle. Inspector Gaspar waited for him down there, looking as patient as the dead.

"I could fetch a cab, escort you back to your dwellings," Gaspar said. "I can wait for you to sort out your... family's concerns."

"I'll be staying here until morning," he said as he sank down on the waiting room's settee. "To see whether my brother returns. I don't want Tia upset any more than she already is."

"Most men wouldn't take such care for a half-owned family," Gaspar noted obliquely.

"They *are* my family," Gabriel snapped. *The man is not a diplomat, is he?* He fished a cigarette out of his case, grateful Ana Maria wouldn't see it. With shaking fingers, he lit the cigarette, drew in a deep breath, and let it go, smoke slipping past his lips.

"You're kind," Inspector Gaspar said. "It's a quality not listed in all the information I was given about you. I think we need you even more now, because that's a trait neither I nor my employer possess. There should always be someone around who will be kind when we will not."

Gabriel took another deep breath, not liking the failure of his talent to determine whether the man meant those words. *At least he seems aware he's not kind.*

"The money can be extended to them," Gaspar said as he crossed to the door. "An annuity, an allowance. Or bring them with you, to Cape Verde or Portugal. My employer can easily afford their living."

Gabriel watched the man let himself out of the house. Once Gaspar was gone, Gabriel settled back on the settee, dragged Ana Maria's quilt over himself, and did his best to relax.

Chapter 11

THURSDAY, 17 OCTOBER 1901
PRAIA, CABO VERDE

Catarina joined Adela for an early breakfast. Adela had grown fond of having a female friend around. The world in which she operated in the Portugals was primarily the domain of men. There she was constantly in competition with them, constantly trying to prove herself worthy of their time. She had little opportunity to enjoy simple companionship, and would miss Catarina once she returned to Northern Portugal.

Unfortunately, their companionable breakfast was interrupted by a visitor forcing his way onto the terrace. The barefoot man wore white trousers and tunic that made her think him a laborer. His straw hat had a tattered brim.

Adela gazed at his hands, dry and hard-knuckled. "You've come from the docks?"

He didn't deny it. "Please ma'am. Please, if you are the Lady, you *must* come."

Adela watched as he twisted a kerchief between his dark hands. His eyes stayed on the stones of the terrace. She was sure he was truly afraid. "Why me?"

"*She* asked for you. The veiled woman," he insisted. "She asked for you. You must come. You must..."

The veiled woman. Adela set aside her drink and rose. "I'll come."

Catarina rose as well. "Shall I accompany you?"

As much as Adela would have liked her company, she had a good idea who waited for her at the docks. "I should handle this alone, Catarina. If it's who I think it is, then I need to bring her back here and, make her comfortable if I can."

The dock worker continued to shift from foot to foot nervously.

"Go on and tell them we're on our way," Catarina said.

The dock worker bowed and jogged away. A short time later, they were in the carriage, heading to the docks. "I'm afraid that you'll find my guest disturbing. Most people do."

Catarina shielded her eyes with one hand. The morning was bright and crisp. "You know who this is? At the docks?"

"Yes. She works for me. She's my... healer."

Catarina turned her dark eyes on Adela. "You say it doubtfully."

Adela sighed. "You shall see, I'm afraid."

The docks of Praia were not impressive—functional at best—but they didn't have to go that far. On the end of the long road into the docks walked a single figure draped in black—a woman in a black dress with a heavy black veil over her head. She came toward the city of Praia, looking all too much like a harbinger of death.

No one approached the woman, as if they knew it would mean their lives to stray too close. Some made the sign of the cross and hurried away. Children playing with a ball on the street picked it up and ran somewhere safer. No beggars held out their hand to her, and the stray dogs all slunk back into their alleyways.

The carriage horses balked, abruptly halting in the middle of the street. Catarina sat immobile, one hand to her chest, an almost greenish cast to her skin. Adela tapped the front wall of the carriage to make certain the driver kept it still, opened the door, and lowered the steps herself. When she'd climbed down, she turned back to face Catarina. "If you'll take the carriage home, I'll take care of my guest."

Catarina stared at that form coming toward them, her breathing shallow.

Adela reached in and grabbed Catarina's knee. The other woman jumped, but met her eyes, so Adela repeated her request. Catarina nodded and made the sign of the cross. Adela merely closed the door, repeated her instructions to the driver, and walked on toward the approaching woman. Fortunately, the driver kept his presence of mind, and she heard the carriage turning behind her.

The woman on the road spotted her and changed the direction she walked. Adela met her not far from the Port Offices, aware what a contrast they would make. She wore white again today, a straw hat perched on her head. Next to her, Nadezhda Vladimirova looked like Death.

She might be wearing multiple layers of black, a heavy veil, and gloves, but Nadezhda wasn't sweltering. She wouldn't be bothered by heat at all. She was, in essence, dead. She wore funereal garb so others would know what she was and keep their distance. An unnecessary step, since most people could sense there was something wrong about her, something dangerous. Only the greatest fools ever disturbed her, for she could leave them half-dead without even touching them.

Being in Nadezhda's presence made Adela's skin crawl, but

like church bells, holy ground, and iron, she could endure it. Nadezhda hadn't, as far as Adela knew, killed a human being in a decade or so now. But if Adela understood correctly, even standing too close to her could siphon away bits of one's life. Fortunately, Nadezhda seemed inclined not to damage her, so Adela had yet to feel the woman's wrath.

Adela smiled and linked her arm with the other woman's. "I did not expect you here."

"I did not wish to come," Nadezhda said in her emotionless voice. "The Jesuits are astir. You should know."

She had left Nadezhda under the eyes of the Jesuit Brotherhood in Lisboa, partially to assure that Nadezhda didn't kill anyone—Adela secretly worried over that possibility despite Nadezhda's promises—and partially to assure the Jesuits didn't start any trouble while she was gone. "Do you know what set them off?"

"Something was stolen." Nadezhda gathered her skirt with her other black-gloved hand as they began walking up the steep road toward the mesa on which the town proper could be found. "I do not know what."

The Jesuits and Freemasons both labored under the strange belief that their way of controlling the magic in the world was the correct one. If there were magical items to be snatched up, both groups would rush to grab them. And they didn't always respect the initial disposition of those items post-acquisition.

In other words, they stole things from each other.

The Jesuits felt that God was on their side, giving them the right to do so. The Freemasons believed that the pursuit of

Science was more important than the Church's whims—although not more important than God, which was a different matter for them. Neither side believed the other had the moral high ground. Both sides needed a nanny to slap their hands on occasion.

Unfortunately, she had to be there in Lisboa to do so.

Adela spent much of the morning arranging for Nadezhda's unexpected baggage to be brought to Miguel's house and settling her in one of the guest rooms. Then she'd had to calm the staff and assure them that Nadezhda wouldn't eat them. Or curse them, or give them the Evil Eye. It had been a trying couple of hours, but she didn't want to cook for herself until Miguel returned, so she made promises that she hoped Nadezhda would allow her to keep. The servants would sleep overnight at a hotel at her expense and would come in only to handle the minimal amount of chores. She'd had to work out similar arrangements wherever she'd taken Nadezhda in the past, so she knew the pattern of it.

After that, though, she saw little point in sitting around at Miguel's house, waiting for someone to tell them what was happening in Lisboa. Then again, Adela knew exactly who *could* tell her what she wanted to know.

And since she'd alienated the man recently, she had no reason not to take Nadezhda with her. The problem would be finding a way to get her there. The distance from Miguel's house to DuBois' wasn't a distance Adela wanted to walk. After a discussion with Nadezhda, Adela asked the cowed-looking butler to arrange for the carriage to be brought around.

"They will stay calm," Nadezhda promised.

Adela wasn't quite as sanguine about that, but Nadezhda had lived this way long enough that surely she knew her own capabilities.

When the carriage came around, she and Nadezhda climbed into it, Adela still in her morning white and Nadezhda looking like a raven. The horses remained eerily calm despite the driver's quivering voice, and Adela wondered if Nadezhda might be drawing out just enough of their life force to still their instincts to flee.

Once they reached the Achada Grande, Adela ordered the driver to stop near an expanse of the gray-green scrub brush that grew on the plateau's wildness. She clambered down from the carriage unaided, and then helped Nadezhda, who had to cope with extra layers of fabric. They walked a good distance from the horses into the scrub brush. The sea breeze, cool and bearing a hint of moisture, tugged at her clothing.

Nadezhda drew in a breath and asked, "No one relies on this for food, do they?"

Adela surveyed the area. The scrub brush all about her wasn't being cut, so it wasn't food. It looked to be some variety of wormwood, something she'd seen everywhere on the island, so it wasn't rare, either. "No humans, I think."

Nadezhda knelt among the wormwood and removed her black gloves, revealing pale and delicate hands, not veined with age. She set her gloves on the dirt and grasped a handful of scrub in each hand.

Adela watched, both fascinated and horrified. She'd seen this before, this theft that Nadezhda practiced. *Better than the alternative.*

The fronds in Nadezhda's hands abruptly turned brown, the entire plants drying out as if they'd had no rain for months. Then the desolation spread, a circle about Nadezhda's black form growing wider and wider like ink spilled in water until all the growth on the plateau was dead, too dry even to feed the birds.

For a brief moment, Adela heard Nadezhda breathing, her shuddering breaths sounding like a frightened child's.

And then her breathing stopped again.

Adela stepped back as Nadezhda rose, tugging on her gloves. "I was unable to feed on the ship," Nadezhda said. "Not unless I wanted to go down in the hold and hunt rats."

That was delivered without any inflection, so Adela wasn't sure whether it was a joke. *Perhaps not.* She had known Nadezhda for almost fifteen years now, and still had no idea how the woman kept moving. Nadezhda claimed she'd only once killed a man in the decades since she left her lake in Russia, but magic usually had a cost. Adela suspected her own life might be shorter now for having crossed paths with Nadezhda Vladimirova.

Without a further word, Nadezhda walked back to the carriage and climbed inside. The horses were no more restive than normal now, as if they knew she was no longer a threat. Adela followed.

They didn't speak in the carriage until they reached DuBois' house. When they stood at the household's door, Nadezhda shifted her veil to assure it covered her face completely. The usual servant failed to answer the door, and when Adela lifted the latch and swung the door open, she saw the bare-footed man on his knees, repeatedly crossing himself and weeping. She swept into the entryway past him, letting Nadezhda follow at her own pace.

Let the man cower. It would set the appropriate tone for the conversation she intended to have with DuBois.

"DuBois," she called. "You withheld information. I want answers."

No one answered. She spotted Nadezhda's dark skirts in the corner of her eye, and glanced back to see the servant crawling on his hands and knees toward the open door. "You there," she said. "Stop!"

He glanced at Nadezhda, jumped up, and ran.

"Do you want me to stop him?" Nadezhda asked.

The barefoot man was already in the drive, past the carriage. Adela didn't relish the idea of chasing him, so she shook her head. Nadezhda probably *could* have stopped him for her, but Adela preferred a more civilized quarry. "Let's go find the brother, instead."

They walked along the main hallway with its azulejos, cool and cheerful. But a metallic smell filled the end of the hall, and when she entered the sunny sitting room off the main hall, she found exactly what had made the servant so afraid.

In the comfortable chair she'd sat in on her last visit, Marcel DuBois sprawled, his neck slashed open. Blood splattered his lovely bookshelves, covered his clothing, stained his carpet, now mostly dried and brown. His death had been violent but mercifully quick.

It hadn't been the servant who did this. Adela hadn't seen a drop of blood on the man.

"Earlier this morning," Nadezhda said after sniffing the air. "Approximately the time that I stepped off the boat."

Well, that would give both of them convenient alibis... if the police were inclined to believe them.

"He went peacefully," Nadezhda added.

Adela took in the scene all about her. Blood everywhere. "How can you say that?"

"I can feel it," Nadezhda said, coming one step closer. "Look at the glasses on the table. They had a drink first, and then... the other cut his throat."

Adela felt her stomach sink. "That's suicide. He would never consent."

"It was not suicide," Nadezhda said, no emotion in that flat voice of hers. "It was *sacrifice*. I can taste it in the air. He gave his life... to protect his knowledge, I suppose."

Adela put one fingertip under her nose to block that tang of blood in the air. The Jesuit Brotherhood put their causes above reason at times, above the black and white interpretation of religious dogma. Surveying the scene again, she had to admit Nadezhda was likely right. DuBois would have seen this as a sacrifice, his duty to his cause. *Martyrdom.*

Chapter 12

THURSDAY, 17 OCTOBER 1901
PRAIA, CABO VERDE

Adela closed her eyes and calculated. If the servant ran directly to the police, they would have an hour perhaps before those worthies arrived. She wasn't going to ask one of Miguel's servants to perjure himself, so the driver would verify the servant's claim that she and Nadezhda were at the house. It came down to whether the physician who examined DuBois' body was competent... and honest. "I do hope we aren't arrested for murder."

Nadezhda turned slowly. "That is not our problem."

Adela opened her mouth to argue.

Nadezhda held up one black-gloved hand as she walked toward the door. "The house is on fire."

Adela didn't care whether the servant or DuBois' killer had started the fire. Either way, it was surely done to hide the death... and whatever evidence had been left behind. "Damn, the man was thorough."

Nadezhda leaned out to peer into the hallway. "Was the priest a painter?"

"The brother," she corrected automatically. "He was a friar. And I've no idea."

"I smell turpentine."

Had that been added after they arrived? She didn't recall smelling it on the way in. "Is the hallway clear?"

"No. The stairwell between us and the door is burning now." Nadezhda stepped back inside the room, unflustered as always, and closed the door. "Perhaps that was what frightened the servant."

Adela had no idea whether Nadezhda could actually die. *I'm fairly certain I can.*

How long did they have? She stared at the sitting room's large windows, calming herself. She needed to think. She could feel heat now, although that might just be in her head. A creak sounded from somewhere above, the bones of the house protesting. She couldn't hear the roar of fire yet, but it was only a matter of time. She pointed to an empty arm chair. "Can you throw that chair through a window?"

Nadezhda didn't argue. She picked up the chair and tossed it effortlessly out the center window. Glass shattered and fell, making Adela flinch back, but she crossed to the not-too-blood-splattered desk on one side of that broken window. She spotted a trash bin underneath the desk, picked that up, and began stuffing every loose document she could find into it, cursing DuBois under her breath as she did so. She jerked open the drawers and rifled through them as the house continued to creak and groan.

Dark smoke, drawn by the chance of escape through the broken window, eased under the door and streamed through the room now. Adela coughed, but continued her search. After a moment, she gave up on the desk. She turned around to see Nadezhda standing next to DuBois' body, one black glove removed. "What are you doing?"

Nadezhda's hand shook. "I..."

That wasn't her normal, emotionless voice. "What?"

"I can feel the life still," Nadezhda whispered.

"He's dead," she said.

"What's in him is not," Nadezhda said, her voice breaking now.

And what harm would it do to kill whatever she sensed in the man's gut? A tapeworm, perhaps? "Then take it. But hurry, I need to search the body."

Nadezhda laid that bare hand on DuBois' forehead. She threw her veiled head back, and then DuBois slumped just a bit, looking ever so slightly *more* dead, if that was possible. *Perhaps it's just the smoke in the air.* Adela coughed again.

Nadezhda stumbled back, her bare hand clenching into a fist. Adele took the opportunity to lean forward. She grimaced, but jerked open DuBois' stinking, blood-drenched morning jacket to dig through the pockets. She located only a scrap of paper the size of a large coin. She thrust that into her bodice and, frustrated, ripped at his trousers' watch pocket. Nothing but a watch.

"We should go," Nadezhda said, her voice returned to its normal coldness.

Adela pushed back from the brother's body. "What did you want hidden so badly, man?"

DuBois didn't answer.

The fire in the hallway was beginning to roar, audible through the closed door. Another creak sounded, this one closer, followed by a loud boom. Not an explosion, but part of the house collapsing. Nadezhda was right—time to go. Adela made her way to the window. The glass had jagged edges, but she used her purloined trash bin to break those edges out, and then grabbed up a throw from one of the intact chairs and laid it over the low sill of the window. Nadezhda climbed through, unconcerned by the fate of her garments. Adela handed the trash bin through to Nadezhda, then followed more carefully, trying to preserve her dress. After all, it would...

She glanced down at her white bodice and saw blood all over it. *No need to save this outfit.* Groaning in disgust, she clambered through the window's opening. Her skirt caught, but she ripped it free. She landed on the ground amid the broken glass and hissed when something cut her palm. Nadezhda helped her up and drew her away.

Once outside, she could hear the roar of the fire unmuted. The house was surely going to burn to the ground. The attics and upper stories were ablaze, those floors apparently set first. They must have arrived here right after the fire was set, making her suspect the frightened servant might have done it after all. That would explain his eagerness to escape. Then again, it meant he was less likely to alert the authorities.

Adela glanced down at her ruined garb and nearly spoke before she heard the clatter of a carriage on the drive. Aha! Miguel's driver hadn't fled. "Come, quickly," she told Nadezhda.

They hurried around the side of the house to where the carriage waited, Adela using her gift to keep them unseen. She didn't want the driver to see the blood on her garments. She opened the carriage door, waited until Nadezhda was inside, and ordered the driver to return to Miguel's house.

"Madam, the house is afire," the driver protested, his tone confused. "We should tell the police."

There was no accusation in his voice, for which she was glad. Perhaps he, too, suspected the fleeing servant. "To the house first, and then you may go tell the police. There's no saving this place."

"Yes, madam," he replied. The carriage began to move, circling the drive to leave.

Adela heard another boom and crash, and through the windows she could see the house shudder as part of the back collapsed with a roar, creating a new flurry of smoke and sparks and heat. With a drought on the plateau, there was no way for firemen to get enough water here to save the place. She coughed and shook her head. "It's a shame."

Nadezhda didn't argue. She didn't agree either.

As the carriage moved down the road, Adele set her trash bin on the seat and glanced at her left hand. There was a narrow cut across the ball of her thumb, more blood than injury, she suspected. It stung, but little more. She ripped a strip of fabric off her skirt and used that to wrap it.

"I can heal that," Nadezhda said.

Adela shook her head. "No, it's shallow."

Like most healers, Nadezhda felt a compulsion to heal others, even now. Adela didn't intend to take her up on it. Not today. It wasn't that she disliked the idea of being healed by Nadezhda, but whenever Nadezhda *did* heal someone, it was at the price of what little animation she did have. If Nadezhda had fed off DuBois' corpse, then let her enjoy the bit of life she'd sucked out.

Nadezhda's veiled head turned away, as if she stared out the window. Perhaps she did.

The driver took them back to Miguel's house, let them down in the courtyard, and then drove away. Adela kept the two of them unseen until they got inside the house. She went to Miguel's bedroom to strip off her ruined clothes and bathe. She had no idea if Nadezhda intended to do the same, but Nadezhda could take care of herself, and none of the servants would look at her too closely. Black fabric hid blood well.

She turned on the taps of the bathtub, poured a brandy to clear the smoke from her mouth, and then stripped off her clothes, letting them fall haphazardly on the tile. The blouse and skirt were ruined. Even if they could get the blood out, the smell of smoke pervaded the fabric. She drew off her corset cover and saw it, too, was stained, as was the corset, DuBois' blood everywhere. She unhooked the busk and dropped the corset to the floor just as she recalled the slip of paper she'd taken from DuBois' jacket. It slid down inside her chemise, forcing her to chase it with blood-stained fingers, one hand pinning her chemise to her belly to keep the paper from falling farther. She finally captured the scrap and pulled it from her chemise.

It was a piece of a telegram. DuBois must have shredded the thing, intending to toss the pieces in the fire later, but he'd missed one bit.

Adela carried it over to the light next to the mirror. Blood stained the paper now, but she could make out the letters on one line.

Alessio Fe, was all it said, the remainder of the name torn off. But Alessio wasn't a common Portuguese name. Actually of Italian derivation, if she recalled correctly.

She licked her lips, feeling satisfaction swell through her.

THE TRUTH UNDISCOVERED

She didn't need to know what the rest of the telegram was about. Whatever had gone missing in Lisboa, upsetting the Jesuits, whatever the remainder of this telegram said, it all had something to do with Alessio Ferreira who had died the previous year in Lisboa.

The man had supposedly been killed in a duel, some argument over a lover. But both parties to the duel had realized the futility of the action and fired into the air instead of at each other. Yet somehow a bullet found its way into Alessio Ferreira's heart.

One person had never believed that claim of accidental death—the infante himself. Among the things he'd tasked her with doing, was finding the truth of how Alessio Ferreira died.

Whatever the Jesuits knew about the man's death, they were willing to sacrifice themselves to hide it. Or at least, DuBois was.

Adela set the slip of paper on the vanity, but then decided it needed more care, so she placed it inside her canister of dusting powder instead. She turned off the bathtub's taps, stripped off the rest of her clothes, and settled into the hot water with a sigh. She took a large sip of brandy.

Why were the Jesuits involved? Ferreira had worked for the infante, a personal friend. Under the guise of his numerous affairs and flirtations, Ferreira had access to many people close to Prince Dinis III of Southern Portugal. He'd relayed messages between Dinis and the infante, who would sooner or later—more likely *sooner* if one believed what seers claimed, which she did—ascend to the throne of Northern Portugal when the current Prince, Fabricio, met his long-awaited end.

There was no reason for the Jesuits to kill Ferreira. They wanted unification as much as the infante and Prince Dinis did. They wanted the North's unreasonable treatment of all witches and non-humans to stop. Their goals were aligned. So why interfere?

She settled back in the water, put the glass of brandy aside, and slowly slid down under the surface so she could give her hair a proper washing.

They were protecting *someone*.

OLINDA, BRAZIL

Gabriel woke feeling better. Tia Ana Maria's influence always made him feel more alive. The house was still dark and quiet, so he sat up, located his cigarette case and matches, and lit his first cigarette. His fingers shook, but they always did at first.

After a few more minutes and a second cigarette, he felt more awake. He went to the water closet, then straightened his clothing and the quilt on the settee. He dug out his watch and checked the time. It was noon.

Shocked, he went and drew back the drapes to find that his watch hadn't lied. He crossed to the bottom of the unlit stair well. "Tia? Are you awake?"

No voice answered that. Gabriel shook his head and began climbing the stairs. He knocked on her door, and when there was no response, opened it. She wasn't there. She must have decided to let him sleep and gone out. He went

THE TRUTH UNDISCOVERED 109

to his brother's room, but that door hung open, the room also unoccupied.

Sighing, he made his way back down the stairs. He steeled himself and walked down without losing his balance. He stood at the bottom a moment to catch his breath, and then lit another cigarette. He had just inhaled when the door banged open.

Ezequiel pushed through the door, his mother cradled in his arms. "Help me," he cried.

Gabriel helped Ezequiel carry her to the settee, eyeing with terror the blood that stained her embroidered blouse. Her head lolled against Ezequiel's shoulder, her breathing strangely labored. "What happened?"

As he laid his mother on the settee, Ezequiel lifted a tear-stained face. "He shot her."

He didn't need to ask *who*. It had been Feliciano. Gabriel began unbuttoning her blouse to see the injury, but her hand lifted feebly to stop him. "No. It's fine, son."

He'd felt dampness on the back of her blouse. The bullet must have gone straight through. Given the odd, wet sound of her breathing, it had punctured one of her lungs. But likely only one. "Tia, what were you thinking?"

"I wanted my son back," she whispered. "Zequinha, water, please. That will help."

Ezequiel dropped her hand and ran for the back of the house to the kitchen. Gabriel knew a drink of water wouldn't help. Her lung was filling with blood. She needed a hospital... or a healer. "Tia, listen to me," he said softly. "You know I'm dying. Use my strength to heal yourself."

She laid that feeble, blood-stained hand against his cheek. "Take care of your brother," she said. "Get him away from Brazil."

"Tia," he began… but stopped as heat seared through his body, his lungs boiling like he'd inhaled a scoop of burning coals. He cried out, but couldn't break away from her feather-like touch on his cheek. "No!"

The burning seemed to last forever, but then he fell away, landing on his back on the tatty rug. He gasped, the agony fading into anguish. Gabriel curled up on his side, unwilling to look, to see what she'd chosen. He coughed, and something vile crawled up his throat, spilling past his lips onto the floor.

"No, Mamãe! What have you done? No!" Ezequiel's voice filled his mind. His words became a formless keening, on and on.

Gabriel lay on his side, watching blood drip from a hole in the settee to the floor. It was too late, and Ezequiel would never forgive him. This would always, forever, be *his* fault in Ezequiel's eyes, even if Gabriel hadn't asked for her sacrifice.

He could turn this on Ezequiel, make this seem to be his fault, but Gabriel knew better. Tia Ana Maria did as she wished, always stronger than the two of them. Seeking out Feliciano had been done to prove to Ezequiel that the man was unworthy. Giving her strength to him had been to make him to take Ezequiel away. He laid there, breathing better than he had in a couple of months, angry with her for forcing his hand this way.

It was *temporary*, Gabriel knew. It wouldn't last. She had pushed back the date of his death, but couldn't heal him.

No healer would do that for him. Tuberculosis was unforgiving that way.

He managed to sit up. Ezequiel was draped over his mother's body, sobbing. Her dark eyes stared up at the ceiling, the labored breathing stopped now. Gabriel rose and stood over her. He took the quilt off the back of the sofa and set that aside on one of the chairs to keep it clean. Then he went to get a sheet from her linen closet to cover her.

He pulled Ezequiel away and let him huddle on the floor. Ezequiel hadn't reached the point of anger and recriminations yet, but Gabriel had no doubt his brother soon would. He gently straightened Tia Ana Maria's body on the settee, folded her arms over her chest, and closed her eyes. Then he covered her with the sheet. "I'm going to go get the priest. Do not leave her."

Tia Ana Maria worshipped the Catholic God with only one side of her mouth, but the priest would know what to do, who to contact to properly care for the body. Gabriel walked out of the house and onto the steep street that led up to the cathedral.

Yesterday this walk would have taken him half an hour, his breath too short to manage it. Today he walked with borrowed strength, a man with a mission. He had an aunt to bury and a brother to get out of the country. Surely with her sacrifice, she'd bought him enough days of life to do that.

Chapter 13

**THURSDAY, 17 OCTOBER 1901
RECIFE, BRAZIL**

Miguel was surprised when Anjos appeared at his hotel room looking less like death than before. The man's Truthsayer's glow was stronger. He stood at the threshold like a man of fifty rather than a man of eighty. The explanation was clear to Miguel; he currently bore the entanglement of a healer about him, strong gold strands that had a sickly dark tinge on the end of them. "I am sorry for your loss, Inspector Anjos."

Anjos' brown eyes raised, pain in them that wasn't physical. "How do you know?"

"I see it. She gave her life, what was left of it. I think she was already dying when she made the choice to pass her strength to you." He stepped back. "Why don't you come inside and sit down."

"I came to make a deal," Anjos said.

"Better to do that inside than to talk outside where we can be overheard," Miguel insisted.

Anjos followed him into the suite, eyeing the sitting area with its overstuffed leather couches, a matching set of ornately carved tables made of Pernambuco wood, and a cherry-wood desk with crisp stationary and a pen provided. "Very nice."

"My patroness doesn't believe in cutting corners." In truth, this room had been held for Adela, not him, but he'd convinced the hotel manager to let him have it by the simple expedient of paying for both the rooms she'd reserved. He rang the bell for room service.

"Good," Anjos said, sitting on one of the couches. He opened his silver case, took out a cigarette, and looked at it oddly. Then he put it away and tucked the case back in a pocket. "I will come with you to the Portugals, with some conditions."

Miguel sat. "We take your brother with us?"

"Yes," Anjos said with a grim nod. "Ezequiel needs a new start."

Judging by Anjos' stiff shoulders, that wasn't the end of it. "Done. And what else?"

Anjos looked at him. "I need you to help me take down Feliciano Morias. He shot my aunt."

Miguel frowned. That explained how she'd died. "The man has a powerful illusion spell, one he did not get legally, I think."

"You're probably right," Anjos said.

A discreet knock at the door told Miguel that the boy from Room Service had arrived. He signaled for Anjos to wait, then went and ordered lunch. A bit late, but the boy nodded quickly, his dark eyes squinting as he tried to recall everything. He left and Miguel returned to his seat across from Anjos. "Now, do you intend to kill him?"

Anjos shook his head. "I can't do that. I'm a policeman."

At heart. Anjos would be no more likely to commit murder now than he'd been when his wife was killed. Miguel nodded. "Then we have to bring him in. Did you have a plan?"

"I cannot touch him," Anjos said, "or I will burn. But you,

you seem unfazed by his protective spell."

"I am immune." Miguel had faced down the illusion the night before. The fact that he'd seen the fire and felt the burn *at all* indicated it wasn't a human magic. Feliciano would have had to trade something valuable to whatever being had given it to him, and in the long run the man would surely face consequences for its use. When he pointed that out to Anjos, the man didn't argue.

"I don't care what he's traded to whom. There are all manner of African deities worshipped here," Anjos said, "and as many native ones. Most people don't believe they're real, but I do."

Determining what manner of creature had given the spell to Feliciano, likely bound in an amulet or other small trinket, *was* academic. It didn't matter whether it was a small god or a demon or a non-human with special powers like an elemental. The important part was getting the talisman away from the man. Otherwise he could never be hauled to a prison.

"Fine," Miguel said. "How do you propose we proceed?"

Anjos rubbed two fingers across his forehead. "I don't... I'm not sure where to find him."

Miguel looked at him. "If my guess is correct, your brother will go looking for him. Why not follow Ezequiel?"

"He's at home, sitting vigil with Tia... with her body."

Miguel drew in a vexed breath. "You know him better than I do. How long will he stay at that post?"

Anjos closed his eyes, jaw flexing. "Fine, he'll stay until I get back. Or until the women come to help prepare her body.

He'll need someone to wail over her."

Miguel suspected the woman's body would be held in the very waiting room where Miguel had woken, perhaps on that same settee. "That will take some time. We'll eat and go back and look for him afterward."

"Eat?" Anjos said blankly.

"You didn't eat last night. Or this morning, I suspect. If we're going to do this, I'm not going to carry you, so you need to eat something."

Anjos seemed prepared to argue, but thought better of it. The timing was fortuitous, since the boy returned then with their food. The steaks were just above rare, so Miguel trusted they were fresh, not something salvaged from the hotel's lunch service. Miguel directed the server to the table near the windows and after the boy set down the tray, tipped him and sent him on his way. Anjos obligingly came over to the table and made a pretense of being interested in the food. Miguel wasn't surprised when, after the man ate a bite of his steak, he suddenly discovered an appetite. Being the recipient of a healing required a meal, almost as much as being the healer did.

PRAIA, CABO VERDE

Adela had her hair mostly dry and wound back up into a respectable-looking coiffure when the police arrived. It was early evening by then and she had just eaten her dinner—with Nadezhda looking on expressionlessly as she always did—and was about to let the remaining servants flee the house for the night.

Nadezhda covered her pale face with her layers of black veils and waited in the hallway.

Adela opened the door herself, and regarded the man the police had sent out, another inspector. The stocky man was more Portuguese than Miguel, but clearly had some African in his bloodlines. "Well, Inspector, how may I help you?"

The man surveyed her with a critical eye. "Would you be the same woman who hired me to gather information about Miguel Gaspar?"

"I would, indeed," she said, "if you are Eduardo Cunha. Would you like to come inside, or do you intend to stay on the doorstep?"

He took a partial step toward the threshold, but saw Nadezhda and paused. "It's only a simple question. I've learned that you visited the house of Marcel DuBois this afternoon, is that so?"

"Yes," she said. "Is that all?"

"The house was set ablaze, as I think you know."

"Oh, yes, we learned that the hard way. We were there to speak with DuBois, only someone set the upper floors alight and we had to flee. We never got to speak with him. Very vexing."

The inspector—Cunha, she finally recalled—blinked a few times. "You didn't *see* him?"

Ah, that was a tell-tale, shifting the question just a hair to test veracity. The man likely had a hint of Truthsayer in him, and was trying to pare down her replies. Unfortunately for him, Adela had ample experience with Truthsayers. "The butler or house servant simply left us alone, so we went in the library to wait for DuBois. I felt... DuBois was trying to avoid speaking with us, as if he had something to hide. He certainly didn't answer any of my questions."

All of that was perfectly true.

Cunha blinked a few more times. "What did you want to discuss with him?"

Time for a distraction. "My associate, Miss Vladimirova, arrived this morning with word that a special item had been stolen from the Jesuit Brotherhood in Lisboa. I went to break the news to DuBois, although I suspect he may already have known. Via telegram, of course."

"Why would DuBois need to be notified about an item taken from the Jesuits?"

"Because he is one," she said in a pert voice. "Did you not know he was one of the Brothers?"

"I see." Now Cunha would spend days looking for DuBois' ties to the Jesuits, which were surely well-hidden. "And the house was on fire when you left?" he asked.

"Yes, I said that earlier. But we had nothing to do with that."

"Why did you not come to the police station and report the fire?"

She was prepared to stamp one foot if it would make her look more silly and petulant. "Because, Inspector, my clothing smelled and I wanted to come home and bathe. I cannot bear to have my garments untidy. However, I sent the driver straightaway from here to alert the police. It was likely only a moment's difference."

Cunha nodded with a touch of unlikely sympathy for a wealthy woman who couldn't be bothered to report a dangerous house fire. "I do understand. Have you seen DuBois since?"

"No," she said. "When you find him, tell him I expect him to call on me here at his earliest convenience."

The flustered inspector left after that, and Adela turned back to Nadezhda once the door was shut, unsure how relieved she should be. "They haven't found his body."

"He *was* dead," Nadezhda said. "Completely."

Well, she would know.

OLINDA, BRAZIL

Night had fallen reluctantly over Olinda. Gabriel walked down the steep street from the cathedral toward Tia Ana Maria's house, keeping an eye peeled for his brother. Gaspar walked at his side, apparently alert to more than sight. The man was watching the spirit world, so to speak.

They stopped at the house where, as predicted, Ezequiel had fled. Two of Tia Ana Maria's closest friends were busy washing the body and preparing her for viewing as a third wailed in the corner. The scent of incense drifted out into the hall like a cloud. One of the women—a plump gray-haired matron—came and kissed Gabriel's cheeks, but didn't let him into the sitting room. She was the first one the priest had suggested he fetch to help with the body, and he was grateful she'd taken over.

"Do you know where Ezequiel has gone?" he asked.

She pinched Gabriel's cheek like he was ten. "He's gone drinking, that no-good boy. Right after I got here."

Gabriel sighed. Even if he'd skipped eating—which he had to admit he'd needed—he still wouldn't have caught Ezequiel. *No-good boy* was right.

"I have to find him," Gabriel said. "May I leave Tia with you and your sisters?"

The women were not closely related. They were, however, from the same part of Africa, so as close to sisters as former slaves could find. "We will take care of her," she said, "but you must be here for the celebration."

"I will. Thank you." He turned back to Gaspar, who'd seemed content to wait through all that. "The bar is around the corner and down."

"Do you not know where Feliciano lives?" Gaspar asked, pointing with his chin to the women in the sitting room. "Or does one of these ladies?"

He hadn't even thought of that, but it was very likely that they might. "Ladies," he asked. "Do you know where I can find Feliciano Morias?"

The wailing woman stopped her keening. She still bobbed back and forth in her seat. "The burning man? Did he do this?"

"Yes," Gabriel said. "And I need to find him and take him in."

She told him an address that Gabriel was sure he could find and returned to her keening. Gabriel led Gaspar out onto the street, marveling inwardly how well he was walking and breathing. A day ago, he wouldn't have been able to have that conversation without sitting down. He had to wonder if the ladies had noticed, and secretly blamed him for Tia Ana Maria's death as well.

As they walked up past the cathedral and toward the neighborhood behind the church Gabriel was looking for—the Church of Our Lady of the Rosary of the Blacks—Gaspar paused and sniffed the air. "Brimstone," he said.

Gabriel smelled nothing on the air other than impending rain and refuse somewhere nearby. "Are you sure?"

"Yes, that's definitely a demon-curse he's got," Gaspar pronounced. "Probably doesn't know that, though, or he would be more sparing in its use."

Gabriel didn't argue, although he had doubts whether demons were real. "Fine, what do you recommend?"

Gaspar frowned. "You stay here. I go on in. I can track him from here."

Gabriel didn't want the man going on without him, but Gaspar could get there on his own far faster. "Go on. You'll pass the church with three arches and then the road splits. Go right, it should be down that way. Number 80."

Gaspar took off running, not concerned about perspiring in his fine suit. Gabriel pushed himself after the man. It wasn't as steep here, but the last of the way to the house in question would be. By the time he reached the church, Gaspar was nowhere in sight. Gabriel trudged up the hill but stopped when he heard a shot.

He ran on borrowed strength, the first time he'd done so in over a year. By the time he'd reached Number 80, the corners of the house were already ablaze. *What happened?*

He stood there and caught his breath, then heard shouting near the back of the small plaster-walled house. He ran past some shrubs to the back side of the house, emerging into an empty lot.

The creature of flame—Feliciano—stood at the house's back door in the falling night, growling his fury. On the other side, Ezequiel lay in the dirt, face down. He might as well be miles away.

"Come get me," Gaspar said to the burning man. "Or are you afraid of me now?"

The creature of fire howled and began advancing on Gaspar. Gaspar backed away, leading Feliciano farther from the house and giving Gabriel room to dash behind the creature to Ezequiel's side. He dropped to his knees and turned Ezequiel over, his chest loosening when he saw his brother breath. Ezequiel's eyes opened, and he blinked at Gabriel, confused. Marks of tears tracked the dust on his face.

Gabriel shot a glance back at Gaspar, who was wrestling the creature of fire alone. "Stay here," he told his brother.

He drew his pistol from his jacket pocket, intending to end Feliciano now, but something flew out of Feliciano's hand to land several feet away in the dirt. The fire all about him disappeared and the empty lot went dark.

Gaspar laughed. "Want to try me now?"

Gabriel could see Feliciano Morias looking about frantically, hunting that missing object. The man spotted the dark object and stepped toward it, so Gabriel fired a warning shot at the thing, sending it skittering farther away. Feliciano, now only human, dove for it anyway, but not before Gaspar caught his arm. Feliciano spun halfway around and landed flat on his back in the dirt.

Gaspar didn't give him a chance to gather himself but flipped him over onto his stomach and settled halfway atop him, using his weight to hold the man face-down in the dirt. Gaspar twisted Feliciano's arms, then slipped off his necktie one-handed to bind the man's hands. "It's a few feet, just under that shrub," Gaspar called to Gabriel.

"You can see it?" Gabriel asked.

"Oh, yes," Gaspar said with a snort. Feliciano yelped, apparently at the tightening of the tie about his wrist.

Gabriel crouched to peer under the shrub and spotted a roughly carved wooden figure. It looked to be of some African deity, only there was a nail driven into its chest. "What is this?"

"Fetish of some sort," Gaspar said. "Local police station where we can take this fellow?"

"Closer to the harbor," Gabriel told him. "Not too far."

As Gaspar wrestled Feliciano to his feet, Ezequiel stumbled over to them. "How could you?" he screamed at the other man "How could you?"

Feliciano just sneered at Ezequiel. Gabriel looked at the figure in his hand and tugged the nail out of its chest.

Feliciano began screaming. Gaspar backed away, catching both Gabriel and Ezequiel in his arms and shoving them toward the house. Feliciano continued to scream, standing bolt upright with his arms still bound behind him, swaying as if touched by wind. Gabriel caught the sickening smell of burning flesh, although there were no flames.

"What did you do?" Gaspar asked.

"I didn't touch him!" Gabriel held his brother back, and Ezequiel covered his eyes.

"No, to the fetish," Gaspar pressed.

"I pulled the nail out." Gabriel pointed with one hand to where the fetish had fallen on the ground. He couldn't see the nail anywhere.

"Do something," Ezequiel begged.

Gaspar picked up the statue and after peering about for a second, located the nail. He stuck it back into the statue's chest. The screaming stopped, and Feliciano collapsed onto the dirt like a doll made of rags.

Ezequiel jerked out of Gabriel's grip and dropped to his knees at Feliciano's side, sobbing. Gaspar put a hand on Ezequiel's shoulder. "Don't touch him, man. He's still burning."

Feliciano's body continued to twitch and jerk on the ground.

"What... what's happening?" Ezequiel asked, gazing up at Gaspar. "What happened?"

"Every bit of flame he's used in the past is roiling inside him now. He is dead already, man. Don't let his movement fool you. Just like wood popping in the fire. It means nothing."

Ezequiel crossed himself, and Gabriel did likewise, almost a reflex. He was close enough now to see Feliciano's handsome face, blistered and charred. The man's dark hands had twisted into red claws.

Gabriel swallowed, but didn't allow himself to be sick. This was going to be his fault, too, when Ezequiel recovered enough to blame him.

FRIDAY, 18 OCTOBER, 1901
PRAIA, CABO VERDE

Adela was the first person to arrive at the telegraph office in Praia in the morning. She'd left Nadezhda outside, but was ready to call her in if the operator proved recalcitrant. "All I want is a copy of the telegram sent to Marcel DuBois yesterday morning. Or the night before. I'm not sure which."

The operator—a slender young Portuguese man in a natty suit—likely lived above his means, as many clerks did. "I'm afraid, my lady, that telegrams are confidential," he explained imperiously. "I cannot simply hand out one person's messages to another."

Adela laid out a sum of money before him that would buy that suit five times over. "It's a simple request. No one will know. I don't know your name, and once I've read it, I'll give the message back to you to toss in the stove."

Those conditions seemed to sweeten the pot, but in the end his face fell and he shook his head. "I can't."

Adela leaned back so Nadezhda could see her through the window and gestured for the other woman to come inside. Nadezhda opened the door, the breeze sending her black veils swirling around her. The young man stood up straighter, eyes wide. He swallowed.

Nadezhda walked to the counter, took a breath, and in a soft, musical voice said, "Give her what she wants."

The young man fought the compulsion for a few valiant seconds before running into the back room and returning with a leather-bound account book. With trembling fingers he opened it and hunted the appropriate page. Then he picked up a pen and copied out the words written there. Adela leaned closer. The writing in the book looked like gibberish, likely the shorthand operators used to keep up with their machines. The young man's eyes jumped up to meet hers, and he handed her the piece of paper before the ink was even dry.

Adela blew on it as she read the words. "Mata," she whispered. "Donato Mata. Now, isn't that interesting, that the Jesuits have an assassin on their payrolls."

Nadezhda, predictably, didn't respond.

Adela folded the paper and handed it back to the cowed young man. "I need you to send a message for me. If it doesn't arrive, I will find out, and this discussion will... come back to haunt you. Do you understand?"

"Yes, my lady," he whispered, all the arrogance wrung out of him.

"To Inspector Miguel Gaspar, Hotel Occidental, Recife, Brazil." She waited until the telegraph operator caught up with her words. "I must return to Lisboa. Find me there. The Lady."

The young man looked up as if waiting for more, but there was nothing more to say. Adela led Nadezhda away, out the doors and back toward the waiting carriage.

"Successful?" Nadezhda asked after a short breath.

As they walked toward the island's plain white cathedral, Adela hooked one arm through Nadezhda's, ignoring the prickles that crawled down her spine when she did so. Though Nadezhda seemed emotionless, she still preferred to be treated in a friendly manner. Adela was determined to honor that preference. "Surprisingly so. The Jesuits had an assassin on their payroll, and they've learned he's the one who killed Ferreira. He's missing now, and the longer it takes us to get back to Southern Portugal, the farther away he'll slip."

"Is there a reason to find the man?"

"Our employer will want to know who hired him. I doubt it was the Jesuits themselves."

"Is that enough for DuBois to kill himself to hide it?"

Adela chuckled dryly. "Oh, no. But I have a list of unsolved murders in the Lisboa area that I now have a name to match with, along with an unsolved attempt on the life of another. And I think I will find that one or two of the most powerful victims were killed indirectly by the Jesuits. Now that... that might be worth hiding."

Nadezhda nodded slowly. "So how will we travel to Lisboa?"

"Well, Miguel's Gaspar's friend does have a yacht. And I suspect that for a few kind words and a lot of money, he'll lend it to us."

Another breath. "Then let us return to Lisboa."

That was exactly what they were going to do. She would simply have to trust that Miguel had come through for her and secured the services of Gabriel Anjos. Miguel would have no trouble finding her in Lisboa if she put it about that she *wanted* him to find her.

And she would, hopefully soon, have a villain to present to the infante of Northern Portugal, proof that his faith in her wasn't misplaced. Adela smiled, relishing the thought of the challenge that lay ahead.

Chapter 14

SUNDAY, 20 OCTOBER 1901
THE OPEN OCEAN, NEAR TERCEIRA, AZORES

Adela stood on the deck of the *Perseverance,* ruing the fact that Miguel was right. As she'd expected, his friend William had agreed to lend them his yacht and crew. The fine old wooden sailing vessel didn't make the kind of speed she would have had on a steamer, perhaps six knots at best.

But... this was the easiest sea crossing Adela had ever had. True, she'd been nauseated on and off for the past two days and had spent more time abed than any active woman would like, but she could endure the nausea. In the past, though, a mysterious bone-deep pain had kept her cloistered for days after a sea voyage. So far, this trip had been free from that.

So while the ocean itself still made her ill—it was moving water, after all—making the journey in a *wooden* yacht changed the whole experience for her. That meant much of her usual illness during sea travel came not from seasickness, as she'd always believed. Instead she'd been reacting to traveling aboard a vessel made primarily of iron and steel.

Because I am *part fairy. Miguel was right.*

It was unfair that she'd spent most of her life in ignorance of the reason behind her intolerance for travel. She could blame her father for that, and the Jesuits who'd influenced him in some still unknown manner to deny his true nature.

She didn't know how the Jesuits were tied into this mess. She had worked with the Brotherhood in Lisboa for well over a decade now, negotiating between them and the Freemasons over every tiny matter of magic that cropped up in the two Portugals. She had kept them from doing unpleasant things to each other. She wondered if it might not have been better to set the two groups at each other's throats, but she was moderately certain that, should there be an all-out conflict between them, the Jesuits would win the day. Their resoluteness would always give them an edge over the Freemasons.

The breeze eased a dark strand of hair loose from her bun. She brushed it aside, pinned her broad-brimmed hat down more fiercely, and returned to gazing at the island city far off their port bow. It was a large city, the tile rooftops orangey-red in the bright sunlight. They would pass it by in the next few hours, and she intended to hide the yacht from any Spanish ship that might come near. The sunlight was straight overhead, giving her an easy light to work with to make the yacht invisible.

A quick patter of bare feet on the wooden deck warned Adela when the crew of the ship left their positions unexpectedly. The youngest—a wiry dark boy of ten or so—clambered up the main mast as if he could escape his fear that way. Adela glanced back to the yacht's aft and saw that Nadezhda had broken her self-imposed isolation and was climbing up to the deck.

A figure swathed in black garb and black veils, Nadezhda Vladimirova looked like Death come hunting. Adela ruefully watched her approach, regretting that the petite woman could not walk among mortal men without inspiring dread. Adela felt it herself, that prickling along her spine, a stinging in her fingers. She was determined not to show any fear, though. She lifted her head and smiled at Nadezhda's approaching form.

Nadezhda reached her side and lifted the heavier veil that covered her face, leaving only the thinnest layer of black silk that rippled in the apparent wind. That revealed her features, something she rarely did, but Adela already knew what she looked like. Nadezhda had been born a Russian princess fifty years past, a delicate-looking woman with fair coloring and a gentle, daydreaming manner that belied her true nature. The creature that Nadezhda was *now* had the clarity of mind that came from a complete lack of doubt or emotion.

She took a breath and asked, "What is that?"

"Terceira," Adela answered. "A Portuguese island, not Spanish. But we're close enough to the trade lanes that we're on the watch for Spanish ships."

The Spanish, with their distrust of witches, would imprison Nadezhda... if they could catch her. The chance of that was slim, as Nadezhda only needed to be in proximity to steal away another's life. And since she was dead already, shooting her wouldn't stop her either.

"Good." Nadezhda's head turned slowly as she considered the three sailors now standing at the farthest distance possible from her, and then she glanced up at the ship's boy clinging to the mast. "How much longer?"

"Two more days, the captain thinks."

"Currents," Nadezhda noted. "I can feel them changing." Adela imagined Nadezhda down in her cabin, sensing the water moving under the wood. She wasn't sure how the rusalka's relationship with water worked, but she was intrigued.

The wind-blown currents were the reason they'd come this

far northwest before turning east to the Portugals. Anyone coming from the south had to go out and around to escape the Canary current. The trip from Lisboa to Cabo Verde had only taken two days, since the current had been southerly there.

Adela turned toward the bow of the ship. "Captain," she called, "my companion says we've crossed onto the Portuguese current."

"I will go back below," Nadezhda said and drew the heavier veil over her face again. She moved away and, a moment later, stepped down the ladder into the lower deck.

As Nadezhda was no doubt moving toward the bow—she'd taken the v-cabin to keep her most distant from the crew—the captain and his two sailors suddenly found reason to move aft. Adela suppressed the smile that tempted her. Better not to antagonize William's crew.

The men adjusted the set of the sails, and soon the yacht began to turn, heeling to port and finally heading toward the Portugals and Lisboa. Adela was more than ready.

RECIFE, BRAZIL

Miguel had been sorting travel options for the last two days while Gabriel Anjos mourned his aunt and arranged for her funeral and burial. He wanted to get Anjos to the Portugals as Adela had requested, but they *could* wait that long before setting sail.

It would take some time to reach Lisboa anyway. There was a Spanish ship leaving Recife on Tuesday that could be in

Lisboa in twelve days, it claimed, but there were burgundy lines all about the ship in his sight, strands only visible in his vision, that warned him the Church held this particular ship. That made it dangerous to a witch like himself. The captain of the *Tijuca*, a German steamer on its way back to Hamburg, said it would be out eighteen days, but Miguel didn't like the colors of the name printed on the harbormaster's charts, each letter glowing a sickly puce as if something bad awaited the vessel. Better not to be aboard when its ill luck caught up to it. The *Ferreira*—the same ship that had brought him from Cabo Verde to Brazil—was scheduled to return from Rio de Janeiro soon. It could make Lisboa in eleven days.

All of those would leave Adela on her own in Lisboa longer than Miguel liked.

Not that she needs me. Clearly, she'd lived and courted danger without his aid for a long time. But she'd left Cabo Verde abruptly, and that spoke of trouble. If she'd sent a letter, there would have been indicators that would tell him more than her words, Unfortunately, the telegraph was an impersonal mode of communication, a creation of electricity. And since she hadn't said in her telegram why she left his home in Cabo Verde, that left her motivation to his imagination. Having been a police inspector for some time, he could imagine a good many things.

"Do you have a date?" Gabriel Anjos asked when Miguel returned to the Hotel Occidental.

The expensive hotel's bar was sleek and modern, with high stools and a high chance of people looking askance at the African sitting there like he belonged. Miguel was beginning to dislike Brazil. Not because he felt threatened himself but because he suspected others like him—like Ezequiel—did feel that way. Miguel settled next to Anjos at the bar anyway, determined not to let the nearby table of white-skinned businessmen stare him down.

"I have booked passage back on the *Ferreira*," he said. "Not the fastest option, but I sailed here on that ship and I trust the captain to get us to Lisboa safely. We'll be stopping in Cabo Verde that way, although only overnight if they stay to their itinerary."

Gabriel Anjos still carried some of his aunt's life within him. The man was breathing more normally than he'd been when Miguel first saw him, his tuberculosis driven back by his aunt's powers. Miguel could still see the healing embrace of that gift, a gentle gold tinge to Anjos' brilliant Truthsayers' aura. Although no healer could cure tuberculosis, they could slow it. If Adela's healer had similar skills—despite being dead—she might be able to keep Anjos alive almost indefinitely.

Miguel was beginning to like the man. Apparently, once Anjos made up his mind, he didn't look back, and he *was* keeping his half-brother Ezequiel under control. Fortunately for all of them, the death of Feliciano Morias hadn't left a body behind to involve the local police. The man had slowly crumbled down to cinders that three of the local wise women had gathered into a clay pot. The fetish Feliciano had used to create the fire-demon with which he'd terrorized others was put into the pot as well, then sealed in with wax and buried... *somewhere*. Miguel could find it if he wished by tracing lines of power that only someone with the second sight could see, but it was better not to know.

Anjos stubbed out the cigarette he'd been smoking and considered his silver case for a moment before putting it away—a sign that he wasn't in too much pain. "How many days before the ship is in port?"

"Two days," Miguel admitted.

Anjos puffed out a frustrated breath. He was a man with pleasing features, a bone structure so regular as to have no distinguishing characteristics. Of average height and build, and having brown hair and eyes and medium skin, the man could slip in and out of any Portuguese-speaking country with ease, the perfect person to pursue and observe their quarry. Until he spoke, that was. His accent was blatantly Brazilian.

Miguel could disguise his own accent but, being half African, he would have a more difficult time passing unnoticed in Lisboa. While in Paris, he'd learned he was distinctive enough that others remembered seeing him.

"I'd like to get Ezequiel out of here before he changes his mind," Anjos finally said.

Anjos had promised his aunt—his wet-nurse, actually—that he'd get his half-brother out of Brazil. But every day Ezequiel came up with more reasons why he shouldn't move forward with his life, why he needed to cling to the life he'd led. He no longer had any ties here, not with both his mother and Feliciano gone, but Miguel could tell that Ezequiel lacked his brother's resolve. The young man waffled back and forth daily, vexing Anjos terribly, as younger brothers were no doubt created to do.

"You said he'd wanted to study healing," Miguel tried. "I might be able to get him taken on at the hospital in Praia."

Anjos licked his lips. "How many days do I have to convince him?"

As long as it would take to reach Cabo Verde. They discussed that for a time and agreed on that effort as a way to get the man onto the ship.

Anjos didn't argue that he wanted his brother closer than Cabo Verde, either. Miguel suspected that Ezequiel would continue to rely on Gabriel to keep him out of trouble as long as he could. A forced separation might be the best thing for the younger man. Ezequiel wasn't a child. He needed to learn to stand on his own feet. At least in Cabo Verde, he would endure less prejudice than he would here.

Miguel could pull the strings to get him a job, although he couldn't keep Ezequiel in that position if the young man didn't do the work. It was a starting point, though, more than many men got in life.

CHAPTER 15

**LISBOA, SOUTHERN PORTUGAL
TUESDAY, 22 OCTOBER 1901**

Although most larger ships landed their passengers up along the Tagus, if the *Perseverance* landed nearer Cascais, it could sneak back out before the Customs Officials noticed its arrival and evade the tariff before leaving. That was what the captain suggested. Adela would have willingly paid any tax, but in truth the crew simply wanted Nadezhda off their ship. It was late enough in the day that if they did dock along the Tagus, the dock master would require any passengers to stay aboard ship until morning.

So the crew loaded their luggage into a small dory and one brave crew member—the youngest—was chosen to row them into the small bay at Cascais. Being a Tuesday, the languid people of Lisboa were less in evidence on the beach, but a few still observed the dory pulling up there... and scattered. The young man tied off the painter and clambered out to help Adela from the boat. She let him lift her over the edge of the boat and waited as he handed her bags onto the sand as well. Then he turned back to where Nadezhda stood cloaked in her black garb and veils. He paused but held out his arms to carry her anyway.

Nadezhda's veiled head turned toward the slender young man. She set a gloved hand on his shoulder and let him pick her up. Adela saw his dark jaw clench, but he took Nadezhda's slight weight and carried her a few steps to the sand and set her down. He backed away to fetch her bag, his eyes downcast.

Adela had already taken her leave of William's captain, but

she stepped back to the edge of the water and took the bag from the young crewman. "Hold out your hand."

His dark eyes darted worriedly, but he complied.

Adela laid a gold ten-thousand reís coin on his palm, along with a bronze five reís coin. "Because you have been kind."

The boy gaped at her, but then secreted the coins inside a trousers pocket.

"Don't mention the gold coin to your shipmates," she said, knowing someone aboard the yacht had likely been watching with a looking glass. "Show them the five instead."

He nodded swiftly, tipped an imaginary hat to her, and pushed the dory off the sands. Then he jumped back in and rowed away, only sparing a glance for her.

"It was too much," Nadezhda said in her flat voice.

"Perhaps," Adela said. "But if he can hold his tongue, his family might be able to change their fortunes with it."

She handed Nadezhda's single bag over, picked up her own, and they walked up the stone steps from the beach to the roadside that ran along the shore. One unnerved cab driver and one hour later, they stepped down before her house on the Praça das Amoreiras.

The house had only three stories. Its plain granite façade was painted buff and gray, with stern gray casings around the doors and windows. Wrought iron balconies stood over the main door, and iron barred the windows. And on the other side of the park in front of it rose the ancient aqueduct.

What was Father thinking?

Although there was a finer house in Sintra—a small palace,

in truth—her father had preferred *this* house. Near moving water, across a small park from the reservoir filled by the aqueduct. Encased in iron. She'd never been comfortable on the balconies, although she could recall her father sitting out on his third-floor balcony every morning to drink his coffee. *Why?*

She tapped the brass knocker and was gratified when Santana, her ancient butler, came to the door. When he saw her there, he stepped back to allow her and Nadezhda inside. He gestured for one of the footmen to fetch their bags. "It is good to see you well, mistress."

"And you as well, Santana." The footman bundled all the bags past them and headed for the stairwell without comment. He seemed inured to Nadezhda at this point, as all her servants did.

"Did the sea voyage not trouble you, mistress?" Santana asked.

He was used to her being a physical wreck after traveling. "No more than your bursitis bothers you, I'm sure."

He inclined his head.

"May I assume that my correspondence is in my office?" she asked.

"Of course, mistress. Shall I have coffee sent in there? Do you dine in, or out tonight?"

"Best to dine in," she told him. "Something light. Let me go through my correspondence and I'll meet with you after we eat." The butler moved away, leaving her to her own devices.

"I will go to my room," Nadezhda announced. "Summon me if you need me."

Adela watched Nadezhda walk smoothly up the stairs before turning down the white-plastered hallway to her first-floor office. She went in and closed the doors behind her, then shut her eyes and breathed in the calming scent of the room: old books and dust, the sharp smell of ink, the whiff of frankincense lingering in the drapes and the pillows. It was her father's favorite place, and had always been hers, too. She opened her eyes and watched dust motes float down through the last of the evening light that streamed in the west-facing window.

My father lived here because it was the last place any of his kind would look for him. Surrounded by flowing water and iron, a house that a fairy would abhor. *Should* abhor.

But inside the house was safe, with ancient wards that had been laid when the house was built. They faded the longer she was gone, but now that she'd returned, they would strengthen and keep her safe from attack. She glanced up at each corner of the room, where the heads of stone horses guarded her office against invasion. Each of the four was still, undisturbed.

Sighing, Adela crossed to the large rosewood desk under the windows. She shoved open the green silk drapes and turned to survey the correspondence Santana had left for her. Three neat stacks—personal, household business, and professional business.

The personal was the smallest, only a pair of letters from her correspondent in in the Golden City, Bastião Vargas. One of the palace guards, he had access to both the prince and the infante of Northern Portugal. Those she would read later, when she was more assured of privacy. The household business letters could simply be turned over to her business manager. It was the professional correspondence

THE TRUTH UNDISCOVERED 141

that concerned her at the moment.

Mostly because there wasn't enough. If the Jesuits up in Campolide had something stolen—or someone stolen—there should be letters from them on her desk regarding the theft. There should be requests for aid. There weren't. There were two letters from the Freemasons, one from the man who called himself Pombalihno, and another from one of the masons in the north, Carvalho, each stamped with their elaborate seals.

It was the third note that captured her attention, though. Unlike the fine stationary of the other two, this one was of the sort of brown paper that might have been used to wrap a sandwich, sealed with a glob of tallow. Not her normal letter. Before she opened it, Adela lifted the thing to her nose and caught a faint hint of what might be grilled chouriço.

She set it back down and went to the office door. "Santana!"

Santana showed up quickly. "Mistress?"

"The letter on the brown paper, no envelope. Where did it come from? The mail?"

His hoary white brows drew together. "Mistress? I'm not sure which letter you mean."

She drew him into her office with her and to distract him before he could comment about the place needing a cleaning, she shoved the letter into his hand. "How did this end up on my desk?"

"I don't recall that one, Mistress. I would remember it. It smells of a workman."

Workman? "Not via the mail then? Or by messenger?"

"No, Mistress."

Adela set the envelope back on her desk. *If Miguel were here, he could just look at it and know if it was safe.*

"If you are concerned," Nadezhda said from the doorway, "I can open it."

She must have heard her calling for Santana. Adela picked up the letter and carried it back to the door. "Could you?"

Nadezhda took it in a black gloved hand and seemed to be peering at it through her veils. Adela hurried Santana out of the office and closed the door. She went back to her desk to watch as Nadezhda broke the seal on the letter.

Nadezhda stepped back, coming up flush against the door. With her veil in place, Adela couldn't see the other woman's expression. If there was some magic at work, it wasn't a visible one. She waited, her breath stilled.

"It reeks of pork," Nadezhda said. "Freshly killed. Farm."

Nadezhda's usual ability to tell time of death unnerved her. "But... nothing magical in it?"

"Yes, there was. A spell, trapped inside the note. I felt it come alive when I broke the seal. I don't know what it was meant to do, but it... didn't affect me."

Because she's already dead? Adela came closer to peer at Nadezhda's veils. There was something caught there, just beyond the edge of her vision. If she looked directly at it, it wasn't there—more like a hint of a reflection. "I can't see it. I'd take off that veil, though. Carefully."

While Nadezhda removed her outer veil, Adela locate one of her father's cigar boxes. The man hadn't smoked, but he'd kept several boxes around. She withdrew one from the books shelves and opened it carefully. The cigars inside were ancient, but still as rich as the day he'd purchased them, no doubt. She dumped the cigars into an empty trash bin, and then held out the open box. The office smelled now of old leather and grass and the earth after rain, the cigars happily giving off their scents after decades trapped in the box. "If you'll place it in here."

Nadezhda put the veil inside the box.

Adela thought she saw movement among the folds of silk, so she quickly snapped the box closed. "That should hold it until Miguel gets here and can look at it."

She set the box aside on her desk and then picked up the brown paper. "Stop looking," she read aloud.

"For what?" Nadezhda asked.

"I have no idea." *Very disappointing.* Someone had sent her a dangerous and cryptic note. It *should* be full of meaning.

"Perhaps the spell was the point," Nadezhda suggested, "rather than the words."

Adela licked her lips. "Or perhaps the entire point was to show that the deliverer got into my office without Santana knowing. And without triggering any of my father's devices."

She surveyed the room again. On top of the shelves, the horses' mouths were shut. If someone with hostile intention had come in here—and someone clearly had—their mouths should have opened.

Then again, she could think of several ways to get around them, the easiest of which was to send an innocent to deliver the item—a child or someone never angry. That person could have sprung the trap, though, or walked into one. She'd left the room un-trapped mostly out of consideration for her staff... and because anything truly valuable or dangerous had been stolen years ago.

She crossed to her desk and opened up the lower drawer, the one that held old files. She thumbed through the labels until she located the one she sought. She was neither an acquisitive person, nor a sentimental one, but she'd kept this file. *Because I hate not knowing.*

Not quite two decades ago, while she was in Paris, this house was robbed.

It had taken some time to discover the theft because she'd been living in the house in Sintra before she went to France. This house had been closed, with the staff coming down from Sintra once a month to clean. Supposedly, the Jesuit brotherhood had been keeping an eye on it as well.

Not for the house itself, but for the contents of the basement.

Her father had kept a workroom down there where he'd tinkered endlessly with small magical devices. As a child, she hadn't been clear on what they were. She'd only become aware that they were magical in nature as she matured. But then her father had disappeared, and she'd been left mostly to her own devices. She had convinced a handful of the Jesuits to train her, but she had never spent much time studying his devices. She'd stuck with magic as theory, not practice.

Yet when she returned from France, she discovered the contents of her father's workroom had been stolen, as well as a handful of books from his office—the ones truly valuable to a practitioner of witchcraft. Her father had kept those only as curiosities. He'd never practiced witchcraft himself.

A magical treasure trove or a large collection of junk. She had never been quite sure which it was.

But whoever had come into her father's office hadn't triggered the horses then, either. And they had left her a note as well, a childish gloating thing, it had seemed. She flipped through the pages in the file. There were the various reports given by the men she'd hired to investigate the theft. A few pages of notes from the Jesuit who'd occasionally come down from Campolide to tinker with her father on his devices. A possible list of what some of those devices might have been. And the list of the missing books. Five books. And tucked at the back, she had the note.

Não tente me encontrar. Don't try to find me.

She laid out the note, written on deckle-edged stationery from a maker in Cascais, and compared the writing to the brown paper that smelled of pork. The letters looked *similar*, but written decades apart as they were, that wouldn't prove anything.

Was the new note meant to remind her of the previous thefts? Or simply left by a criminal who couldn't resist tweaking her nose? A signature?

She sat down and mulled that over while Nadezhda waited silently, unmoving. And some of the pieces fell into place, painting a picture that made sense of it all. "In the morning," she told Nadezhda, "we will go up to Campolide and talk to the Brothers there."

WEDNESDAY, 23 OCTOBER 1901

The distance between the college of the Jesuit Brothers in Campolide was less than a mile from Adela's home, but it seemed farther than that. Lisboa hadn't grown out this far, so the college was surrounded by countryside.

Santana had hired a cab for her, and the driver remained silent throughout the drive. He was intimidated by Nadezhda, of course, not her. In her current mood, Adela was likely the more dangerous. More reckless.

He finally set them down in front of the college, a long building of granite, three floors high. It was a stern place, with only a curved pediment in the front over the two main doors. Towers rose in the back, though, giving it a fanciful look. The many windows were shuttered, to keep the students within focused on their work.

Adela wasn't interested in the college itself, but in the chapel next to which it had been built. This version of the chapel was more recent than the college, but older than the newest renovations to the college. The Jesuits kept enlarging the two buildings. Adela directed Nadezhda down the path that led from the front of the college to the chapel, giving them a fine view of the aqueduct off to the west as they walked.

A pair of students approached, heading in the opposite direction, their black cassocks and caps lending them an air of authority in this place. When they were no closer than a dozen feet, one stopped and raised a hand. Perhaps eighteen, the boy's narrow features suggested an ascetic nature, and his tone was disapproving. "Mistress, there are no visitors allowed on weekdays."

Well, stern, but not rude. I won't kill him. "I am here on business, to see Father Serafim."

"Serafim?" the young man repeated blankly. He shot a glance at his companion, who merely shrugged. "There's no Father Serafim here, mistress."

"And that is why it's a waste of my time to talk to you," Adela snapped. The boy was likely new here, in his first year, and didn't know there was more to his college than was made public.

Nadezhda simply walked on, forcing the two boys to scatter out of her path, clutching their books and notebooks to their chests as if mere paper would protect them from her flapping veils. Sighing, Adela followed, not looking back at the duo... who would tell all their compatriots about the terrifying woman who'd swept down on them. Nadezhda would likely be much taller in their rendition of the story.

The college chapel was a plain building, the sort one associated with mendicant orders, plain granite walls and little ornamentation—only a circular window. No ornate masonry about the doors and no tilework to enliven it. The brown doors stood open, but Adela didn't enter. Stepping over that threshold would make her skin crawl.

She had no idea what it would do to Nadezhda.

Instead she walked on, around the square tower at the edge of the church. On the back side of that was another door, one never accessed by students. She removed a brass key from her handbag and opened the door outward, revealing a stairwell that led down to the subterranean parts of the college.

Given the subjects studied in this part of the college, the tunnels had deliberately been excluded from the consecration of the chapel. So Adela felt only the slightest twinge in her gut as she lifted her skirt and stepped over the threshold onto the landing. She waited for Nadezhda to follow and locked the door behind them.

By the time they reached the level of the tunnels—all neatly plastered in white, of course—one of the brothers had come running to intercept them. Fortunately, she knew Brother Tomas. He stopped abruptly when he saw who it was and gestured for them to proceed.

"Bother Tomas, where is Father Serafim?" she asked before he could get away.

"In the storerooms, Lady," the brother said quickly. "There's no…"

Adela brushed past him, Nadezhda in her wake. Tidy workrooms lined either side of the tunnel, each with large tables and glass cases and scientific equipment and books. Adela didn't stop for any of those. The storerooms grew off the far ends of the tunnels, vast chambers of shelves and glass cases that held more than a century's worth of acquired magical artifacts for the handful of students in this part of the college to study. Most of the study here was done by select priests and some brothers who also happened to teach in the college. It was an attempt to understand magic scientifically, a movement that was gaining ground—even though mostly in secret—around the world. The Jesuits merely had more experience with the matter than anyone else.

She reached the door of the main storeroom. When she pushed it open, she could see that the gaslights were turned up, a sure sign someone was in there.

"Father Serafim?" she called, advancing into the storeroom

THE TRUTH UNDISCOVERED 149

without invitation. *No point in being civil now.*

It smelled of antiquity and disuse in there. A few dozen rows of shelves held an odd assortment of objects, each meticulously tagged and documented: glass globes, small machines that looked like the innards of clocks but likely had far different intent, items illicitly made of sereia skin and selkie pelt and human flesh. The tags listed creator and date of creation and possible uses, along with verified uses; one of the things the Church wanted documented so that those uses would not to be confused with miracles. As she walked along the center aisle, the artifacts became older and older, some predating the Jesuits themselves. She had never been as far as the artifacts of the Templars, but there were so many ancient protections on *those* shelves, she wouldn't dare it.

"Father Serafim!"

A tall man in a black cassock abruptly emerged from between two rows of tall shelves. For a brief second his lined face seemed friendly, then his dark eyes fixed on Nadezhda. "What have you done, bringing that monstrosity down here?"

Adela stopped where she was. She wanted to take him to task for calling Nadezhda that, but she needed to pick her battles cautiously today. "What have I done? Serafim, you have spent the better part of my life manipulating me. I am not in the mood to be insulted by the likes of you. The man you hired to steal my father's magical creations has been back in my house again. What was he after this time?"

In her experience, most priests had the good of their flock in mind. They cared for their people and guided their steps out of love. Serafim was an exception to that. He'd acquired this collection with blithe disregard for kindness or ownership or, as it turned out, honesty. Nearly two decades past, she'd addressed the theft of her father's creations and books with him, and he'd told her he had no idea who'd been behind it.

"I don't know what you're talking about," Serafim said. "That creature is likely influencing you."

"Was it not you, Serafim, who whispered in my ear that I should go to Paris and find her? I can only imagine Brother Marcel's horror when he realized whom you'd sent to France. To get me out of my house, you jeopardized his control over the Meter. All for a few trinkets that I'd bet you still don't understand and can't use."

Serafim came closer, the light shining on his sparse white hair. "I know you talked to Brother Marcel," he said. "What has he told you?"

Something in those words tipped her off. *Has.* "You don't know that he's dead."

Serafim made a dismissive gesture. "Don't be melodramatic, girl. He's missing. That's all."

"He is dead," Nadezhda said in her soft voice. "His throat cut."

Serafim glanced at Nadezhda's dark form, an inky blot under the gaslights, and retreated one step before stopping himself. "What do you mean?"

Adela sighed. "He was dead when we reached his house. Before it was set ablaze. His throat had been cut, and someone else did it for him."

And that someone apparently hadn't sent news of his actions back to the Brotherhood here. Serafim's mouth fell

THE TRUTH UNDISCOVERED 151

open, although the crafty fox snapped it shut a second later.

Nadezhda walked closer. In a faintly sing-song tone, she said something in Russian.

Serafim laid a hand to his chest, as if struggling to breathe. His mouth opened. He was fighting not to talk.

"Did you pay Donato Mata to steal the contents of my Father's workshop seventeen years ago?" Adela asked.

His mouth worked as Nadezhda reached his side. She ran one gloved hand down his arm and gave him another command.

"Yes," he ground out between his teeth.

"And you came up with a pretext to get me out of the country so that the wards on my house would die down enough for him to enter. Is that right?"

Nadezhda wrapped her small hand about his forearm. His eyes fixed on her as he fought whatever coercion she was using on him.

"Yes!" he said. "Make her let me go."

"And because one of my investigations might get close to Mata," she lied, "you hauled him in and held him prisoner, so that I wouldn't incidentally find out what he'd done for you. Is that how he came to be in your charge?"

"Yes!" Serafim said, voice shaking now. "Call her off!"

"And then he escaped, didn't he?" It was the logical conclusion.

"Yes." Serafim slumped, his shoulder leaning against one of the shelves now. It looked as if Nadezhda was holding him erect. "And he took it all with him," he volunteered in little more than a whisper. "All the artifacts from your father's workroom. All the books."

Nadezhda let go of his arm. Serafim slid down against the side of the shelves until he sat gracelessly on the floor, cassock poofed up around him. He breathed hard like he'd just run to Campolide all the way from the mouth of the Tagus.

Adela knelt by his side, catching the scent of perspiration and damp wool. "You never needed to hire a murderer to steal from my home. I have known you most of my life, Father, and always respected you as a teacher. I understand your desire to hide these things—these tools—from the world. If you had asked, I would have *given* you the contents of my father's workshop. I would have given you my books. Freely."

His dark eyes darted toward her, and he patted her hand.

"This man, Donato Mata, will come back to haunt you." Adela rose. "Your God *can* use bad men to achieve His designs, but you... are not as wise as He is."

CHAPTER 16

**PRAIA, CABO VERDE
MONDAY, 28 OCTOBER 1901**

After discussing it with Catarina and William, Miguel was content to leave Inspector Anjos' brother loosely in their charge. In their one day in port—the *Ferreira* was only taking on basic supplies here, not cargo—he had introduced Ezequiel to his cousin and her husband, the hospital's administrator, and found the younger man a room to rent in a house of an old couple who needed a well-paying tenant. Then he'd left him with Anjos to make their parting, which Miguel hoped was the last he saw of Ezequiel.

He'd found Ezequiel exhausting company. The younger man had alternated between grief and self-recrimination at first, but with a growing amount of time being spent on how unfair Anjos was to him. Anjos had shown amazing restraint throughout his brother's accusations. Even so, Miguel suspected Anjos would feel much better when the ship sailed in the morning... without Ezequiel.

His own problem was best addressed at the police station. Eduardo Cunha reluctantly made time to talk with him, although the inspector became more amenable when Miguel suggested they enjoy an ale at the café around the corner. Little more than a room in the owner's house opened out, the café had a half-dozen cramped tables bearing grimy white table-cloths. It was heavily frequented by police officers, and a friendly relationship between them and the old lady who owned the house assured that their conversations would remain private.

Cunha took a great swig of his ale as if he'd had nothing to drink all day. Summer was drawing to its end, but the drought hadn't receded in the weeks Miguel had been gone. "So," Cunha began when he sat down his glass, "by the time I reached DuBois' house, it was little more than rubble and ashes. Still burning in a few spots."

Cunha was a man with only a faint Truthsayer's gift. He did his job primarily with his intellect and perseverance, something Miguel appreciated. "And DuBois?"

Cunha shook his head. "I have nothing to tell you. He hasn't shown up since."

Miguel took a sip of ale to cover his surprise. Adela's letter had clearly stated DuBois was dead. Very very dead. "Is there any chance he died in the fire?"

Cunha shook his head. "If he did, he whisked his own bones away."

Well, that's not possible. Miguel pondered that conundrum while Cunha spoke of stopping by his house to question Adela, then the search for the missing manservant, whom Miguel's driver suspected of starting the fire. Fortunately, it apparently never occurred to Cunha that Adela could have started the fire. Or that she could be responsible for DuBois' disappearance. That was a relief. When the man reached the end of that story, Miguel asked that if DuBois did resurface, Cunha would relay his concern for DuBois' welfare. And with that, he left Cunha sipping a second ale and regaling the owner with the tale of chasing vandals out of the cemetery at Várzea.

That incident turned out to be nothing more than a pair of lovers seeking a place to tryst, according to the caretaker of the cemetery. The elderly man told Miguel that none of the graves had been disturbed, either. That eliminated the first place Miguel thought to look for a hidden body.

DuBois' body wouldn't be in the cathedral, either—a new burial would be too easily noted there—so Miguel discounted that. But if DuBois was a Jesuit, surely, he would wish to be buried on consecrated land. Would whoever killed him and removed his body do that for him? A few moments of quiet contemplation reminded Miguel that there were other churches nearby. He climbed back into his carriage and instructed the driver to take him out to the old city.

Cidade Velha had been abandoned for well over a century; Cassard, a French naval officer seeking spoils, had laid waste to the town in 1712, and it had never been rebuilt. Despite the town's early career as a hub of the slave trade—or perhaps because of that—it had held well over a dozen churches. Miguel settled back in his seat, doing his best to ignore the ill-maintained road.

The old Church of Our Lady of the Rosary, he suspected, was his best bet. After an hour of jouncing along the terrible road, he stepped down from the carriage into the town, a place of ruins amid the rising plateaus. He spotted small movements, traces of magic and everyday ties that told him people were living here in the broken buildings, but nothing spoke of violence or danger. He closed his eyes and sniffed the air. Beneath the dry dirt and a touch of sweat, he caught the sweetness of decay. He opened his eyes and followed that scent right into the church grounds.

Only one wall of the church still stood, an irregular archway opening out in the direction of the sea. Miguel walked across crunching bits of broke stone and stopped under that arch. It must have been the main door of the church once. Some of the finer stone remained as well—footings for pillars, lintels, perhaps the stairs leading up to the chancel, such as it was. Miguel turned his back on the open doorway and walked along what would have been the central aisle of the church. And there, buried under a smattering of loose stone, he could see strands of power hidden beneath.

He swept away the rubble with one foot, locating an old grave marker with a coat of arms, words written in Latin. The marker had been pried up and carefully replaced, small stones and dust sprinkled back over it to hide it. But the edges glowed in his sight, the burgundy ties of holy rites being performed—the extreme unction. Someone had given DuBois his last rites before sticking him in a nobleman's grave.

DuBois would like that. Miguel smiled at the conceit of DuBois, tangled together with the nobleman until their resurrection, arguing about the rights of man.

"Desecration," a voice hissed.

He caught sight of a white-haired woman near the ruined doorway. Her wizened frame hunched as she watched him come toward her. She held a cane in her wrinkled hand, so he made certain to stay out of its reach.

"What desecration?" he asked.

"Opening the old graves," she said, pointing with her chin.

"Did you see them do that?"

Her head bobbed up and down. "Two men. In the night, so I didn't see their faces, but one was a priest. Wore a cassock."

Someone *had* administered last rites for DuBois, so there had to be a priest involved somewhere along the line. The other man could be anyone. "Did you notice anything else about them?"

She came up the step into the ruined building, a faint breeze blowing the white skirts around her thin, dark legs. "They put a keystone into the grave with him." She tapped her cane against some of the rubble, old stone that had once been part of an arch. "Like this one."

Miguel went to see what the woman pointed out. There amid the broken stones was one that had clearly once been a keystone. It was broken in half, the symbol partial. Not Jesuit, but the square cross of the Military Order of Christ—the Templars.

LISBOA, SOUTHERN PORTUGAL

Adela strode into her office and flung herself into the chair behind the desk. When that didn't abate her annoyance, she considered getting up and doing it again, but doubted that would help. And she would probably damage her blue walking suit, one of her favorites.

Her hired investigators had gotten nowhere in locating Donato Mata, absent thief and assassin. It had been days, and nothing. She was accustomed to swifter results. Interference from the Jesuit Brotherhood was confounding things. Father Serafim, no doubt in retaliation for her bringing Nadezhda into their disagreement, had spread the word that no one was to talk with her hired help. That meant either lying about who she was when she hired men to ask questions or waiting around until better investigators arrived.

Miguel could do it—since a man with ties to the church is visible in his eyes.

She sat back in her chair and crossed her ankles atop her footstool, taking in the familiar scent of her office and allowing herself to think lustful thoughts about Miguel's eventual arrival in Lisboa. Sooner rather than later, she hoped. Santana cleared his throat, catching her daydreaming. "Yes?" she asked.

"I've completed the inventory you asked for, lady," her butler said, holding a book tucked under his arm. "It appears that only one book is... gone."

This time. "Which one?"

"Order of the Knights of Christ," he said, then opened his mouth to add something.

"Wait," she asked. "Is that the old one in Latin? From Father's library?" It wasn't a book she paid much attention to, or it would have lived in her office where she could find it easily.

"Yes, lady," Santana said. He tried to add something but stopped when she went on.

"How did no one notice a book that large was missing? Not that I blame you, Santana. You have your hands full here, but I hadn't noticed it, either." She'd had time to glance through her father's books herself and hadn't seen a space for a missing volume.

He removed a large book from under his arm and held it out to her. "It's not completely missing, lady."

She took the book from him to inspect it. The words picked out in gold on the tall leather-bound spine read *Order of the Knights of Christ*, but there was clearly something amiss with it. She opened the errant volume only to discover that it was merely the cover. The pages had been hacked out. She sighed and mentally cursed whoever had abused the poor book, but the reason was clear, now. A second book had been secreted inside the cover, this one with no imprint on the cover or spine. Of plain brown leather, the spine itself was bound with colorful twisted threads—a journal.

While Santana waited, Adela opened the journal and peered down at the neat script, the ends of the letters a bit more florid than her own writing. Black ink on some pages, here a day with burgundy ink, one with brown ink. She turned to the endpapers and found no name written there and found none at the front of the journal either. A slender ribbon marked a page near the end, so she turned there. Nothing exploded, fortunately... although Santana had probably already thumbed through this to make certain there were no traps hiding inside. "Did you figure out whose journal this is?"

"No, lady," Santana said, running fingers through his gray hair. "The writer only uses initials throughout. You'll see that he calls himself A, lady."

"Were the missing pages of the other book located?" she asked, glancing away from the puzzle.

"No, lady. The thief must have taken those with him."

"Is there anything else?" she asked, wanting to get to reading.

Santana drew himself up stiffly. "The footmen have demanded a rise in pay, lady. I promised I would discuss it with you."

Santana had worked with her long enough that she never took his concerns lightly. In her line of work, loyal servants were invaluable. "This is about Miss Vladimirova, yes?"

"Yes, lady," Santana said with a regretful inclination of his head.

"What do you think is fair, Santana?"

He succinctly laid out terms for an increase in pay for the household servants, and she nodded swiftly. Dealing with Nadezhda was trying on the nerves. Adela was simply glad they hadn't all quit when she and Nadezhda returned.

"Your terms seem quite reasonable, all things considered," she said, tapping fingers on the journal. "If you'll write that out for me, I'll forward the instructions to my man of business. Please include yourself in the increase, as well as the maids and the cook."

"The kitchen boy?" he asked.

"Him, as well," she said. "And Santana, I will have two more guests arriving soon, both gentlemen."

"I will arrange rooms for them, lady."

"One of them will take my father's room."

Santana stilled. It was only an instant, but long enough to betray surprise. "Yes, lady."

Her father's room had remained empty since her father's death. It adjoined with the room that she now used, though, and would make life simpler for her. "Although I do not intend to make the news public, Santana, Inspector Gaspar and I were married while in Praia."

"In Africa, lady?" he asked, as if the location might make the sacrament null, rather than the lack of her signature… or the dispensation required for her participation in such a sacrament as she was not Catholic.

"Yes, in Africa." She hadn't thought *Santana* would be the one to disapprove, but the narrow line of his lips said otherwise. "And yes, he is African."

Santana's shoulders stiffened. "Will there be anything else, lady?"

She gazed up at him, at a loss. *What do I say now*? "He is... my husband, Santana, and the darkness of his skin does not diminish that station. He is a gentleman, educated at the Sorbonne in Paris, and a man of means."

Santana flushed. "My apologies, lady."

"I do not want to hear complaints against him if they are simply veiled distaste for his ancestors. He should arrive in the next week, which will give you ample time to clarify that to the staff."

Santana bowed, cheeks still ruddy. "You may count on me, lady."

Once he'd whisked himself away, she let out a shaky breath. Santana was, if nothing else, absolutely professional. He would make her position clear to the staff and would enforce it. But it hadn't occurred to her before today that she would need defend her choice at home. Miguel had warned her, but she'd considered his concerns only in terms of the Freemasons and Jesuits she worked with. She hadn't thought it would extend down to maids and kitchen boys.

Perturbed, she forced herself to focus on the hand-written pages in front of her instead. She sat poring through the journal for a time, then rose and paced her office, still reading. There were dozens of people named here, only by initials, though. When recounting what some other person had said to him, the writer referred to himself as A.

The bookmarked page told of his meeting the aunt of his closest friend, R. He mentioned walking along the Rossio and running into her in the company of the Marquis of M., chatting about the quality of the seafood at one of the local restaurants, and then leaving to accompany another friend back to his home. He went on to describe *their* evening together, but Adela didn't care about that.

She remembered that day, a little over a year ago now. She had walked along the Rossio with the Marquis of Maraval, as he tried to convince her to move to Northern Portugal and the Golden City. She called the man her godfather, although that wasn't a formal relationship. But they had strolled the Rossio, discussing the various attractions of the two cities. She had never, for a moment, believed Maraval wanted her to move north to partake of the joys of the Golden City. He wanted her there so he could keep a closer eye on her.

While on that walk, they'd encountered Alessio Ferreira, the son of a businessman in the Golden City. Alessio's father had been a man whose industry and wealth caught the eye of the current prince's father, prompting the prince to grant the title of cavalheiro to a commoner. Adela had met the handsome Alessio a few times before, primarily when he'd attended the university at Coimbra and lived in the same *republica* her nephew did. The two had become fast friends.

But that day on the Rossio, they had talked about seafood before parting ways. A week later, Alessio Ferreira was dead. This journal had to be his property.

Nadezhda stepped inside the office, all black veils and skirts. The feel of cold and death crept in with her. "What have you found?"

"Santana found it." Adela set the journal atop her desk. "I like to think that people are intelligent, Nadezhda."

"Half of all humans are of below-average intelligence," Nadezhda said in her emotionless voice.

Adela laughed softly. "I suppose that's true."

"It is, without doubt." Nadezhda appeared to dither for a time before deciding to sit. "Why does this bother you?"

"Because I too often ascribe cleverness to others' actions when they might be no more than pettiness or spite." She leaned back against the desk. "This appears to be the journal of Alessio Ferreira, my nephew's friend who was murdered. Donato Mata, if he was the one who broke into the house recently, left it for me in the place of a book on the Templars that he mutilated. Hidden inside the carcass of that book, so that I would have to be actively looking at the book to find it. And yet... I keep thinking there should be a great significance to the choice of book to destroy."

"But you don't see what it is?"

"Frankly, no. Also, if this is, in fact, the journal it seems to be, then I must ask how Mata came to possess it."

"When he killed the young man."

"No, Alessio Ferreira was participating in a duel when he was killed, so he wouldn't have had it with him. It would have been in his hotel room."

Nadezhda shrugged. "Easy enough to steal from a hotel."

Adela nodded absently, wondering briefly if Nadezhda had experience stealing things from hotels. "And why the book on the Templars? It isn't a particularly important text, in itself. Is this a reference to some nobleman or soldier given those honors by the throne?" Southern Portugal had long ago secularized the military order, so that it now was little more than a trifle. "Or is this meant to be a reference to the Freemasons, since so many conflate the two groups? Or... actual Templars, returning despite the papal ban? Perhaps the Pope himself is involved."

Nadezhda ignored the wild speculation. "Or perhaps the book was chosen solely for its size. Pointless to worry without more evidence."

Yes, Nadezhda would say that. Nothing worried her or troubled her. In her current state, she could cut off her own hand and be unperturbed.

Adela sighed. "The truth is that I'm having trouble seeing Mata as a complicated man. I think he must, in truth, be rather stupid. I think he was simply spiteful and wanted to rub my nose in the fact that he'd not only broken in here twice, but also killed a young man I liked and got away with it."

Chapter 17

TUESDAY, 29 OCTOBER 1901
SINTRA, SOUTHERN PORTUGAL

Adela breathed in the air of the mountains, cool and misty. The Quinta da Regaleira was named for the baroness who'd owned the vast estate for much of the previous century. It was a lovely place, spilling over the mountains near Sintra, where the prince of Southern Portugal held his court. The name of the estate suggested a vineyard had once stood here, but Adela suspect that was more a romantic fancy on the part of the baroness than the truth.

The present owner of the estate was of more concern to Adela than the baroness. António Augusto de Carvalho Monteiro was a vastly wealthy man who'd returned to his parents' native land from Brazil to purchase this place. The current house was grand, but nothing strikingly special. Adela would have preferred it stay that way, but men with money often felt a need to display their wealth and cleverness to everyone else. Carvalho Monteiro had dreams of making the estate into a showplace. It would feature several buildings, all with clever nods to his various occult fascinations—alchemy, Gnosticism, Rosicrucianism, and of course, the Freemasons and Templars.

She sighed and led Nadezhda toward the house. "I hope I haven't wasted our day driving up here."

Nadezhda, an inky blot in her regular blacks, glided on toward the steps. "I would like to meet the man."

Adela suppressed a smile. Nadezhda held strong opinions about people who tinkered with magic for amusement. And men in general. "We can't afford to kill him."

"I will keep that in mind."

"We're not here to meet him anyway." Carvalho Monteiro might have one of the most extensive Camonian libraries—full of rare manuscripts tied to the nationalistic fever dreams of Luís de Camões—but he was a *collector*, not a true practitioner of... well, *anything*.

She lifted the knocker and let it fall. It took only a moment before the door was opened, revealing Carvalho Monteiro's whippet of a butler, a wiry fellow not quite as tall as Adela. "Lady," he said, inclining his head. "It has been a while. Shall I take you to see her?"

"Thank you, Tomar. I've been traveling." Adela stepped over the threshold, feeling the chill inside the house that likely hadn't been there when the previous owner held the place. The entry hallway was papered in a deep red, punctuated by a leaf pattern. Heels ringing on the white marble floors, Adela and Nadezhda followed Tomar—who never seemed to react to Nadezhda like other people—through the house to a large receiving room with a terrace that overlooked a garden that spilled down the slopes below.

"She is outside, Lady," Tomar said, inclining his bow more toward Nadezhda than Adela herself.

The wide stone terrace was guarded by a stone balustrade to keep any careless visitor from falling the twenty or so feet to the garden below. Adela stepped out onto the terrace and headed toward the western end where a still form huddled, to all appearances gazing out across the mountains toward the sea. Ifigénia Carvalho wore a white walking dress that had seen better days. Stains around the hem showed she'd been walking in the garden. Her dark hair was unbound, spilling down almost to her waist in tangled locks. It made her long face seem even longer, more austere.

She shuddered when Nadezhda stepped onto the terrace. "Lady," she said in a rusty voice, one at odds with her youth. "I see that you've brought Death with you."

I see was not an accurate statement. Ifigénia Carvalho was blind, the consequence of a mistake made in complete innocence.

"Miss Vladimirova likes the mountain air," Adela said blandly.

"Humidity and mist?" Ifigénia laughed. "I suppose she must."

"Water is water," Nadezhda said, apparently unoffended by being called Death… or being spoken of as if she wasn't there.

"Why are you here?" Ifigénia asked. "My cousin is away on Madeira."

Ifigénia Carvalho was a distant cousin of Carvalho Monteiro's mother, hence her being deposited here in this house far from the rest of her immediate family. After the incident, her father—a blustering nobleman who lived in the Golden City—hadn't wanted her near him, a constant reminder that he was a careless man. He'd sent Ifigénia away from her sisters and mother, dropping the girl into a spiral of loneliness and bitterness as she tried to cope with her sudden inability to see. Adela came to visit her, but not often enough, she knew.

"I wanted to talk to you," Adela began. "About a book."

Ifigénia crossed her arms over her chest, sending her hair cascading to one side, trailing to the floor. "I have no answers for you," she snapped. "As you've none for me."

Ifigénia often grew belligerent with Adela, mostly because she'd never found what Ifigénia needed. Adela had never deceived her—there was very little chance that the girl would ever see again, even if they did find the book in question. Very little. But Ifigénia still had hope, and Adela had never brought her good news.

Adela settled on the balustrade, picking at her blue skirts until she was satisfied with how they fell. Nadezhda moved until she stood back against the wall, out of her way, although Adela doubted it was far enough that Ifigénia couldn't sense her presence. "This is about a different book."

"I heard eagles earlier," Ifigénia said as if Adela hadn't spoken.

Adela held in her sigh. Ifigénia often changed the topic when frustrated. There likely had been eagles, though. The mountains between Sintra and Cascais was on the western edge of the eagles' range. "It seems a bit late in the year."

"They have to eat," Ifigénia responded. "Maybe you should just let her kill me."

Her would be Nadezhda, not one of the eagles. "She has chosen to abstain," Adela said. "You're barely what? Twenty? You have a long life ahead of you, Ifigénia."

"A life without sight. I think of it every day, you know," Ifigénia said. "Jumping over the edge. One day I'll do it."

Adela wasn't going to discount that. Ifigénia's life had not been easy over the last two years. "I'm sorry I haven't visited. I've been traveling."

"People come, stare at the blind girl, then they leave." Ifigénia pushed herself out of her chair abruptly. "I'm going inside."

The girl knew the way well enough that she didn't hesitate when she reached the door. She fumbled for the latch for only a split-second before she opened the door and stepped inside. Adela rose and followed, leaving Nadezhda to bring up the rear of the procession. Ifigénia crossed to the pale stone hearth, the fire already lit, and paced in front of it. Her stained hem dragged on the ground—she'd grown thinner since losing her sight—and her bedraggled hair tangled with her arms.

She's going to convince others that she's mad. Adela wondered if that was Ifigénia's intention, perhaps to punish her father. Or perhaps it was genuine frustration with her situation. "Ifigénia, I need your help. There's a slight chance that the same person who recently destroyed a book in my home is the same person who took that book from your father's house." *That book.* They always referred to it that way. "Can you describe the book in your father's office for me? The one you read?"

Ifigénia stopped with one hand on the mantel, her lips turned down in a grimace. "The book was just over two feet tall, opened about three feet wide. There was a bookmark. It was burgundy, satin. I have answered this before."

She had, but Adela listened with new attention, since the description was familiar. "Do you remember seeing any title? Any author's name at the top."

Ifigénia pounded her hand against the mantle. "One word," she shouted. "I read *one word.*"

Ifigénia had always been the most intelligent of Lord Carvalho's daughters. The eldest, Genoveva, was the one expected to marry well. She'd been taught to dance and make her way through society, but little else. The youngest girl, Constância, had the brains of a rabbit, but a loyal heart. Ifigénia had been her father's favorite, the one who'd learned Greek and Latin, the one who might one day go to the university in Coimbra... until the day she'd read that book.

The book in question had been left lying open on her father's desk. Lord Carvalho had thought nothing of leaving arcane tomes lying about, and his daughter paid the price.

"What was the word?" Adela asked.

Ifigénia closed her eyes, as if to shut off sight she didn't have. "*Obcaeco*," she said. "But that's not what I said."

"What did you say?"

"*Exoculo*," Ifigénia answered, her voice soft. Resigned.

In some books of arcane nature, the writers imbued the volume with a curse intended to prevent females from reading it, although Adela had never heard of a curse this severe being attached to one. Young Ifigénia had merely been reading aloud, with no intent to speak a spell. Some curse had twisted the word in her mouth, though, and thus she'd blinded herself with her own tongue.

Adela blamed the girl's father. The man had left a dangerous book lying open where his curious and intelligent daughter might stumble upon it. He might not have known of the curse on it. "And your father said it was a text on the Templars, right?"

"An insignificant text," Ifigénia said. "That's all I know." Her voice had risen again, her words ending on a shout.

"Please, Lady, leave her alone," a voice said in accented

Portuguese. A youngish man stepped out of a side hallway, a book clutched to his chest, a slip of paper protruding from the top. He was a soft-spoken fellow of fair coloring and slightly shabby attire. His spectacles gave him a studious appearance that befitted his training. Johannes Konrad had been a teacher at a boy's school in Lisboa until last year when he'd literally taken refuge in this house to escape a winter storm. He'd been here ever since, taking a position that earned him almost nothing—as a librarian handling the owner's valuable rare books.

Adela knew better than to think the young man would steal anything of his master's despite the abysmally low pay. Konrad wasn't here for the books. He stayed for Ifigénia... who seemed not to notice his interest in her.

Adela sighed. "Mr. Konrad, I may have a new lead on the thief."

The young man stepped closer to Adela. "You should not get her hopes up," he whispered. "Not if it's *may have*."

"I can hear you," Ifigénia snapped. "Don't talk about me like I'm a child." To punctuate that, she pushed the nearest item off the mantle—a brass candlestick that clattered as it hit the marble floor.

"Then don't behave like one, Miss Carvalho," Konrad said in his soft voice. "Do you want me to read you this letter from your sisters or not?"

Ifigénia's fingers gripped the stone mantel, her knuckles momentarily white. Then her hand relaxed. "Yes. I'd like you to read it. Will you wait for me in the library?"

Konrad's eyes fixed first Adela and then Nadezhda with a warning glare. He nodded toward the library. Then he bowed his head to Ifigénia, as if she could see him do so. "I will be waiting when you are ready, Miss Carvalho."

He took himself out of the room without a glance backward, trusting that Ifigénia would be good for her word.

"Will you just get out now?" Ifigénia said in a defeated voice.

That wasn't meant for Konrad, but for her. Adela inclined her head and pointed for Nadezhda to go to the library. "I've a couple of questions I must ask of Mr. Konrad, and then I'll leave, Miss Carvalho."

Ifigénia waved one hand absently, her head turned away. She slouched down into a low chair set before the hearth and laid both hands over her face. Adela left her there, letting Nadezhda decide whether to follow or not on her own.

When she entered the library, it seemed dark, a stark contrast to the brightly lit main room. This house still didn't have electric lights, and Adela doubted that Carvalho Monteiro would have them installed while he had other plans for this estate. Mr. Konrad reached to turn up the gaslight above the desk where he usually sat, cataloging the estate's books.

"Lady," he said in a voice that betrayed his annoyance with her. "What have you come here for?"

Since she knew he wouldn't suggest it, Adela sat in the chair on the other side of his desk. "A book in my home was damaged recently. Someone tore out the pages to put another book inside the cover. This morning I made the connection that... the book involved was a minor text on the Templars. The book is a folio style, approximately two feet tall and three feet across when opened." She opened her small handbag and took out a slip of satin. "This is what

THE TRUTH UNDISCOVERED

was left of the bookmark."

Konrad picked it up, his lips twisting a bit as he contemplated the scrap of fabric, no bigger than the last digit if his finger, but it was burgundy satin—just as Ifigénia had described.

"I wish I had made the connection sooner," Adela admitted, "but there was nothing magical about that book. And yet... it matches the description of the one that took her sight."

Konrad handed back the slip of fabric. "I don't know much about magic, but is it possible for one book to be enspelled and another not? Copies of the same book, I mean?"

"Yes," she said. "Or, the book might have been created with a key that, when spoken, brought it alive, so that some copies of the book have been activated while others have not."

Konrad pulled out his chair and sat, eyeing her warily. "Then every library in Portugal is dangerous."

"Libraries are, by their very nature, dangerous."

Konrad shook his head. "I do not mean access to knowledge, Lady, but access to magic. How many other young women could be blinded by such creations?"

It had happened enough throughout the centuries that Carvalho should have been more careful. "I have always assumed her father was lying about the book," Adela admitted. "About what book it was. But I have been searching my mind, trying to decide why the copy in my father's library was destroyed and wondered if there might be a tie."

"What was the book called?"

"*Order of the Knights of Christ*," she told him. "No subtitle, no author's name on the spine. When I looked at my father's catalog this morning, the attribution said *Anonymous*."

"That is not helpful," Konrad said, brow furrowing.

"True, but if there's some connection, however tenuous, it might help in the search for the original book." To remove the curse, they would need the exact book that Ifigénia had looked at, and if that one had been stolen as her father claimed it was, it could be anywhere in the world by now. "I thought it might be worth asking if you have a copy here. It is the kind of basic book that any Camonian library should have."

Konrad sat still for a moment, his eyes narrowed as he calculated. He rose. "If you'll let me go look, Lady."

He disappeared into an area of the library hidden from her view by a freestanding rack of shelves. She heard pages turning, and then a ladder rattling along a rail. Using the time to look around, she saw that Nadezhda hadn't followed her into the library. She felt bad for leaving Ifigénia to Nadezhda's limited mercies, but Ifigénia could call for the butler's aid if she became alarmed.

Konrad appeared around the edge of the bookshelf, a large tome in his hands. He laid it out on the desk. "Is this it?"

Adela reached for the book to search the pages for signs of an overarching spell, but Konrad slammed one hand down on top of it. "Under no circumstances are you to open this."

Adela gave the young man a dry look. "I do not intend to read any of it aloud."

"Is it the same book?"

"Yes," she admitted. "I'd like to look at it to see what…"

"It's going into the vault," he said stiffly. "Until I have a way to know there's no chance it will hurt her again, I don't want anyone to touch it."

"Don't be silly," she said.

"I am never silly, Lady."

She likely had a different definition of *silly*. "I can steal this from you without your knowing it."

"I have no doubt," he said, lifting his chin but keeping one hand firmly atop the book. "But I trust that you will leave it here so I may continue my search for the book that hurt her."

Adela inclined her head as gracefully as possible when vexed. After all, she'd only come here to look at the book, to see if there was a copy in this extensive library. She could give in… for now. She rose. "I have a friend who will be able to tell us whether the spell on that is active," she said. "May I bring him here when he arrives?"

Konrad's eyes narrowed. "Very well."

"We'll come as soon as we can."

"Carvalho Monteiro will be back in a week," Konrad said. "I'd suggest you come before then."

"Absolutely." With that arranged, she took her leave of the young man, hoping that when Miguel arrived he could do more to reveal the reason behind the destruction.

She left the library and emerged back into the brightly lit main hallway. Ifigénia still slumped in her chair before the hearth, but Nadezhda now sat across from her. She leaned forward, closer than would be comfortable for most living people, and spoke softly to Ifigénia, drawing in a breath before every sentence.

"Miss Vladimirova, are you ready to leave?" Adela asked in an intentionally bright voice.

Without answering, Nadezhda rose smoothly and came to join Adela, bearing that creeping sense of death with her. Ifigénia remained her in chair, hands clenched on the arms, her jaw working with some distress.

"What did you tell her?" Adela asked once they had gotten far enough down the red-papered hallway that even Ifigénia wouldn't overhear them.

Nadezhda drew in a breath. "That by the time I was her age I'd been married off to a man I didn't know, passed around like a whore between his uncles and cousins, and drowned by my own husband's hands. The time for her complaining should end."

In this form, Nadezhda showed little sympathy for others. "Did you not tell me that you stayed at the bottom of your lake for a decade before you left it?" Adela pointed out.

"I was dead," Nadezhda said. "And I believed I was supposed to remain there forever. She has other options."

As Adela recalled her story, Nadezhda had lurked in the bottom of the lake her husband drowned her in, drawing in and killing every one of her husband's kinsmen who came near. It wasn't until her brother had come to the lake and begged her to stop that she walked away from the watery existence of a rusalka to become something else—whatever she was now. But Nadezhda still smelled like lake water, all the time.

"Evil things happen," Nadezhda added, "but we must move on."

Since Nadezhda was still dead and Ifigénia still blind, *moving on* had to be considered a relative term.

CHAPTER 18

**THURSDAY, 31 OCTOBER 1901
LISBOA, SOUTHERN PORTUGAL**

The Pombaline Baixa—the downtown—of the city of Lisboa could have held Miguel's attention for days had he not felt he needed to find his wife. In the letter she'd left him in Cabo Verde, Adela had intentionally omitted where she lived, and they hadn't discussed it before, thinking at the time they would be traveling to Southern Portugal together. But Fate had intervened, and they'd come here separately.

Fortunately, he had an idea where to start. The cab driver carried him and a travel-worn Anjos out to the countryside to the college run by the Jesuit Brotherhood out in Campolide. Miguel wasn't sanguine about visiting the Jesuits, not given what he knew of DuBois, but the dead man's name would give him some credibility with the Jesuits, while it might not help with the Freemasons at all. Hence the choice of the Jesuits.

The college turned out to be a long building with two towers behind it—likely stairwells. Miguel stepped down from the cab and instructed the man as Anjos followed. The driver turned his cab down to the bottom of the road before the school to wait for them. They stood on the drive before the college, clearly not belonging there. Miguel's fine suit was rumpled from the drive, and Anjos' baggy brown frock coat—admittedly cut from cheaper fabric—looked like he'd slept in it.

Young men in black cassocks and caps hurried past to the main entryway, their serious faces all turning away from

Miguel's darker one. These would all be young Portuguese men of good family, not the children of workers who'd immigrated from former colonies. Miguel saw little sign of magic among them, but multitudinous ties to the Church, to each other, and for one pair that carefully walked at an arm's distance from each other, the tie that spoke of recent sex.

"Which end of this dragon do we assault?" Anjos asked, peering at the stately building rather than the students. The temporary flush of life that his aunt had bestowed on him had faded over the last few days of travel. Anjos was back to being the weary man dancing with death Miguel had met that first day in Recife, his breath short and his gait slow.

"I think we should start with the chapel," Miguel said, "since my gift tells me it's the head of this particular dragon." If there was any place on this campus that bore the myriad glows of magic in his eyes, it was there.

"I'm sure they wouldn't like us referring to it that way," Anjos said ruefully.

"I am not concerned about their opinion." Miguel led the way down the paved walk to the chapel. The chapel was small and plain on the outside. Once they removed their hats and stepped through its brown doors, they found an interior equally severe, all carved wood and plastered walls. No gilding here. The smell of incense surrounded him, amber and dusty in his eyes. His ears picked up the hum of the bell, as if the very air in the chapel made it ring silently. Ignoring the confusing sensations, Miguel walked along the nave, leaving Anjos to catch up after performing his genuflection. A lone priest stood filling a censer at the front of the chancel. In Miguel's perception, the old man

THE TRUTH UNDISCOVERED   181

was heavily cloaked in the glowing burgundy vines that told of his ties to the church.

"I am Inspector Gaspar, late of Cabo Verde," he said to the man. "I have news of Marcel DuBois. To whom should I speak about him?"

The old priest's face gave away nothing, but weaving through the burgundy vines about the man, Miguel saw something odd—a single strand of black, the like of which he'd never seen before.

"Let me fetch Father Serafim," the old priest said before Miguel had time to focus clearly on that anomaly. "He can better deal with whatever news you carry."

With that, the man scurried away—it looked like *scurrying* to Miguel—to the side of the chapel and down a stairwell. When Miguel glanced that way, he saw a wall, but the illusion lasted only a split-second. There was a stairwell sequestered there instead, leading only downward. It was a complicated thing, that illusion of a wall, and not normal within a church. Surely that stairwell led somewhere interesting.

"Do you want to chase him?" he asked Anjos half-heartedly.

"No," Anjos said. "It wouldn't be dignified. Or are we in a hurry?"

"I'd like to see how long it takes for this priest to show up," Miguel answered. "Find out how urgently they want news of DuBois."

Miguel went to the first wooden pew and sat, leaving Anjos to decide if he would do so as well. After a moment, the Brazilian man did likewise, conserving his energy. There *were* other things they could be doing with their time, so the wait was an annoyance. Miguel would have loved a chance to bathe at this point, before he met Adela again. Accommodations on the *Ferreira*, while adequate, had not included bathing facilities. He felt dry and dusty, and his suit wanted cleaning.

A priest emerged then from the sequestered stairwell. He seemed flustered, as if Miguel's arrival worried him. *It should.* The man approached them and immediately turned to Anjos. "How can I help you, son?"

Miguel gazed at the priest, evaluating the man's clear ties to the Church, his affection for large quantities of wine, and his sloped shoulders. This was a man whom others preyed on, he decided, a tool, not a predator.

"I think you mean to speak with Inspector Gaspar," Anjos said stiffly, indicating Miguel with one hand.

The priest turned his watery green eyes on Miguel, then, harrumphing to cover his embarrassment. "I didn't realize. Inspector Gaspar, you said you have news of Marcel DuBois. How did you know him?"

Any Jesuit who knew Adela would likely know what DuBois' relationship with Miguel was. And that suggested that this man was *not* the one he needed to speak with. Miguel glanced over at Anjos. "Does he actually not know who I am, or is he dissembling?"

Anjos' head tilted as he considered that query. "Try asking him a direct question."

"Father Serafim," Miguel said, "do you know who I am?"

"No," the priest answered, spine stiffening. "Should I?"

THE TRUTH UNDISCOVERED

"Go back," Anjos said. "Ask his name."

Miguel tried that, to which the priest stammered that he *was* Father Serafim. Anjos merely shook his head. Miguel turned back to the man pretending to be Serafim. "Why don't you go find the real Father Serafim for me?"

The old man frowned but harrumphed his way off to the stairwell.

"That was not very helpful," Anjos noted dryly.

"They have things to hide." During the voyage to Iberia, Miguel had explained his relationship to DuBois to Anjos, provoking dismay. Not only did Anjos not approve of the idea that Miguel had lived before, a clear violation of the Church's beliefs, but because Miguel was immune to witchery, Anjos couldn't judge his truthfulness as he did other men's. That apparently made every word a challenge that Anjos hadn't had in some time. Miguel suspected Anjos still didn't quite believe his claim of having lived other lives.

"I understand that," Anjos said. "Why send a fake?"

Miguel laughed softly. "*You*, my friend. They had to know the Lady was trying to hire you, that she planned to go to Brazil to find you, so sending up a fake Serafim limits how much information you can get out of them."

Anjos puffed out a weak breath. "I'd rather be eating lunch."

"As would I" Miguel said. "I've always heard the dining on Rua Augusta is marvelous."

Anjos looked at him questioningly.

"From others who've visited here," Miguel clarified. "I've always wanted to come but have never been able."

Anjos pondered that for a moment. "Do you feel... at home here?"

That was a complex question. *Too early to answer it.* "I have to admit, the welcome so far has been sparse."

"I could learn to like it here, I think. Then again, I'll die here, most likely."

Miguel had no argument for that. Fortunately, a new priest emerged from the stairwell, saving him from speculating about the length of time Anjos had left. This man was tall and dark eyed and approached them far more warily than his predecessor. As expected, the ties of the church wrapped around him. They were joined by that unexplained black strand again, although it quickly submerged under the other ties. That made two priests so far on whom Miguel had seen it.

Very odd. Miguel rarely saw anything *new*.

"I am Father Serafim," the priest said, "And you are Miguel Gaspar, the Meter."

Ah, this was definitely the man he needed. "I am. Therefore you know I had dealings with DuBois back in Cabo Verde."

"I did," Serafim said quietly. "What news do you have of him?"

"I'm offering a simple trade of information," Miguel said. "Tell me where I can find the Lady, and I'll tell you where DuBois is buried."

Serafim considered that option, mouth in a thin line. "Do you have paper to write it down?"

"I do," Anjos said, drawing a notebook and pencil from a jacket pocket.

"30 Praça das Amoreiras, near the aqueduct," the priest said.

Anjos wrote that down. "It's the truth."

"You would be Gabriel Anjos, the Truthsayer," the tall priest observed coolly, surveying Anjos from head to toe. "Brazilian, of course, but that accent makes it obvious."

"I would think so," Anjos said mildly.

Miguel resisted the urge to laugh at the priest's pallid attempt to sneer at them. Both he and Anjos had dealt with enough criminals over the years to have been insulted in every way possible, so this man wasn't impressing either of them. "DuBois is buried in the old abandoned Church of Our Lady of the Rosary in Cidade Velha, in one of the tombs along the nave, with a Templar's sigil laid atop his body."

When he spoke those last words, that thread of black surfaced amidst all the burgundy wrapping around Serafim.

"And someone did administer last rites," Miguel added as he rose.

The priest didn't look happy about the whole thing but nodded to Miguel once. "Tell her that I would rather deal with you in the future."

Miguel let one of his eyebrows rise. He had no doubt Adela would laugh at that restriction. If she wanted to talk to Serafim, she wouldn't let his desires stop her.

Gabriel Anjos was already exhausted by the time they reached the house on the Praça das Amoreiras. He'd barely slept the last few days of the journey, renewed pain in his lungs making him fitful at night. He'd smoked a couple of cigarettes on the ride there. That comforted him but didn't make him feel more awake.

It was disheartening to feel death creeping back into his body when a week before he'd felt hope. No, it was cruel.

He let the footmen gather his tatty luggage from the cab, watched Gaspar pay the driver, and followed as they all went inside the house. The house itself was not large, only three stories, in stern grays and browns, with wrought iron rails and balconies. A very *Portuguese* house, he decided, much like those in the better parts of Recife, where the citizens looked back to their homeland for inspiration.

The footmen carried off their luggage, up a flight of stairs that didn't look too steep. Gabriel waited with Gaspar in the white-plastered hallway for a moment until the elderly butler returned to deal with them. "If you will join me in the sitting room," the butler requested, "the Lady will be down in a moment."

The butler led them down the white hallway and opened out a pair of doors to reveal a vast sitting room that looked more masculine than Gabriel had expected. Green velvet draperies filtered the afternoon light, showing heavy sofas in a brown stripe. Gabriel suspected it was all silk. Expensive, and suited to a very wealthy sponsor. Large potted plants stood in the corners and, on the far side of the room, a black shadow waited for them.

As soon as he looked that direction, a frisson of fear slid down his spine.

That is Death. Not like the sticky fingers of the consumption that fouled his lungs and made it hard to breath. No, this was the sharp knife, quick and painless if he sought it.

THE TRUTH UNDISCOVERED

"What is *that* doing here?" Gaspar asked, speaking to someone beyond the door behind them.

Gabriel tore his eyes from the black shadow, forced himself to take in a breath, and turned to face his employer.

The woman had walked in behind them, but even without an introduction, he knew she held all the power in her hands. She had light eyes, pale skin and inky black hair, and carried herself with the assurance of a general. "Miguel, Miss Vladimirova must stay somewhere. Better here with me."

Gabriel licked his dry lips. *Ah, yes, the shadow of Death has a Russian name, Vladimirova.*

His employer came closer. "And you must be Inspector Anjos," she said. "You may address me as Lady."

It wasn't a name, but he didn't intend to demand more. She was paying his brother's tuition and housing at the hospital back in Cabo Verde, after all. "Lady. I am pleased to meet you."

Gaspar stepped closer to the Lady, causing Gabriel to turn halfway back to see the woman in the corner of the room, so many veils about her that he could only tell she was of diminutive stature. She stood almost like a statue, unmoving or unmoved.

"It is dangerous to have that thing in your house," Gaspar said urgently, one hand on the Lady's elbow now. "Vampires lack self-control."

Out of the corner of his eye, Gabriel thought he saw the shadow flinch. It was a small movement, but Truthsayers learned early to associate motions with emotions. *She doesn't like being called That Thing.*

"This is my house, Miguel," the Lady said imperiously, "and if I want her to stay here, she will."

This was about to turn into a full-blown argument, Gabriel realized by the tone, and it would all be carried out in front of everyone. Despite his tiredness, it only took a split-second for him to talk himself into doing the proper thing. Ignoring the fearful thumping of his heart, he walked over to that far corner of the room. He held out one arm for the black-veiled woman to take. "Miss Vladimirova, I wondered if you would like to walk around the neighborhood for a time."

There was no obvious reaction to his words, but after a moment, she laid a gloved hand on his arm. "That would be wise."

Gaspar and his lady had moved out into the hallway to continue their argument, so Gabriel simply led Miss Vladimirova out of the room and past them. A footman hurried to open the front door for them and stood stiffly to one side, clearly terrified of the woman on Gabriel's arm. Gabriel ignored that and led her along the row of houses, her heels clicking on the stone walkway.

Her head barely came to his shoulder, and the gloved hand on his arm was narrow. He wondered how old she was that she felt the need to hide her face. Or perhaps she was disfigured.

"If you wish to see the aqueduct," Miss Vladimirova said, "turn left."

Her voice was oddly even, without the nuances he usually used to judge truth. Not like Gaspar's, where his truthfulness was simply missing. Hers seemed flattened instead, like a curl of hair pulled to straightness.

THE TRUTH UNDISCOVERED

"I have never seen an aqueduct," he allowed, although he *was* seeing it at the moment—the aqueduct ran off into the countryside, taller than the houses around them. But since he wished to keep her out of that house for a time, he did as she suggested. The plaza teemed with amoreiras—mulberry trees—their foliage so dense it masked the houses on the other side. With the aqueduct overhead, the walkway seemed confined.

"You did not need to escort me out," Miss Vladimirova said. "I am accustomed to aversion."

He heard no inflection in those words, but it *was* a lie. Gaspar's words had hurt her somehow. "Inspector Gaspar is a good man," he offered. "He is not, however, kind. He has told me that himself. He sees only what is, the surface of things. Not what potential a person may hold."

Her black veils fluttered in the afternoon breeze that carried the whispering of the trees with it. "There is no potential left in me."

"Most would say there is no life in me, either," he pointed out. "I know what it is like to have others shy away from me."

"Because you are ill?" she asked. "I can feel it all about you."

"I am dying. I have already lived longer than the doctors expected."

"A healer has tried to chase out your sickness."

They were approaching a gray stone building of straight lines and massive dimensions. "You can tell that?" Gabriel asked, noticing the smell of her garments for the first time, the scent of water—like that of a lake, not the sea.

"Yes. It is a terrible thing," she said.

"I agree." There was little more to say about the plague that was slowly consuming his life.

"Go in here," she said, pointing to a tall wrought-iron gate that surrounded the stern building. "Through the gate."

"There's a lock," he pointed out.

"I have the key. I made the watchman give it to me." She lifted her hand from his arm to fish the key out from a pocket or purse hidden within all those layers of black cloth.

How did she make the watchman give it to her? He felt a chill again, having forgotten for a moment that she was dangerous. She opened the lock with the large iron key and pushed the gate open with a loud creak.

Looking up, Gabriel realized that the aqueduct seemed to end in the roof of the building, so this must be where all the water ended up. "Is this a reservoir?"

"Ah, that is the proper word." She walked on up the ramp into the building, leaving him behind, so Gabriel moved swiftly to catch up. By the time he did, she was at the building's front door, for which she also held a key.

She opened one of the tall doors and he followed her inside. The scent of water wrapped around him, a cool humidity that swallowed his senses. It was quiet, only the sound of water falling. She closed the door behind them, and then led him forward.

The reservoir was huge inside, with stone arches on tall stone supports—marble, he guessed by the hard feel underfoot. The ceiling was plastered white, though, softening of the echoing qualities of the stone. Light came in from arched windows on each wall, reflecting off those white surfaces. A walkway edged the entire reservoir, with a platform extending out into the middle of the water, a short railing around it all to prevent anyone from being drawn into the water. On one side of the reservoir, water spilled from the mouth of an ornate stone dolphin and tumbled down a man-made slope. This was, indeed, the very end of the aqueduct.

Miss Vladimirova walked out onto the platform, not intimidated by the high arches or the deep water all around them.

Gabriel watched her, reminding himself that she was supposedly a rusalka, a water spirit, and she could use her magic to draw him into the water and drown him. That was what rusalki did, if he recalled Gaspar's tales. Instead, she merely stood there, veiled head tilted, either listening to or scenting the waters. Perhaps she sensed the water on some other level that he didn't grasp. For a time, he stood near her, taking in the vastness of the reservoir about them.

"It is alive," she said then. "Not the water itself, but it teems with life. Life so tiny that no one can see it, but I know it's there."

"Bacteria?" he asked.

"Yes, and other things." Without warning, she walked to the edge of the platform, took off one of her gloves, and leaned over the short rail to touch the water with her bare hand.

Gabriel felt a slight pressure... and the scent of the air about him suddenly changed, now *burnt* like a dry, hot afternoon. He heard a faint gasp, as if Miss Vladimirova struggled to breathe, as if she'd sobbed. "Are you unwell?"

She rose to her feet and came at him. She wrapped her bare

hand around his throat, shockingly strong. He went still, unable to resist her grasp, as if his feet were bound to the platform. And warmth flowed into his body through her touch, burning him like it had when Tia Ana Maria tried to heal him... but this touch was gentler, more controlled.

"I am broken," she said in a soft voice, higher pitched, with inflections under the words. A voice that sounded young and lost. "I am a pitcher that cannot hold life, cracked in too many places."

Miss Vladimirova let him go.

Gabriel dropped to his knees, leaving her standing over him. His eyes fixed on her bare hand framed against her black skirts, droplets of water hanging from her fingers. It wasn't the wrinkled hand of an old woman as he'd expected, but the creaseless hand of a girl. *Who is she?*

When she spoke again, her voice had returned to that emotionless tenor. "But I can pass life on if I choose."

CHAPTER 19

THURSDAY, 31 OCTOBER 1901
LISBOA, SOUTHERN PORTUGAL

Adela waited in her office for Anjos to return. The man had spirited Nadezhda out of the house, apparently so she wouldn't have to hear Miguel's arguments against her continued existence. Adela wasn't particularly surprised that Miguel felt that way. After all, in his last life he'd hunted vampires in Paris under the aegis of the Jesuits. He must have carried forward strong opinions about creatures who were mostly dead.

In the end, they'd agreed to let the argument lie. She couldn't prove to him that Nadezhda was actually alive, and his augmented senses told him she wasn't. *A walking corpse*, he'd called her. All in all, Adela was grateful that Anjos had taken Nadezhda away. Now she simply had to hope that Nadezhda didn't eat the man... and that he returned before dinner.

Anjos didn't disappoint her. He knocked on the door in a gentlemanly fashion—Miguel had warned her that Anjos was a gentleman, even if impoverished—and entered the house looking rumpled. When directed by Santana, he came to her office. "Please sit down, Inspector Anjos. I want to speak with you before dinner is served."

He took his chair without argument, which pleased her. *Accustomed to taking orders from a woman.* Or at least the man wasn't going to argue with her every word because she was a woman. She got enough of that from the Freemasons.

"Now, as to Miss Vladimirova," Adela began. "Did she not

come back with you?"

"She said she would stay at the reservoir," Anjos said.

Adela sighed. Becoming accustomed to his broad Brazilian accent would take a bit of work. "That's acceptable. She rather likes it there. Although it's easier for *me* to have her stay in the house, it's not her first choice."

Anjos merely nodded.

Adela wasn't certain whether he looked healthier than he had before. She'd been too distracted by Miguel to pay much attention to Anjos when they'd arrived. He did, however, look very preoccupied. "So... as you'll be working with Miss Vladimirova, I will ask that you be the one to share a carriage with her. Miguel has already refused to do so."

"How old is she?" Anjos asked.

Ah, a personal question. "She was born in 1851, so she would be just over fifty now."

"I see," Anjos said softly.

"You'll quickly discover that she was murdered by her own husband," Adela added, "so for much of that time she's been... well, *dead.*"

He nodded again as if that made sense, causing Adela to wonder whether Nadezhda had shown the man her true face.

"I've already told Miguel," she added, getting down to business, "but we'll be going up to Sintra first thing in the morning. I advise getting a good night's sleep."

"I will need to attend Mass in the morning first," Anjos said.

"Mass?" she repeated. "Why?"

"It's All Saints Day," he told her.

She *was* familiar with all the major holy days. It wasn't as if she hadn't lived in the Portugals most of her life and worked with the Jesuits. Santana had even had the cook prepare soul cakes for the children who would inevitable appear at the front door to ask for them after Mass. "I realize that, Inspector Anjos, but do you actually mean for us to wait on you while you pay your respects?"

"Yes," he said firmly.

She waited for him to use the argument that he was soon to meet his God and must genuflect at every opportunity, but the man simply left his answer as it was. "Very well then, much of the staff will likely go to early Mass tomorrow. Gather up Miss Vladimirova on your way back and we'll leave immediately afterward."

"Thank you," he said, inclining his head.

Well, he's polite, if nothing else. She had to make a team out of these people, one that could work together to achieve Raimundo's aims. Anjos' politeness gave her hope.

FRIDAY, 1 NOVEMBER 1901

Gabriel woke when one of the servants knocked at his door as requested. He thanked the young girl—likely the lowest of the maids, given the way these houses usually ran—and sat on his bed once she was gone. He took a deep breath, as much as he could, and lit a cigarette. Clerics could argue endlessly whether this was breaking the fast before Mass, but if he didn't have a smoke now, he would be shaking by the time the service ended. The smoke calmed him.

The room he'd been given was painted a light cheery blue. It wasn't overlarge, clearly a guest room, and he wouldn't have thought his new employer vastly wealthy judging by the contents of the room. Admittedly, the woodwork was fine, lovingly carved, and the white jacquard coverlet was spotless. And the attached bathroom was a thing of beauty. He hadn't lived in a place with a private bath since he'd left his father's house decades ago.

The servants, however, told him that this was their mistress' smallest house, tiny when compared to a palace in Sintra. There were other houses in the north as well, although the servants here didn't staff those. Their words painted for him a picture of great wealth, old wealth, that made Gabriel less inclined to interact with the Lady. He had more in common with her servants than with her.

Miguel Gaspar was also comparatively wealthy, but he'd worked as a police inspector, which gave them a common ground for friendship. Gaspar seemed to understand poverty, too, which meant he grasped that most people's world didn't include access to a bath, much less a private one with hot- and cold-running water.

Gabriel glanced around the room and finally spotted a silver salver on one of the dressers. He picked that up and carried it back to the bed with him, a makeshift ashtray. He didn't want to foul the white coverlet. After a time, he stubbed out the end of the cigarette and went to bathe, quelling his normal morning nausea with a mental promise of breakfast and another cigarette on the way back from Mass.

An hour later he was clean, dressed, and following a pair of the footmen to early Mass in the dark. The Church of Santa

Isabel was nearby, less than half an hour's walk, so he wasn't too tired when he arrived. And the Mass itself was pleasantly familiar, with the usual instructions to model his life after the saints. Something he could recognize in this different place with their murmuring accents.

Afterward, he walked back, stopping at a café to pick up a couple of pastries and drink a cup of coffee. He smoked as he walked on to the reservoir to find Miss Vladimirova. He'd been making himself not think about what had passed between them. She'd given him back weeks, taking his health back to the moment when his aunt had healed him. But she'd done it differently.

A witch was a witch, but training made all the difference. Surely a Russian-born healer would use her power differently than an African-born one. It was a question he could ask Gaspar, he suspected, but clearly Gaspar was not well disposed toward Miss Vladimirova.

What truly stuck in Gabriel's mind was that brief moment when she had gasped, when she'd called herself a broken pitcher, one not capable of holding life. *She was alive then.*

If he'd not heard that, heard the inflections of truth in her words at that moment, he would believe Gaspar's assertion that the woman was dead. But there was more to her than that.

When he reached the reservoir, he found the gate unlocked, and likewise the main door. The damp air of the reservoir clutched at him when he stepped inside, although the smell was still off. Gooseflesh ran along his arms, a sense that something was profoundly wrong. His mind knew the danger she presented. He ignored that and walked forward.

He found Miss Vladimirova standing exactly where he'd left

her. "Do you feel the passage of time?"

"Not as you must," she said in that other voice—the flat emotionless one. "I need no food, no rest, so there are no pressures."

"You must consume *something*," he said.

"Water is full of life," she replied. "In here, I lack for nothing."

She'd said that the previous evening. Was that why rusalki lived in water? To feed off that teeming life? "I brought you a pastry," he said anyway, holding out a paper-wrapped bundle. "Should you want it."

She turned away from the water and faced him for the first time. She still wore a veil, but not one as heavy as before. Even so, he caught only a vague glimpse of a pale oval of a face and light hair. "It is not necessary," she said.

He held it out anyway. "If you should change your mind."

For several breaths—his, not hers—they stood there, his hand extended. Then she took the wrapped pastry and tucked it into her garments somewhere. He wasn't sure with all her veils.

"Thank you," she said. She'd had to breath in before speaking, and then stopped.

"It was nothing." He gestured toward the open door. "The Lady wishes to travel to Sintra this morning. Are you ready to leave?"

"Yes."

Nothing more. She simply walked past him and out the door, waiting for him there so she could lock it behind them.

THE TRUTH UNDISCOVERED

While Miguel had found Lisboa interesting because of all that he'd heard of it before, Sintra was another matter. The town up in the mountains held the palace of the southern royal family, but that wasn't the cause of it, either. Instead the air itself, damp and cool and misty, vibrated with magic. Strands of it thrummed in brilliant hues through the sky, linking the whimsical royal palace, the old Moorish castle on the nearby mountains, the myriad other palaces and fine homes. It left a taste of cardamom and sweet queijo pastries in his mouth... no, that last one he was actually smelling, from a pastry maker somewhere nearby.

From his own past, he knew that sections of Paris were like this—particularly around the Sorbonne. It was a place where magic was commonly used, not restricted in any way. He'd once told Adela that he thought perhaps five percent of people in Cabo Verde were witches. In this town it would be a much higher percentage.

"What are you seeing?" she asked him, peering out the carriage window as if she could see what he did.

"Chaos," he told her, "and magic. Freedom."

"Hmmm. I wouldn't have thought that." She sat back. "You like it?"

He laughed at her offended tone. "Not truly. Chaos is dangerous. It can foster growth, but it can also bring the world crashing down around us."

"Ah, so you lean more toward the Jesuit view than the Freemason's view."

He knew what she meant. The Jesuits had a long history of witches in its ranks, but their actions were always controlled by the stern order of the Church. The Freemasons preferred science over dogma, which led to experimentation with magic, as if it was a chemistry study at seminary. "Experimentation with magic can be dangerous."

"True," she said.

The carriage took a turn off the main road and headed out of the town toward the estate she was seeking. "Is it true you own a palace up here?"

"I do." Adela sat back and straightened her skirts. "I rented it out to my godfather last year or I would move us up here."

"Godfather?" he asked. "How can you have a godfather?"

"It was never formalized," she said, a flush appearing on her cheekbones. "My father said, *this is the Marquis of Maraval, your godfather,* and I shook his hand."

"How old were you?"

"Seven," she said. "And very serious."

He hoped there was a photograph somewhere of her at that age but doubted that one existed. "And now you see him…?"

She waved one hand dismissively. "Once every few years. He lives in the north most of the time. He's the Minister of Culture for Northern Portugal. He merely wanted a place in Sintra so he could forge ties with the local aristocracy, possibly steal away a few artists. That's about it."

"But he knew your father?"

"Magical circles are small in the Portugals," she said. "Like my father, he studied witchcraft, but didn't practice it. He helped my father construct some of the devices he'd come up with."

When it came to the Church's teachings, magical devices fell into a no-man's-land. They weren't witchery, not natural outgrowths of God-given talents. And although some craft was required to create them, it wasn't considered proper witchcraft. So a priest could still hold a magical device in his hands and use it, but it wouldn't be considered witchcraft to do so, even if most of those devices did require a small sacrifice of human blood to work.

"I suppose more than anything else," Adela went on, "he was there at a time when my father felt he needed to find an additional person to bear responsibility for me. In case."

That made sense. Fairies were supposedly capricious. "And when your father passed away?"

"Disappeared," she said. "I was thirteen. I didn't need Maraval's help by then. Father Serafim was nearby, as well as a few of the Freemasons who'd known my father, so I simply went on with my studies as if nothing had happened."

She gazed at him, her expression daring him to question whether she'd needed a father figure at thirteen. He didn't bother. She would merely wrinkle her nose and say, *Certainly not*. So he changed the subject to the estate they would visit and listened while she told him everything she knew of the past owner and the current one.

When they reached that estate, he led her inside without waiting for Anjos and his dead companion to emerge from the other carriage. "We might as well wait," Adela said.

"Why?"

"Making Tomar lead two sets of people to the library separately creates more work for him," Adela said.

The butler peered narrowly at Miguel, as if offended that he would even consider such a thing. A thin man of short stature, he was wrapped in a virtual cocoon of ties of varying sorts—church, power, sex, and a hint of magic—enough so that Miguel knew he was the sort who would extract a petty revenge if angered. He smelled of cigar smoke, and his hands fidgeted constantly, even though he was trying to control the motion. He reminded Miguel of a pickpocket, always watching for a tidbit to steal.

"Fine," he said, and did his best not to react to the creature when Anjos led her up the steps and indoors.

Interestingly, the butler watched her without not fear, almost a hint of avarice clinging to him. This was the sort of man, Miguel decided, who when faced with a vampire didn't want to kill it but serve it instead. Tomar wasn't dangerous save in the fact that he wanted to be close to dangerous people. *I will tell Adela that later.*

The little butler led them down ornately decorated hallways—nothing too out of the ordinary—until they entered the library. There an earnest-looking young man bent over a folio copy of a book laid out on a tilted-top desk. There was nothing of magic about him, which set Miguel at ease, given that everything else in this room seemed to be laden with magic of various types. Witchcraft spun webs around some books, while others bore the marks of witchery—natural magic permeating the pages. There were ties between many of them, one a rather comically blunt spell that attempted to seduce the reader into purchasing other tomes from the same publisher.

THE TRUTH UNDISCOVERED

"This library is chaos itself," he told Adela.

The young man drew up as if stung by Miguel's words. "I have worked hard to create order here, sir."

Miguel didn't laugh at the earnest young man. "I am talking about the magic in here, not the ordering of the books. That's something you cannot neatly tuck away."

Adela blew out a vexed breath. "Mr. Konrad, this is Inspector Miguel Anjos, late of Cabo Verde. He's an expert in magical things, come to look at that book of yours."

The young man folded his arms over his chest. "Expert? More than you, Lady?"

She gave a self-deprecating laugh. "Of a different type."

He was going to ask her about that later. He'd never heard her sound like that, as if she was unsure of herself, or... remorseful.

"You've brought Death with you again," a woman's voice said from behind them.

Miguel looked back and flinched, an involuntary breath hissing between his teeth. Whoever she was, he couldn't make out her face for the marks of magic that covered it. It was like someone had taken a photograph of her and scratched out her eyes with a knife tip dipped in the ink of black magic.

"And who else?" she asked. "I know there's someone else here. Someone disgusted by my ugly face, I think."

Miguel sighed. "I cannot see your face, miss."

She laughed shortly. "Are you blind, too?"

"This is Miss Carvalho, isn't it?" he asked Adela.

"Yes," she said. "Miss Carvalho, I have two newly arrived guests, Inspector Anjos, who is standing near the door with Miss Vladimirova, and Inspector Gaspar, who is standing next to me near Mr. Konrad's desk."

"So if you're not blind," the young Miss Carvalho asked, "why can you not see my face? I've actually put my hair back today."

"You look lovely," Adela said in a soothing voice. "Is the dress new?"

"One of Genoveva's castoffs," the young woman said, a hint of bitterness in her voice. "She can't wear the same dress more than a few times or people will know Father's short on cash."

It was a blue dress, Miguel could tell that much. He closed his eyes and tried to drive out the scratch marks he saw over the young woman's face. *It's all in my mind.*

When he finally opened his eyes he saw a plain young woman with a thin face, dark hair drawn up into a thick bun atop her head, and eyes that stared at nothing. Then the visual ghost of the scratching reappeared, obliterating her face.

"That's a curse," he said. "I see it. A rather nasty one. A lot of anger behind it."

"You see it?" the young man said. "You can see a curse?"

Miguel turned to gaze at Mr. Konrad, easier on his eyes. "That's my gift. I see magic... among other things."

"Miss Carvalho," Konrad said in a softer voice. "Perhaps you

THE TRUTH UNDISCOVERED 205

should leave. I'm going to get the book."

The faceless girl drew herself up straighter. "It can't do anything more to me than it's already done."

The young man nodded and headed back into the library. As they waited, the young woman came forward, giving Miss Vladimirova a wide berth as she did so. Apparently, she sensed the dead woman. Miss Carvalho came to stand near Mr. Konrad's desk, her head moving slightly as she tried to place all the others in the library by sound.

"And what will this Inspector Gaspar be able to tell us?" she asked Adela.

Adela shifted to look up at the younger woman, who was taller than her by a few inches. "I hope he'll be able to tell us why that book is important enough to put a guard dog of a curse on it."

"And the one at your home?" Miss Carvalho asked.

Miguel had inspected the book at Adela's home, or rather the remains of it, earlier that morning. The cover and its cut bits of pages bore signs of magic, but so trampled in that destruction that it seemed nothing more than a hash of colors to him. "It was too damaged."

"Ah, so it was magical?"

"Yes." Miguel saw the young man returning, a leather-wrapped object in his hands. Peeking out of the leather he could see strands of magic trying to escape, like the tentacles of an octopus captured in a net. "You should all stand back."

The young man's earnest blue eyes lifted to meet his. "Is this thing dangerous?"

"I don't know," Miguel admitted. "I'll have to open it to see what sort of magic is trapped inside."

"Did it blind her?" Konrad asked, a flick of his eyes indicating Miss Carvalho.

"I suspect so," Miguel said. "But I don't know why. I suggest that everyone clear back."

Konrad laid the book in its wrapping on the desk, and Miguel crossed around to that side so he could see the pages better. "Me, too?" Konrad asked.

"Yes," Miguel said. "Until I know what I'm dealing with."

The young man obligingly moved back, giving Miguel plenty of room to unfold the leather around the book. He set that aside and centered the book on the desk. Magic fluttered around it, the crimson magic of the Church, the purple of the Freemasons, the red Miguel associated with the Templars, and even a hint of blue and white—something tied to the thrones of the Portugals—but none of them had true power. It was as if the author or the publisher had tried to tie all those influences together but hadn't quite succeeded. "Well, that's a proper mess."

He opened the book out and peered down at the frontispiece. There was nothing about it other than a red glow. The other bits of magic were like extra mouse tails waggling in his vision. He sniffed the book, and caught the scent of burning, like the air after a close thunderbolt. He rubbed fingers down the title page and touched them to his tongue. *Metal,* like wires. "Electricity," he said. "This book is more about electricity than magic."

"Electricity?" Adela repeated. "How is that possible?"

THE TRUTH UNDISCOVERED

He shook his head and began flipping through the pages. Nothing stuck him as particularly noticeable. This was a basic text, apparently a history of sorts. There was nothing in it to suggest...

He turned the page to one marked *Chapter Conclaves*.

Words tugged at his eyes, as if they wanted him to read them. He shook his head to dash away that impulse, and that was when he saw it, a horrible creature of hate, all flailing limbs and angry teeth, living inside the page. He stepped back, but not before the creature sprang directly at his face.

CHAPTER 20

FRIDAY, 1 NOVEMBER 1901
SINTRA, SOUTHERN PORTUGAL

Gabriel had watched Gaspar as he pored over the book's pages, grumbling over the poor application of magic in them. For the most part, Gabriel trusted Gaspar's evaluation.

When Gaspar jumped back from the table with a startled exclamation, Gabriel saw nothing... but something *was* wrong. Gaspar cried out and covered his head with his arms as if something attacked him. Blood bloomed on his jacket sleeves, even though nothing was there.

"Miguel!" The Lady jumped forward, but Miss Vladimirova shoved her back. The Lady fell to the ground, eyes wide with shock.

Faster than Gabriel's eyes could follow, Miss Vladimirova moved to where Gaspar fought his invisible foe. Her hands rose to clutch something a few inches before his crossed arms. As if pulling away an octopus, she yanked it loose. Gaspar dropped to his knees and drew a great breath.

Miss Vladimirova took a step back, and then another, still imprisoning the unseen thing between her hands. Fire erupted between her fingers, catching her veils, her sleeves. She pressed her gloved hands closer and closer together as if squeezing the unknown thing between them. The flames engulfed her... but her garments didn't burn.

Demon fire. Gabriel ran to aid her, but she growled at him, the sound of a rabid wolf. And as he watched, she pressed her burning palms together, the air went acrid like the smell of the sky after lightning. And the flames abruptly died.

For a moment, she stood there, her palms pressed together, then crumpled to the ground with a soft, breathy cry.

Gabriel rushed forward again.

"Stay back," she begged in her softer voice, the one he'd heard in the reservoir.

Gabriel stepped back again, aware suddenly of Gaspar sitting on the floor, the Lady between them, clutching his bloodied hands. The young librarian had come around the table and stood in front of Miss Carvalho, his blue eyes wide with both fear and determination.

And Miss Vladimirova hunched quietly on the floor, the smell of burned skin emanating from her now. As Gabriel watched, she laid her gloved hands on the carpet. The fibers of the carpet twisted and burned without flame. Miss Vladimirova breathed hard, panting, and then slumped down against the floor, the scent of overheated wool, much like burned hair, surrounding her.

Gabriel laid one hand on her back. Heat still radiated through her garments, but she had stopped moving.

She isn't breathing. He drew back. After a moment, she pushed herself up and held out one hand, so he helped her rise.

"What happened?" Miss Carvalho asked sharply, likely not for the first time. "What happened?"

The young librarian set a hand to the blind girl's elbow. "I'm not certain Miss Carvalho. I..."

Gaspar had regained his feet. "That was a demon, Mr.

Konrad," he pronounced in a matter-of-fact voice.

The younger man's lips pressed into a straight line, betraying a lack of belief.

"It was," Miss Vladimirova confirmed, her voice back to the flat tone than Gabriel knew all too well now. "I destroyed it."

He had no way to judge her words, not when she was like this. "How?"

Her veiled head turned toward him. "I ate it."

Gabriel made himself not stare at her. She might very well have eaten it, the way she'd consumed the life in the reservoir. Only this had half-melted the carpet.

He wasn't going to ask. He had no idea what it meant this time, but surely a demon's life force would have been a horrible thing to ingest. Unfortunately, he couldn't see her face to be sure she was well. Surely, she couldn't feel well after swallowing a demon whole.

Gaspar tugged off his jacket and handed it to the Lady, and then rolled back his shirt sleeves, revealing dozens of narrow slashes along his arms. Whatever had done those had managed to do so without affecting his jacket and shirt.

"It tried to throw its curse on me, but couldn't touch me with magic," Gaspar said. "So it attacked me physically. I owe you my thanks, I suppose, Miss Vladimirova."

Gabriel's jaw clenched. Gaspar didn't mean those words, the sub-text beneath them clear even though Gabriel couldn't detect truth from the man.

"I will go get some bandages," Mr. Konrad said into the awkward silence that followed.

"Send for the butler," Miss Carvalho suggested.

"I'd rather not," Konrad admitted, eyes drifting toward the ruined area of the rug. "I'll be back in a moment, sir."

Gaspar's jacket was ruined—not from slashes but with blood—his shirt as well, so the Lady loosely wrapped the jacket around his forearms to protect them until Konrad returned.

"I need water," Miss Vladimirova said. "I will leave."

She walked out of the library without waiting for a response. The Lady tilted her head toward Gabriel. "Best if you keep an eye on her."

He didn't want to deal with Gaspar at the moment, so Gabriel went, trailing Miss Vladimirova out of the library, across a wide sitting room, and out to a terrace behind the house. She headed down the stairs that led to the gravel below, almost running. Gabriel hurried after her. *If she keeps up this pace, I won't be able to stay with her.*

He caught up with her farther down the path, though, as she walked on determinedly. "Where are you going?" he gasped.

"Water," she said. "I am unclean."

The path lead through the unkempt gardens but at one point, she veered off toward a wall of stone. A slender fall of water splashed down the rocks and a low wall surrounded a shallow pool at its foot. Miss Vladimirova lifted her skirts to clamber over the wall and stepped directly into the knee-deep water. Uncaring about her garb, she laid down in the pool. Her skirts held air at first, belling up, but slowly sank to settle about her.

THE TRUTH UNDISCOVERED

Gabriel stood there, watching. She had curled up on her side, her veils waving about her in the moving water and giving him tantalizing glimpses of pale skin and a wheat-colored braid. But the surface of the water was too rough and distorted everything.

He settled on the low wall. It didn't look like she planned to leave the water any time soon. He fished out his case of cigarettes and lit one, inhaling deeply. Hurrying down the walkway had left him with pangs in his lungs. He slowly smoked two cigarettes while watching Miss Vladimirova do nothing other than let the rough water flow over her.

I am unclean, she'd said.

Miss Vladimirova had barely been eighteen when her husband drowned her. While in the carriage on the way here, she had told him something of her existence since then, first in her lake and then in Paris, where she'd hidden in the libraries of the Sorbonne for years. It sounded like a dull existence to him, save for those rare instances when she'd been moved to kill someone.

Was she answerable for sins committed after her death? If she felt unclean, then surely she had some moral compass that suggested she knew right from wrong, good from evil. He had no doubt that the woman he'd spoken with in the reservoir, who'd called herself a broken vessel, had *feelings*. He had sensed that in her. She could not be what Gaspar thought. She could not be dead, could she?

She's lying at the bottom of a pond, he reminded himself. *Like a corpse.*

As he thought that, she rose from the water, lifted her sodden skirts, and stepped back over the low wall. Gabriel stood regarding her with dismay. Her clothes were soaked through, her shoes and gloves likely ruined. And she would soak the carriage on the way back to Lisboa. "Perhaps Miss Carvalho has a dress you can change into."

The veil-covered head tilted, and then she held one gloved hand over the pool. Water began to dribble from her fingers. The skirts that had clung to her slender form began to loosen—to *dry*, he realized—and then her blouse and veils. After only a minute or so, the fall of water ceased, and she stood before him, looking much as she had before she'd stepped into the water. The odor of burnt flesh and hair had left her, though, replaced by her more usual scent of lake water.

She controls water. Gabriel stubbed out his second cigarette against the stone wall, tossed the butt end onto the damp earth, and ground it out with one foot. "Shall I escort you back up to the house?"

"Not necessary," she said in her flat voice. But then, a moment later, "I appreciate your consideration."

Gabriel offered an arm, hoping she didn't intend to walk back uphill at the pace she'd come down. She walked with him tamely enough, letting him choose the pace.

"I had to use what was left to heal myself," she said.

"I thought I smelled... burns," he responded. "Are you in pain?"

"No."

The air was warming, the scent of the garden around them rising. "Are you healed now?" he asked.

"I am."

Their conversation in the carriage had been similarly one-sided, almost an interrogation. He felt awkward pursuing the subject, but etiquette had been trained into him. "I am glad you're better."

"Thank you," she finally responded. "I would want you to know that I would be grateful for your concern."

A very convoluted sentence. "I don't understand."

"If I were alive," she said, "I would want you to know."

Gabriel paused on the walkway. "Is that how you decide your reactions? Trying to remember how you would have felt when alive?"

"When I am alive, I remember what I have done, so it is better if I do what is right."

When I am alive. "So you are alive, at least part of the time?"

"It seems so," she said, "although it may only be a dream. Or a hallucination." She walked on up toward the house, leaving him staring after her.

How painful it must be, not even to know whether you are alive or dead.

Adela pinned the end of the bandage around Miguel's left forearm. The demon that had attacked him had left him with dozens of slender cuts along his forearms. They didn't look deep enough to require stiches, but she had no idea what poisons a demon might carry in its claws. Miguel insisted the cuts were clean, though, and she wasn't going to squabble with him in front of these two children.

Mr. Konrad had fetched a shirt and coat from his own armoire for Miguel to wear. The frock coat was a tatty thing, brown with a hound's-tooth pattern, and far below Miguel's usual sartorial standards. He thanked Konrad anyway, and promised to have the garments cleaned before returning them. They fit well enough, although being of Germanic stock, Konrad was bulkier.

Miguel pointed with his chin toward the abandoned book. "Now that its guard dog is gone, let's take another look at that thing."

"It's gone?" Ifigénia asked. "What does that mean?"

Miguel rose from the chair. "I'm afraid, Miss Carvalho, that it means reversing your condition is almost certainly impossible."

Adela pinched the bridge of her nose, wishing Miguel wasn't always quite so blunt.

Ifigénia stood her ground, undaunted. "Why?"

"Because reversing a human curse is one thing," Miguel said. "Reversing one cast by a demon is another. It will eat your soul before giving you anything. You have nothing else it wants."

"And there still lies the problem of finding the correct book," Adela reminded her. She tried to sound kind, to soften the sting of the bad news.

"Enough," Konrad interjected. "If we haven't made any progress, then there's no need to hash over it."

"I can, I think, tell Miss Carvalho *why* she was attacked," Miguel said, then glanced back at Adela. "And why your book was destroyed."

THE TRUTH UNDISCOVERED 217

The young librarian's brows rose. "And?"

"These books are being used to communicate, like... telegraph stations. The demon set at this terminus was there to prevent anyone unapproved from accessing the wires, so to speak."

"Who can set a demon to watch a book?" Konrad asked.

"Someone practicing witchcraft," Miguel said. "Not a particularly tidy job of it, either. The demon should not have been able to slip its bonds to physically attack me."

"Who?" Konrad repeated.

"I have no idea," Miguel admitted. "I have no familiarity with the practitioners here, much less those old enough to have been involved in the casting of this particular spell."

"So it's old," Adela stepped in. "Any guess as to how old?"

He gazed at the book for a moment, mouth twisted to one side as he considered whatever it was that he was seeing that she couldn't. "At least a decade," he said, "but it could be two. The magic in it is stale and brittle."

"And my copy of the book? You saw nothing of a telegraph station in it."

He tapped the open page of the book. "It's anchored to this heading about conclaves. Whoever ripped the pages out of yours wanted the link gone."

"Removing evidence that only *you* can see?" Could someone have realized the Meter was coming here and destroyed her book to prevent him from seeing it?

Miguel's smoky eyes rose to meet hers. "Anyone with enough second sight might have been able to see it. Possibly your father knew of it, given his origin."

Adela sighed. She would ask him later not to tell others her father had been a fairy. "I don't understand the point, then. Destroying my copy drove my attention to this one." Or perhaps that *was* the point, trying to entice her to look at this copy and trigger a demon's attack. "What else can you tell us about the magic involved?" she asked. "Other than it's old."

He smiled mysteriously. "Well, I think it would be best if we went onto the rooftop."

Adela wanted to roll her eyes but settled for a mental promise to make him pay for his teasing later.

The roof of the house had a flat area for observation of the overgrown gardens. A faint breeze blew, lifting the perpetual mist of Sintra only a bit. It carried with it the smell of damp soil and trees, the dusty old scent of nobility and pride, and the ever-present vibrations of the magic of the town.

Miguel dug a compass from one pocket and instructed Konrad how to lay out the map of Iberia on the folding table he'd carried up with them. Then Miguel opened the book and set it carefully atop the wide granite balustrade about the observation area. He turned to the appropriate page and began reading aloud the words there.

Adela tugged him away with one hand. "What are you doing?"

"Harmless now," he reassured her. "The guardian of this book is gone."

THE TRUTH UNDISCOVERED

She stepped back, still not happy. "If you're certain it's safe."

"I am." Miguel started again, reading past the words that had tried to ensnare him earlier. He finally reached the one that must serve as the trigger. Above him, magic flared to life, a network of lines that smelled of metal and electricity and glowed with tattered bits of magic like prayer flags on a line in Tibet—red, purple, gold, and blue.

He was surely grinning like a madman. It was beautiful in its own way. One line came down out of a junction that reminded him of... no, he had that backwards. The line extended from the book *up* to the overhead lines, much like the pole rising from the top of a streetcar. In fact, the magical lines he saw in the sky strongly reminded him of the trolley and streetcar lines he'd seen in Lisboa.

Someone has adapted that invention to magic.

That in itself was fascinating. Someone had taken scientific principals regarding electrical current and stretched them to work with witchcraft, a clever new adaptation of magical thought. The Chinese had tried to tie magic to lightning, he recalled from somewhere in his multi-layered past, but that had only ended up enhancing fireworks.

And whoever constructed this system had tried, less successfully, to set the imprimatur of several groups on the magic. Those tattered flags of magic were attempts to make this whole creation look *Templar*. To force all the other magics to serve a common *soi-disant* Templar purpose, Miguel suspected.

He relayed that to Adela, who rubbed a slender finger across her chin. "Like burying Brother Marcel under a Templar sigil, even though the man was a Jesuit?"

He agreed with that assessment of Marcel DuBois. He'd never seen anything remotely resembling Templar magic about the man. Only his ties to the Jesuit Brotherhood.

"Jesuit?" Konrad asked. "Are they involved in this?"

Adela gazed at Miguel for only a second before turning to the young man. "The entire body? No. This might instead be the work of a few rebellious souls within the Brotherhood."

"But not DuBois," Miguel said firmly. Something had passed between Adela and DuBois in Cape Verde that had set her firmly against the man, an incident or discussion she had refused to divulge to Miguel.

Adela sighed dramatically. "Very well, as you say."

He gazed back up at the lines above him. "I suspect that you, my dear, will need to unravel that end of the equation, but Mr. Konrad and I can help... if you give us some time to work on this."

Adela waved one hand in a vexed manner and went to join Miss Carvalho, who waited by the landing with a white-knuckled grip on the stairwell's rail.

"So what am I to do, sir?" Konrad asked.

"We're going to chart the direction of these lines." Miguel picked the one that was strongest in his vision, pointed in that direction, and then glanced down at his compass. He read the direction off to the young man, and then waited while Konrad carefully drew a red line from Sintra in the corresponding direction.

"Lisboa," the young man said.

"Anything more specific?"

"The path passes roughly through Queluz, Reboleira, Damia, Campolide, Xabregas."

That made sense. He would bet the Jesuit College in Campolide held the terminus of that line. He picked out the second brightest thread and read off that measurement to Konrad. The young man drew dutifully and said, "The Golden City."

It could end anywhere between, but Miguel would bet on that northern capital instead. He took the next measurement, which Konrad identified as Coimbra, the university town. The breeze picked up and Mr. Konrad was forced to cling to the map, but they continued their work. That went on for nearly half an hour as they tried to transcribe the network of lines that only Miguel could see onto a map. He was picking out a fainter line when the whole thing flashed once… and disappeared from his sight.

He was left with the normal ambient glow of Sintra and its mystical surrounds, a very earnest but very human young librarian, and a certainty that the sudden failure of the magical network was not his doing.

Someone else shut it down.

Miguel slammed the book closed. "We need to leave here now."

Chapter 21

Friday, 1 November 1901
Sintra, Southern Portugal

"This is your fault," Ifigénia snapped as Adela tried to pack a bag for her. "I was happy here. I know this place, and now…"

"And I would prefer not to see you murdered," Adela finished, her voice rising in turn. The girl had inherited more than her share of her father's pig-headedness. "What other dress do you want to bring with us?"

Ifigénia froze before she could launch into her next complaint. "I don't recall what they look like," she said after a moment, her angry jaw now replaced by a trembling lip. "I don't…"

Adela leaned back to peer out into the hallway. As she'd expected, Konrad was out there, already carrying his sole traveling bag. "Mr. Konrad, which color is her favorite gown?"

He set down his bag and came into the bedroom. Ifigénia had calmed herself by then, concentrating on keeping her nose in the air. "I believe you like the light blue one," he said to her. "The one with the lace collar—is that right, Miss Carvalho?"

"Yes, that's the one," Ifigénia said quickly. "I remember now."

Adela spotted that one hanging in the wardrobe, drew it out, and when Konrad nodded, she set it aside to fold.

"And the gray one," Konrad added, pointing.

Adela almost argued that they didn't have time to pack a

third gown—a gown of dove gray with an overdress of charcoal gray netting and a beaded hem. Simple, with no train so Ifigénia wouldn't trip over it. Konrad had picked out the sole gown that could be worn for evening with a proper wrap, likely given to the girl because it wouldn't suit her older sister. A good choice, too, in case Ifigénia needed to do something other than wander through gardens in the afternoon. "Very well. I'll pick out some underthings."

"I'll do that," Ifigénia snapped, her face flushing. "I'm not helpless."

Because I said something in front of Konrad. "Fine, I'll start packing the dresses. Mr. Konrad, if you'll wait for us in the sitting room."

The young man darted a glance at Adela, but merely told Miss Carvalho that he would carry her bag for her when she was ready to go. Then he carried himself away, off down the hallway.

"Don't embarrass me in front of him," Ifigénia hissed at her. "He's my only friend."

Adela was not going to argue with this child about whether she should be counted as a friend as well. How unfortunate that Ifigénia's annoying father hadn't even sent a friendly housemaid with his daughter into her exile. "Mr. Konrad sees your garments, so he recalls what color they are."

"I'm not stupid," Ifigénia snapped, one hand balling into a fist.

"I know. Will you please help me pick out some undergarments? We need to be gone before anyone reaches this place. I don't want anyone to find Mr. Konrad waiting in the sitting room."

That galvanized Ifigénia into motion. She made her way to her wardrobe, opened the drawers, and began touching various undergarments to make her selections. "This is your fault," she said anyway, under her breath.

The carriage rattled along the road away from Sintra. It was jarring to leave this place in such a hurry, but the Lady had insisted they go ahead, and Gabriel didn't argue. If anyone pursued them, they would have to choose which carriage to chase. And honestly, he was safer with Miss Vladimirova sitting at his side.

"Have you killed a demon before?" he asked her once they were on the main road to Lisboa. The roads were steep, but regularly maintained.

"No," she said in her cold voice.

Her gloved fingers twitched on the fabric of her skirts, and he spotted a place where one of the finger seams was coming unraveled. How old were her garments? Were they ones she'd worn since she died? "It took courage, then, to try."

"I have heard that it could be done. Stories of my ancestors."

"One never knows how true those are," Gabriel noted. Miss Vladimirova had risked herself for Gaspar's sake, for a man who clearly didn't like her. And he'd barely been civil in return. "I am sorry your efforts were not more kindly received."

For a time, she remained silent. "I do not feel anger, nor do I feel wounded. Not at the moment."

But she would later? Perhaps in one of those short spans when she spoke with a softer voice and he would hear the truth behind her words—when she was *alive*. "Does it trouble you? To continually isolate yourself for the sake of others? To feel you must hide your face?"

He waited as she put together an answer to that question. She startled him by lifting her hands and tugging her outer veil off. She set that in her lap and reached up again, unpinned her hat—he could see now it was a flat cap with a veil—and drew that off as well, revealing her profile to him. Then she turned and lifted her light eyes to meet his.

He couldn't breathe for a second.

It wasn't her face that made him catch his breath. It was the coldness of her eyes. The bleakness of them. There was no humanity in them, as if Gaspar was correct and she was a monster.

She closed her eyes, and the icy hand grasping his heart let go.

Now he saw a young woman.

Her skin was clear and fair, but no flush touched her cheeks. A thick wheat-colored braid lay over her far shoulder, shining in the afternoon light that peeped in through the carriage's half-shaded window. Not particularly beautiful, but attractive, with delicate features. A straight nose, pale lips, long blonde eyelashes that brushed her cheeks.

Then her eyes opened, and the young woman disappeared like a magician's trick. The scent of lake water seemed to rise about him, filling the carriage. Gabriel felt it clogging his lungs, a crushing pain in his chest, dragging him down under with her. Those cold eyes would be the last thing he saw before he drowned.

And just as suddenly, that horrific grip released him. He blinked, and she was hiding her face again with the veiled cap, pinning it calmly in place as if nothing had happened.

"I hide my face so I will not see how others fear me," she said, her voice softer now.

Somehow, he'd convinced himself that people were afraid of her because they *couldn't* see her face. Little did he know. The cloying fear he felt whenever she walked near was nothing next to the reaction he'd just suffered. "I... did not expect to react that way."

She pulled the second veil over her head, hiding her face. "You are a man," she told him, "looking at his death."

"The consumption will take me long before you do, Miss Vladimirova." His heartbeat had stopped racing, at least.

Her gloved hands stilled in her lap. "I can keep you alive until I decide to eat you."

He had no idea how he should respond; he couldn't sense truth or falseness under her words. "Are you planning on killing me?"

The veiled head turned toward him. "That was a joke."

He licked his dry lips.

"I never was good at jokes," she said then.

Of that I have no doubt. "Ah. Do all healers control water? I do not think my aunt could."

"No."

He waited a moment, and then persisted. "But you can? How is that possible?"

Her head turned toward him, then back to the front, then back again, as if she struggled to decide whether to answer. Finally she said, "There is a legend in the Vladimirov family that centuries ago, one of my ancestors married a water dragon."

He would love to know if she was speaking the truth. "Are dragons real?"

"I have never seen one," she told him. "That I know. Perhaps I saw one in human form. How would I know? But my great aunt told me that last dragon died not long after the Patriotic War."

The Patriotic War sounded like it was a specific war. "I don't know your people's history," he admitted. "When would that have been?"

"1812, when the French invaded our country."

Less than a century past, then, there had been a dragon living somewhere in Asia. Of course, before last month he hadn't known that there was a Meter, much less one who had lived other lives before. He hadn't known what a rusalka was. *Why not believe in a dragon?*

"And that is why you control water? Why not use that to defend yourself when your husband... attacked you?"

Her hands twisted together on her lap. "I did not know I was a healer. My family thought the talent had bypassed me. I never felt it inside me until that very moment, and then, I did not know how to use it. It was too late."

He wondered if her family had known how she was treated

THE TRUTH UNDISCOVERED

by her husband's family. Or perhaps they hadn't valued her as they should because she didn't come into her power as a child normally would. Either way, those would be horribly personal questions to ask. "But you learned to use your powers afterward?"

"Yes. To kill."

Pursuing that statement would probably be unwise, too. "I suppose after ten years in the bottom of a lake, I might learn to control water, too."

Her head turned toward him again. "You would not. You are neither healer nor dragon."

"That was a joke," he told her. "I was never good at jokes, either."

For a moment they were both silent as the carriage rattled on, now on the main road toward Lisboa. She had talked more on this part of their journey, though, which made time seem to pass more quickly.

"She does not know," Miss Vladimirova said then. "About the dragon. I have never told her."

"The Lady?" he asked.

"Yes. It is a... family secret. I would want you not to tell her."

She had told him something about herself that even the Lady didn't know. She didn't want the Lady to know, likely because the lady in question would want to know everything about her family and that long-dead dragon.

Of course, if Miss Vladimirova plans to kill me, she can confess anything without fear.

It was a cynical thought, but one that bore remembering.

He fished out a cigarette and lit it, surprised to realize it was his first one since climbing into the carriage.

Miguel had some doubts as to the wisdom of the rooms in the hotel. Adela had settled Konrad and the Carvalho girl in one of the palatial suites in the Hotel Avenida Palace under the name of Schmidt. And then proceeded to book three more rooms on that same hall for an indefinite period, never once blinking at the exorbitant price the manager demanded. The man had to move less illustrious—or less financially-liberal—guests out of two of those rooms, though, so extra compensation made sense.

"Tomar will definitely squeal like a pig to anyone who will listen," Adela said once the porters had left them alone. "That little weasel of a man has been looking for an excuse to cause problems for me." The usual glittering of her skin was stained pink with vexation as she strode back and forth across her rented room. It was larger than his, a suite with an area for them to meet, and a wide bed more suited to the non-existent Lady Luisilda Malheiro.

His room was booked under his friend William's name—the first thing he could come up with—and she'd also booked one for Anjos, not bothering to assign the inspector an alias. Since Adela evidently frequented this place enough that the manager recognized her and her fake title, Miguel supposed she considered it a safe haven. If the weaselly butler did tell anyone who'd stolen the questionable book from the Quinta da Regaleira along with the estate's two young inhabitants, they would surely go straight to Adela's house on the Rua das Amoreiras seeking them.

"So what do we have?" she asked, pausing mid-stride to regard him with narrowed eyes.

"Clarification?" He'd learned that when Adela became frustrated, her speech bounced from one topic to the next. *And she is frustrated.*

She flung herself onto an elegant striped sofa that had borne more than its share of lovemaking couples, judging by the aura of heated passion that stained the air near it. "My employer wants us to find Alessio Ferreira's murderer. Donato Mata was hired to do it, and at some point, the Jesuits had him under wraps, but he escaped them, then conveniently left evidence in my office suggesting that he was the assassin."

"Why would he do that?" They had discussed this already, but it never hurt to rehash information in the hope that new connections would emerge in the process.

"It doesn't make sense," she conceded. "And what does that have to do with DuBois and that idiotic book." Her eyes narrowed to slits as she worked that over in her mind.

For a second, his sight of her faded, as if a filmy copy of her sat on the sofa. Miguel watched her, wondering whether she even knew she was fading from view.

A knock came at the door, and she rose from the sofa. She moved out of sight of the doorway and gestured for him to open it. When he did so, it was to find a porter of no particular unusualness carrying a thick missive on a silver salver. Miguel took it and tipped the young man. As the paper bore no hint of magic about it, either, he handed it to Adela.

There were layers of envelope inside, and she read the first, dropped that on the floor, and unfolded several sheets that lay inside the next envelope. She read through them, making him wait until the end. Miguel considered the sofa but chose to sit on a wooden chair instead.

"Finally!" She slapped the sheets of paper against her skirts for emphasis. "One of my investigators turned up the location of Mata's family home. If Mata is still anywhere around Lisboa, he will have been in touch with his father. The man might be a thief and assassin, but he apparently cares about his family. How touching."

"And where do we go?" Miguel asked. The sun was setting outside, so they could surely pursue that lead tomorrow.

"A small cork farm, out in the countryside." Adela glanced at the papers again. "Not far. Easy to get there and back in one day."

"Do we go in the morning, then?"

"Hmm," she mused. "No, I think this is something that calls for Anjos' particular skills. We want to truth out of the elder Mata. Between Anjos and Nadezhda, I'm sure they can get it."

Miguel knew better than to think she didn't already have other designs for him. "And what will we be doing instead?"

She leaned back against the wall next to the door. "We will go and visit the Freemasons and the Jesuits. That will let you get a look at them. Perhaps you might recognize someone who touched that communication system."

That seemed like a decent plan but would immediately expose their location to those they questioned. "You are aware that the German boy can't hide himself or his paramour like you can, aren't you?"

Adela choked out a laugh. "I doubt she's his paramour."

"Not yet," Miguel admitted, "but soon, I suspect. I'll let you know when that changes."

The corners of her lips lifted into a calculating smile. "I'll bet you fifty reis that he sleeps on the couch in the sitting room tonight."

He was confident about the *eventual* outcome of leaving those two youngsters unchaperoned in the suite one over. Although he doubted the clearly-smitten Konrad would impose himself on Miss Carvalho in any way, he suspected that hot-tempered young lady had other plans. "Done. And will I be sleeping in the other room tonight?"

"I have a feeling we'll both be up rather later than planned," she said airily, "going over my notes again to figure out some pattern for all this nonsense."

Gabriel rose when the door to the reservoir opened, letting in the cool night air. He subbed out the cigarette he'd been smoking and set one hand on his pistol, but relaxed when Gaspar called his name. "I'm inside," he called back.

Gaspar strode into the reservoir, eyes surveying the vast columns and marble walls before settling on Gabriel where he waited. "You're the only thing alive in here," Gaspar said.

He wasn't going to argue with Gaspar over whether Miss Vladimirova was alive or not. The man *believed* his words, which made them truth for Gaspar, at least. Truth was absolute, but individual's truths were sometimes subjective. "Why are you here?"

"There's a hotel room for you at the Avenida Palace, next to the train station. When you didn't show up there, she sent me to find you."

The butler had told Gabriel of the hotel room. He simply hadn't wanted to leave yet. As soon as they'd arrived here, Miss Vladimirova had thrown herself into the water—clothing and all—and promptly sank to the bottom. There were lamps here, but Gabriel couldn't see her; the reservoir was too deep. So he'd decided to wait for her to surface again. "I was waiting to be sure that Miss Vladimirova was safe."

Gaspar crouched by the edge of the platform and gazed over the low railing into the dark water. "Why?"

"Why?" Gabriel repeated.

Gaspar's head turned in his direction. "Why would you worry about that creature's safety? She's already dead. What are you afraid someone will do to her?"

Be unkind to her.

Gaspar would merely laugh at that sentiment, of course, so Gabriel didn't say it aloud. He chose not to answer.

"The Lady wants the two of you to head out to the countryside in the morning," he said. "Visit a farm owned by Mata's father and see if you can find out where Mata's gone to ground."

Gabriel crossed his arms over his chest. "We can do that."

Gaspar rose. "We'll be checking with the local Jesuits and Freemasons, to see if the book turns up any further ties. I suggest you return to the hotel with me, get a good night's sleep."

He'd been considering sleeping here, not wanting to walk all the way to that hotel, but the wooden platform was hard enough to make him reconsider. "Could you give me a couple of minutes?"

Gaspar shook his head but walked out of the reservoir. When the door shut, Gabriel relit his damaged cigarette. He needed to refill his case anyway. "Did you hear all of that?" he asked.

There was a swishing sound in the water, and then Miss Vladimirova's head appeared at the edge of the platform, uncovered. She lifted herself enough to cross her arms on the platform, but stayed there, bare head atop her sodden sleeves. Her eyes were closed, sparing him. "I heard him."

Gabriel took another drag from the half-crushed cigarette. "Will you be safe here? If I leave you alone?"

She didn't move, but suddenly the water rose all about him with a roar, ocean waves higher than his head coming into shore on all sides of the platform. Gabriel threw up his arms to protect himself...

...but the water stilled. It remained in those curled waves above him, almost as if frozen there. He could see the water shifting and moving within those waves yet held back from sweeping him off the platform. The rushing of the water hadn't ceased, either. He drew a few cautious breaths, trying to overcome the inborn compulsion to flee the looming waves.

And then the waves subsided, not falling straight down onto the platform as water should but withdrawing gently into the reservoir. A moment later, the surface was still again, almost reflective, the normal drip and trickle of the water coming in from the aqueduct the only sound.

"You should go," she said. "Sleep in a bed. It will be better for you."

"I'll come for you in the morning, then," he said.

"Good night." She slipped back down into the water, disappearing from Gabriel's sight.

Gabriel rubbed his neck with his free hand, then walked out of the reservoir, feeling superfluous. In this place, Miss Vladimirova was safe. Safer than any of them.

CHAPTER 22

SATURDAY, 2 NOVEMBER 1901
LISBOA, SOUTHERN PORTUGAL

Making an early start of it, Gabriel had the driver stop at a bakery to grab a quick coffee and a cheese tart along with some pastries for the driver to eat while they travelled out to the Mata farm. He picked up a second paper-wrapped tart and carried it away with him in the carriage. He had no idea if Miss Vladimirova had eaten the pastry he'd given her the day before. Perhaps it was still in a pocket hidden within her black garments, now rather distressingly sodden.

When the carriage stopped before the reservoir, he stubbed out his cigarette, then stepped down and went to fetch her. He hadn't had any idea what to expect when he entered, but Miss Vladimirova stood motionless on the wood platform, her back to the entryway. The windows let in light from all sides, making her a dark blot in the center of the place.

"Miss Vladimirova," he said, "are you ready to go?"

She settled her second veil over her head and came to join him. "Yes. I am."

"I brought you breakfast," he said, handing her the paper-wrapped tart. As before, she took it after a moment's hesitation and secreted it into the folds of her clothing. When she walked next to him to the doorway, he asked, "Are you well this morning?"

She walked on without answering. He kept pace with her and helped her into the carriage when they reached it. He climbed up, then settled next to her. "Do you mind if I smoke?"

Her head turned toward him. "No."

He hoped the drive out to the countryside wouldn't continue like this. He opened his case and took out a pair of cigarettes, tucking one into his breast pocket for later. Then he lit the first and drew in a deep breath of smoke.

"I am never well," she said. "You do not need to ask again."

A chill settling in his heart, Gabriel sat back. The carriage began to move, heading toward the edges of Lisboa.

Miguel and Adela were enjoying breakfast at the hotel still, only receiving a few questioning glances. He didn't let it worry him. Lisboa was a metropolitan city with plenty of visitors from the former colonies in Africa. The waiter was polite, no hint of magic clung about him, and that was enough for now.

As they sipped their coffee, Konrad finally arrived with Miss Carvalho clutching to his arm. He surveyed the table, then selected the chair next to Adela for the girl. He held the chair while Miss Carvalho felt the back of it and then sat. Then he settled next to Miguel, who decided for now to say nothing, since the young man seemed deathly serious.

"I have wired my mother," Konrad said without preamble. "I plan to take Miss Carvalho there. I know that you have the skills to keep her safe, Lady, but you cannot be around at all times."

"To Germany?" Adela asked gently. "Have you sent word to

THE TRUTH UNDISCOVERED

your parents, Ifigénia?"

Miss Carvalho's head turned her direction. "My father would rather I was gone anyway; you know that. And telling Father might be the same as telling whoever uses those books where I've gone. I'll... I'll write to Genoveva when I'm ready."

"When we know it's safe," Konrad inserted.

Adela licked her lips, her regret causing Miguel's perception of her glittering skin to fade to a bluish shade. "I am likely to run into your family when I go north to the Golden City. What do you want me to tell them?"

Ifigénia's face with its scratched-out eyes turned down as if to look at the table. "Nothing. Don't tell any of them."

"That might not work," Miguel said. "The butler—Tomar, I believe—has to know that you left with us."

"That doesn't mean anyone will tell my father," Miss Carvalho said. "He's not known for keeping secrets."

Miguel took another sip of coffee, savoring the earthy smell. From what Adela had told him about Carvalho on the way to Sintra the day before, the man sounded like a boastful pig. How he'd ended up in a position of power among the Freemasons of Northern Portugal likely had to do more with an old family name and money than intelligence or integrity.

This would ruffle their plans to visit the Jesuits this morning, but having the young people out of the country would give them one less worry while they pursued this riddle. "We'll see you to the station," Miguel offered, "and make sure that you are safely on your way."

"I would appreciate that," Konrad said sincerely.

For a moment, silence settled over the table. The waiter returned, presciently bringing two more cups of coffee and a plate of pastries. When he left, Konrad leaned close to Miss Carvalho and whispered something to her. Her hand slid onto the table and located the coffee cup. She touched it carefully, as if judging where it was, then carefully lifted it to her lips and sipped.

"Lady, I don't want you to think I don't appreciate your efforts to help me," she told Adela after she set down the cup. "It sounds less and less like recovering my sight is possible, though, and I want... I want to get on with my life."

The girl was holding her temper in check, clear from the whiteness of her knuckles on her napkin, but the sentiment of the statement was polite. Gaspar expected Konrad's hand in that.

Adela's eyes dropped to the table, the corner of her mouth in a sad moue. "I do understand, Ifigénia."

This is not the time for any personal observations, Gaspar reminded himself. He could hold it in until later.

Adela didn't ask any personal questions either, neither what the girl planned to do in Germany nor what the young man intended toward her. It was trust in Konrad that made Adela hold her tongue—that, and a determination not to say something that would make Miss Carvalho feel criticized. Miguel found her restraint charming, given that he could see that she wanted very badly to ask.

But they ate in relative silence, the young man discreetly tucking the leftover pastry in a napkin and slipping it into a jacket pocket for later. Konrad was accustomed to poverty, Miguel guessed, and that pastry would likely end up as his lunch. When Miss Carvalho finished her coffee, Konrad said they both needed to go upstairs and pack. Miguel let the two young people go ahead while he strolled to the elevator with Adela on his arm.

"I owe you fifty reís, don't I?" she whispered.

"You do," he said.

Gabriel wasn't surprised by the lack of cooperation. The small farm outside the town of Ulgueira held cork trees that spilled down the side of a hill to the west. They couldn't see the sea from this point, but if they went farther uphill, Gabriel suspected they would. It was a pleasant place, and if he had been set to inherit it, Gabriel would have stayed here working with the trees every day. Apparently, that wasn't the case with Donato Mata.

His father, Virgilio Mata, had refused to come down from his ladder. Although the cork harvest was long over, their stripped tree trunks reddish now, the old farmer's secondary stand of olives had produced what looked to be a fine crop. Small black-skinned olives littered the tarp near Gabriel's feet.

"I don't know where he is," the grizzled old farmer said from the ladder he perched on. "He comes and goes as he wishes. I haven't seen him for…"

Gabriel's senses told him all of *that* was true, but the pause while the man considered when he'd last seen his son indicated that the next statement might not be.

"Months," the man finally decided.

He hadn't looked at Gabriel when he said it, and everything about that word rang false in Gabriel's ears. *A lie.*

"And if I talk to your other son?" Gabriel asked, "Jorge, I think his name is?"

The Lady's information hinted that the younger son was *simple.* That could mean any of a thousand things, Gabriel knew, but the Lady's investigator claimed the father was protective of Jorge.

Sufficiently provoked, Mata climbed down from his tree. He folded thick arms over his barrel-like chest. "You will not speak with him."

The man was afraid now, stress bouncing off every word in Gabriel's ears. "I have little choice," Gabriel said reasonably. "I'm investigating a theft in Lisboa, and Donato left evidence at the scene showing he was there. And not alone."

The last part was a lie, but Gabriel felt safe testing the waters with that claim.

"Ask one of his criminal associates," the farmer snapped, stepping closer, his angry eyes peering up into Gabriel's.

"The man who entered the room in question could not have been a criminal," Gabriel said. "It was someone without ill intentions. Crossing a magical ward, you see, could be done by someone like your Jorge, there only to please his brother, I suspect."

That was the Lady's theory, that Mata had used his younger brother as his proxy. Jorge Mata, an innocent by all accounts, would have been able to walk past the wards her father had set up on his workshop and library precisely because Jorge had no ill intentions in his heart.

The farmer swept one arm angrily, almost hitting Gabriel's chest. "I don't know what Donato was involved in..."

That statement had the air of self-delusion. *The man knows exactly what sort of criminal his elder son is.*

Gabriel waited for the man to finish, but the farmer's voice had petered out. A familiar shiver worked itself down Gabriel's spine, and he knew Miss Vladimirova was making her way up the hillside to join them. The farmer's eyes grew wider, his jaw working as if that black-draped figure was the shadow of Death come to collect.

Gabriel turned to catch a glimpse of her. The light wind tugged at her veils. It bore the scent of the sea, not hard to understand so close as they were to the ocean. When he turned back to Mata, the farmer had backed away a few steps.

"Do not run," Miss Vladimirova said in her flat voice.

Gabriel's feet stayed firm as if they were growing roots in the rocky soil. He couldn't have moved if he wanted. He gasped in a breath, then another.

"Let me go!" Mata cried.

"We will not chase you," she said. "But I will not allow you to leave, either."

The man's dark eyes flicked between Gabriel and her, frustration showing in the twist of his mouth. "I don't know where he is!"

"But you know where he goes," Gabriel managed. "And how long he's been gone. Tell us, and we will leave your other son alone." He didn't like the manipulation, but Miss Vladimirova had raised the stakes of this encounter by revealing that she was a witch, and he had to back her play.

"He left yesterday, sent to Sintra," the man yelled. "I don't know who, but he was contacted and told to go there."

"And is that the only place he might be?" Gabriel asked. Miss Vladimirova had reached his side by then, a motionless dark presence, the smell of lake water overriding the salt of the sea now. She hummed under her breath, a low drone that was the source of the compulsion to obey her.

"He goes to the island," Mata ground out. "The little one."

"Which island is that?"

Mata shook his head. "The little one, past the bear beach. I have heard it called the *Ilha da Fada*, but I have never seen it on a map."

The little island past the bear beach? Were there bears here in Southern Portugal? Gabriel hadn't thought so. "How far?"

Mata struggled to raise one arm. He pointed toward the sea. "Just off the shore. Not even an island. Just rocks. He goes there every week when he is able."

Gabriel chased that around in his mind. Every word had rung true; they simply didn't make much sense to him. "Miss Vladimirova, does the bear beach mean anything to you?"

"On the maps," she said, "it is called *Praia da Ursa*, for the rock formations."

Further questioning did reveal that there was a beach just to the west of them with that name, and it was from there that Donato Mata took a boat out to the *Ilha da Fada*. Regularly, like clockwork. Gabriel finished with the questions in his quiver. "Miss Vladimirova, do you have anything else to ask?"

She stopped humming. "I know what I want."

Virgilio Mata, suddenly freed from the grip of her magic, fled into his trees without a glance back. Gabriel's feet were free as well, and he turned to gaze out toward the sea. "I suppose we should go look at this beach."

"It is headlands," she told him. "Easier to go to the lighthouse."

One of the things he would do when they got back to Lisboa was borrow a map and try to learn something of this coastline. "Fine, we'll have the driver take us there."

They made their way back down to where the carriage waited, Gabriel relieved that it was downhill rather than up. Once on their way, she told him of studying maps of the Portugals before coming to Lisboa with the Lady. It seemed a wise effort now, one he probably should have tried.

The lighthouse they sought was out at the Cape of the Rock, the westernmost point in Europe, and from there nothing but sea would stand between him and Brazil. He imagined that as he partook of another cigarette, blowing the smoke out the carriage's window.

It wasn't much over a mile, the driver had told him, but the roads were poor, so it took some time to get there. While they drove up the last of the slope to the lighthouse—an old one, perhaps more than a century, judging by the style—a handful of tourists clambered down from their own conveyance and ambled up a narrow path toward the cape itself. The driver pointed Gabriel in the opposite direction, though, to the north side of the lighthouse.

A bare-footed young boy ran up to them, offering to point out the rocks for a few reis, but he paused when Miss Vladimirova came closer. Since neither of them knew this territory, Gabriel held up one hand to warn her back. "Will you tell me which one is which?"

The boy agreed, finally, casting only one wide-eyed glance back at Miss Vladimirova's veils. He grabbed Gabriel's hand and dragged him along a footpath to the north, promising the best view. They walked along a path through low scrub to the edge of the cliff. When they reached the high point, the boy stopped and dramatically waved one hand to point out the panorama before them.

Gabriel had trouble catching his breath. This was nothing like the beaches of Recife. It must be well over two hundred feet from where he stood to the water below. High rocks littered the shoreline in strange shapes, some golden in the afternoon sun, some gray. The boy patiently pointed out the largest gray formation in the distance, standing in the water just at the foot of the cliffs. That was the Giant, he claimed, and then pointed out the Bear—another tall gray formation that came to a sharp point. The Horse was a golden ridge of stone that jutted out into the water, and the Sentinels stood to either side.

And not far past the Horse, out in the water, was a small outcropping of rock. Hardly an island at all. "Is that the *Ilha da Fada*?" he asked the boy.

The boy nodded quickly. "If you take a boat out there, you will become lost. It's fairy-cursed."

"Has it always been called that?"

The boy shrugged.

Gabriel handed the boy a five-reís coin. "Thank you. You can go back up to the lighthouse, now."

The boy ran away like a shot, clutching his prize. He gave Miss Vladimirova a wide berth, and then was gone from Gabriel's sight. While waiting for her to join him, Gabriel lit a cigarette, surprised that he could keep a match lit in the salty wind.

When she stood at his side, Gabriel pointed out the Bear to her. "The one that's rounded on top."

She tugged off the outer veil, and then lifted back the second, exposing her pale face. "I see it."

He made himself look in her direction when he spoke to her, although he didn't meet her eyes. He pointed to the outcropping. "The boy said that's the *Ilha da Fada*."

She peered at the rocks. "That? Why would Mata visit that?"

A good question. It was too small to hold much, perhaps a stash of money or illegal goods of some kind. This shoreline—at least what Gabriel could see of it—looked too dangerous to make smuggling worthwhile, though.

For a time, they both gazed at the rocks. Gabriel still wasn't sure what he was supposed to be looking for, but a *feeling* grew in his mind. Something was out there.

"There is a disturbance in the water," Miss Vladimirova said finally. "It disrupts the flow of the waves just enough that I can see it."

And if anyone knew how water should flow, it was her. "Can you tell what it is?"

She shook her head. "A low wall, perhaps? Without getting

closer, I cannot say."

Perhaps it was just the reinforcement of having someone else note it, but Gabriel felt surer now that he sensed something out in the water. *A lie.*

I am looking at a lie. That is why I can sense it.

"The boy said that if anyone took a boat out there," he told Miss Vladimirova, "they become lost. That's why it's called the Island of the Fairy—because it's supposedly cursed."

The wind tugged a lock of her hair loose from its braid. "I think we should go out there."

The cliffs appeared difficult to scale, but they could sail up the coast. "Do you control sea water?" he asked.

"Water is water," she said, tucking that loose strand behind her ear.

"I think we should bring Gaspar here," he said. "Let him look at it first."

"Yes."

As noon had passed, he nodded with his head back toward the lighthouse. "Let's go back to Lisboa, then."

Miss Vladimirova nodded and replaced the veils that hid her face. Moving at his slower pace, she walked back with him to the lighthouse where the carriage waited. "Mata went to Sintra yesterday his father said, so where is he now?"

"A good question," Gabriel allowed, a bit out-of-breath. He began to cough, but managed to rein that in. The pain remained, though, spreading through his chest. He took out a cigarette to calm himself and lit it with shaking fingers. Fortunately, Miss Vladimirova had stopped when he did. "My apologies," he managed.

"Unnecessary," she said, and walked on.

The carriage took them down from the heights, rattling along the rough roads as Gabriel tried to ignore the pain that his coughing fit had brought on. Miss Vladimirova seemed to realize his current condition—perhaps she could sense it—and simply waited in silence.

After a time, he could breathe more normally. Miss Vladimirova turned her head to look out the window, and coolly remarked, "We've left the main road."

Gabriel had left his shade down, so he raised it and peered out. She was right. They were on some narrow, graveled path now, drawing close to a farm. He leaned forward and pounded on the front wall of the carriage to get the driver's attention. "Where are we going?"

"Back to Lisboa, sir," the driver shouted down. "One of the other drivers told me this was a shorter way."

Gabriel leaned farther out, peering along the road ahead. The road seemed to lead only to a grazing field. Two dozen buff-colored cows stood among the low shrubs, eating contentedly.

"No." Miss Vladimirova said. "We are going north now, parallel to the shore."

"Stop the carriage," Gabriel called up. When the driver pulled to a stop, Gabriel opened the door and stepped down. With a wave to the man, he walked to the front to get a better look at the path ahead. They were on a farmer's land. From where Gabriel stood, he could see the hillsides of low shrubs tumbling to the south of them. He had little idea of the terrain of Portugal, but they had definitely gone the wrong way. He turned back. "The driver who told you this, did you know him?"

"He was a local fellow," the man said. The corners of his mouth curved down, recognition that he'd made the wrong choice. "I apologize for the delay, sir. I'll get us turned around."

Gabriel took a step toward the carriage's open door, but gunfire cracked across the hillside. He ducked down instinctively, reaching for his pistol. The driver slumped across his seat, and slowly toppled to the ground next to the horses.

On this hillside, we're completely exposed. The driver had fallen to the left, so the shooter was to the right.

"Nadezhda!" he yelled. "They're off to the right."

The carriage swayed, and she tumbled out the door he'd left standing open, a bundle of black cloth collapsing on the gravel.

"Are you hurt?" he called.

"No," she said, her voice utterly calm. "Where is Mata?"

Yes, it has to be Mata. Perhaps he'd followed them out of Sintra the day before. Gabriel rose, keeping the bulk of the nervous horses between him and the shooter. "Stay down. I can't see him."

With the low shrubs, the man could be hiding almost anywhere.

"I must see him to control him," Miss Vladimirova said, coming to her feet. She stepped behind the carriage, one hand raised as if to stare into the distance.

THE TRUTH UNDISCOVERED

A shot rang out before Gabriel could reach her.

She swayed as if from a gust of wind, but remained standing, peering toward the distant fields. Gabriel ran. A third shot sounded and her body jerked, but she didn't fall. Gabriel slammed into her, carrying her with him to the ground.

Another shot followed. Fire bloomed through his chest.

Gabriel had no breath left, the world around him darkening as the black fingers of death finally pulled him down.

Chapter 23

**SATURDAY, 2 NOVEMBER 1901
NEAR CABO DA ROCA, SOUTHERN PORTUGAL**

Gabriel Anjos watched the Russian woman as she smoothed down her skirts. He was too dazed and shocked to do anything else. A hot flush still colored his chest, roughly the size of Miss Vladimirova's small hand. No mark of any bullet could be seen.

The afternoon wind whipped about the hillside, and the cattle on the far side of the road were lowing as if perturbed. Less than twenty feet away, the Lady's driver lay on his side in the gravel where he'd fallen from the carriage's seat, eyes blindly fixed on the underside of the carriage. He was very dead. *Why him and not me?*

Gabriel's skin prickled, and a surge of nausea caused him to roll to his knees and cast his meager lunch up on the ground next to the farmer's fence. He sat down on the gravel and wiped his mouth with his bare arm. He touched his chest again and saw that his fingers were stained red with his own blood.

He'd been shot. He knew that feeling, having lived through it before in Brazil. *I was shot.*

Yet she had healed his wound completely, which went far beyond a normal healer's power.

Most healers wouldn't touch deep wounds like a gunshot. How she could have managed such a feat was a mystery—she had no life to give him.

His lungs felt strange, too, as if they'd been washed and laid out to dry. He'd been bleeding into his lungs, he was sure. But now even their normal tightness had eased, making it easier to breathe. Had she cured that as well? Healers had always told him it was impossible to cure consumption, so surely, she hadn't.

Then he saw the bull on the other side of the fence, its hulking form unmoving in the field. Gabriel started at it numbly. After a time, he forced himself to turn about and face her.

Nadezhda Vladimirova's pale fingers trembled as she tried to rebutton the black fabric of her bodice. Her veils had been ripped aside, one caught now under the wheels of the carriage. The other fluttered against the wooden fence. Her wheat-colored braid was disordered.

"Miss Vladimirova?" he managed. "Did I hurt you?"

Her eyes lifted to meet his, tentative. It was very unlike her usual hard and uncanny gaze. "I did not mean to upset you," she said softly in a voice that carried truth.

Upset *him*? Shouldn't it be the other way around? He had simply fallen on her. She hadn't even fought him. She had seemed to welcome his... advances, but that made no difference. He had never in his life treated a woman like that. "I must apologize for what I... It was..."

"Not your fault," she said, eyes lowered to the ground. "I knew when I healed you. I *triggered* that reaction."

She had healed him, saved his life, knowing he would then treat her like a common whore?

Gabriel grabbed up his blood-stained shirt and undershirt. Both were ruined. She had torn at them in her haste to examine his wound. Spotting his suit jacket a few feet away, he pushed himself to his feet and retrieved it. It was marked with blood as well, but he drew it on and buttoned it as best he could.

Nadezhda Vladimirova still sat on the pebbled roadside, sweeping grit from the road off her black suit with pale fingers. Gabriel offered her a hand to help her up, all too aware of the gravel dust all along the back of her garments. When he'd drawn her up next to him, he helped her brush that off, then plucked her veiled cap off the fence and handed it to her. "Again, I must apologize."

Her eyes met his. "I cannot regret it, Inspector Anjos. For now, I am alive."

Alive. His hand stilled, almost touching hers. He'd thought there was warmth in her hand when he'd helped her up, and a flush to her cheek. He tilted his head and saw a pulse fluttering in her slender throat. "Your heart is beating."

"For minutes or hours, yes," she said, pale lashes fluttering, "but it will fade like morning fog over water."

He could sense the truth in her words, as he could not when she was the other. The times he'd sensed this before, it had only lasted a moment or two. This was the longest he'd seen her *alive*. And that life would soon trickle away. *How horrible.*

She wiped at the corner of one eye with a bare finger and discreetly touched that to her sleeve to dry it. Then she tugged on one glove, seeming inclined to dismiss the whole incident.

Gabriel could see now, since she'd not yet donned her veil, that a bullet had torn into the black cloth on her shoulder, a spot of skin peeking through there. Another showed on her bodice, near her waist. Mata had been shooting at the carriage, and she'd stepped out to try to locate the man... so she could call him to them. Gabriel recalled seeing her body shake with the impact of each bullet. "You were shot."

She took her hat and pinned it on. "I am healed now. Do not... It is not important."

"How did you do that?" he managed.

Her eyes slid toward the bull's carcass, then she reached up to untangle the cap's veil. "Death is powerful."

She could kill people to remain like this. *To remain alive.*

"Please, wait," he begged. "I don't understand what happened."

Her eyes stayed on his hands. "I saw you were dying, so I let Mata go. I could not have called him to me in time and saved you. I am sorry."

"I don't give a damn about Mata escaping."

She shook her head. "The Lady will. I called the bull to me instead and took its lifeforce to heal both of us."

But not the driver. Had he already been dead? "Why save me?"

"You are always kind to me," she whispered, her pale eyes lifting to meet his, then. "People generally aren't kind to monsters."

Unable to stop himself, he touched her cheek with blood-stained fingers. "You aren't a monster."

Tears glistened in her eyes. "I am," she said, her voice

quavering. "I have killed enough men to earn that title."

"Not for me," he told her.

Her eyes hardened, suddenly cold again. She stepped away from his hand and tugged down her veil. Just like that, the young woman was gone, leaving behind only the Nadezhda Vladimirova everyone feared. A shiver fled down his spine.

"We should put the driver's body into the carriage," she said, her voice like stone in his ears now.

CAMPOLIDE, OUTSIDE LISBOA

The morning had not gone as Adela planned. It had taken hours to get the children safely off onto their train headed for Germany. That would take them a few days, rattling over the mountains into Madrid, and from there to the Spanish-French border, and there catching a new train across France to Germany.

While the two packed, Miguel had cashed in their third-class tickets and arranged for Ifigénia and Konrad to have a private compartment under the names of Mr. and Mrs. Schmidt instead. Adela felt better for that, at least. As much as she hated the pair leaving her control, having them safely and comfortably out of their way would make the hunt for answers simpler. Fewer risks.

It was only after luncheon that she and Miguel made the drive to Campolide. When he came around and helped her down from the carriage, Adela noticed immediately the change in the air about the college. Students in their black cassocks and caps huddled past on the walkway from the chapel to the main entrance of the college, their heads bowed.

Miguel glanced up at the bright sun.

The students' behavior seemed like fear of a coming storm, but Adela saw nothing above but bright blue skies. "Do you sense anything?"

The driver pulled away, leaving them standing in the drive. Miguel's eyes dropped to fix on the chapel. "I think we should head down there."

Adela walked on his arm, unconcerned for the moment what the brothers might construe about their relationship. "What did you see?"

"Torn ties," Miguel said, "as if someone had cut down all the cables for the electrified trams."

She cast a worried glance at him. "Torn? How?"

"Brutally," he said. "Whatever happened here, it was unpleasant."

She led him past the main chapel entrance and around to the side entrance behind the square tower. She took her key from her handbag, opened the special door, and started down the stairwell that led to the subterranean parts of the college. The white-plastered tunnels were eerily silent. She made her way toward the storerooms where, most of the time, she could find her nemesis. "Father Serafim!"

No answer came in the silent hallway. *This place is never abandoned.*

"Brother Tomas?" Adela called. "I must talk to Father Serafim."

She continued down the hallway but stopped when something unusual in one of the workrooms caught her eye. She stepped back and peered through the door's small window. Laid out on two of the work tables were sheet-draped forms, the like of which would be recognizable anywhere. *Bodies.* Adela tried the handle, and the door opened inward. She found herself drawn to the first table, where she cautiously drew back the sheet. Miguel came to stand behind her.

Father Serafim lay on the table, his face set in a rictus of pain. His hands were clenched atop his chest.

Miguel leaned closer. "Strychnine," he said. "Perhaps last night."

Adela moved to the second form and uncovered the ancient priest who worked in the chapel above them. She'd always disliked the old man but rarely saw him, so she didn't even know his name. "Why poison Serafim? And why him?"

Miguel nodded to the second priest. "When Anjos and I came here, I noted that these two had the same strange black mark about them."

Adela turned. "Black mark?"

"It was hard to see, hidden," Miguel added, his dark brows coming together. "But... it was there. A tie to some other thing I hadn't seen before."

"Have you seen it since?"

"The butler," he said pensively, eyes on the dead priest.

"Santana?"

"Ah, no. The butler in Sintra." The corner of his mouth lifted in a hint of a sneer.

"Tomar?" She disliked Tomar, too, but because he was a sycophantic little weasel. "Interesting. Why do you think they're down here? Not up in a chapel?"

"Perhaps they want the rigor to pass before... well, that could take days." Miguel sniffed. Then he frowned and drew back the sheet a bit farther, revealing Father Serafim's narrow chest. There was a burn on it, a brand the size of his palm, but without a hint of charring—a Templar cross. "That was done magically," Miguel said. "And recently, perhaps within the last hour. A device, I think, not natural magic."

"So it could have been anyone."

His head tilted to one side. "If we had any doubt this was murder rather than an accident in the labs, that clears it up."

So murdered earlier, yet marked just a while ago? That made no sense. "Let's see if we can find Brother Tomas. If he's not dead, too."

They went back into the hallway and continued toward the storerooms. That was one place she couldn't imagine the brotherhood leaving unguarded. As they neared, a footstep sounded behind them. Adela looked back, and a form in a black cassock emerged from one of the workrooms they'd passed.

Miguel thrust her behind him. Adela stumbled over her heel and fell to the floor. Color bloomed all around her in jumbled images of fire and ice. It passed over and around Miguel, like water spraying to every side. It was icy cold then steaming hot, wet then dry. The loud bong of a church bell caused her to grab her ears to muffle it. Smells bombarded her, like the cooking of a thousand kitchens, a charnel house, and a flower shop all jumbled together. Gagging, she managed to untangle her heel from her skirts and got to her feet just in time for Miguel to shove her back toward the storeroom. "Go!" he yelled.

Adela ran, Miguel only steps behind her. She reached the room and slammed the door as soon as Miguel crossed the threshold. He reached past her and threw the bolt home as another wave of brilliant light splashed against the door's small window.

He stripped off his jacket and jammed it into the opening under the bottom of the door, then set his back against the bolt. "Shit. Where are we?"

"What happened?" She couldn't make out his expression in the faint light, so she stretched across a worktable to turn up the gaslight on the wall. When she looked back, she saw him cringe. "Are you hurt?"

"That was... uh... that was not human magic." Although he was immune to human magics, non-human magics could baffle him momentarily. "Where are we?"

"In their storeroom." She could turn up the lights, but she had a feeling that would only make his discomfort worse. "What was that?"

"I don't know," he admitted, blinking madly. "Some sort of magical bomb. He threw it at me and it engaged a few feet from my face."

Colors still streamed against the small window to one side of his head. "A bomb?"

He cringed again and closed his eyes tightly. "Yes. I didn't get a look at him, so I couldn't tell if he was a witch or using a device."

"What did he do to you?" The colors outside the window were beginning to fade now, although she wasn't sure what that meant.

"I don't think..." His breath shuddered out and in. "I don't think that was meant to harm anyone. It was just lights and sounds and smells, but..." He stopped and ground the heels of his hands against his eyes, then pinched his nose. "Oh, God."

He slid down against the door until he sat on the floor, hands over his face.

Adela suddenly grasped what was happening to him. With his heightened senses and confused responses, so many different stimuli must be overwhelming his mind. She took a careful breath, and then collected the shadows around him, effectively plunging him into a world with no light. "Is that better?" she whispered.

She could tell from his posture that he'd relaxed, even if he didn't answer. She knelt closer but didn't touch him in his dark shell. "I'll find a way out," she whispered. "We're safe. Just wait here."

If he heard her, he didn't even try to argue.

Adela rose and surveyed their prison. The storeroom held rows of shelves that contained magical objects collected by the Jesuits over the centuries since their formation. Each was tagged and documented: glass globes that seemed to contain the night sky, small clock-like machines, illicit items made of sereia skin and selkie pelt and human flesh.

THE TRUTH UNDISCOVERED

As she walked along the center aisle, the artifacts became older, but she didn't look at them. She could investigate these devices all day, but too much information would only be a distraction.

No, this had to be simpler. She had always been told there was no other way out of this storeroom than the door, but given that her father's possessions had been stolen from this room, that couldn't be true. Mata could not have simply carried them right out through the main hallway. He had to have had some other way out of here.

She closed her eyes and tried to think her way around her own limitations. Surely being half fairy had advantages other than being able to play tricks with light.

She listened to her senses. In the corners of her mind, she could hear the devices on the shelves—some of them, at least—clacking and chattering as if straining to be free. Others wanted blood, those made with a need for human sacrifice, even if just a drop. Miguel would hear all those things clearly, no doubt, but to her they were mere whispers.

In her breastbone, she felt the faint thrumming of being trapped under consecrated ground. She could ignore that. To one side of the room, there was something that bothered her more, making her teeth ache worse than that church bell sound in the hallway. She listened to that for a time, feeling it tug at her.

Tesla coil, her mind told her.

She had seen a Tesla coil demonstrated a couple of years past, while she'd hidden up in a balcony at a Freemasons meeting in the Golden City. It had electrified the air about the masons, striking out at this metal object and that within its sphere, always humming and angry, wanting more.

This was like that, a hungry spot in the world, in the storeroom. She opened her eyes and turned to face it, only there was nothing but empty shelves in that direction. Adela walked farther along the main aisle until she'd come even with the source and looked directly at it. No, nothing but more shelves. This was where her father's books and devices had been stored, she realized, before Mata stole them.

She closed her eyes again, seeking that humming sensation. It was down the aisle next to which she stood, so she turned and took a few steps that direction. She stopped when her hand touched a wall. When she opened her eyes, she saw nothing. She was standing in the middle of an aisle, empty old wooden shelves on each side. No wall.

But when she closed her eyes, she could feel the wall again. It was there, right in front of her.

Adela swallowed. If there *was* a doorway here, where would it go?

A hand settled on her shoulder. Adela jumped, and brought one heel down on the foot behind her, only managing to soften the stomp when she realized it was Miguel. *Of course, it's him.* At least she'd managed not to scream.

He'd left his shadows behind, but his eyes were still tightly closed. She grabbed his sleeve, then put his hand on the shelf. "Stay right here," she whispered to him.

She made her way back to the front of the workroom. The door was still locked, colors swelling against it again as if trying to break their way inside. Whoever was doing that hadn't fled.

THE TRUTH UNDISCOVERED

Hurriedly, Adela searched the drawers of the worktable, looking for the brothers' cleaning tools. There were balls of cotton for carefully swabbing devices, and she found a length of linen cloth. She ripped off a long strip as quietly as she could, then ran back to where she'd left Miguel.

"That isn't human magic," he managed, pointing with his chin toward that humming spot.

"It's a door." She took two of the balls of cotton and stuffed one in each of his ears. Then she wrapped the linen around his eyes and tucked the ends in.

She closed her eyes, took one of his hands in her own, and then walked to toward the wall. She tried to push her way through it, but it wouldn't budge.

"It needs a key," he said.

She thought of the keys in her handbag, but she'd dropped that back in the hallway when the first attack had come. She inhaled, the familiar scent of dust and old books filling her nostrils, even though there were no books nearby. *What*?

The easiest course was often the correct one. "Open," she commanded in Latin.

Nothing happened, so she tried again in Portuguese. Then French. And variations on *open*, in every language she could recall.

At the storeroom door, she heard the distinct squeal of metal bending. "Papa, please!"

And she fell forward onto the carpet in her own office, Miguel landing halfway atop her.

Chapter 24

SATURDAY, 2 NOVEMBER 1901
LISBOA, SOUTHERN PORTUGAL

Adela lay back against the carpet in her office, sweat prickling against her spine in a very unladylike fashion. What had she said that got her through the doorway to this place? *Please?*

That was a little too non-specific. It was the *Papa*. Her father—who always preferred that she call him *Papa*, a French term for father—had created that door, although she had no idea when. Before he disappeared, evidently. *Fascinating.*

Miguel was breathing hard and trying to get his bearings by touch alone. He'd landed sprawled halfway atop her, as if they'd both tripped over a threshold. He found the leg of the desk after a moment and used that to drag himself to his feet, off her.

Then Adela remembered the squeal of metal. "We have to get out of here."

Despite the cotton in Miguel's ears, his head turned. He reached out a hand, seeking hers. Adela placed her hand in his and let him haul her to her feet. He caught her in his arms and held her a moment to steady her.

Her skirt's hem had ripped out in the back at some point, but she didn't have time for that. Her mind raced, trying to come up with a plan. She took one of Miguel's hands and laid it on her desk. "Wait here."

She opened her desk drawer, drew out the little pistol she

kept inside, and stuck that in Miguel's hand. He felt it carefully while she dug out the folders she wanted and a case to put them in. She grabbed his free hand and walked swiftly down the hallway. "Santana!"

She had almost reached the kitchens by the time her butler peeked out in answer to her calls. Miguel bumped into Adela, making her recall what an odd picture they must present. She with her briefcase, and he blindfolded and coatless with a gun in his hand. Santana seemed unruffled.

"A man might show up in the next while," she said, "in my office. Don't try to stop him. I want all the servants out of this house, as quickly as possible. Dinner on the town, as fine as you like. I'll pick up the tab. And don't come back until sundown, at least."

Santana nodded. "Yes, Lady."

And with that, she led Miguel through the kitchens, out the back door, and into the back courtyard. A cab was not going to be easy to find.

LISBOA

Miguel trailed at the end of Adela's arm, his mind spinning with rampant sensation. He couldn't tell what was real and what wasn't any longer. He managed to get the little icy pistol tucked into one pocket as she hauled him across rough footing toward *something*. Fireworks played behind his eyelids, the ghost of color flares lingering far longer than they should, making him smell lily and iris and bat guano, accompanied by the tinkling of a thousand tiny bells and the very high-pitched squeaking of bats in flight.

Her hand felt alternately insubstantial in his and then hard, but like clay, not flesh. He could tell when she stopped, when those hands made him climb into a vehicle, and when that ship swayed sickeningly on a sea of scentless water. He smelled vomit and wasn't sure whether it was his own or just his mind supplying false information.

After a long time, the ordeal ended, and those hands propelled him along hard floors and then slowly lowered him to the side of a bed. That was Adela, surely, because she fished the pistol back out of his pocket, then pushed him gently until he was lying down. *Thank God.*

Miguel woke some unspecified time later. He pulled off the blindfold. The room was dim, near to dusk. The world still spun faintly, but nothing like before. Bearable, at least.

He cautiously removed the balls of cotton from his ears. Somewhere nearby, Adela was shuffling through papers that sounded like the breaking of thin sheets of glass. Everything else he heard was harsh and metallic. The smells his mind perceived were still a mix of overripe fruit and flowers and manure. Whatever that man in the tunnels had thrown at him, it had left his senses all out of whack.

It *was* getting better, though. He could tell that much. He didn't know how long it would take to return to normal, but this would render him useless for a time. That worried him. He never doubted that Adela could get herself out of that situation, but she'd had to drag *him* around like dead weight, and that worried him.

She rose from the table, then, the scraping of the chair's feet on the floor sounding like thunder. Her hand touched his cheek. Her fingers felt spongy, but fairly solid now. More like actual flesh than clay. "Any better?"

The words tinkled like bits of glass sparkling onto a tin floor. Miguel held in a cringe only by gritting his teeth together. He forced himself into a sitting position, eyes half-closed to keep what he saw to a minimum. "I'm going to go down to the bar. I think getting drunk might help."

He could tell he'd offended her by the way she moved, withdrawing like a crab going back into its shell. She didn't believe in *excess*. He went anyway, making his way down halls too brightly lit, into a foyer that smelled of gray and rain. He stumbled into the much darker bar, dropped a twenty mil-reís bill on the counter, and asked a shadowy bartender who smelled of oyster sauce to give him a bottle of brandy.

The man handed him a glass and a bottle, and Miguel made his way to a white-clothed table in one of the corners. It was early enough that patrons were still stopping for a quickly drink before heading out for a night in the old downtown, the scent of coming rain notwithstanding. *Is that smell even real?* He poured a glass with a shaking hand, and then gulped some down without even trying to appreciate the stuff. To his eyes, the world burst into flame, violent and orange... the color he should be seeing.

A relieved breath shuddered out of him. *Something normal.*

He closed his eyes and sniffed the brandy and was rewarded with orange against his closed eyelids. When he opened them, the flames that licked along the edge of his table and tablecloth had paled to yellow.

He took a careful sip this time, and it behaved the way that brandy should, hard in his mouth, with a stinging air that tried to escape through his nose. *Better.*

Out of the corner of his eye, he spotted a man entering the

bar from outside. Darkness was falling outside, so the man was clearly visible in the electric lights of the bar. It took a moment for Miguel to recognize Anjos in this altered reality, but the man bore the blue-white aura of a powerful Truthsayer, so he couldn't be wrong. And he was surrounded with the golden light of a recent healing. And sex.

Miguel wanted to lay his head on the table, but waved Anjos over instead.

Anjos came to the table and sat heavily, the smell of lake water all about him. His suit coat was buttoned, and bizarrely pinned at the neck with a hat pin as if this were some new fashion among the youth of Lisboa. A black scarf wrapped about his neck hid the fact that he wore no shirt under the jacket. If the bartender realized that, he'd probably kick Anjos out. So Miguel waved the bartender over himself, asked for another glass and bread and olives, and then handed the man another bill. Oyster-man's brows rose, but he left to procure the requested items. Anjos sat hunched over the table as if he wanted to lay his head on it, too.

"Dead," Miguel said. "What is it about that concept that you don't grasp, Anjos? She's *dead.*"

The bartender brought the glass and a tray of olives and bread. He cast an odd glance at Anjos' attire but left as Anjos poured himself a drink. He downed it in a single gulp, gasping as it burned its way down his throat. Then he poured another.

"I did not plan for that to happen," Anjos said once he got his voice back. "Mata shot me. She killed a bull then healed me. Apparently, the sex... was a side effect."

Miguel felt his brain starting to clear, inasmuch as it ever did. The brandy might be fine, but the olive he tried tasted bizarrely like butterscotch candy. "You saw Mata? Perhaps you should start from the beginning."

Gabriel poured a third brandy, far more than he usually drank. Then he started from the beginning and told Gaspar of his day full of mishaps. He started with the informative interview with Mata's father, the visit to the cape to view the *Ilha da Fada* where the father claimed his son often went. Then the side trip by the driver, who'd been taken in by someone's proposed short cut back to Lisboa.

"That was when the shooting started," Gabriel said. "The driver was killed right off, and I was shot trying to protect Miss Vladimirova."

"Can you truly shoot a corpse?" Gaspar asked, his face twisted in disgust as he ate another olive.

"She was shot at least twice," Gabriel admitted, "but healed those wounds when she healed me."

"That's where the bull comes into the equation?"

"Yes. She let Mata go and drew the bull to her instead. Then took its life to save me." His emotions about the bull's death were mixed. It was only an animal, but it had a right to live, too, didn't it? "It was only after that, I suppose, that I... fell on her."

"So Mata got away?"

"Yes," he said. "It's likely he was the one who advised our driver to take that side road. It never occurred to me to check."

Gaspar just shook his head. "Can't plan for everything. Tell me about this island of yours."

Gabriel picked through his memories, trying to piece together those sensations that had made him suspect he was seeing a lie. In the end, Gaspar agreed it was something he needed to go see for himself… once he was back to normal.

Then Gaspar took his turn relaying the day's events, from Mr. Konrad and Miss Carvalho's precipitous flight to Germany, to the death of the priests, to the explosion of a bomb that had rendered him senseless—or rather, overloaded those senses—which forced the duo to take a secret doorway that somehow connected the Lady's house to the underside of the Jesuit college.

Gabriel wasn't sure which of the two of them had the worse day. He finished his brandy, thanked Gaspar, and made his way out of the bar and down the hallways to his bedroom. Fortunately, he still had the key in a jacket pocket. He kicked off his shoes and ran a hot bath, one of the advantages to having a rich patroness.

He'd wiped most of the blood from his chest with his ruined shirt and undershirt, but he felt sticky and suspected he was beginning to smell. And now he wanted a cigarette. Or five. His hands were shaking again.

Gabriel flicked the stub of his cigarette into his toilet.

Miss Vladimirova had walked into the reservoir without a single parting word to him. Not a flicker of recognition of the fact that they'd become, for a lack of a better description, lovers. She claimed she'd triggered his reaction, but he was the one who'd—actually, he didn't even recall the act itself.

For a short time after her healing him, Gabriel had *been* the bull, that animal's life force—and other urges—flowing through his body. It was an image he didn't want to contemplate, hence the brandy.

The water grew cold while he sat in the tub, smoking and trying to soak away the idea that *he* was a monster.

He hadn't thanked Miss Vladimirova, Gabriel realized, for saving his life. He should have thanked her. Gaspar had pointed out that Miss Vladimirova didn't have any feelings to be hurt, but Gabriel wasn't so sure. Underneath all that coldness lay buried the woman he'd talked with that afternoon, the woman who'd shed tears.

She'd only been eighteen when she died, and that had been over thirty years ago. And in those thirty years, she'd only had rare moments of being alive. What was it like for her between those rare moments?

He heard the door to his bedroom open, keys in the lock. Gabriel hurriedly wiped one hand on the towel that lay over the edge of the tub and picked up his pistol. "Miguel?"

"No," the Lady responded airily. "It's me." She pushed open the door to the bathroom and gazed down at him. "I want to talk to you."

He set the pistol back on the chair. *The woman has no shame.*

But he knew she wasn't going to pass out from embarrassment merely because he was nude, and she wasn't going to go away until she had her say. He grabbed the towel that lay over the edge of the tub and covered his privates. "What do you want?"

"Miguel told me what happened, that Nadezhda killed a bull

to save you," the Lady began, striding around the small bathroom, waving one hand. Thankfully she wasn't looking at him. "I'm going to have to reimburse a farmer."

Perhaps he should just get up and put on his dressing gown. But that was hanging on a hook on the back of the door. "You can take it out of my pay, Lady."

"You clearly don't know how much a good bull costs." The Lady turned her keen eyes on him. "You learned something of her today, did you not?"

"Of Miss Vladimirova?" He could be coy with his employer, but he wouldn't lie to her.

"The best analogy I've heard for it," she continued, crossing to gaze out the high window, "is that it's like flint and steel. A spark is created when they... come into contact."

He had no idea what she meant and told her so.

The Lady leaned back against the wall. "She used the strength stolen from the bull to heal you. Imagine that... she killed the bull and for a time was fully alive. She gave that up to save you."

"I understand." He wished he had another cigarette, but they were over on the toilet stand. *Damn.*

"I doubt that you do," the Lady said. "Think how tempting it is to see a starving beggar and know that if she takes his comparatively worthless life, she'll feel whole, even if just for a short time." She picked up his silver cigarette case and emptied out the contents into her palm, about a dozen slender cigarettes. She turned and dumped them into the toilet. "She could walk through a crowd and steal a year of life from each person, but she doesn't. She denies herself every day, every hour. She forces herself to go on without true life. Because she has *decided* it's immoral to kill or to steal. For no reason other than that she is disciplined."

She disapproved of his smoking, worried that he'd let his need for a cigarette distract him from her business. "You've made your point, Lady. Are we done?"

"But I haven't made my point, Anjos." She went to the window and turned back to face him. "How much do you know about Healers?"

"I'm sure it's not as much as I'm about to hear."

Her head tilted as she glared at him. "Don't be an ass. When a healer has a lover, some healing theoretically takes place during the sex act. That's why healer's lovers are usually in good health. Every time, so it would be a mutually beneficial arrangement."

Mutually beneficial arrangement?

"If you were her lover," the Lady continued, "she might be able to, over time, ease your illness. In turn, she would feel, at least for a while, whole again."

Consumption would kill him eventually, he'd lived with that knowledge for a few years now. But at the moment it was only a tight chest and coughing. The pain could be ignored. He licked his lips. "Did she ask you to broker this deal?"

"Not at all," the Lady said lightly. "But since Miguel told me you've already... broken the ice, so to speak, I decided I should make you aware of the possibilities presented by your situation."

Broken the ice. What a hideous turn of phrase to choose. Gabriel groaned and covered his eyes. Why would she not go away?

The Lady ignored his reaction. "Miss Vladimirova is too shy to pursue a lover, I suspect, so I thought I would take the matter into my hands."

Gabriel pinched the bridge of his nose, feeling a headache starting behind his eyes.

"...and she likes you."

"She has no feelings about anyone." He felt guilty saying that, knowing it was untrue.

The Lady stepped over next to the tub and kicked the side of it, sending the water rippling about him. "I would kick you," she said, her voice sharper than normal, "but I don't want to get my shoes wet. Do you think she enjoys being a monster? Being the thing that children shrink away from? I think you know better. You treat her in a gentlemanly fashion. You *try,* which no one else does. Miguel certainly doesn't."

No, Miguel Gaspar never drew his punches. Things were black and white for Gaspar, *absolute.* He saw Miss Vladimirova as a corpse and nothing more, despite the evidence of her walking and talking.

"You are a kind man, Anjos, which is one of the reasons I like you. I'm merely suggesting that you give her something she craves more than you crave your cigarettes." With that parting shot, the Lady walked out of the bathroom, leaving him blessedly alone. His hotel room door shut behind her, the lock clicking.

Gabriel climbed out of the tub to get a cigarette, only to recall she'd dumped them in his toilet.

He tramped back into the bedroom, dripping water as he went, and dug a box of cigarettes out of his portmanteau. Sitting on the edge of the bed, he fumbled out a match with shaking fingers, lit the cigarette, and inhaled smoke before blowing out the match. The head of the match crumbled and landed on his bare thigh. He hissed and swept it off onto the floor where it continued to glow. Its light winked out between one second and the next, making him recall that afternoon, when he'd watched Nadezhda Vladimirova's life do the same.

Miss Vladimirova could kill to get her life back. Or she could find a dozen men to lie with; that would, apparently, do the trick as well. She could find a brothel and keep herself alive indefinitely. But she'd clearly decided not to pursue either option.

Miss Vladimirova had principles, something a corpse couldn't have.

Chapter 25

Sunday, 3 November 1901
Lisboa, Southern Portugal

Miguel woke to the feel of cloth brushing his skin, a *normal* feeling. The fabric felt of silk, linen, and hot places… not rubber trees, cumquats, or stone. That was a good sign.

"I need your clever brain," Adela's voice said, bells ringing in it, "so wake up."

Her fingers touched his hair, and that felt normal as well. Miguel dared to open his eyes and saw her glittering skin, the dancing of motes of dust on the sunshine slanting in through the window, and her strained smile.

His head was pillowed in her lap, so she must have been trying to wake him for some time. Her black hair trailed unbound over her shoulder, the scent of lilies drifting from it. Actual lilies, not phantom smells in his mind. "Fine, I'm awake."

Adela slid off the bed, letting the back of his head hit the mattress. Apparently, her sympathy was over. "So, about what Anjos told you yesterday…" she began.

If it was what Anjos had said yesterday, he had to have told her *after* returning from the bar. Miguel didn't recall having a conversation with her then, but he'd been moderately drunk by that time.

"Do you recall if he said *when* he saw Mata?" Adela asked. "I've been trying to piece together a timeline of when and where Mata was, and I don't think he could have been the man we saw in the tunnels."

Miguel pushed himself into a sitting position. His head ached, but that could be ignored. "Anjos said afternoon, but not much more than that."

Adela sighed. "Even if Mata used a door like we did, I don't think he could be in Cabo da Roca and Campolide at the same time."

She moved around the room as she spoke. Miguel didn't follow her motion since the light was so bright. He closed his eyes instead. "I thought you believed it was Brother Tomas in that hallway"

"Brother Tomas has been at that college for decades," Adela said dismissively. "He wouldn't have hurt Father Serafim, so it must have been someone else. Someone in a cassock and cap."

Miguel sat up, intrigued. "The man we saw wasn't the same man who killed them, or likely not. The bodies had been dead for hours, but that branding was recent. Two people, Adela."

"I still can't imagine why Brother Tomas would brand them in that way, much less attack us." She was pacing now, her footfalls on the soft rug small thuds in his ears.

He sat up and began to contemplate whether he should try to escape to the toilet. "But you've ruled out Mata?"

"For yesterday afternoon. Not for anything else. He could have killed DuBois, Father Serafim, and Tomar, but couldn't have been trying to take out Anjos at the same time that we were in the tunnels.

"Tomar?" he asked, his brain finally in motion.

"The butler at the estate in Sintra," she offered. "I had a telegram this morning, and Santana had it delivered here. Someone slit Tomar's throat last night."

Miguel opened his eyes. "Looking for the book?"

"Possibly," she mused, pausing to gaze out the window. The sunlight glittered around her. "Or simply tying up loose ends like DuBois."

"And our second man is going around and burying them? Or marking them, at least? Some form of final rite?" He pinched the bridge of his nose. It didn't make sense.

"Not any last rite that I'm familiar with," she said.

What am I missing? He'd had that feeling before—that he was missing some obvious detail that would tie everything together neatly. "Has he marked that butler yet?"

Her head turned toward him, early light cascading across her glittering skin, the dark of night in her black hair. He smelled lily-of-the-valley, surely not present this time. "I have no idea," she said, "but that might be something to watch for. DuBois was buried later, didn't you say? And Serafim will be as well."

Miguel rose from the bed. "If I get to Sintra first, I can watch for whoever shows up at the estate."

"You should take Anjos with you," she said as he walked toward the bathroom. "No, he'll have to go to Mass first."

Given the sunlight, Anjos has already missed early Mass. "I doubt it. He'll want to go to confession first," Miguel pointed out. "Atone for whatever it is he thinks he did wrong."

Adela sighed. "I read him a lecture last night, so he's likely to avoid me for a time."

When was that? "Last night?"

"After you came up and told me about him and Nadezhda, I thought he needed to hear my take on the situation."

"You went to tell him he's a fool for doing such a thing?"

She laughed lightly. "Not at all."

Gabriel Anjos paused in the doorway of the reservoir. *I am a fool for being here.*

The soft scent of the water inside mingled with the rain-damp air outside. The clouds had lifted, sending light streaming through all the windows of the reservoir, shining on the surface of the deep water. He let the door close behind him.

He'd had time to work through everything the Lady had told him the night before. It made sense in a bizarre way, that healers could gain strength via sex. It was something he hadn't given much thought before last night, and certainly a topic he would never have raised with Tia Ana Maria.

Between one breath and the next, Miss Vladimirova appeared on the platform, water streaming from her black garments. The veils were missing, but she still wore the same dress with its bullet holes showing small bits of her unmarked skin. Gabriel felt a sudden urge to go to her, to assure himself that she was whole.

"Inspector Anjos," she said in her cold voice, her eyes closed to spare him. No emotion, no hint of anything passing between them other than strict necessity. "Does she need us?"

Frankly, this morning Gabriel didn't care what the Lady needed or didn't. He wouldn't be settled in his own mind until he talked further with Miss Vladimirova. If he lost his position over failure to be available for the Lady's whims, so be it. "I wanted to speak with you," he said. "Not by her bidding."

Miss Vladimirova waited. There was no sound other than the trickle of water coming in from the aqueduct. Water still clung to her skirts, but her hair was dry now, he noted. Her sleeves as well.

Gabriel stepped onto the platform, out to where she could easily drown him and drag his body to the bottom of the reservoir. "What happened between us yesterday... is that something you would wish to... pursue again? Without the influence of the bull?"

Her head tilted the other way. Her skirts were dry, the water streaming away only a trickle now. "Did she suggest that?"

He wasn't going to lie to her. "Yes."

"Why?"

"She believes it would help you feel more alive," he said. "And it would improve my health as well."

"Logical extrapolation," Miss Vladimirova said dispassionately. "But true."

I am propositioning a dead woman in a reservoir on Sunday morning when I should be at Mass. Gabriel licked his lips.

God would surely have strong opinions about this choice of his. "I cannot tell how you feel. I can't read your response."

She stepped toward him. A shudder fled along his spine, but he made him feet stay where they were. "I think I would not be unwilling."

That was a reference to the *other* her, the one he'd seen the day before.

She gazed at him, no doubt on her face. No expression at all, to be truthful. She began unbuttoning her jacket, pale fingers moving on the buttons.

He stepped closer. "Let me,"

Her hands stilled. His request seemed to give her pause, as if no man had ever undressed her before. Perhaps that was the case, as he'd no idea what sort of relationship she'd had with her murderous husband... or any other man in the intervening decades. Gabriel tugged her closer by the edges of her jacket and slipped the last button free. He opened the jacket, pushed it off her shoulders, and down her arms.

If it had been wet, that would have been a struggle, but the black fabric was completely dry.

There *was* an expression on her face now, closer to confusion than anything else. Her eyes went to the jacket where it fell on the stone platform. She wanted to pick it up, he guessed.

Her eyes lifted. "It will be wrinkled."

A strangely mundane concern. "Can you not put it in the water and pull it out again?"

She drew in a small breath. "Oh. Yes."

He stooped down, picked it off the floor, and laid it neatly to one side, flat. The last thing he wanted was for her to be thinking about her garments the whole time. When he turned back, she was undoing the cuffs of her grayed old shirtwaist. He set his fingers to the buttons down the front, tugging it loose from her wide belt as he did so. She turned when he suggested, and he peeled the shirt from her, then moved on to the fastenings of her belt and skirt. Once they were gone, he unhooked her stays, suddenly all too aware of the body under his fingers. A moment later she stood in only a chemise and stockings.

When he'd lain with her on the side of the road, he'd done no more than throw up her skirts. He truly hadn't any idea as to her figure. Undressed she had the shape of a young girl, almost boyish. Her breasts were small, her hips straight. He'd never fancied shapeless women. He smiled at her anyway.

She'd seen his reaction, though. It didn't show on her face, but her chin dropped, her eyes flitting back to the floor as if she were still eighteen, the age she'd been at her death. He wondered if the woman hidden underneath her mask *was* still eighteen in her heart. She'd been a wife for three years. What had her husband done to her? How had he talked to her?

Gabriel laid one hand against her cool cheek. "Look at me, please." Her eyes lifted, and he could see it then, a hint of fear. Somewhere deep inside she was afraid of being rejected, no matter the pragmatic nature of this strange arrangement. "Will you take down your hair?"

She began unpinning her hair, carefully collecting the pins and setting them on the platform's railing, so he removed his shirt and undershirt as she did so. She'd seen him without a shirt before, so that shouldn't trouble her. As he removed his first shoe the coil of her hair fell loose, a stream of wheaten gold that reached past her waist. If the sight of her in only a chemise hadn't roused him, her hair made up for it. She stroked her fingers through it, dividing it into loose tendrils. He pried off his other shoe without unlacing it.

"Your hair is beautiful," he said, sounding as breathless as if he were eighteen himself. He wrapped it about his hand. It felt like satin about his fingers. He leaned closer and pressed his lips to hers.

Despite the dampness of the reservoir, her lips were cold and dry. Gabriel set one hand against the back of her waist and drew her against him. Her hands went to his bare shoulders, cooler than he expected. Her slight breasts pressed against his chest, and whatever misgivings he'd had about this enterprise fled.

He licked his lips and kissed her again, and she surprised him by letting out a whimper. He drew back. "Do you not...?"

Her cool hand wrapped about his neck and yanked him back to her. Evidently, she had set aside her misgivings as well.

———

She had come alive as he'd touched her, her skin slowly gaining warmth, her eyes softening to human eyes. Afterwards she'd fallen asleep in his arms. The wood of the platform was cool and hard, and they lay atop her petticoats and his clothes, no doubt wrinkling them horribly. He'd found himself watching her as her throat moved with her breath, a pulse fluttering at the side of her neck.

She was alive, although he had no idea how long it would last.

She wasn't beautiful. Her face was too thin and her jaw too square. He lifted a hank of hair to his lips. That *was* beautiful, shining in the light that came through the windows, gold with streaks the color of sand. A shame it was hidden under veils all the time. He coiled the lock of hair around his fist and brought it to his nose.

It smelled of lake water. Her skin carried the scent of lake water. Her mouth tasted of lake water. Did she know that? Likely not, and he wasn't going to mention it. It wasn't natural, but it wasn't unpleasant either.

There had been no deception involved here. They had both agreed to this.

And yet, he felt guilty.

It wasn't as if he could marry Miss Vladimirova. Even the most understanding priest would draw the line at performing a wedding where one of the celebrants was dead.

The thing that made him flinch was her apparent youth. She might be over fifty now, but she *looked* half his age. He felt like one of those middle-aged men who took lovers younger than their own daughters, thinking that would make them young themselves.

But in truth, how was this different? He did feel better than he had last night, the ache where a bullet had torn into his chest eased away. He felt no urge to rise and seek out a cigarette, either, as if she'd quelled that urge at the same time.

And none of that mattered. He watched the pulse flutter in her neck and drew her closer, asking himself over and over what he could do to make her fleeting life last.

Miguel had left for Sintra, and Adela remained behind to pore over the paperwork she'd patched together the night before. The pieces had come from the desk of Marcel DuBois on the day he'd died. Or rather they came from his trash bin. She'd picked it up to gather the papers off his desk before escaping his burning house. Nothing she'd put in the basket had been particularly revelatory. Apparently, DuBois had been going through the expenses of his household on Cabo Verde, a pathetically normal day in the life of a landowner. Nothing on the desk revealed anything about the man who'd come to the house and slit DuBois' throat. The only thing that the gathered papers had revealed was a half-torn note that announced that someone was coming to consult on his library. Adela set that one aside, but it hadn't revealed anything other than a vague promise.

But someone *had* come to the house, slit DuBois' throat—apparently with his cooperation—and set the house afire. DuBois' body was later buried in the old town under the floor of a church, a capstone with a Templar mark on it buried with the man.

She was surely dealing with two people, one killing, and one cleaning up the scene behind him, taking care of the bodies. And yet...

I am missing something.

A knock came at the door. Adela picked up the pistol and,

secreting that between two folds of her skirt, went to answer. She opened it enough to see it was one of the porters with the coffee she'd ordered. She unchained the door and let him bring the tray inside.

"Your name?" she asked the young man.

A young man of no more than eighteen, the porter seemed flustered. He set the tray down on her sitting room table. "Shall I pour, Lady?"

"Your name?" she pressed.

"Tomas, Lady," he answered.

"I'll pour for myself," she told him. "That will be all."

Tomas surveyed the room as if he'd never been in one of the hotel's better ones. *Perhaps this is his first day.*

Adela walked past him and caught the scent of dust and old books. Her eyes narrowed as she turned back to peer at him. He blurred around the edges, like an image printed on a frayed bit of linen. Adela stepped back, lifting the pistol. "Who are you?"

Between one blink and the next, the frayed image resolved into Brother Tomas. "I need to speak with you. Put down the gun."

She had no intention of doing that. She took a step back, though. She'd allowed a shapeshifter of some sort into her room. She wasn't going to compound that mistake by giving in to his request merely because he looked like Brother Tomas. For all she knew, Tomas was dead. "I'd prefer not," she told him, a chill stealing along her spine. "Move over to the door."

Brother Tomas took in a vexed-sounding breath, as if she was a troublesome child. His dark hair—always hidden by a cap before—looked rumpled. "I promise you will remain unharmed."

"And I'd shoot you if you tried," she said. Brother Tomas didn't normally demand much of her attention, so she wasn't sure if he looked much different than normal, other than wearing a porter's garb.

He took one step closer to her, hand out. "Put down the gun."

She shook her head. "I think not."

His dark eyes met hers. "Adela Liberté Lafayette Soares, drop the gun."

Adela's breath went short as she fought to control her own hand. Her fingers loosened even as she ground her teeth together.

He used my name. My full name. No one had done that for decades. No one *knew* her full name, the name she now understood could compel her to do their will.

The pistol dropped to the carpet.

Brother Tomas leaned down and picked it up. "Now we can have a proper talk."

CHAPTER 26

SUNDAY, 3 NOVEMBER 1901
LISBOA, SOUTHERN PORTUGAL

At Brother Tomas' command, Adela settled on the couch. Still holding her pistol, he took the armchair opposite her. "Do you remember me?" he asked.

He could force her to answer, but the more he did that, the more she granted him control over her. Compliance was a better choice. "Are you actually Brother Tomas?"

"Sometimes," he said, "when it suits me to be."

She let out a vexed breath. The implication was that, of course, he wasn't Brother Tomas. She'd seen with her own eyes that he could change his appearance, so there was no way to tell who he was. "The Brother Tomas I knew wouldn't have attacked me in those tunnels."

"I didn't attack you." He sat back, crossing one leg over the other. "I drove you, toward the doorway. I needed you gone."

He didn't deny it, then. "Why?"

"Because I was trying to catch that prick Mata before he got away, and he might have shot you. He's indiscriminate about who gets hurt."

Well, the man was an assassin and thief for hire. Adela flicked a fold of her skirt to one side, trying to work out what she needed to know from this person. "Why are you hunting Mata?"

"Mostly I'd like to kill him," the man said. "Their system is collapsing, and someone's using Mata to confuse the trail."

Confuse the trail? Adela licked her lips. "*Their* system. Whom do you mean?"

"These fake Templars, those who play at being the men who will control the Portugals. The communication system that once bound them all is being dismantled from the inside. Intentionally, so that none of the others at distant poles know what's happening and why."

That would be the network of strands of light Miguel had seen extending out from the book, which—once he'd had a good look at it—was shut down. From somewhere else, if she recalled correctly. Someone must have realized they were being spied upon. "How do you know that?"

"I built that system," the man said.

"For them?" she asked.

"I built the system because I wanted to see whether it would work. It does, but unfortunately someone put it to other use than simple long-distance communication. Lashed demons onto the end points, making it a rather dangerous system for anyone to use without permission."

"Yes, a young friend of mine was blinded by one of those creatures."

The fake Brother Tomas shrugged with one shoulder. "They feel some sacrifices are inevitable."

"For what?" she asked. "What is their ultimate plan?" It was annoying to talk in terms of an unclear *they*, when the man seemed certain he knew what was happening.

"Frankly," he said, "I don't think anyone I've questioned so far knows. They're being manipulated but are so caught up in the glory of their conceit of a glorious unified Portugal that they don't understand they're merely puppets for someone else's plan."

Actually, she could see that happening. Like soldiers who never knew the true reason they fought a war. "Who have you talked to so far?"

He gestured mildly with the pistol. "DuBois, Serafim, Contreras, Tomar."

All dead now. At least she assumed that Contreras was the chapel priest killed at the same time as Serafim. "Did you kill them?"

He paused for a moment. "DuBois, yes, and Tomar. When they realized why I'd come, rather than reveal anything, Serafim and Contreras killed themselves."

That would neatly explain the differing modes of death. Adela lifted her chin. *I am sitting in the presence of a self-confessed murderer.* "Are you going to kill me?"

"Of course not," he said. "Why would I do that?"

"It seems that other people who speak with you end up dead."

"But not you, of course, Adela."

A subtle reminder that he knew her full name and could just as easily order her to kill herself as he'd ordered her to drop her gun. "Even so, you attacked us in the hallway."

"I told you, I was driving you to the storeroom."

"What you did to Miguel was excruciating for him," she said.

The fake Brother Tomas shrugged again. "His welfare does not concern me. I am pleased, however, to discover that there's something that works against the Meter. I know he's supposed to be immune to magic, so I presented him with… sensation."

Then it *had* been deliberate. "Do you intend to sell that information on elsewhere?"

He chuckled. "No, I'll keep that to myself, for use should I ever think he mistreats you."

She peered at him through narrowed eyes, wondering if there was a guise she could see through. "Why would you care?"

He smiled. "Because you're my daughter."

Miguel banged on the front wall of the carriage and waited for the driver to come to a stop. He'd finally recalled what his blurry mind had forgotten the night before, what he'd forgotten to tell Adela. Anjos' bleary report about a place where the air and water seemed to be lying.

"I want to go to the cape instead," he called up to the driver once the carriage stopped. "Can we get there this afternoon?" He frankly wasn't sure how far they'd driven toward Sintra, but the cape was in the other direction.

The driver assured them they could get to the cape and back by nightfall, or not much later, so Miguel bid him go there instead. Anjos had seemed to think whatever he'd seen—or not seen—was important. Adela might rail at him later for letting Mata slip away, but he'd had only a slim chance of catching the man anyway.

He closed the door and sat back down, wishing he'd

thought to bring a newspaper or a book to read. Instead he crossed his arms over his chest and closed his eyes, resting his senses while the carriage bobbed and swayed its way down to the ocean.

A few hours later, the driver stopped the coach at a place that bore the scent of the sea and storms—stone, blue, green, water, and plants. Miguel breathed in for a moment, accustoming his nose and mind to the many smells before forcing his eyes to see it too. Seagulls cried all about the spot, the wind carrying them inland this time of day. He opened the coach's door, climbed down, and peered out toward the sea.

He had always liked watching the sea. It was powerful and yet without ties or magics. It simply did what it did, without any care for human's wishes or plans. Nature was calming in that way. Pure. Always there. He let out a pent breath, and some of his tension slipped away with it.

"Can you wait for me here?" he asked the driver.

The man merely shrugged, as if people came out here daily. He drove the coach off to one side and climbed down to loosen the traces.

Miguel tried to recall Anjos' story from the night before through the remembered fog of brandy and disjointed sensations that had cluttered his head. Anjos said they walked to the north to look over the rocky outcroppings there. That was where this *Ilha da Fada* lay. Anjos had then added something bizarre about guards or sentinels and something about *bears*, and Miguel hoped he could figure that out, or the long drive out here would be wasted.

He followed the pathway along the coastline, wondering how he was going to recognize the spot. There had been a couple of other carriages at the cape, but the inhabitants had gone the opposite direction, toward the lighthouse. That path had a small sign that promised a better view of the rock itself. He was looking for something else. He took a path that split off to the north and proceeded toward the rocky headlands.

The path ended at the edge of a steep drop that looked out over the fantastical outcroppings below. This was where Anjos had stopped in his tale and listed off the series of nonsensical names for formations.

Miguel didn't need to know any of those.

It was right there. *Right in front of everyone's eyes, and they can't see it.*

Perched atop one of the small rocky outcroppings—a tiny island farther out than any of the others—was a creation of air and magic. A giant sphere of golden circles, almost like gears, slowly turning against one another. Smaller wheels turned within those, some in the opposite direction, and even smaller wheels within those. Constant movement, and colors constantly changing. It was both baffling and unspeakably beautiful.

That is not human magic. He was looking at fairy magic, far more complex than that simple glamour that was natural to their kind, that even Adela could produce. This was magic that had been... formalized. It had been fitted onto a geometric structure, a pattern repeating over and over, growing smaller with each iteration. Miguel couldn't tell what that structure was supposed to do, but it had surely been constructed with some intention other than its beauty.

He doubled back along the pathway until he found a narrower path that made its way through the scrub and rocks down to the closest spot to that magical sphere. Miguel followed it as far as he trusted and sat down on a large rock, his feet resting on the succulents that grew there.

Even at low tide, the only way he could reach that sphere was with a boat. Well, he could swim that distance, but reaching it wet might not be a good idea. From this close, he could hear it, the humming of it like the purring of a large housecat. He sniffed the air, still catching the blue and green of ocean smells, but a faint scent of ozone floated there was well, as if lightning had just struck. Closer, he could see more colors in the wheels, browns and oranges. More complexity.

I could watch this thing all day.

Gabriel knocked on the door again. He had hoped to convince the Lady to go out to see the strange spot in the water near the cape, or at least to send Gaspar. "Perhaps she's gone."

"I can sense someone inside." Nadezhda had come with him to the hotel to add her voice to his.

Anjos had to admit that he simply didn't want to talk to the Lady alone. Not after their last encounter when she'd invaded his rooms to lecture him and make odd suggestions. His eyes flicked to Nadezhda's veil-draped form. Nothing about her current demeanor hinted that anything between them had changed. Her voice was as cool as ever, no intonations of truth or falsity behind her words.

Her life hadn't taken long to die away after their earlier... *encounter*. For a time, she'd been the human Nadezhda, the one he was beginning to care for. She'd spoken with him, touched his lips with gentle fingers, and even laughed once. That had been a beautiful moment, to see her laugh. But it hadn't lasted.

He had no idea how she felt about that fading of her life, but she was aware of it, else she would never have agreed to lie with him that morning. No matter her dislike for the men in her past, she had decided to trust him, to make herself—that younger self—vulnerable to him.

But she can't feel anything now.

"There might be two people," she added.

Gabriel weighed her odd answer. "You're not certain?"

"No."

Deciding to err on the side of recklessness, Gabriel turned the latch and pushed the door inward. No sound came from within. Motioning Nadezhda back, he stepped into the sitting area.

It was a larger room, the baroque style of the décor even more pronounced here than in his room. The furnishings were white gilded with gold, stark against the burgundy velvet draperies. That was why it took a split-second to notice the Lady, her white skirt and blouse making her blend into the couch. "Lady?"

Her dark head swiveled toward him. Tears glistened on her face, something that struck Gabriel as intensely wrong. She wasn't the kind of woman who cried over things. He crossed to where she sat, halfway aware that Nadezhda had followed him into the room. "What's wrong, Lady?"

"I don't know." Her pale eyes flicked up to meet his. Her

voice held a hint of confusion, very unlike his experience with her.

She meant those words. Gabriel dug a handkerchief out of his pocket and handed it to her. After a brief hesitation, she used it to dry her cheeks. "What time is it?"

"Four," he said. "We came looking for you."

The Lady's eyes sought out Nadezhda's form.

She hadn't come far inside, and stood with her head turned toward the wall, not toward them. She reached out one black-gloved hand as if trying to grasp something unseen, but her hand found nothing. Her veiled head turned toward them, then. "I sense that someone was here."

Gabriel turned back to the Lady. "Did someone come to see you?"

"I don't know," she replied again. "How can it be four already?"

Gabriel tried to figure out that strange query as Nadezhda joined him by the couch. A fresh shudder chased along his spine. *So, I'm not inured to that instinctive reaction, even if I did lie with her.* He felt the sudden craving for a cigarette.

"What time do you think it is?" Nadezhda asked.

"I rang for coffee just after luncheon," the Lady answered, gesturing toward the table where the coffee service sat. "I don't remember anyone bringing it."

Gabriel touched the side of the little coffee pot. It was stone cold. "You don't remember?"

The Lady brushed her hands down her skirt and then rose. She handed the handkerchief back to Gabriel, sent a quick glance flying between him and Nadezhda, and then put her nose in the air. "Well," she said in a brisk voice, "I seem to have lost track of the time. A good few hours of it. That is *not* normal for me."

Gabriel surveyed the room, looking for any hint that someone else had been here. Someone had to have delivered the coffee tray, at the very least. He laid a bare hand on the various cushions, checking for warmth. The armchair felt slightly warmer than the others, but not enough for him to be sure someone had sat there.

The Lady pulled up the cushion where she'd been sitting. "Damnation, my pistol is gone."

He resisted the urge to ask her to amend her language. "Are you sure?"

Her head tilted, her pale eyes vexed. "That's why I'm looking, Inspector. That pistol was one of a kind. Titanium, specially made for my father in Switzerland."

Titanium as opposed to steel. How odd. He helped her remove all the cushions from the couch, anyway, then crouched down to peer under the furniture. That position set off a fit of coughing, and he held his handkerchief over his face while he waited for the moment to pass. After a moment, he had it under control, and by then she had uprooted every pillow from each seat.

"Damn!" The Lady stamped her foot, but stopped, mid-rant. "Who closed the door?"

Gabriel followed the direction of her pointing finger. The door *was* closed, even though none of them were near it. Nadezhda stood nearer the windows now. She could not have crossed the mostly white room to the door without him noticing, even if he had been coughing. He wiped his mouth and shoved the handkerchief back in a pocket.

"I was watching it," Nadezhda offered. "It closed on its own."

Chapter 27

SUNDAY, 3 NOVEMBER 1901
LISBOA, SOUTHERN PORTUGAL

Adela shooed Nadezhda and Anjos out of her hotel room as soon as she could. Then she sat back down on her couch and covered her face with her shaking hands.

I lost hours this time.

Something had happened, and she'd lost at least two hours of her life. Perhaps three. It had happened before, her coming to herself with no idea what had happened in the past short while. If she was more concerned, she would have tracked it in a journal, but there was no need. Even if she didn't know what had happened during those intervals, she recalled the occurrences themselves.

She had always suspected that *something* happened. She was not a forgetful person. She wasn't prone to lapses in memory. In those instances, she didn't doubt herself.

But this was the first time anything had ever gone missing. Or shown up. The appearance of the coffee tray combined with the disappearance of the gun offered itself as *evidence*. Adding to the tally, Nadezhda's belief that someone else had been there told her that the instances of memory loss were *not* some activity of her mind. It was being done to her.

If Nadezhda and Anjos hadn't arrived, would the coffee tray have been removed, taking away much of the evidence? Would the gun have been left behind?

Would it have been like all the other times? Merely a gap in time with nothing to prove her mental assertion that she wasn't losing her mind.

Adela dropped her hands, shook her head to clear it, and rose.

She had done nothing to help herself this time, either. After the first time, she had planned to leave some manner of message for herself to explain it, but clearly, she hadn't done so. No, the gun and the coffee tray hadn't been that message. Those had been someone else's mistake—the person who was making her forget.

It *was* a person. A person who stole her father's special gun. A person who could leave the room unseen by Anjos... and only suspected by Nadezhda, who could *smell* the life force she wanted to consume.

The only other person she knew who could cause others not to see him was her nephew, the son of her much older half-sister. Raimundo had inherited that talent from his mother and had learned young to simply make himself disappear. It had stood him in good stead, giving him an avenue to escape from the palace in which his brother held him prisoner. It had given him a measure of freedom and a way to familiarize himself with the city he would one day rule.

Adela had learned of her own ability accidentally, when she'd wished to avoid her instructors as a child. She would make them pass her by, as if she was invisible. She was moderately sure Raimundo had discovered his talent the same way.

She crossed to the window, tugged the heavy draperies aside, and gazed out at the people strolling along the street. Under the early evening light, men walked past in search of dinner, ladies in their finest frocks on their arms. Innocent people passing the hotel, all unaware that someone could be moving among them unseen.

Not her, not Raimundo, and not her long-dead sister, who'd died at Raimundo's birth.

No, my father is out there somewhere.

When Miguel reached the hotel, it was to find Adela packing her bags. She had apparently dumped everything onto their bed and was folding it there, too impatient to wait for one of the hotel's maids to come do it for her.

"Are we moving to another hotel?" he asked as he stood in the doorway to the bedroom.

The face she turned to him seemed strained, her pale eyes reddened. "Yes, we can go back to my house. It's safe now."

Miguel caught the smell of tears from across the room, the taste of them gray in his mouth. She'd been crying. "What happened, Adela?"

She shook her head and glanced up from the dress she was setting into her trunk. "What did you find in Sintra?"

"I didn't go there," Miguel admitted. "I recalled that Anjos wanted me to travel to the cape to look at an island there."

Her shoulders slumped. "Ah, yes, he told me of that earlier."

Miguel glanced back to survey the sitting room and caught a faint hint of the glow that told him Anjos had been in this room recently, as well as the accompanying air of deadness that spoke of Miss Vladimirova. But he had the sense of another person in the air as well, a glittering presence that tasted of magic and ozone. "Who was here?"

Adela paused, mid-motion. Then she deliberately set the hair brush she held into the trunk. She perched on the edge of the bed. "Damnation. I forgot you would... know."

He waited for a moment, thinking she would find a way to say it. He'd had plenty of time in the carriage to consider who could have created that sphere out in the water. Over and over, he'd been drawn back to a circumstance in her past she had never actually explained to him. When she gazed at him helplessly, he asked, "Adela, what happened to your father?"

"He disappeared," she said, hands held wide.

"When?"

"When I was thirteen," she said.

"Tell me about it," he said. "Were you at home when you found out? At school? Who told you?"

Her jaw clenched. She shook her head, still not looking at him. "He disappeared."

"Who told you that?"

Her pale eyes lifted to meet his. "He disappeared."

Miguel nearly spoke her name sharply, intending to ask again, and then realized he would be using her true name to force her to speak... something he had promised not to do. He crossed to her side, sat next to her, and took her hand in his own. "Can you say anything else?"

She shook her head.

She's under a compulsion. If whoever had done this was human, it would be witchcraft and illegal. But he suspected a different culprit. "Have you ever looked for him?"

"No," she said softly.

"Did you never think to try?"

"He disappeared," she snapped, as if that made everything obvious.

And it does. He sighed, wishing they had endless time to piece this together. But he suspected they didn't, not as fast as the deaths were piling up. "The island Anjos talked about is a little off the coast, surrounded by moving water. There is a... prison atop it. Not a physical building, but a creation of magic. I can see it."

Adela licked her lips. "A prison?"

"I think so, or perhaps just a single cell. The magic involved isn't human. It's far too complex, and... I can't imagine what it's designed to hold other than someone not human. Someone who's supposed to be impeded by moving water. The little island is close enough to access when needed, but supposedly far enough to keep the prisoner from coming ashore."

She took another breath. "Anjos said something about Mata going there regularly."

"That may be the case," Miguel said. "I suspect he's the tie between that prison cell and some jailer on the mainland."

Adela looked away from him, the glittering of her skin faded. She was not a woman who liked displays of emotion, and this day had evidently drained her.

"We've started this problem in the wrong spot," he said. "Haven't we?"

She let out a vexed huff of air. "I think we may have."

Interesting that she could say *that*, but not directly speak about her father's absence. No doubt that was part of the way the compulsion was worded. Fairies were governed by *exact wording* of bargains, if he recalled correctly, rather than the spirit or intent of them. "We were starting with Donato Mata's murder of Ferreira, but we need to think further back, to the theft of the items from your father's library and workshop. Or even further back than that, to your father's actual disappearance."

Her fingers balled into a fist, her face turning away.

"Please look at me," he said.

She met his eyes. "I am looking at you."

"Your father made magical devices, is that correct?"

Her shoulders loosened. "Yes, he did. They were designed to work without actual witchcraft, usually just a touch of blood or a hint of talent."

So... she could talk about her father's work. "And did he create them for anyone in particular?"

She shook her head quickly. "No, he merely liked trying out different things. It was curiosity. He kept up with a number of technical journals and thought up ways to apply the same scientific principles to magic. He loved studying batteries and... electricity."

Miguel recalled the electrical hum of the magical telegraph system that had joined the supposed conspirators, not unlike what he'd heard out at the island. "When I talked about that communication system with the books, did you wonder whether it was your father's creation?"

"My father disappeared," she said softly.

Miguel let go of her hand and rose. Some manner of bargain or adjuration prevented her from even thinking of it... or speaking of it, at the very least. But she hadn't denied it, either. "Adela, is it possible that your father..."

No, that won't work. He closed his eyes, catching the smell of her, and lights sparkled behind his eyelids. *How do we talk about something she can't talk about?*

"Let me tell you a story," she said then. "Once upon a time, there was a princess who thought her father was the smartest man alive."

"A princess?" he repeated, gazing down at her inky black hair.

She peered at him from under a lowered brow. "It's always a princess in stories."

He leaned back against the bedroom wall. "So what happens to our princess and her clever father?"

"Someone locks him away," she said. "And tells him that if he tries to escape, they'll hurt the princess."

There was logic to that idea; that if her father had been imprisoned somehow, he had cooperated out of concern for her. No way to know without asking *him*... or the man who'd imprisoned him. "And then?"

"And she grows up, never knowing where her father went. Until one day she loses an hour. And then it happens again and again, and she realizes the only person who can make her forget those hours is her missing father."

Forget? "Did the princess' father make her forget where he went in the first place?"

Adela licked her lips. "I think for the purposes of the story, we have to assume so. I can't imagine who else might do that to her."

"If that father ever escaped his prison," Miguel asked, "would he have reason to kill some of those involved in his imprisonment. Do you think that..." He caught himself before he said the word *your*. "Would this princess' father be the sort who would seek that sort of revenge?"

Adela didn't hesitate. "The princess had a very bloody-minded father."

Gabriel stood on the street outside the gates of the reservoir, smoking a cigarette. Night had fallen over Lisboa, a night where his world had become considerably stranger than it had been that morning. And that was shocking. Not only had he taken a lover, one who was alive and dead in turns, but his understanding of the possibilities of humanity had grown as well.

Or not humanity. That wasn't the correct term—fairy. *I was aware of demons, so a fairy shouldn't surprise me.*

The fact that a fairy had been able to procreate with a human made no sense, but horses and donkeys begat mules. He would have to resist the urge to call the Lady mulish. That thought made his mouth twist with an ungentlemanly whisper of humor. More like something Gaspar would say.

As if summoned by that thought, Gaspar strode out of the darkness between streetlights and mounted the stone steps of the reservoir. He came to where Gabriel stood. His eyes flicked toward Gabriel's cigarette.

"You want one?" Gabriel asked.

Gaspar laughed softly. "Still no."

For a moment they stood silent, the wind in the trees and the flow of water in the aqueduct the only sounds. Then Gabriel asked, "What does she say now?"

Evidently the Lady was able to work around some fairy compulsion by talking in abstracts, but that didn't help relay exactly whatever it was that had passed between herself and her father, if that man was indeed the one who'd been in that room with them. Nadezhda claimed it must be so, that the unseen presence in that room had, like the Lady, tasted not quite human.

It should worry me that Nadezhda can taste *another's life force.*

"She wants to go out there," Gaspar finally answered. "See this prison, first thing in the morning. The tide should be out then, she reckons."

More likely the Lady had sent her butler Santana running off to find the most recent tide charts to do the reckoning for her. Of course, Gabriel suspected that whether the tide was out or not, Nadezhda could get them to that island. But she hadn't told the Lady of her secret talent, so Gabriel wouldn't either. "Ready at six?"

"No Mass?" Gaspar asked.

Gabriel thought his understanding of Gaspar had improved, even if he couldn't hear any truth or falsehood behind Gaspar's words. The way he'd said it, Gaspar didn't mean that query as an insult. He was simply asking about his plans. "No. I'll be there."

Gaspar nodded his head and began the short trek back to the Lady's house, alternately visible under the streetlights and not. Gabriel turned to toss away the butt of his cigarette, but then stubbed it out on the reservoir's stone wall. He made his way inside and closed the outer door behind him.

Nadezhda Vladimirova sat on the wooden platform out in the middle of the reservoir, striped down to her chemise, her knees drawn up with her arms about them. She looked small and frightened. She was breathing, a faint ragged sound.

He knelt by her side. "Nadezhda?"

"I cannot hold onto it much longer," she whispered, her eyes flicking up to meet his. "I am trying, but..."

There was a hint of panic behind those words. She'd been waiting for him to return, hanging onto that thread of life she stole from the miniscule creatures in the reservoir. And knowing what she needed, Gabriel sat at her side, drew her closer, and kissed her.

Chapter 28

MONDAY, 4 NOVEMBER 1901
CABO DA ROCA, SOUTHERN PORTUGAL

The boat was tiny, suited to tooling around the coastline, but all four of them fit on the benches. Miguel sat on the aft bench, while Miss Vladimirova had the fore one. He felt better with her at that distance. Adela and Anjos shared the middle bench—a little cramped, no doubt—but Anjos wouldn't be able to row for long, so Miguel had taken that chore himself.

As he rowed closer to the small island, Miguel watched the sphere of interconnected circles move in their paths, a faint metallic smell surrounding them all now. He could almost taste the electricity in the air. The sphere was just as beautiful as it had been the afternoon before, many-colored circles moving together like gears, the patterns repeating and shrinking with every iteration until they were too small to see. He would have to resist the urge to stare or the boat would end up aground. "You can't see anything?"

"Again, no," Adela snapped, glancing at him over her shoulder.

Yet he could see it quite plainly, this spherical, moving prison. Miss Vladimirova detected oddness in the flow of the water about the little island, she'd claimed, probably related to her being a water spirit. Anjos saw it as a *lie*. Save for Adela, they could all *see* something was wrong here. She likely thought it unfair this was hidden from her.

He rowed until they reached the island's rocky sides. This close, the sphere hung huge above them, the hum now converted to the thumping sound of a train running over smooth-laid track. If Miguel glanced up, he could still see the movement, but it also seemed alarmingly ready to fall on him, so he kept his eyes on the familiar water and rock. This close to it, the taste of ozone in his mouth was overwhelming.

Miss Vladimirova extended one black-gloved hand into the surf, and the waves around them stilled. A shiver ran down Miguel's spine at that casual display of power. Evidently a rusalka had more control of water than he'd understood.

"There's an opening on the far side," Miss Vladimirova said in her odd, flat voice.

They'd approached the island from the south. Miguel lowered the oars to row around to the northern side of the island, but the boat moved on its own, as if someone was hauling on the painter to draw the boat into dock. The boat slipped around the west side of the island on the placid waters, and a moment later they stared at a cleft in the rock that made up the small island.

"Let me look," Miss Vladimirova said, and tumbled over the side of the boat fully clothed.

Miguel couldn't help his instinctive lunge to save her but sat back when Adela cast him a dry glance.

"She's fine," Adela said.

Anjos hadn't moved, so he must be aware that... well, that Miss Vladimirova didn't fear the sea.

Then suddenly, the boat began to sink... no, the water level itself was falling. A wall of water rose a few feet away from the island as the boat lowered down and then came to rest on the rocky sea floor. The sand and stone smelled wet, and

Miguel could taste water all about them now, blue and green and *hungry*, more powerful here than even the sphere above them.

Still draped in her black veils, Miss Vladimirova stepped out of the tall wall of water onto the now-bare stones and sand of the sea floor. She pointed to where the crevice between the rocks widened out, a spot previously under the waves. "We will have to crouch down, but we can get inside there."

Adela rose slowly, hoping the boat wouldn't tip her out. Nadezhda might have banished the water—a demonstration of power Adela hadn't known was possible—but the boat's bottom wasn't flat, so as she rose, it tilted. She laid one hand against the wet rocks to balance herself.

At least she'd worn trousers for this expedition, making it easier to get over the side of the boat and onto the sand in a dignified manner. She tried to listen, as she had back in the storeroom, for any sound that might be a portal, but the prickling of her nerves kept her from focusing. Her stomach churned in the presence of so much water moving about her. She forced that reaction down. Half *human*, she reminded herself. *I can do this.*

Miguel took hold of her arm to steady her, and once she was squarely on her feet, he let her go and crouched down to pass through the crevice. Anjos had exited the boat first and was already gone, leaving her last to enter the tight space.

It opened out, though, into a small cay in the island's center that would normally be full of water, almost like a clearing in the forest. Rocks rose around them on all sides, and here—with the water held at bay—Adela could sense something similar to what she'd felt in the storeroom, reminding her of the vibrations of a Tesla coil. A portal or doorway?

Anjos surveyed the rocks about them with a frustrated twist to his lips. Adela had no idea how Nadezhda was reacting under her veils, but Miguel gazed upward, as if the unseen thing above him called his name. "There are stairs," he said, indicating something to the left of them.

She let out a vexed breath. *I still can't see it.*

Miguel drew his gun and stepped upward onto nothingness. "I'll call down if there's trouble."

Adela wanted him to stop, but he was the most logical choice to go first. If there was a magical trap, it wouldn't affect him. A physical trap was another matter. She started that direction only to be held back by Nadezhda. "I'll go."

Adela grabbed her sleeve. "And what happens if you're startled and you lose control of the water out here? Anjos and I will drown."

For a moment, Nadezhda didn't move, but then she stepped aside, allowing for the superior logic of that. Adela went instead, putting her foot about where she'd seen Miguel set his. There *was* something there. By now she could see only the bottom of one of Miguel's legs, so she hurried, climbing a stairwell she couldn't see up into nothingness.

Everything around her faded into whiteness as the passage took her upward, her feet not touching anything any longer. Her teeth ached as they did near church bells, but one step farther and the light abruptly failed. She emerged into a pitch-black chamber, only able to discern that because the steps had ended. She felt a floor beneath her shoes. An echo suggested a large room. The smell of old papers and books and moldering wood surrounded her.

How can it be dark here when it's daylight outside?

A hand out of the darkness—Miguel—drew her gently away from the unseen stairs. "Can you make light?"

That was an aspect of her ability to manipulate shadows and light that she rarely bothered with because it was feeble at the best of times. Given the darkness, though, she focused her energy into sending the shadows away, just enough to let them see where they were.

Light blazed into the place, hanging above them like a small sun. The huge room in which they stood had shelves lining the walls, save for one which sprouted a set of worktables, some flat, some tilted, like a drafter's. Papers lay scattered about those, and small machines, taken apart. One of the shelves held a few books, but the rest were empty.

Adela crossed to the where the books lay and began reading the titles. "I know these books."

"Don't touch anything," Miguel said sharply.

Adela glanced back at him and saw Anjos had come up the stairs to join them. Alone. "Where is Nadezhda?"

"She couldn't enter the stairwell," Anjos said. "It... rejected her. That's how she said it." He stood still for a moment, apparently catching his breath after that short climb. Then he said, "I can breathe."

Adela gazed at him, wondering at the strange sound in his voice. "What do you mean?"

He held one hand to his sternum and took another deep breath. "I am not having trouble breathing."

"Do not touch anything," Miguel repeated, more loudly.

Adela stepped back from the almost-empty bookshelf. There were only five books there, ones that had been stolen from her father's library long ago. They were volumes of witchcraft, plain and simple, ones her father had never bothered much with. "What's wrong?"

"Look up at your light," he said.

Adela glanced up and saw that the light she'd created now covered most of the room's ceiling, a false blue summer sky stretching endlessly up above them. There should be clouds, she noted... and immediately they appeared, light and fluffy shapes scudding across the apex of that sky. Adela held her breath. *I did that. I can make real magic here.*

"I don't have that sort of power," she said. "I shouldn't be able to control light like that." Shadows, yes, but not light.

"No," Miguel said softly. "Not in the human world, at least. But that's not where we are."

Gabriel breathed, his lungs filling like they hadn't in years. Not like when his Tia had healed him, nor when Nadezhda had. This felt as if he'd never been sick at all. "Where exactly are we?"

"I think we're somehow in the fairy realm," Gaspar said, hesitation in his voice.

That was oddly phrased for Gaspar, who rarely qualified

anything. Gabriel licked his suddenly-dry lips. "You're not sure?"

Gaspar glanced back at him. "My gift is... not working."

Gabriel stared at the other man as Gaspar continued to survey the room, the sky-ceiling, the floors, and then himself and the Lady.

"This is..." Gaspar began. "It's so... quiet. My God, this is how you all live, all the time, isn't it?" He closed his eyes, a rare smile lighting his face. "There's nothing there."

I can breathe, his gift is gone, and the Lady has more power than before. "Do you think God is tempting us?"

"No," Gaspar said, eyes snapping open. "This is the fairy realm, not God's hand. I don't know much about this realm, but I know there are a thousand ways to trick you into staying here, so don't touch anything."

There was a door on the far side of the room—an actual wooden door with a brass latch—and Gabriel could only wonder where it led. Perhaps there was a whole world out there, one where he didn't have to feel his body dying all the time. He could...

He laughed softly. It didn't matter what was out there, beyond that door. He had promised Nadezhda he would come back, and he didn't break his word. Even if it meant going back toward his death. "What are we looking for here?"

Gaspar shook himself. The Lady had moved from the near-empty bookshelves to the worktables and stood peering down at one of haphazard piles of papers. "This is my father's hand," she said. "These are his notes."

"What was he doing?" Gaspar asked, going to join her.

"It looks like mostly the same thing as before," she said bending closer to peer at the papers on the desk. "Devices to access magical power." Not looking away from the papers, she pointed to small golden device that sat atop a wooden box one corner of the table. "That's what he was working on here, I think. Oh... that's clever."

"What is?" Gaspar asked, leaning closer.

"Together they're a compass," she said, "but instead of pointing to the north pole, the small one points to the box."

"In case we're separated?"

"Well, yes," she said. "Or you could sneak the box into someone's carriage and you would know where that person went. They just require a few drops of blood to make the pairing work."

Gaspar leaned back. "Bloodthirsty little things."

She went around him to peruse what lay on the next table, one of the tilted ones, so it held only papers. "Now this is something totally different."

Her voice sounded troubled enough to prompt Gabriel to join them in staring that the cluttered papers on that table. "What are we looking at?"

"This is an..." She licked her lips. "An incredibly complex spell. I need time to study this."

"We can't stay here too long," Gaspar said. "Time may be different here."

Despite Gaspar's warnings, she started shuffling through the loose papers, assembling them into a pile to take with her. "We need to get all of this back to my office." She

THE TRUTH UNDISCOVERED

pointed toward the few books on one of the shelves. "Those, too."

After a flash of a frown, Gaspar went to fetch the books in question. He located a leather satchel at the side of a desk and began putting her purloined goods inside. "We didn't come here to rob the place."

"We came to find out what was happening here. To learn if my father was here. Clearly, he's not." She tapped the sheaf of papers against the table to straighten them. "Anjos, can you grab those devices?"

She'd pointed with the tip of her nose at the first table. Anjos pocketed the smaller device and picked up the wooden box. The size of a football, the contents of the box ticked and whirred alarmingly as he moved. "Is this going to explode?"

"No," she said. "It's not active."

"So where *is* your father?" Gabriel asked her.

"He was definitely here, but now? I have no idea." She turned her back on the worktable and squinted at the vast room as if trying to see something that wasn't there. "Papa, where are you?"

A bright light flared behind Gabriel. He turned in time to see a tall man step out of that light.

Chapter 29

MONDAY, 4 NOVEMBER 1901
ILHA DA FADA, SOUTHERN PORTUGAL

The whirring box in his hands, Gabriel wondered if it might not be wise to jump back down the invisible stairwell. Surely that would be safer than waiting to see what this man wanted.

The tall man stood before the ring of light, his silhouette slowly resolving as that faded. Like the Lady, he had black hair and pale eyes, along with a marked widow's peak. He wore a well-tailored suit and would be considered handsome if that otherworldly air that he carried were not so... otherworldly.

The man was not human, Gabriel was sure of that. *Her father.*

His pistol was still in its holster, but he couldn't reach it without dropping the box, so he turned to place that on the table and free his hands. Gaspar set the satchel he held on the floor.

"Papa?" the Lady said. "What *are* you doing here?"

"Why are you in my prison, girl? I told you to stay away."

Gabriel turned back in time to see her throw her hands up in frustration.

"But you made me forget," she said. "Why tell me and then make me forget?"

The tall man came closer, and Gaspar stepped in front of the Lady. "He's not ready for you to act," Gaspar inserted, eyes fixed on the newcomer. "Are you?"

"Do you know how long I have wanted to kill you?" the man asked in return. "And I dare not, for her sake."

"What are you talking about?" the Lady asked. "Papa, what do you mean?"

The man's eyes stayed on Gaspar. "Do you remember it, de la Cour? That day you exposed us to the Jesuits? That day my freedom ended, and my child's?"

Gabriel reached inside his jacket to set one hand on his pistol. If there had been any question after seeing the man's pale eyes, there was none now regarding this being the Lady's father. He'd referred to Gaspar as *de la Cour*, a sign he'd known Gaspar in his previous life.

"I don't know what you're talking about," Gaspar answered flatly.

Gabriel wished he had some way of knowing who was telling the truth here, but he was behind Gaspar and couldn't see his face. And he couldn't watch that other man's face too long without discomfort.

The man let out a bark of laughter. "You were dead drunk, you fool. You pointed at her and asked that prick DuBois how she could be half-fairy."

The Lady shook her head. "What are you talking about, Papa?"

"He betrayed you to the Jesuits, and how could they not guess then about me? They held me in iron chains until I gave them my parole. Not long, since they had you. Do you want to remember that time?"

From behind, it was hard to judge the Lady's reaction, but she laid one trembling hand on Gaspar's shoulder. "Yes," she said softly, "tell me."

Adela watched her father, baffled. Why must he make everything so difficult? Why could he not have told her everything the day before? Why not simply enlist their aid? Why repeatedly find her, and then make her forget?

"I release you from your word, then," he said. "Remember..."

Adela closed her eyes, almost dizzy with the sudden filling of her mind, the sense that everything she'd ever missed in her life had come back to her.

"I was raised in Paris," she whispered. How could she not have recalled that? When she'd returned to Paris in her twenties, so much of the city had been oddly familiar.

She'd been thinking it was memories of a past life that brought her to that house in Paris, but she'd gone there *as a child*. She'd stood outside on the street, watching for something, mesmerized—at five years old, then six, day after day. Her father had come after her, patiently, every time.

And I never knew why I wanted into that house. I banged on the door with my fist, and he didn't answer.

Until that day that Etienne de la Cour had come out on the step and peered at her with drunken intensity. He'd said something to the shadowy half-seen man who waited behind him, but her father dragged her away before she could reach that half of herself she never found again. She recalled crying, brokenhearted, as her father packed that night, desperately, only the books he loved best, his silver and bronze tools, his diamonds…

But it was too late. The priests came, many of them crowding into their elegant flat. Adela ran to hide as her father bid her, confused by this sudden intrusion into their quiet lives. One of the priests grabbed her up. He said calming things, but she screamed over and over again—part fear, part fury. Until they held a funny-smelling handkerchief over her mouth.

She had been used to force her father's compliance.

Adela licked her lips. She had never truly known whether her father loved her. He was a peculiar, capricious creature, by turns concerned and dismissive, charming and taciturn. He'd encouraged her curiosity but save for where it concerned that mysterious house she wanted into so badly. He had disappeared without a word to her.

I never should have doubted. He gave up his freedom for me.

"That's why you killed DuBois," she said. "I didn't understand why *him*, because he wasn't part of the pattern."

"Mata loved to tell me all about his doings, thinking that I could never leave this room. Mata was leaving the next day on a steamer to Cabo Verde to silence DuBois, taking along a questionable archivist-priest to collect the man's papers. Papers concerning the Meter… *and you.*" Her father let her consider that for a second. "I got there first. DuBois knew exactly why I'd come. Honestly, I was surprised you'd let him live, once you knew."

That explained why her father had set DuBois' house alight—to destroy any records the man had concerning her before the Jesuit brotherhood could reclaim them. Records she now knew went back to when she'd been six.

She closed her eyes, recalling the times when she'd walked the streets of Paris at twenty-five, so certain she'd seen those cafes and bridges before. The cathedral and churches she'd never entered, shivering at the sound of the church bells. Queasy when she crossed a bridge over the Seine. She hadn't *known* then what she was. When the Jesuits took custody of her she'd forgotten, all of that, protection for her... and for them.

She laid one hand to her stomach, the unfamiliar waistband of the trousers she wore, and forced herself to breathe evenly. Her father had made her forget her early life because it was too easy for a child of six to slip up and admit what she was. He had made her forget her lost Paris, and what she was. That was his special Gift, to tinker with the memories of others. The Jesuits had believed him able to manipulate light and shadow. They hadn't understood that about him... and to protect himself *and* her, he'd made her forget, too.

And then they were at Campolide and they were Portuguese again and she never remembered any different tale for herself. Her father bought the house in Lisboa, near the reservoir, with enough moving water to keep out others of his kind. Where he'd hidden what he was, even from her, to protect her. And the Jesuits had let her go her own way, under the tutelage of her trustees and godfather... and under Father Serafim's watchful eyes.

The threat was forever there. As long as she lived, she would be a weapon to be used against her father, all thanks to a few words spilled between de la Cour and DuBois. She met Miguel's eyes.

"I recall that now," he said to her softly. "That was the night Etienne de la Cour shot himself."

She took his hand in hers, tacit forgiveness. They could talk about this later. DuBois was the one who'd sold her father into a life of captivity, and her as well, in a way. And the man would have done it solely to keep the Meter away from her as long as possible. No, to keep *her* away from Miguel.

"Why the others?" Miguel asked. "What's worth killing over? Or dying to hide?"

"That," her father said, "I still don't know."

Miguel scowled at the man, who looked like no more than a man to him. His senses told him nothing special about this creature. No stray smell, no special glittering, no ties of power and magic. He looked like a man—a frightening man, given—but his visage didn't waver under Miguel's continued regard.

"Does he look human?" he whispered to Adela. "To you, I mean?"

She cast a sharp glance his way. "It's a seeming. He's making himself look human."

And that meant—along with everything else here—her father's glamour affected *him*. Not much differently than it affected Anjos, he would guess. He glanced up at Adela's fake sky and couldn't see through it to the rafters that had been there when they arrived.

I am susceptible to magic here. Did her father know that? Did he realize that human witches had no power here? *Of course he knows.*

That meant he was only still alive because her father forbore to kill him. Given how much stronger Adela's skills were in this realm, her father must be nearly all powerful. A prickling went down Miguel's spine, the flare of excitement of discovering something *new.*

"Father Serafim and Father Inacio took strychnine," her father said, "to avoid telling me anything. It was self-sacrifice, rather than suicide, I suppose, so they are within their rules. And even though that sycophantic weasel Tomar was involved in the plot, he gave me no other names, mostly because the only one he knew was Mata."

"And you have no idea what this plot is?" Miguel asked.

"None, save that it involves these new *soi-disant* Templars. Even Mata doesn't know who's pulling his strings," the man answered. "He does as he's told, by whoever pays him the most."

"Father put the book with the journal in my house," Adela said softly, "after Mata confessed to him that he had it."

Miguel recalled that the journal of Alessio Ferreira had been found secreted inside the damaged copy of The Order of the Knights of Christ, the book on the Templars that had been used by the conspirators to communicate. "Why tear out the pages of that copy of the Templar book, though?" Miguel asked her.

"To be sure that no one in the household picked it up and read it, triggering the protections on it," her father answered instead. "I would not wish Santana or some overzealous housemaid to suffer. I created that system to allow humans to communicate over distances, but they took it and turned it to their own purposes. That's what concerns me now. I do not know where all my work has gone."

Miguel cast a quick glance at Adela, who nodded. He saw then that Anjos stood ready, one hand near his holstered pistol. "Your work?"

"His devices and plans," Adela answered. "The ones stolen by Mata from the Jesuits, and from his workspace here."

"Unfortunately, Mata doesn't know, either," her father added. "Whoever pulls his strings is very careful about hiding his identity, and Mata's not the brightest star in the sky to begin with."

"But what is this person trying to achieve?" Miguel asked, pressing again.

"Whatever it is," the man said, "it's a huge scheme. Serafim and Inacio were here to watch my daughter and I both, Tomar was to access books in Carvalho Monteiro's library, Mata is to make the crimes, but many more of the conspirators are up north."

"Are you chained here," Miguel asked. "Or can you leave?"

"I can leave for short periods—a day at most—but I am pulled back here every time," the man said. "It's only a loophole."

"Gaspar," Anjos inserted, "there's water."

Miguel glanced back at Anjos and saw for the first time that water stood in the center of the floor, behind where the four of them stood, a circle that was quickly growing. Miguel snatched up the satchel that held the books and papers Adela had collected and settled it with the strap across his chest. He put one hand to Adela's elbow. "Is she doing this?"

Adela looked uncharacteristically flustered. "If she is, I don't know how. Father?"

The man laughed softly. "Well, that's very interesting. I knew they were scared of that woman, but I had no idea why... until now."

Water had begun to burble out of the center of the wooden floor, as if there was a fountain there, barely held back by the wood. And then the wood burst inward, water spraying up about them as planks flew toward the sky-ceiling. They instinctively cringed back but were too late to keep sea water from splattering them all.

"What are you doing?" Adela demanded of the water, stepping behind Miguel again. "You're letting it in!"

A form resolved out of the water—Nadezhda Vladimirova standing on the water itself, her black garb soaked and hanging about her. A veil still covered her face, clinging to her features. "I have waited," she said, her voice seeming garbled. "You must return."

"How long?" Anjos asked her. "How long have we been here?"

Miss Vladimirova eerily spun atop the burbling stack of water to face him. "You have been gone for a month."

Adela's father laughed. "Child, you have made your pet dragon angry."

Chapter 30

MONDAY, 4 NOVEMBER 1901
ILHA DA FADA, SOUTHERN PORTUGAL

"This isn't my fault," Adela snapped. "How can we have been here a month?"

Her father seemed unconcerned by the water rising about them, now up to mid-calf, but *she* was. Her skin crawled with the feel of it, her stomach churning. "Time is different here, in this place."

She took a careful breath, blowing it out her nose. The smell of sea water was filling her head now, and her trousers were soaking it up. It was cold, but not freezing. "What is this place, then?"

"You must release them," Nadezhda interrupted.

Her father just shook his head. "I cannot."

"You must," she repeated.

Adela stepped in. "What do you mean you can't release us?"

Her father faced her, his expression sorrowful. "This is a *prison*, child. That's why you weren't supposed to come here. When I built it, I left a loophole so I could get in and out through the other side, but that won't work for anyone else. Not even you."

The other side—then he sneaks off via the fairy world. That wouldn't work for the others because they were human. But if she was half fairy…

"Didn't Mata come here?" Anjos asked. "Regularly, I was told."

"The Jesuits sent him here to check on me," her father said, "to steal more of my work. But he has a key. You don't."

Another reason to catch that man.

"We're trapped here?" Miguel asked.

"Nadezhda, you must stop the flooding," Adela told her. The moving water was making her feel ill.

And it was getting darker. Adela glanced up and saw that the bright sky she'd created had dimmed, storm clouds building there now instead. *What exactly did I do?* "Father, what is this prison made of? Are we... in the fairy world?"

"You should have asked that before you came here. This is neither here nor there. It's a doorway, blown up like a balloon to hold me trapped between."

"But you made this?"

"Yes," he said.

She crossed her arms over her chest, trying to hold in her fear of the water. "Then there must be some way to break us out."

"If I break this place, a door between will be left standing open."

Adela glanced down at the water now swirling around her thighs. Her teeth started to chatter. "Nadezhda, I don't know how to swim."

"I will stop you from doing this," her father said, addressing Nadezhda. "They can remain safely here."

In this prison? Was her father insane? Adela opened her mouth to protest.

"What is she going to do?" Miguel asked.

"Destroy the prison," Anjos said from behind them. He jumped toward the table and grabbed up the wooden box, just before a wave of water swept him off his feet.

Miguel wrapped one arm around her and dragged her against him. Then Adela was flowing away on a wave of moving water that made her stomach roll and the world turn black.

Miguel held to Adela, hoping he could keep their heads above water. He could swim, even if she couldn't. The current swept them up, higher and higher toward that ceiling that was a false sky, into the storm clouds arisen from Adela's fear.

The darkening world around them was filled with the roar of water. The smell of the ocean overlaid everything now.

"Don't fight her," he yelled into Adela's ear, trying to still her struggling. "She's holding us up."

He managed to get his other arm wrapped about her waist, the satchel he'd been collecting papers in now squashed between them. Adela stilled, though, lying half atop his chest now in the water, her eyes squeezed tightly shut. Miguel kept his eyes open, thinking one of them should

The swirling movement of the water took on a dizzying spiral shape, not matching the visual contours of either that wooden ceiling or the false sky, warring in his senses with what his eyes saw. At times they passed through the wood of the roof, into the storm clouds, then back again into the room.

Miss Vladimirova was filling the sphere with water. Was

this simple physics rather than magic?

If the pressure inside is greater than outside, it should...

The swirling movement continued, and then a sound roared through Miguel's senses, a horrific high-pitched squeal that his mind recognized as the tearing of metal. His eyes turned upward as light spangled through widening cracks in the world.

Miguel hung on to Adela tighter. "Take a deep breath," he ordered her. "And hold it."

He felt her lungs fill as he did the same. And then the world was flying in a chaos of colors, the sounds of seagulls screaming leaving the taste of guano in his mouth, the scream of violated space making his flesh crawl and his ears ring. The scent of ozone filled his nose as the walls spun away in tiny squares, the beautiful patterns and iterations shredded into brown and gold threads of magic floating away like corn silk on the wind. His heart hurt with the loss of that beautiful prison.

We're hundreds of feet in the air... and we're not falling.

He barely had the time to register that thought before they did begin to fall... slowly. It wasn't quite a fall; it was a *lowering.* Careful not to shift Adela, he wrenched his head about and saw the headlands of the Cabo da Roca not far away, the seagulls spinning about them as they dropped toward the stones of the Ilha da Fada, cushioned by a tower of water that bent unnaturally out and over the stone. "We're safe," he said into Adela's ear.

She let out a sobbing breath. "I'm going to be sick."

This much moving water must be horrible for her. They

passed down below the level of the rocky headlands, below the sentinel rocks standing out in the ocean, and down into the ring of stone that made the Ilha da Fada itself.

Something angry buzzed in his mind, something that wanted to eat the world.

Gabriel Anjos waited on the rocky island, and Miguel experienced a jarring sense of unreality when he saw that the man's clothes were completely dry, rippling slightly in the wind. The wooden box sat on the rocks near his feet, and Anjos held his pistol in one hand. With the other, he reached down to help Miguel up.

"Easier if you're standing," Anjos said incongruously.

After shifting a limp, sea-sick Adela to one side, Miguel took the offered hand and Anjos jerked him to his feet. The satchel landed on the stones with a wet squish. The small island did, indeed, have water in its center, calmer than the sea outside.

It was mid-day. Miguel could taste the warmth of the sun, a weak-tea taste for early winter—because Miss Vladimirova was right that time had passed while they were gone. It was December now; he could feel that in his bones, the loss of time. He was hungry, too.

Once he was standing, he could see the source of the buzzing in his mind. It was making his teeth hurt. A glowing circle stood there, its center displaying a field in evening, shown as if through wavy glass—the door between, just as the fairy had claimed. Lightning bugs glowed among that distant field's grasses, far larger than they should be, even through the distortion. And that circle was growing.

As Miguel stood there gazing at that wonder, the water

drained from his clothes, dribbling onto the rocks about him. The leather of the satchel straightened, and its color lightened as it dried.

She's not just a rusalka. Miss Vladimirova's powers were far too strong just to be those of a water spirit, dead or alive. Miss Vladimirova was nowhere in sight, even though he could sense her, taste the dread of her in his mouth. What had Adela's father called her? *Your pet dragon?*

"What have you done?" a black-syrup voice demanded, thick and bitter.

Miguel jerked in that direction, realizing suddenly why Anjos held his pistol in his hand. A creature cloaked in shadows and light waited there. Anger flowed around him as well, red coruscating lights in ribbons flexed about the shell formed of moving strips of shadows.

How can she be half fairy? Etienne de la Cour had asked that question because he hadn't thought it likely his mate would take that form. A cross between this creature and a human woman must be fraught with complexity. Miguel stared, trying to spot anything human at all among all those wisps of shadow.

"It had to be done," the ocean finally answered in a voice as ancient as stone. It rasped along Miguel's senses, gently wearing him away until he would one day be nothing. "I would not let them die merely so you could pursue your vengeance."

"They stole my life away!" the shadows oozed. "They stole my life's work! How dare they use it for their own foolish aims."

"And what of your daughter's life?" the water demanded. "You must close the gate now, or it will consume our world."

THE TRUTH UNDISCOVERED

"You are the one who caused this breach," the shadows answered... and the strips of shadow and light fluttered away on the wind.

Gabriel groaned and holstered his gun. He hadn't even been sure it would fire anyway, soaked in seawater as it had been. He set his hands against his thighs and bent over, the ache in his lungs back now with a vengeance. He coughed for a moment, coving his mouth with his hand. When he drew it away, blood speckled his palm.

It didn't hurt there, but it was *getting worse.*

He straightened, fighting the weariness that dragged at him. "Nadezhda, where did he go?"

The water in the center of the ring of rock answered. "Everywhere, and nowhere."

He glanced up at the circle of light above them. Oddly, it was deep night in the center of it now. "Then how do we close that?"

"He created it, only he can close it," she answered from behind him. Nadezhda stood now on the edge of the rocks, veils fluttering around her.

Gabriel wanted to tear them away to see how the expenditure of all that power had affected her, but not in front of Gaspar. He glanced toward the other man and saw Gaspar helping the Lady to sit up. Her pale eyes fixed on the portal above them.

"Oh, no," she said, then glanced down at her man's trousers

and paused as if surprised to see them dry already. She stood then, surveyed the tableau around her as if taking command once again. But she still held one hand to her stomach. "What happened?"

"Miss Vladimirova destroyed the prison," Gaspar told her.

Her eyes fixed on Nadezhda, and Gabriel had to force himself not to step between them.

"How is that possible?" the Lady demanded. "I thought the prison was a part of faerie, not this earth."

"It was," Gaspar agreed. "But the doorway could let in things of this world... and not let them *out* without a key. Miss Vladimirova merely forced in enough water to overwhelm the doorway."

The Lady licked her lips. "That wasn't a solution."

"I don't know about you," Gabriel inserted, "but I'm in far worse condition now than I was when I went in there."

"Sooner or later you would have been forced to consume something," Nadezhda said in her toneless voice. "And that would have trapped you there forever. There would have been no choice."

The Lady glanced down again at her trousers, then held out the waistband an inch or so. Clearly even she had lost weight in the prison. "Damnation."

"We have to get him back here," Gabriel inserted, "to close that thing." He turned his gaze to take in the others, the four of them trapped on the stones of an angry ocean, some distance from the shore. "How do we do that?"

Chapter 31

ILHA DA FADA, SOUTHERN PORTUGAL

Gabriel covered his face with his hands, ruing the predicament that had forced this. Nadezhda had broken the prison to protect *him*, he had no doubt of that. But in that act, she had left an open doorway that even he could see.

And it was growing larger. He had no idea what would happen when it encompassed the very rocks on which he stood.

Apparently only the Lady's father could close the thing, and short of threatening the Lady's life, he had no idea what would draw her father back to this spot. "Do we stay here and try to fix this now?" he asked, dropping his hands. "Or do we swim for shore and try to find that man?"

"I can't swim," the Lady said again.

Standing next to her, Gaspar folded his arms over his chest as if to reinforce that protest. It wasn't that far, but if one couldn't swim, it was an impossible distance. Gabriel knew better than to think he could cover the distance himself, not as tired as he felt now.

"Not necessary," Nadezhda said coolly. "The boat is coming."

"You kept it here all the time?" the Lady asked.

Nadezhda's black form turned toward her. "A different boat. I lost track of the first one."

"How long has it been?" Gabriel asked. "How many days?"

"Twenty-eight," Nadezhda said.

That made this the thirty-second of November, Gabriel decided. Or the second of December. He wasn't sure what day of the week it was, though. He was too tired to work that out. "What boat is coming?"

A horn sounded, prompting them all to turn seaward where a police patrol boat stood off in the waters. A smaller boat came toward them, rowed by a single officer.

"And how do we explain being out here?" Gabriel asked.

Gaspar shielded his eyes from the light. "We won't have to. That man knew we would be here."

"How?" the Lady asked.

"He's a seer," Gaspar said.

The boat came close enough that Gabriel could see the man better, a stocky fellow with dark hair and a strange symbol on his cap. "His cap... Is that the right sigil for the police?"

The sigil was that of an opened hand, and he didn't recall seeing that on any officer in Lisboa so far. Gaspar's eyes narrowed, but Gabriel doubted the man knew any better than he did. They were both foreigners here.

The Lady frowned and squinted at the man under the shade of her hand. "Damnation!"

"What is it?" Nadezhda asked.

"He's northern," the Lady spat out. "Special Police. He bears the sign of the Open Hand."

That answers that.

Gaspar shook his head and climbed down the rocky islet's side to give the man a hand up from the boat.

"I can drown him," Nadezhda said very softly.

"No," the Lady said with a sigh. "Let him come."

It was a little late to stop him now—although Gabriel was sure Nadezhda could drown the man even when he stood on relatively dry land. Gaspar wedged the bow of the boat in the rocks and held the painter while the policeman climbed over the side onto the rocks.

The police officer shaded his eyes, peered up at the burning circle that still hung above them, and made a humphing sound. Then he turned his attention to Gaspar. "Captain Pinheiro, Special Police of Northern Portugal."

He hadn't lied about that part, Gabriel knew, even though the man seemed young for that rank.

Gaspar crossed his arms over his chest. "You had a feeling you might be needed here today, did you?"

Pinheiro shot him a concerned glance but lifted his chin to point to the doorway. "Is that thing up there what's killing all the fish?"

"The fish?" Gaspar asked. "What do you mean?"

"Last month or so, there've been no fish on these beaches. Some wash up on the shore, but they don't even rot. Or not normally, at least."

That was all truth as well, his gift told him. The man was here because of fish. Gabriel kept his mouth closed. He knew what had been happening to the captain's fish; Nadezhda had been feeding off them.

"Why does this demand the attention of the Special Police? Particularly so far out of your jurisdiction?" the Lady asked, delicate nose in the air.

The captain removed his cap and tucked it under one arm, revealing wavy dark hair. "Madam, I am not here to arrest anyone. A friend in the police in Lisboa asked me if I could come look at the place since I have more experience with magical oddities than he does. We're just trying to ensure that fishermen can work this winter. So if that's what's causing this, we need to shut it down."

"That's all true," Gabriel said softly, just loud enough that the Lady could hear.

Her head tilted and she peered at the newcomer. "And how do you propose to do that, Captain?"

He glanced at each of them in turn, not visibly reacting to Nadezhda, at least. "I was rather hoping one of you would know."

Miguel nearly laughed at the man's vexed tone. Pinheiro glowed with the blue spark of the seer's gift, although he probably rarely exercised it. He was likely as unsure why he was here as his words suggested.

What he did see in the man reassured Miguel. Pinheiro had ties of the Church about him, old and strong. Not the Jesuits, though, and no sign of that black mark that had appeared on the priests and the butler. No, his ties reminded Miguel more of the Brothers of Mercy, so perhaps this man had been an orphan.

There was a single long red tie fading off to the north, a fated partner somewhere, although given that the man hadn't had sex recently, perhaps he hadn't met them yet. And ties to family, one twined with irritation and resignation—an *embarrassing* family member.

Miguel agreed with Anjos' assessment. This was an honest man, an honorable one. And if they were to investigate the Special Police in the north, this man was a good one to start with. Gaspar suspected that Pinheiro, like Anjos, was *kind*. He could help them when they reached the Golden City. If they reached it before this cataclysm

"We were just discussing among ourselves how to do that," he told Pinheiro. "Once we close it, the fish should come back soon enough."

"Only a fairy can close it," Miss Vladimirova said in her dead voice.

Miguel suppressed the urge to step farther away from her, which would be into the ocean. "Yes, and the fairy has fled."

"A fairy. I see." Pinheiro humphed again. He was apparently one of those people who took things in stride. "Is there any kind of substitute we can try then?"

"I can try it," Adela said then, trepidation in her voice. "I... *may* be able to do it. From the other side, I think."

Miguel turned on her. "No. Absolutely not."

"Turns out that once I have my memories back, I know a great deal more about fairies than I thought," she said, her hands shaking. "In theory, I should be able to go in there, close that door, and use his backdoor to escape."

"Escape to where?" His tone was sharper than he'd intended.

Her eyes flashed. "Do not think to rule me, Miguel," she

snapped. "I am the only one who has a chance of doing this, and even then only if he built in a way for me—and me alone—to escape. He certainly wouldn't have made room for you." Her hands were shaking as she said that.

Recalling his audience, Miguel climbed back up to where she waited. He took her hands in his. "Take me with you."

"Did you hear what I said?" she asked, jerking her hands away.

He stepped closer and lowered his forehead so it touched hers. "Take me with you," he said softly. "and if either of us is trapped, it will be together, at least. We could survive there."

Her lips trembled. "I can't give you that. If I fail, Miguel, I need you to carry on for me. I need you to take charge of the group. To start your investigations, to find Mata, to find out who controls him, who's taken my father's work, and what they intend to do with it. There is so much undone, and I cannot fix this..." She gestured toward the ring of light. "...not having left someone here to take on my work."

God help me. He understood exactly what she was asking of him. Because she might not make it out. Or might not survive the attempt to close the door. And she would not take no for an answer. He had to let her go, so soon after having found her. "I won't wait forever."

"Time is different there," she said. "You have to give me time."

"Don't eat anything," he told her, stepping back to give her room.

She rolled her eyes. "I know that."

In the corner of Miguel's eye, he saw Anjos toss something

to Miss Vladimirova, who caught it out of the air without even glancing that way. Neither argued with Adela's plan. How could they? Pinheiro was still standing to one side, watching the interplay. "What is happening?"

Miguel spoke through a clenched jaw. "She's going to close it."

Ignoring the captain, Adela turned to face Miss Vladimirova. "Can you lift me up to the circle?"

A tower of water began to form in the middle of the islet. Pinheiro stepped back toward his boat, finally startled by something. Adela, one hand to a stomach that must be roiling, stepped onto the tower of water when it reached her feet and was slowly carried upward to the burning circle.

With one last glance down at him, she stepped through the circle to the other side.

Miguel felt a pang, as if every last tie to her had suddenly snapped.

Adela fell into darkness.

There had been no place to set her foot, so she simply fell, landing somewhere not too hard and smelling of green. A meadow perhaps, or a field. At least the giant fireflies were gone. The opening still burned behind her, a bright glaring spot in her dark world, but that other side had already begun to darken with sunset. Time passed faster there.

How long do I have?

She'd lied to Miguel. She had no idea what she was doing

here.

But there hadn't been any other option, had there? There was no one else to fix this, and her father, in his current fit of pique, was unlikely to return to take care of his mess. She didn't care that he blamed this on Nadezhda; she knew very well who had created this scar on the surface of the world.

She forced herself to her feet and faced the burning circle, the evening light shining through the circle causing the dark world around her to seem even darker. She couldn't see Miguel on the other side; the circle was still too high above the rocks. Instead she only had a vision of darkening sky, facing off to the north above the sea.

Adela stepped back, rubbed the back of one hand over her mouth, and said, "Close."

The burning circle ignored her. If anything, it was slightly larger than when she'd first looked at it.

She tried again in French, in Latin, in Greek. She added *Please* to her request, and that had no effect, either. *What if this requires some language I don't even speak?* She took a deep breath and closed her eyes as the circle continued its bone-jarring hum.

Had she ever seen her father use one of these things? The memories she'd regained were mostly from the perspective of a child, a young one. She tried to recall seeing one of these circles and found nothing there in her new memories. The only time she'd ever used one herself was only days ago, that doorway between the campus at Campolide and her own office. And that had closed after she went through, hadn't it? Which made it different than this... *thing*.

She peered at the tattered edges of the glowing circle. This was a mistake, not an actual doorway between Portugal and faerie. Her father had described his prison as a bubble in the doorway. And by destroying the prison, Nadezhda had left an open wound instead of a door. She couldn't close it because there was no door to shut. It would have to be healed instead.

She had a basic understanding of healing magic. The healer touched the patient and then used their talent to urge the body's flows to correct themselves, to heal. Could this be done that way?

She opened her eyes and gazed at that humming circle, the blue-gray skies of dusk now showing through. Miguel would be getting impatient, and if she didn't do it now, he might come tumbling through it at any second. She put her hand out and grasped the lower edges of the circle.

The humming in her mind turned into a vibration that shook her bones. Her teeth clattered together, so she clenched her jaw and focused all her attention on bringing to two edges of the hole together. They didn't move at all.

Healing wasn't about physically closing a wound by pulling the edges closed. That helped but wasn't actual healing. Healing was subtler, suggestion rather than force.

She closed her eyes again, listening to that hum, trying to find a single strand, something small enough that she could manipulate. There, on each side, a broken strand of the same frequency. She let go with her right hand and traced a connection between the two, holding that frequency in her mind the whole while, imposing it on the world around her.

When she opened her eyes, there was one single strand

crossing the gap. Holding.

And she felt as if that thread had been torn from her soul.

Adela swallowed. She'd taken on this task knowing there was a good change she would never get back to Miguel. This might take the rest of her life, until she collapsed from exhaustion and withered away in this dark meadow. But if she was to protect the Portugals from destruction, she had to do this.

She closed her eyes and found another broken strand to trace. And then another. And another.

And each consumed her.

CHAPTER 32

ELSEWHERE

Adela was a shadow, every breath an effort now.

This must be how Nadezhda felt when her life was flowing away, thin like moldering paper about to crumple to dust on the next breeze. Her bones ached, her teeth grit together so long that her head would never forgive her.

The other side of the circle was dark now, night fallen on the shreds of Portugal that she could see. She had covered only about half of the circle: a strand here, a strand there, until there were spots that looked opaque. Until the rattling thrum of the circle had quieted to an almost bearable state.

And then, as if a dam had broken, the circle began to fill in on its own.

Barely daring to breath, she stepped back, hands dropping away.

Lines fled across the surface of the night, night in Portugal disappearing and night in this place, wherever it was, supplanting it. The smell of crushed grasses rose around her. She had fallen to her rump, she realized. She crossed her aching arms over her knees, bowed her head, and sobbed.

How long she sat there, she didn't know, but after a time she rolled over and pushed herself up onto her feet. She swayed but got her first look at the featureless night of the landscape she inhabited. The occasional sound of insects told her some life existed here. At least she hoped those were insects.

She took a couple of slow breaths, closed her eyes, and mentally searched for the buzzing sound of a doorway, like she had in the storeroom. The gash that had stood before her no longer hummed at all. It had closed, on its own. That was a relief. At least she hadn't sacrificed herself and failed.

But nothing else presented itself in her mind, no other sound that could be one of those doors.

What do I do? She had no map, no idea how to get back to the true Portugal, and every moment she delayed doing something, days might be passing over there. Miguel had said he wouldn't wait forever. He'd had an odd look in his eye when he'd said those words, and she only hoped that he had meant before coming to look for her, not that he would take his own life to cause their intertwined cycle of death and rebirth to repeat.

Her eyes had adjusted to the night, enough that she could see she was in flat territory with nothing moving. Moonlight filled the sky, although she couldn't see the moon itself, an oddity when there was no true place for it to hide beyond the flat horizon.

She stuck her hand into her jacket pocket, seeking a bit of paper she might tear up to leave a trail, but instead found something hard, metallic, and wet. She drew it out and peered at it in the darkness. It was her father's compass—the half that *followed*. Water trickled out of it onto her hand, and then it clicked and whirred as if waking from a watery nap.

She laughed in sheer relief. Whether it could work between worlds, she didn't know, but that small lifeline gave her hope. "Light," she whispered.

A pale light shone around her, just enough to show her that

she stood among shin-high grasses and that the compass needle pointed off to the left.

She let the light go—it would only attract attention—and began trudging through the dark in that direction.

That was when she heard the hounds.

MONDAY, 2 DECEMBER 1901
ILHA DA FADA, SOUTHERN PORTUGAL

Miguel refused to go even when darkness fell. The tide began to come in, forcing him farther up on the islet's rocks. He stayed there, though, his stomach rumbling with hunger. The police captain rowed Anjos and Miss Vladimirova to the boat anchored farther out in the water, and after a time returned to stand watch with him.

The circle was still growing, not dropping toward the surface of the water but extending up higher and wider. He wasn't high enough to see Adela framed within it, getting only a sidewise glimpse of the circle's surface now.

Pinheiro calmly unwrapped a sausage roll in brown paper and offered it to him, but Miguel couldn't eat. Not while so many questions were unanswered. He waited in silence.

On the northern point of the rocky outcropping, Pinheiro was the first to spot a slender strand of light crossing the darkness. "What is that?"

Miguel carefully crossed the rocks to stand next to the man. True enough, he could see Adela now, moving almost imperceptibly slowly as she drew one hand across the opening. A glimmering strand of burning light traversed the circle, confusing what he could see of her. She slowly tugged a second strand into place.

"She's not closing it," Pinheiro said, "she's reweaving it."

Of course, he'd been a fool not to see it wasn't a door—it was never a door—it was a tear in the fabric between this world and faerie. "Will she succeed?"

"Are you asking me?" Pinheiro asked, brows puckered.

"You're a seer," Miguel said.

"I..." Pinheiro snapped his mouth shut.

"Yes, you are," Miguel said. "I can see that about you. It's my gift, to see what others can do. So answer."

Pinheiro's jaw flexed, but then he closed his eyes. "Yes," he said after a moment. "It will work."

Miguel licked his lips. "Will she come back?"

That took longer. "I don't know," Pinheiro said. "Too many variables, I think."

Miguel tore his eyes from that slow-moving distorted image of her. That there was a possibility at all surprised him. "She was lying to me," he admitted. "There's no door there, no way for her to come back. She will have to create a way."

Pinheiro's brown eyes had opened and watched him. "You knew that?"

"She was going," Miguel admitted, "no matter whether I protested or not. She had made up her mind, so I didn't argue the point."

Pinheiro made that noncommittal sound, and then said,

"Inspector Anjos said something about a compass. That she has half of it. Is that something that can help?"

Miguel glanced up to the circle again where a second strand now glowed across the distorted surface. "Perhaps."

"Then hang on to that hope," Pinheiro said. "I'm going to sit down since it seems we'll be here a while." In the presence of a hole in the world, the man calmly settled on the rocks, unbuttoned his uniform jacket, and set his cap aside. He ruffled fingers through his dark hair and gazed back up at the circle. "Does this happen often?"

The man evidently intended to stay with him until he agreed to leave the islet. Miguel gave in and sat down nearby, wondering when this feeling he'd been stabbed in the heart would ease.

Gabriel sat on the bench running across the aft of the patrol boat, his chest aching. He wanted to lie down on the planks and sleep, but as weak as he was, he had no surety he would ever get back up.

The two officers manning the police boat had fled to the bow of the ship to escape Nadezhda. Despite the darkness that had fallen, she wore her veils, hiding her face from them. But they didn't need to see her face to fear her.

"You are about to be very hungry." Nadezhda had one arm extended over the side of the boat, and as Gabriel watched, a shark's huge nose appeared out of the water, its maw revealing rows of white teeth as it rose toward her outstretched hand.

Heart pounding, he jumped to grab her back... only to watch the shark fall away into the dark water. For a split-second the air sizzled about him, dry and dead, then warmth flowed into his body, his lungs and chest boiling again as she sobbed out a pained breath.

He let go of her arm, trying to break the bond between them. She was breathing still, and her head tilted toward him. "I'm sorry," she whispered.

He rose to his feet and walked the ten feet across the deck to the port side, then across to the starboard, back and forth, unable to stop himself. Fortunately, the anchored patrol boat was large enough that his movements didn't rock it. His stomach began to rumble. "What is wrong with me?"

"It is his nature, to always move," she said in her small voice, "to hunger."

He wanted to see if she still breathed, but his feet forced him to move on. At least he was *able* to walk now. Over-warm, Gabriel stripped off his jacket. He'd been so caught up in his physical misery that he hadn't noticed her drawing the shark to them.

"You waited there for a month," he said as he paced. "Living off the fish?"

"Yes," she answered softly. "If I let it, the doorway would have closed."

Leaving them prisoners in the faery realm. Where he hadn't felt ill, but his body had been deteriorating anyway. And to stay alive they would have had to eat, which would have trapped them there in faery permanently if he understood the rules correctly. He paced back and forth a few more times as he contemplated what Nadezhda's situation must have been in all that time. How tempting it would have been for her to have abandoned them and eaten all the fish in the sea. The seas were vast, and she could have kept herself alive indefinitely.

Although she would never be able to sit still again.

"How long will this last?" he asked the next time he paced toward her.

"It will burn off in an hour or so," she said, her voice gone cold and dead.

No. Gabriel kept his sigh to himself, regretting he'd not had the chance to talk with her while she was still alive. He paced off to the bow of the boat where the two policemen were cowering. "Is there any food?"

The younger of the duo gazed at him, mouth open, as if a dead man had come asking him questions. His cap bore the cross of the Portuguese crown on its badge, making him an officer from Southern Portugal. The other officer, a grizzled old fellow, pointed toward a large chest secured against the railing. "The captain said you would be hungry."

Of course, Gaspar had said the captain was a seer. Gabriel opened the chest and found several grease-stained paper bags. He plucked up the nearest one. Inside were a half dozen sausage rolls, slightly stale. His mouth started watering anyway, and he gulped one down in three bites before he recalled his manners. "Have you eaten, gentlemen?"

"There's plenty in there, son," the older man said. "Thought the captain was crazy, bringing that much food along, but it looks like we might be sitting out here all night." He pointed toward the islet, where Gaspar and Pinheiro sat on the rocks companionably now as if watching a game of football.

Gabriel nodded and carried the bag back to where Nadezhda waited. He held one out to her.

"You should eat that," she said. "You hunger, I do not."

Not exactly true. He continued to hold out the paper-wrapped sausage roll. After a moment, she took it with black-gloved fingers and hid it somewhere in the folds of her dress. He took a third roll and managed to chew it more slowly this time as he walked back and forth across the aft of the boat. Then a fourth.

Nadezhda had opened the satchel that Gaspar had saved—now completely dry—and peered through her layers of veils at the pages. Gabriel wished he could stop walking long enough to look at those pages, but given that his fingers were greasy now, he would only ruin them, if any were legible.

Teeth gritted together in frustration, Gabriel walked on as the sun set. He ate far too many sausage rolls. *I will be sick in the morning.*

But better than he had been.

ELSEWHERE

Adela stuffed the compass back into her soggy pocket and ran. She was already so tired.

The hounds that pursued her were sounds rustling through the grass, but she couldn't see them. They bayed—off to her left, off to her right—and far behind her a horn sounded.

THE TRUTH UNDISCOVERED

She knew the sound of a hunt, and she was the fox.

There was nowhere to hide in this moonless nighttime landscape. She paused to catch her breath, and something rustled in the grass only feet away. It nudged her boot, and she jumped back. "Light!"

Light flared around her, almost as bright as in that false house they'd been in. Something brushed her leg, growling. She jumped back, but there was nothing there. She sucked in a terrified breath, gazing about frantically for the animals.

The grasses parted, something slipping between them, but nothing was there. *Invisible hounds.*

Adela sobbed out a breath.

In the distance she saw riders, men of women of strange beauty mounted on stags that hurtled toward her. The horn sounded again as another unseen beast bumped her leg, harder this time. She stumbled but kept her feet.

I can't run anymore.

She was too tired from healing the hole in this world, too tired even to spare her own life. She wanted God to help her, but she wasn't sure He could come to her aid in this place. There was only one who would.

The riders would be on her in a moment. The unseen hounds crowded around her now, their growling promising a painful death.

"Papa, please help me," she begged.

Wind whipped around her, strips of shadow flowing past her sphere of light and toward the riders. They grew more solid until they blocked her light and rattled together like dry leaves. Beyond her sight, a gunshot sounded, answered by angry cries from where the riders must be. Adela held her breath. A second shot after that. She wrapped her arms about herself, holding on to that little bit of light still inside the rustling wall of shadows that surrounded her now.

"Papa?" she whispered.

A third shot sounded, followed by a sharp whine, and the hounds were suddenly gone.

The strips of darkness around her abruptly spun away as if caught in a dust devil and then settled, draping themselves one at a time about the approaching silhouette of her father, cloaked in shadow and light.

Chapter 33

ELSEWHERE

"You made the wrong choice, child," her father said as he moved past her toward the hunters.

Adela slumped down to the ground, too exhausted to complain about being called a child, too relieved to argue with him. Wherever the hounds had gone, they were leaving her alone. She took a deep breath, then lifted her eyes to watch the confrontation her father's arrival promised.

The Jesuits might have imprisoned her father, but in that very acknowledgement of his existence, they'd made him stronger. *Belief* gave fairies power, even if that belief came in the form of fear.

Streams of light and shadow threaded out across the night, obliterating the distant fields as he remade this world—or at least this part of it—into what he wanted. Howling sounded on the dark wind, and wild bellows came from the stags the hunters rode. Adela clapped her hands over her ears and squeezed her eyes shut, trying to block it all out.

A hand touched her back, rousing her from sleep.

Adela jerked to a half-sitting posture. She'd been sleeping prone, face pressed to dewy grasses. Her breath was ragged, more surprise than fear. She gazed at the world around her, green fields as far as she could see.

Daylight. That got her to her feet. She turned about, looking for her father, heart pounding.

He stood behind her, a cool and distant creature wrapped

in a cloak of shadows. Much taller than her in this form, his face was still familiar enough that she recognized him. It held a cold perfection he'd never worn in the human world. "Foolish child."

"How long have I been sleeping?" Adela begged.

"As long as you needed," he said. "Does it matter?"

"How much time has passed back in the Portugals?" she asked then. "I have to go back."

His sigh came like a cold breeze, making the grasses sway. "You will stay."

Adela squared her shoulders. "No, I have to go back."

"And how do you think to do that, foolish one?"

She pressed her lips tight. "You can make that happen. I know you can."

"Can, but won't," he answered.

"Why not?" she cried. "I need to go home."

Her father strode around her, circling her now, his shadows clutching him as he paced. "This can be your home, child. You are half my kind. Here, you will live forever."

Adela swallowed, parsing through what he was offering. She did have greater power here, but she would only ever be a flawed version of his kind. "Why would you want me here?"

"You are my child," he said.

She folded her arms over her chest, feeling exhaustion drag at her again. "Your foolish child."

The still face regarded her with narrowed eyes. "The Hunt

wanted your blood. I made a bargain to defend your life, child. Now I must stand guardian here until some other comes to claim this place."

Bargains. He'd made a bargain of some sort, and now he was trapped here. But he'd done it to protect her, like so many other things in his life. He protected his children, if nothing else because they believed he existed and that, too, gave him strength.

"If I do not return," she tried, "then your enemies will continue to corrupt your work. To stop them, I must go back."

It grew warmer around her, as if his anger was the sun. "If you return you will die."

Adela checked her pocket for the compass. It was still there, no longer damp. "I was meant to die one day, Papa. Then I will live again."

"No," he said. "There will be no more lives. Why do you think the Jesuits watch him so closely? Why did they react to you in such a way? It is because their seers have predicted this is the Meter's *last* life, that your being born only half human is the sign of that. This is his only life, and yours, child. You must be more cautious of it. You can stay and live forever."

As his prisoner, for lack of a better term. "Without him? No, Papa."

"You will die for his sake, then?" The question had the flavor of a bargain about it, like he wanted an essential truth for his cooperation.

"Yes," she said, turning to follow his movement. "And I must keep my word to Raimundo, to aid him when the time to change comes. He is your grandson, and his children will know your name." It was an appeal to her father's vanity, the promise to have future generations remember him. It was also a promise of power. "If you are trapped here, Papa, then let me go and finish your work. Let me go and finish *mine.*"

He stilled. "Promise me you will stop these men, before they use my work to destroy the world."

Was that what this odd posturing of his had been about? She didn't believe for a moment that he'd actually wanted her to stay. Not when he'd spent so much time out in the world. He had too much at stake there, and nothing here, surely. But he could not stop himself from pointing her at his enemies. "Tell me everything you know about them, and I promise I will try with my every last breath to ruin their plans."

He bent close to her ear, so much farther than he must in the human world, and whispered words that carried more than their own meanings, words full of portent, words full of whispered knowledge.

But no name. He still had no name for the man who headed this conspiracy.

He drew back, taking a moment to stare into her eyes. "Goodbye, child."

She took in a shuddering breath. He meant that. This would be the last time she ever saw him. "Farewell, Pa..."

The smell of old books surrounded her, and the fluttering of shadows like ravens' wings baffled her eyes. She fell, or flew, or tattered away only to come together into herself, standing in her office.

Adela caught her breath, wondering at the sense of loss that filled her. Her chest ached with it.

It was morning, and there was a chill in the room—no fire in the fireplace. Why had Santana not...?

She was wearing trousers, an odd thing. Something mechanical clattered at her, and she reached into one of her jacket pockets and drew out a small metal device, no bigger than her palm. A compass, the needle pointing dead north.

She'd lost time again.

Adela set the compass down and pressed the heels of her hands to her eyes. She was hungry and tired, and now she'd lost time.

She opened her dry eyes and glanced up to check the horses in the corners of her office. All stood in their normal poses, so no one had been in here. "Santana! Where are you?"

She waited for a response, and then went into the hallway to search for her butler. "Santana?"

The old man came jogging around the corner, tugging his suit jacket on as he came. "Lady?"

"I am... unsure of the time, Santana. What time is it?"

Her butler blinked at her for a second. "You've been gone for four months, Lady. It is March 2nd, Lady. Sunday."

Oh, I know that. The knowledge had unfolded in her mind, a tidbit of memory her father had allowed her to keep. Annoyed, Adela licked her lips. Most of her servants would be enjoying their time off this afternoon. "Have there been any... untoward incidents?"

"Other than your absence? No, Lady." Santana paused, then added, "Well, the Inspector did destroy a cigar box in here."

She'd forgotten all about that stupid cigar box she'd stuck Mata's curse in. She should have seen it destroyed herself. She was as bad as Carvalho, leaving magical things sitting around. "Um... where is my... where is Inspector Gaspar now?"

"He told us you instructed him to go ahead to the Golden City, Lady." Santana wrung his hands. "Were those not your instructions?"

She did recall that now, a parting from Miguel where she'd bid him to carry out her task. She hadn't truly expected to return, had she? "Yes. Yes, Santana. Could you have a bath drawn for me? And did he leave anything for me?"

"In the safe, Lady. I'll send Mafalda and then I'll fetch the papers for you."

Half an hour later, Adela sat in her warm bath, sorting through the papers Miguel had left for her. There were the water-stained papers her father had left in his workshop, half-legible plans for some new device with a circular design, although she had no idea what it did. There were a sheaf of letters her father must have removed from Tomar's possession before he killed the man, all written by Donato Mata, three of which complained about his difficulty in killing Alessio Ferreira, who had regularly slipped from his grasp. Interesting to know that Mata and Tomar had been correspondents, and further proof that Mata had been hired to kill Ferreira, but she wasn't sure of the letters' value otherwise. They didn't give up the name of the chief villian, and that was what she needed most.

THE TRUTH UNDISCOVERED

There was a deed for a house in the Golden City, on Boavista Avenue, across from the military hospital. It was in Miguel's name and dated early in 1902.

Adela ran her fingers over that inked date. It was hard to believe it was 1902 already, the change of the year having slid by while her father held her in his world. He had done something to her memory, and at this rate she would likely never know what.

With a sigh, she set that deed aside on a chair next to the tub. There were a handful of what appeared to be weekly reports from Miguel, written in a paltry code, where he spoke of William and Catarina and Ezequiel. It took her only a moment to decide that Miguel had cast himself as Ezequiel, Anjos' younger half-brother. And of course his best friend and cousin from Cabo Verde stood in place of Anjos and Nadezhda. He wrote of books read in the library, and how several dozen—at the time of the last letter—were now sorted into piles to either keep or remove. Books would represent officers of the Special Police, some of whom would be purged from the force when Raimundo became Prince of Northern Portugal.

Evidently Miguel, Anjos, and Nadezhda had become an effective team despite their difficulties with each other. It was a relief to learn that much of her mandate had been achieved in her absence, without her lifting a finger.

Adela set the last of the papers on the chair, closed her eyes, and leaned back against the tub's cool porcelain. She needed to get herself to the Golden City. That was where she would be able to solve the mystery of Alessio Ferreira's death, catch whoever was behind the scheme to use her father's plans for ill, and reassure herself that Miguel was still waiting for her.

MONDAY, 3 MARCH 1902
THE GOLDEN CITY, NORTHERN PORTUGAL

"It's getting louder." Gabriel pointed at the wooden box that sat on the corner of Gaspar's desk.

The compass they'd brought out of the workshop of the Lady's father seemed to be halfway alive. Gabriel bled for the thing every morning, a few drops from a pinprick to a finger. Gaspar's blood didn't work for that, apparently a side-effect of his immunity to magic. But Gabriel's blood seemed to keep it alive enough, and it had started clattering wildly the previous afternoon, the first time it had done so since they'd brought it here to the Golden City.

Gaspar rose from his seat and opened the lid of the box to peer inside. Gabriel wasn't sure what he thought he would see since the metal gears never changed. Making an annoyed sound, Gaspar sat down again, a scowl on his dark features.

He wasn't faring well, Gabriel reflected. Gaspar had admitted once that he'd considered suicide. In his mind, that it was a mortal sin didn't matter, because he and the Lady both lay outside God's normal plan. Although Gaspar had not mentioned it in more than a month now, Gabriel knew that idea *often* crossed his friend's mind. Why should he go on when she might be months dead by now?

Arguing over it again would only distance him from Gaspar. Gabriel sighed and returned his attention to the paperwork on his desk, a new batch of officers to question.

Despite the strain of the last three months in a city none of the three of them knew, they'd accomplished a great deal. With the aid of Pinheiro and a handful of sympathetic officers in the Special Police—those who favored the infante, Raimundo, over his brother, Prince Fabricio—they'd begun a thorough and systematic investigation of the ranks of the Special Police. He and Nadezhda had already interrogated many of the officers, and they had separated out a couple of dozen they trusted. Those now staffed this new police office.

Others were marked as members of the Open Hand, that dubious group who supported the conspiracy that had raised its head in Lisboa, Sintra, and even Cabo Verde. Until the infante succeeded his brother, though, their ability to purge those men from the Special Police was hampered. Whatever that mysterious cabal was doing, they'd not yet been able to determine.

And Mata was still a free man, under the protection of someone powerful enough to have him instated as a member of the Special Police yet keep him hidden. They had no idea who had hired Mata to carry out his various thefts or the murder of Alessio Ferreira. But it all had to be related somehow.

Unfortunately, they had little access to the magical elite of the city, if such could be said to exist. Unlike Lisboa, the Golden City frowned on magic and persecuted non-humans. The Freemasons would not talk to Gaspar, nor a mere Inspector like himself. Without the Lady's influence, they seemed unable to form any deeper ties in this city.

With a sharp rap of his knuckles, stocky Captain Pinheiro peered into their office. "Inspector Gaspar, you might want to head down to the train station."

Gabriel blinked at the captain, wondering what could provoke that sort of statement. "Has Mata been seen?"

Pinheiro's dark brows came together. "No. The night train is arriving from Lisboa in half an hour. There's a cab waiting outside the station."

Gaspar cast an equally puzzled glance at Pinheiro, then his eyes turned to the compass. He shot to his feet, grabbed his suit jacket and hat off the wooden valet near the door, and rushed past Pinheiro and down the stairs.

Gabriel rose, his gaze staying on Pinheiro. "Is she coming today?"

For a brief instant, Pinheiro looked ready to deny his seer's foreknowledge, but changed his mind. Apparently, he'd grown more comfortable admitting it aloud. "I believe so. Strongly."

Pinheiro's gift seemed to deal with probability, not certainties, but as Gabriel understood it, each seer was a little different. Now it seemed that their investigations would finally begin in earnest with the Lady here to lead them.

Pinheiro moved away from the door jamb, walking on down the hallway to escape the arrival of Nadezhda. Not even glancing at the captain, she walked into the office and sat in the lone chair in the corner. Gabriel smiled for her. "Good morning."

Mostly out of a lack of familiarity, they all lived in this house Gaspar had purchased, with their private rooms on the first floor and the police offices below on the ground level. Although he and Nadezhda had separate rooms, they often shared a bed. He didn't think she slept. At times, though, she lay down in the fountain in the house's Spanish-style

THE TRUTH UNDISCOVERED 371

courtyard and slept there. It was not an adequate replacement for the reservoir in Lisboa, but Gabriel knew it comforted her.

"Where has he gone?" she asked.

Despite working together for months, Gaspar still held Nadezhda at a distance, mistrustful of her. It was a thorn in Gabriel's side, one he could not pull free because in some part, Gaspar was right: most of the time she was dead. But there were times when she was not, and Gabriel doubted she would ever spend one of those fleeting moments proving that to Miguel Gaspar.

"To the train station," Gabriel answered. "Pinheiro thinks she is arriving today."

He heard a distinct sniff from under Nadezhda's veils, as if she was trying to catch the scent of the Lady even from this distance. He drew out his case and lit a cigarette, reckoning his long-missing employer was going to show up any moment and toss his cigarettes into a nearby chamber pot. *Might as well smoke them now.*

Nadezhda never complained of that, his smoking to lessen the pain. Here in the Golden City, there was ample life for her to draw on to keep him alive, but she refused to kill. And even if she were to do so, he would rather she hold it in herself, keep herself alive, if only for minutes longer.

He hated that one of them had to die. Constantly, if they wished to maintain this delicate balance. For a time he smoked, thinking of all the ramifications of the Lady's return from wherever she'd been.

"I would be pleased that she is still alive," Nadezhda finally said in her inflectionless voice, no truth or falsehood in his ears. Although he knew that to be the truth, because she didn't lie.

Not to me. She sat unmoving in the corner of the office, a presence that still sent shudders along his spine at times, no matter how well he knew her.

He loved her. He had told the other Nadezhda that a hundred times in hushed whispered conversations when no one knew they were together, both tenuously alive. That time was always too short.

"Do we interrogate Officer Machado?" she asked as he stubbed out the end of that cigarette in a porcelain bowl on his desk.

He considered a second cigarette. "I suspect she will want to know everything that has happened."

"Yes, she will," Nadezhda said, knowing the Lady far better than he did.

Gabriel pressed himself to his feet, determined not to let her see him wobble when he stood. "Then I'll go dismiss Machado. We can bring him back in a couple of days."

Nadezhda said nothing as he left her. They could talk later, when she actually had feelings about his words.

Miguel wished the cab would move faster, trundling along Rua do Heroismo toward the station. *Faster than the tram, at least.*

He had feared she was dead. Every day had been an exercise in frustration, with duty the only thing that propelled him out of his lonely bed in the morning.

What had happened to her in that faery realm? What had held her there so long? Would she be changed? Why had she not sent a telegram?

He kicked one foot against the front wall of the cab. It was childish to be annoyed by that, of all things, but he was. He had waited so long for word of her.

The cab neared the train station, a neoclassical building of granite and white stucco. Miguel jumped out of the cab, tossed the driver his fare, and jogged through the building to the platform behind. The train from Lisboa was just pulling up under the platform's shelter. He paced back and forth as the train came to a full stop, and the porters moved the steps up to the first-class cars.

It didn't take long, then. The doors to the cars opened, and the porters began moving luggage, a scramble on the platforms. Miguel kept to one side, eyes peeled.

Adela came regally down the steps, her hair tucked up neatly under a blue hat. Her eyes swept the platform and settled on him. She smiled.

His irritation fled. She came toward him, one hand extended to take his, even in this public venue. He held both her hands in his, the fragility of the moment so clear to him now. He could lose her at any time. Other passengers pushed past them toward the station, so Miguel drew her back against the wall.

"The porters will take my luggage on to your house," she said.

At the moment he could not care less about her luggage. "Are you unhurt? What happened to you there?"

She gave him one curt nod—better to keep things professional here in public. "My father returned to save me," she said. "He sent me back here to finish his work. To find the person heading this conspiracy and stop him from using my father's work to destroy our world."

A simple charge, then. "Not ambitious at all."

Her cheeks colored, just a bit. "Do you doubt we can do it?"

"Never for a moment," he said. "Together we can do anything."

She licked her lips, her eyes on his lips. "My father had a lot to tell me before we parted ways, but much of it he buried in my memories. I have no idea how to access that."

Her father did have a history of toying with what she could recall. "Did he tell you who that person is?"

Her mouth firmed in vexation. "No, he never found out. But he did tell me is that DuBois researched us for decades, the relationship between you and me. And with my being born half-fairy, the Jesuits believe it is somehow at an end. Neither you nor I will be reborn again. Perhaps that's why you're able to remember the past."

He stared at her face, wishing he could know whether that was the truth. Not whether she believed *her* words, but whether her father had lied to her. "What does that mean for us?"

"Other than please don't die?" She gripped his hands harder. "This makes us like any other husband and wife, Miguel. I am not your death, not this time around."

And that meant there might be children as well, did it not? Before this moment, he hadn't let himself consider that. He hadn't let himself dream of having a normal life, a family.

That possibility spread before him like looking out onto the ocean for the first time. It was a world he'd never truly lived in, not in all his lives. For a moment, stunned hope took his breath away.

This was not the place to discuss that, though, nor to make plans to catch their conspirators, so he let go of her hands and drew one instead through the crook of his arm. "Let's go home."

For now that would be enough.

THE END

Cast of Characters

Cabo Verde

- Inspector Miguel Gaspar—Police inspector and Meter, able to see, smell, or taste magic, but immune to it himself
- William Monthaven—Gaspar's closest friend, Englishman
- Catarina—Gaspar's cousin
- Marcel DuBois—landowner and, secretly, Jesuit brother
- Teresa dos Santos—Restaurant owner
- Eduardo Cunha—Police inspector

Brazil

- Inspector Gabriel Anjos—Police inspector and Truthsayer, able to perceive lies
- Ezequiel—Gabriel's half-brother
- Ana Maria—Gabriel's wet nurse and Ezequiel's mother, healer
- Feliciano Morais—Ezequiel's lover

Portugal

- The Lady—Trained in the study of magic, negotiator between the Freemasons and Jesuits, Aunt of Infante Raimundo of Northern Portugal, tasked with gathering a team to investigate Northern Portugal's Special Police

- Nadezhda Vladimirova—Rusalka, Russian by birth, Healer
- Santana—the Lady's butler
- Brother Tomas—Jesuit brother at the Campolide college
- Father Serafim—Jesuit priest at the Campolide college
- Donato Mata—hired assassin and thief
- Antonio Auguste de Carvalho Monteiro—landowner in Sintra, purchased the Quinta da Regaleira
- Ifigénia Carvalho—young woman staying at the Quinta da Regaleira
- Johannes Konrad—librarian at the Quinta da Regaleira
- Tomar—butler at the Quinta da Regaleira
- Raimundo—Infante of Northern Portugal, younger brother of Prince Fabricio
- Captain Rafael Pinheiro—officer of the Special Police of Northern Portugal
- Inspector Joaquim Tavares—inspector for the police in Northern Portugal
- Marquis de Maraval—the Lady's godfather, bureaucrat in Northern Portugal
- Alessio Ferreira—(dead) friend of Infante Raimundo of Northern Portugal

HISTORICAL NOTES

Brazil and Cabo Verde are, in this alternate version of history, both *former* colonies of Portugal. However, as it was in actual history, both were heavily involved in the slave trade, with Brazil having brought in approximately 12 slaves for every 1 slave in the USA. Many of those were funneled through Cabo Verde, which has little in the way of natural resources but is in an excellent location for warehousing items for shipping. In a post-slavery society, social acceptance of mixed-race individuals (*mestiço*) varied from place to place. Brazil, the last country in the Western world to end slavery (1888—only 13 years before the setting of this story), would still be the harshest toward their African brethren.

The Jesuit college at Campolide still exists, although now it's the state-run New University of Lisbon. It's worth noting that when the new government of Portugal took over the college in 1910, the army and the public streamed in to investigate what were commonly believed to be subterranean areas of the college. Were there actually tunnels beneath the college? That I haven't found, but it was certainly suspected at the time.

Antonio Auguste de Carvalho Monteiro (Monteiro the Millionaire) did purchase the Quinta da Regaleira in the late 1800s. The wealthy transplant from Brazil—an entomologist—redesigned the estate into a curiosity that is still a popular tourist attraction today, featuring strange and ornate towers and an Initiation Well that has been the subject of many photographs. Carvalho Monteiro's fascination with all things esoteric inspired that estate's omnipresent references to the Jesuits, the Freemasons, the Rosicrucians, Tarot, and the Templars. He is also known for gathering one of the largest Camonian libraries (libraries with works related to Luís de Camões.) However, his renovations did not begin until a few years after this novel takes place, so what's present there now is not what would have been there in 1901.

The Mãe d'Água (Mother of Waters) Reservoir sits at the end of the Águas Livres (Living Waters) Aqueduct. Not a Roman aqueduct, it was built by the Portuguese in the early 1700s to bring water into Lisbon. It was one of the small percentage of structures that survived the great earthquake of 1755 intact and stands today over Lisbon. Although it ceased to supply water for the city in the 1960s, the reservoir still regularly hosts art exhibits and the occasional wedding.

The clipper ship FERREIRA actually still exists as well, and I was lucky enough to be able to walk across its decks in 2014 when I visited London. The ship is likely more familiar to readers by its English name, CUTTY SARK.

The CUTTY SARK was best known for transporting tea at top speed, but that trade slacked off due to the rise of steamer ships. She was eventually sold to a Portuguese firm in 1895 and renamed FERREIRA. The then-Portuguese ship transported goods between Portugal, Brazil, New Orleans, Mozambique, Angola, and Britain. Since changing the name of a ship was considered bad luck, the Portuguese sailors persisted in referring to the ship as the *Pequena Camisola*—essentially the direct translation of 'cutty sark'. By 1922, the FERREIRA was the very last clipper ship operating anywhere in the world. After putting into a French harbor during a storm, it was spotted and eventually purchased by a Welsh captain who moved the ship to the UK and returned her to her original conformation and name. She last sailed in 1938 and is now permanently moored in London as a museum.

(Special note: I am told most Portuguese sailors do not refer to ships as 'she', causing me a bit of a headache as to the proper pronouns to be used in the above paragraphs.)

Although travelers who have been to Porto (the Golden City) will recall that the magnificent São Bento train station is downtown, right at the end of the Street of Flowers, in this alternate fantasy world where the prince stunted the industrial growth of Northern Portugal, that building is still a decrepit monastery. Therefore when Gaspar goes to the train station in Porto, that means the Campanha station at the (then) eastern edge of the city.

And a final note for those who have visited Porto and are curious why there is no or little mention of the azulejos (tiles) that cover the sides of many buildings like the Church of Our Lady of Carmel or the São Bento train station: those lovely walls of azulejos were mostly added between 1910 and 1930, and thus would not have existed in 1901-1902. A shame, because they are creations of great beauty and historical significance, and well worth touring the city to see.

SPOILER WARNING

The following snippet is set the day AFTER the events of **The Golden City** and **The Seat of Magic**, and thus might spoil some aspects of those books.

If you haven't read them yet, please skip this section.

Bonus Scene

SUNDAY, 2 NOVEMBER 1902
THE GOLDEN CITY

Gabriel woke in a cool, sunny room, hearing the noise of distant voices and street traffic. The sound of church bells ringing pulled him from a light doze into full awareness as he counted the sonorous peals. Nine in the morning, surely.

He sat bolt upright, his mind abruptly recalling where he'd been—the palace, with...

I'm in a hospital. The room he was in was white-plastered, the window covered with fine white curtains. It was large enough to hold another bed or two, but his was the only one there.

The last thing he recalled was pain, his right arm feeling as if every blood vessel had burst. Blood, there had been blood everywhere. He remembered a burning that had cut through him like a sword, searing his lungs. He remembered coughing up blood.

He sat up. Eyes closed, he took a deep breath as the most distant bells fell silent outside.

Nothing hurts. Nothing, not even his lungs.

He slid out of the bed and crossed to the window, amazed by the energy he felt, as if he could run a hundred miles. This was not like when his Tia Ana Maria had healed him, nor when Nadezhda first brought him back to life. This was... a miracle.

He pushed the fine curtain aside and saw that passersby were dressed in their finest, surely leaving Mass.

"Ah, you're awake," a man's voice said from behind him.

Gabriel turned and saw Inspector Joaquim Tavares standing at the doorway, a leather satchel in his hand. "Is it Sunday?"

"Yes," Tavares said. "You've been sleeping for days. To sweat out all the poisons, Miss Vladimirova has claimed. Even so, the prince wanted you at a hospital, so you were brought here, to Santo Antonio."

"Where is she?" Gabriel realized he was standing there in a nightshirt. While someone had apparently cleaned away all the blood, he didn't smell pleasant. "Is she here?"

Tavares set the satchel down on the end of the unmade bed. "No, back at the police station on Boavista."

His mind was racing with far too many questions. "Who survived?" he finally managed.

Tavares nodded once. "Miss Vladimirova has taken to her rooms and refuses to come out, so I cannot tell you how she fares. Inspector Gaspar has a couple of broken ribs, but he's up and moving around. The Lady seems unhurt. Duilio, Oriana, and I are fine. Pinheiro is fine. Raimundo is well, and Prince Fabricio died yesterday."

Nadezhda wouldn't come out of her room? That wasn't unusual, as she tried to discomfit others as little as possible, most of the time. Perhaps she thought that without his presence, others might be uncomfortable should she appear.

Gabriel shook his head and tried to focus on the other news. If the prince was dead, that meant Northern Portugal had a new prince, one who would re-engage with the world. But that had to have come at a high price. He turned to regard

Tavares' solemn face. "How many died?"

"Five members of the Special Police, six palace guards, a valet, and Ambassador Alvaro," Tavares said. "That we know of at this point. A group of bodies were only found a day later in a secret closet in the palace, so it's possible that number could grow. They are still working to account for all the guards, and a couple dozen members of the Special Police have disappeared, making it difficult to be certain whether they died or fled."

Those would be members of the Special Police they suspected of being part of the Open Hand. They had to know they were marked and were fleeing the city. Gabriel tugged at his borrowed nightshirt. "Does that bag have clothing in it?"

Tavares laughed. "Yes, I brought some from the station house. Can I assume you're well enough to mount an escape?"

To get out of this place without the normal reams of bureaucratic paperwork required? That sounded like an excellent idea. "Yes."

"I'll wait in the hallway, then," Tavares said.

A few minutes later, Gabriel was walking at Tavares' side along the hallways of the Hospital of Santo Antonio, trying to look like he belonged in these stern hallways of white plaster and gray granite. They managed to make it into the entryway foyer and out of the front door without attaching the notice of any of the doctors or nurses.

Tavares led the way toward the station. The traffic was subdued for this time on a Sunday morning, the city thrown into mourning by the death of their prince. Whether a household had liked the prince's policies or not, black ribbons were worn, black armbands and garb, black bunting set on window boxes.

They stopped in the rococo Church of Our Lady of Carmo, and after making his genuflection toward the gold-crusted altar, Gabriel went to light a candle and pray mercy for the souls of the men who'd died. In a way, those men had sacrificed their lives for him. Not intentionally, but he had been the ultimate beneficiary of their deaths. Belatedly he added a prayer for the soul of Prince Fabricio, who'd been misled unto his death. He could not bring himself to pray for the defrocked priest, Salazar, the doctor Serpa, or Maria Melo, the three who had caused all this death and destruction. Perhaps in time, but not today.

Gaspar might have been impatient with his prayers, but Tavares—who had once considered the priesthood, Gabriel knew—understood.

Normally Gabriel would have wanted to locate a tram, but this morning he wanted to walk. After being chained in the prison of a dying body for years, it was freeing to feel the crisp morning air filling his lungs. They arrived at the station to find it lightly staffed, many of the men off to celebrate Mass with their families. Captain Pinheiro stood in the station's small courtyard, in front of the bubbling fountain, a small box in one hand. He clapped Gabriel on the shoulder. "Did you get out of the hospital without notice?"

"Yes," Tavares answered for him.

"Good," Pinheiro said. "We've been keeping quiet about your condition, Inspector Anjos, as we don't want anyone to start talking in terms of miracles. I think Miss Vladimirova would dislike the attention."

And that explained why he'd woken in the hospital alone. They hadn't wanted to draw attention to the man who'd been healed of tuberculosis. If it became widely known that she'd cured him, Nadezhda would be hounded to cure others for the rest of her life, no matter the cost. There would always be men who thought the sacrifice of others' lives worth it to preserve their own.

"I should go up and talk to her," Gabriel said. "Thank you, Inspector Tavares."

Tavares clapped him on the shoulder and headed out toward the Massarelos Station where his own work waited. Pinheiro walked with Gabriel toward the stairs. "Perhaps you might bathe first," Pinheiro suggested as they began to climb. "You are a bit ripe."

Gabriel's nose had warned him of that. But it was also very interested in that box in Pinheiro's hands. "I suppose I can do that. Then I'll stop to talk with Miss Vladimirova and afterward come down to see how I can help out."

"Take the day off, man," Pinheiro said with a laugh in his voice. "I can handle the station alone." He dug a set of keys out of a pocket with his free hand and set the key to the door lock. "They salvaged these from the remains of your suit."

Still weighing whether he should check on Nadezhda or bathe first, Gabriel set the satchel inside the door and turned back to thank the captain. Pinheiro just handed him the keys and the box. "Don't eat too many of those," he warned. "You haven't eaten in a few days, and your stomach may need some time to adjust."

Once the door closed on his room, Gabriel lifted the box to his nose and sniffed, catching the scent of sausage. His stomach gurgled. He'd had a failing appetite for well over a year. Now it surged back, reminding him that eating could be a pleasure. He set the keys aside, sat on the side of his bed, and opened the box to reveal Pinheiro's generous gift of a half-dozen sausage rolls.

He managed to keep himself to two as the water ran for his bath, uncertain how his gut would feel about the offering. Then he let himself sink into the blessedly hot water, grateful for the luxury of a private bath.

He swiped a hand towel along his arm and paused. There should be a scar there—a pair, actually—from a bullet that had torn through his bicep. On both sides, the scars were gone. He bent his right knee a few times, trying to tweak that old injury gained while chasing a thief in Olinda. He hadn't noticed a twinge when he'd walked here with Tavares. Was that gone as well? He sat still a moment, mentally taking stock of old cuts and scars, all of which seemed to be gone.

He wasn't craving a cigarette. Usually after a healing, he would have a few hours without that craving beating against the walls of his mind like a trapped bird. But he felt nothing now, four days later.

Truly a miracle.

What would he say to Nadezhda? She would likely just ignore his gratitude, her emotions shut away in her living death. Perhaps he could coax out the hidden side of her, the girl who cared for him enough to heal him, and thank *her*.

The better part of an hour later, he felt presentable. He had dressed in a new shirt, one that didn't carry the scent of cigarette smoke yet, and his best trousers. And even though she didn't need food, he picked up the box that still held

THE TRUTH UNDISCOVERED

three of the sausage rolls.

He went next door and knocked.

"Go away," her voice came through the door, hoarse and rougher than her normal emotionless tone.

"It's me," he said. "Gabriel."

"You should..." There was a hesitation. "You should go away."

There was something behind that voice, a hint of a lie. She didn't want him to leave. And the only time he sensed her truth was when she was alive.

She's alive. His breath stilled as that realization flowed over him. She should not be. When she healed him her own life flowed away with that healing, her strength coming into him. Her life always faded away like the glowing ember at the end of a match.

She's alive.

Desperate now, he knocked again. "Nadezhda, please, let me in. Please."

The door opened a sliver, only the top of her head visible to him. "You need not come to me any longer."

He wrapped his hand around the edge of the door. "Why do you say that?"

"You no longer need me to heal you."

That was truth, but it told him nothing of how she felt. "Months ago I told you that wasn't why I came to your bed. I love you, Nadezhda."

The eyes that lifted to meet his were reddened and puffy

from crying.

"Please, let me in," he repeated.

After a moment, she opened the door wider to let him in. Gabriel went in and let her close it behind him. He set aside the box of sausage rolls and gazed at her. Nadezhda wore a linen nightdress, her hair bound back in a simple braid. She looked like a girl, out of place in all this.

She licked her lips, still unwilling to look at him. "Men say what is expedient."

Did she actually think that of him? Or simply men in general? Given what he knew of her husband, he suspected the latter. "Please look at me," he begged. When her eyes lifted hesitantly to meet his, he said, "I have never lied to you. This is not about expediency."

She pressed her lips together, tears forming in the corners of her eyes. He cupped her cheek with one hand. One tear slid down, and he wiped it away. "I'm not accustomed to this," she whispered, sounding aggrieved now. "I'd forgotten what this is like."

He leaned down to peer into her face. "This? What do you mean?"

She sighed heavily and closed her eyes. "To feel… all the time. I can't escape it."

When she'd retreated into death, her feelings never followed her. They didn't trouble her. Only when she'd come to life again did she have to face them. He drew her into his arms and held her close. She began to weep softly.

If she'd been sitting alone in this room stewing for the last few days, she must have worried herself into knots. He sat down on the edge of the bed, drawing Nadezhda into his lap. She didn't fight him, so he laid his cheek against hers and let her cry.

He hadn't loved his wife, Graciana, like this. It didn't compare, or perhaps his memory of Graciana was so faded that she seemed unimportant. He had been rather melodramatic about her at eighteen. About everything at that age.

Nadezhda's marriage at fifteen had been arranged, though. Her husband had been a complete stranger who cared little for her beyond bedding her. He'd not tried to win her affection during the three years of their marriage, and the women of the household neither liked nor supported her. There hadn't been anyone to confide in, and the other men of the household had treated her like a whore. It would have been a hellish existence, capped by her husband's drowning her. In the thirty years since, she would have had little time to resolve how she felt about what had happened.

He didn't know how to fix this for her, how to make it better. He doubted he could understand what was going on inside her. He settled for holding her in his arms, hoping that he could provide some reassurance, even if it was three decades too late.

His life had changed, but hers had as well. He didn't know whether things would be the same. He hoped that she would still want him.

It surprised him how fervently he wanted that.

Gabriel's eyes fluttered open. He wasn't certain what had woken him.

The room about him was dark, all the lights turned down. He was still dressed. He lay curled up in bed, farther down than was comfortable, with a blanket over him and a pillow crammed under his head. Nadezhda lay beside him, her head on his chest.

He'd fallen asleep on her. Not precisely romantic. Perhaps he wasn't done sleeping off the healing yet. He yawned and tried to ease out from under her.

Her hand caught his sleeve. "Stay."

"Are you certain?" he asked her.

"Yes," she whispered. "Please."

Gabriel turned to face her and was gratified when she shifted to lie in his arms. He wasn't going to press her, but...

"You smell different," she whispered, surprising him.

"I haven't had a cigarette in days. Was it something you did?"

"I set everything aright," she told him.

Gabriel rubbed his cheek against her hair. He sniffed, and then noticed for the first time that her hair smelled of lavender. Not lake water. Lavender, like the soap she used, the scent of which never clung to her skin. She had always smelled like lake water. Her skin had always tasted like lake water. He had never talked to her about that; he'd thought it indelicate to reference the lake in which she'd been drowned. But now her hair smelled of her soap.

"Nadezhda, I am sorry I fell asleep. I did not mean to..."

"It is the healing," she said. "It will take time until everything is settled."

THE TRUTH UNDISCOVERED

Good to know. "I feel better now than I have in years, and I owe that to you, but that is now why I'm here. I came here because I love you."

She shook her head, pressing it once more against his shoulder, her face hidden. "I am a murderer, Gabriel. You cannot love me."

He suddenly understood why she'd shut herself in this room. She was dealing not only with the violence done to her, but with what she herself had done after her life was taken. "You are not. I am a killer, Nadezhda. I have killed men, and a couple of women as well. But never murder, and I cannot believe you a murderer, either. I will accept that you have killed, but not…"

He could not say it wasn't out of malice, because she had drawn her husband's male relatives to her lake and drowned them. It wasn't self-defense, either, as he knew she could have used the water to push those same men away. It wasn't a crime of passion, because in that form there had been no passion in her.

"…not as yourself," he finished. "You are not that person."

"I could be," she said, lips trembling. "I know what it takes, Gabriel. I know what to do to become that person again. And what will I do here if I am not her?"

Because she wouldn't now terrify men into answering their questions. Hadn't that ability to subvert their wills come from being a rusalka? Did that mean she was no longer one? He sighed. "Police will always need healers, Nadezhda. I would feel better knowing one as talented as you was nearby should I be shot again."

She sniffled. "Gabriel, if I kill to save your life, I will go back."

"I would never ask that of you. Promise me that if you must do so to save me, you will let me go. I have already cheated death once."

Her head burrowed against his chest, but she didn't answer.

"Promise me," he insisted. "I will not buy my life at the cost of your soul."

She drew away just a bit. "Do I still have a soul?"

He shifted down and cupped her tear-stained face in his hands. He knew she'd been a devout Christian before her husband murdered her, but thirty years of living death may have changed that. "God would not have brought you back without one," he guessed. "Now you have your change to seek forgiveness for everything that the other you did."

"No priest would ever grant absolution," she whispered.

He had questions. Would her repentance count since it had not truly been her who killed her husband's family? What sort of penance could she make for that? And would a priest even believe her. He suspected that Tavares could find the right man for her to talk to, someone who would answer those questions for Nadezhda. "Have faith," he finally said.

She raised one hand to wipe at her eyes with her sleeve, forcing him to let go her face. "I am glad you think there's some chance of it."

He did. He had to believe God wouldn't hold her crimes against her since she abhorred what she'd done. And given that...

"When we find a priest," he said, "I would like to talk about marriage, Nadezhda. It was not possible before, but would you consider it now?"

THE TRUTH UNDISCOVERED

"You can't marry me," she protested, light brows drawing together.

"Do you not want me?" Had he simply assumed affection on her part?

"I..." She blinked, her blue eyes filled with confusion. "You can't want to marry me."

He'd had the better part of a year working with her. True, he'd only known *this* Nadezhda in snippets of time, a stolen hour here or there, but he knew her well enough that he had no doubt what he wanted. He wanted a chance to build a life together with her, no matter that she looked far too young to marry a man in his mid-thirties, no matter that she was Russian at heart and controlled water—could she still do that?—and no matter that other people might doubt her humanity. He knew who she was and didn't fear her. "Yes, I want to marry you."

She sniffled again, tears returning to her eyes, but her weak smile told him they were tears of joy, not pain.

He cupped her cheeks with his hands. "However long this takes, I will be here for you. If you merely want me as your friend, I will understand. I would be your lover, your husband. Whatever you wish."

"You would have to convert." she said softly, without inflection.

Convert? That gave him pause. He hadn't thought he would have to go that far. There were vast differences between the Orthodox Church and the Catholic Church. Surely a civil ceremony would...

She laughed softly, a good sign. "I was not serious, Gabriel."

Thank God. "Then you will marry me?"

Her blue eyes lowered, then raised to meet his again. "Yes."

And under her words he could tell she was speaking the truth, the sweetest thing he'd heard in a long time.

THE END

ABOUT THE AUTHOR:

J. Kathleen Cheney taught mathematics ranging from 7th grade to Calculus but gave it all up for a chance to write stories. Her novella "Iron Shoes" was a 2010 Nebula Award Finalist. Her novel, **The Golden City** was a Finalist for the 2014 Locus Awards (Best First Novel). **Dreaming Death** (Feb 2016) is the first in a new world, with the books of *The Horn* coming out in 2017, and the books of **The King's Daughter** and sequels to **Dreaming Death** in 2019

Other works by J. Kathleen Cheney

The Golden City Series
The Golden City
The Seat of Magic
The Shores of Spain
The Seer's Choice
After the War

Palace of Dreams Series
Dreaming Death
In Dreaming Bound (coming 2019)
Shared Dreams

The Horn
Oathbreaker, Original and Overseer

The King's Daughter Series
The Amiestrin Gambit
The Passing of Pawns
The Black Queen

Iron Shoes: Tales from Hawk's Folly Farm
The Dragon's Child: Six Short Stories

For more info on any of these books, please visit www.jkathleencheney.com.

A Dream Palace Press Book

Made in the USA
San Bernardino, CA
16 January 2019